ALWAYS YOU

Always You

Bridger Falls
Book 3

Erin Branscom

Want to listen to the Always You playlist. Scan here:

Content Warning

This book includes "on-page" adult content and language unsuitable for minors. If spice isn't your thing, they're easy to skip over. :)

Chapter 1
Poppy

Always You by Trey Lewis

"If you keep driving this thing like a gorilla stole it, I'm going to call time of death on it," I tell Jimmy as I think about how his truck practically limped into the bay yesterday, sounding like a dying cow swallowing a harmonica.

Random music spills from my office, coming from my little brother Owen's phone, and I glance over, distracted, before turning back to Jimmy. "I mean it. You aren't going to have this truck much longer if you don't bring it in for regular maintenance."

I swipe at a stray lock of hair that fell out of my ponytail and shout toward the office, "Owen, if you're watching videos again instead of finishing your homework, I'm selling your Switch to buy new tires for the truck!"

And I really do need new tires. But no, I would never sell his game. I'm broke, but not heartless.

"I'm literally doing math," he yells back with his sixth-grade attitude.

"You lie like an experienced politician." I shake my head but can't help smiling. There's no way that kid is doing math right now. I see his thumb moving up and down over his phone as he's kicked back in my office chair, feet up on my desk.

Jimmy laughs as he watches this play out. "Kid's got your spunk, Poppy."

"Oh, trust me. That kid inherited my attitude, temper, and my ability to detect bullshit. The world is screwed, Jimmy. There are two of us."

Jimmy whistles. "Poor world."

"Right?" I say in agreement as I twist my wrench hard and tighten a loose bolt. I'm getting Jimmy's truck finished up, and it's been a long day. I want to go home, eat dinner, shower away the day, and go to bed.

Jimmy chuckles. "I gotta say, Poppy, it's no wonder you're single. You're a little scary."

"Good," I grunt. "Fear keeps the assholes away."

"Well, if anyone is an asshole to you, Poppy, they're gonna have to deal with me," Jimmy says, looking like the protective grandpa-like figure that he is. And the truth is, Jimmy wouldn't hurt a fly. He's a big jokester. A teddy bear.

I lean in, giving the engine one last look. The engine was hot and temperamental like a drunk, fire-breathing dragon when he brought it in. Basically, I've worked miracles here, and I deserve a giant gold star. Jimmy stands beside me, as if to offer his own mechanical wisdom. He absolutely will not be doing that. Jimmy doesn't even come in for routine oil changes.

"I thought maybe it was the spark thingy," he suggests, scratching his head, trying to be helpful.

I give him a deadpan look. "Yes, the spark thingy. Revolutionary wisdom, Jimmy."

He lifts his hands, laughing. "All right, genius. Please enlighten me. What was wrong with it?"

"Everything," I say, tightening one more bolt. "You wore it out driving like oil changes and routine maintenance are suggestions. Spoiler alert, they're not. You need to get this in regularly, Jimmy, otherwise it's going to the truck graveyard."

"I need this truck, Poppy. I have had this old girl for over twenty years now," he quips, eyebrows pinching with worry.

I crank the engine, and it starts right up, purring like a kitten. He whistles through his teeth. "You sure know what you're doing."

"I hear that a lot. Although usually it's in an anxious tone and as a question," I tease as I shut the hood and pat it.

"Nah, don't listen to any of that nonsense. You're a damn good mechanic. I sure am thankful for ya."

"You're welcome, Jimmy. Now, here's a card with your next oil change scheduled on it so you do not forget, okay? Put it in your wallet. There's even a sticker on your windshield to remind you."

"Sounds like a plan." He nods thoughtfully as he pulls out his card to pay.

As he's leaving, he leans out the driver's side window and says, "If you ever wanna date a good man, you give me a holler."

"Well, you let me know if you meet any," I reply sweetly.

His laughter booms and echoes through the bay as he drives his truck out, and I lower the garage door behind him.

I love working with guys like Jimmy. They give me crap, but there's respect under it. They're not treating me like I don't know what I'm doing. I love giving people shit, and I don't mind receiving it when it's respectful and fun for everyone. Around here, it's a sign that people care. If they're straight-out mean and disrespectful, that's where I have a problem. And I get plenty of that around here, too. I went to school to be a mechanic, and I know what I'm doing. I have been working in my dad's shop since I could practically hold a wrench. I started doing my own oil changes when I was eight.

I start cleaning up when I hear the front door slam shut in the cold January wind. "Murphy?"

Inwardly, I groan. For one, I wanted to be done for the day. I can't afford to turn away business right now, though. I need the money. But this customer, I truly wish I could turn away.

It's Randy Garvin, who once told me women shouldn't be mechanics while he pointed and laughed at me at The Black Dog with his friends. Today, he's here with his broken-down Ford and wearing a defeated expression. He looks like he doesn't want to be here, but he has no other choice.

"Hey uh," he starts, scratching his neck. "So, there's this weird noise. Sorta like a *thwap thwap thwap*. Or maybe a *clunk.*"

"Wow," I shoot back. "What happened to your mechanic with a penis, Randy?"

He knows damn well what happened to his mechanic. That was my dad, Sully, and he hasn't worked here for several years now. He also knows he has no other licensed mechanic in Bridger Falls to help him, other than me, or he'd have to drive over an hour away to get his truck fixed.

His face flushes red, frustration twisting his features, and he bites out, "I know what I said. But I need your help, Murphy."

"Murphy was my dad. I'm Poppy," I remind him, kneeling to check his tire. I don't like being associated with my dad or the Murphy last name. When I took over this shop, I wanted to start fresh. The name Murphy might still be on the building, but this place is practically mine, now. "Did you rotate these yourself?"

He shrugs and looks away. "Maybe. It's been a while."

I pop the hood and try to lift it, and it's stuck. I plant my foot on the bumper and jerk with both arms until it pops loose with dramatic force.

Randy watches, slack jawed. "Nobody could get that off."

Interesting. So, he did try to go to someone else before he came to me. I'm his last resort. Not surprised.

I use my machine to quickly pull off the lug nuts. I see the look of surprise on his face when I zip through them in record speed. I lift the tire effortlessly because I do this every day, and I'm in hella good shape now. There was a time back in high school when I was bigger and got made fun of for my weight. These days, though, I'm feeling pretty good about myself. I'm strong and confident. I still have my curves, but to be honest, I like them. I need to be strong to do this job.

I inspect the tire. "How long have you been driving around like this?"

He blinks. "It didn't get that bad until recently."

"Yeah, right," I mutter. I don't like Randy Garvin, but I love a challenge, and I need the money right now, so I'm going to fix it for him.

He looks around. "So, Poppy, you got a man?"

I snort, shaking my head, and glance up at my giant poster of a bear behind my toolbox. The bear. I will always choose the bear. And why is everyone so interested in my love life? If they want to be interested in something, they could get interested in my never-ending grocery bill. Or the other bills that I'm behind on.

I glance up at him, eyes sharp. "The line of applicants starts at the back of the parking lot. By the dumpster. I need references."

He stammers, looking confused. "What kind of references?"

"I prefer a letter from your therapist," I grunt as I lift the new tire and place it on the machine and turn it on.

He shuts up after that, and I see the irritated recognition on his face that I'm teasing him and it's never happening. First off, Randy Garvin is old enough to be my father, and I'm not into the whole age-gap romance. And another thing, Randy Garvin is a sexist pig. I wouldn't date someone like him if he were the last person on the planet and mankind were at stake, needing us to be together. Sorry, mankind, you are dying out and taking Randy with you. It's probably best that his lineage is extinct after his personality. My love life may be on life support, but I'm not and never will be that desperate. That's why God made battery-operated machines.

I fix his issue, take his payment, and send him on his way. I don't have time for this sexist bullshit. I know none of these assholes ever came in here and asked my dad if he had a woman after my mom died. Number one, I don't want to think about my dad's love life, and my dad was probably already screwing anyone he could. He is not a good man and never was. I still have no clue what my mom saw in him. And number two, my dad would have knocked their teeth out for talking to him like that. These assholes better start respecting me, or they're going to get a different version of me and a reminder that my last name is still in fact Murphy.

I get my bay ready for tomorrow and swipe a swig of water. Today has been nonstop, but it feels good when I get my work done, and everything is going relatively well.

As soon as he leaves, the door opens again. Mrs. Harmon, our neighbor from across the street, strolls in with her gray poodle, Bernita, in tow. She offers me a Tupperware of banana pudding like a tribute. Now this is a nice way to be treated by a customer at the end of what feels like a never-ending day.

I hug her and smile. "This looks so good, Mrs. Harmon. You spoil us."

Every week, she drops by a random treat. We never know when they're coming, but they never disappoint.

"You look tired, dear," she says as she looks around at the chaos.

"I am," I reply. "Being iconic takes a lot of energy."

She laughs and pats my cheek. "You are definitely iconic. Anyway, I was just out walking my Bernita and wanted to drop by a treat for you and Owen."

"We will never turn down your treats, Mrs. Harmon. Thank you. You are the best." I lean down to scratch Bernita's ears.

She waves to Owen through the glass window of my office and heads out. He's definitely scrolling again. He barely looked up when she came in and he usually loves seeing Bernita. He has begged me for a dog, but there's no time for a dog. I barely have time for Owen. I'm drowning here, and something needs to give. I need a miracle at this point.

I might be exhausted, broke, and drowning a little here. But I remind myself that I'm Poppy Murphy, and I can fix anything. As long as it has an engine. Life, bills, and stress, however, I haven't figured out how to fix yet. That's an after-work Poppy problem. Here in this shop, I can fix things I know how to fix. And fixing things makes me feel better.

Overall, it was a pretty good day. I wrapped up several projects and made money to cover at least half of the bills I have stacked up. Half is better than nothing.

I decide the day is finally over and get washed up. Owen is still curled up in my chair. He looks like he's napping now, phone resting on his chest.

The air in the shop shifts, heavy and tense. That's when I see a shadow beyond the threshold. Then, Dad fills the doorway, and everything in me goes tight.

He has that sagging, tired look that used to make me worry about him when I was younger. I started realizing he never worried about us, though. I was only sixteen when my mom died, and he pretty much died when she did, too. I had no parents after that. Not only did I take over raising Owen when he was barely a few months old, but I had to finish raising myself, too. I was pretty much like a teenage mom with no support from my still living dad, who also worked me like a dog here at the shop so that I could support him and my brother.

Slowly but surely, he stopped working the shop and disappeared for weeks on end with his friends. At first, I pretended my dad was in the back working. But really, he was gone, and I just fixed everything and kept the shop going. I got through high school working nights and weekends to cover bills. After high school, I took classes at the local trade school to earn my auto-mechanic certifications. Maggie, a close friend and basically a fairy godmother to our town, paid for my certifications. I kept the shop going during that time, too. My certificate is proudly displayed on the wall in a thrifted frame. I look at it sometimes and remind myself that I did that.

I wipe my hands on a rag and toss it over my shoulder, trying to be casual, when I really want to scream at him for being the piece of shit father that he is. "Sully."

No greeting in return, not even a friendly smile or even a glance at my face. He states, "I came for my check."

No, how's Owen? Or how are you guys holding up? No, do you need anything? Just here for the check. Typical Sully. He doesn't care about anything besides getting my money, which I earned, and that he feels entitled to because legally his name is still on the shop. It's bullshit, but if I want to keep Owen safe and the shop going, I have to play his games. And my dad is a real asshole if I don't do what he wants.

I glance toward the office and see Owen shift and blink awake, like he feels the tension. His eyes find my dad through the glass. I see his face light up for an instant, then dim quickly. And I hate it when Sully does that. I hate it, loathe it. He breaks

Owen's heart every single time he comes around just like he used to break mine.

"Give me a minute," I tell Dad. I want him to go as fast as possible.

I crack the register, count out the contents, and slide it over to him as he watches me.

His eyes narrow as he counts out the cash. "This is short."

I nod. "It's either pay you or buy groceries. And Owen also needs basketball shoes. You'll have to get the rest next week."

He doesn't even blink at the mention of Owen's name. His gaze flicks up toward the office as Owen steps through the doorway. Dad's eyes move to me and narrow. "You're worried about groceries?"

"We have to eat." I stare at him.

He lets out a humorless laugh. "I'd be more worried about the house and where you're going to live. You need to manage your money better. You know what is owed to me, and I expect it when I come. Not a week later."

I do my best to keep a neutral face and not show any emotion. Because if I do, he'll use it against me, and I've learned to give him what he wants so he'll be gone quicker. But this time he's got me worried.

"What's going on with the house?" I stammer, trying to sound casual. We had an agreement.

"It's going into foreclosure. You'll have to figure something out." He glances up the back stairs to the apartment that Ollie rents above the shop. "Move in with your little boy toy."

I ignore that jab and say, "That's our home, Dad. The only home Owen has ever known. You said you'd cover the mortgage payments until he's graduated."

"Yeah, well, things change," he clips out.

"What do we need to do to get the house out of foreclosure?" I ask, frustrated, mentally calculating how much money I could come up with, and it's not a lot.

"Figure it out," he huffs with irritation in his voice.

"Why are you even here?" Owen asks, glaring at him.

Dad says something under his breath as he stuffs the money in his pocket, turns, and leaves without acknowledging Owen.

Bastard.

"What are we going to do, Poppy?" Owen asks, worry making his brows crash together. "Where will we live?"

"That's my job to figure out as a grown-up. And your job is to pack up your backpack so we can go home and eat dinner," I say, smiling at him and trying to center him back to normal—something we both have to do after Sully pops up. I've had twenty-seven years of practice being disappointed. Owen's only had eleven. I'm better at this than he is.

Inside, I'm fuming. I've played nicely. I've put up with far more bullshit from my dad than a person ever should have to do. But now, I'm close to done. I am going to figure out how to make sure he never gets another dime from us and leaves us alone for good.

Chapter 2
Poppy

Wanna Be Loved by The Red Clay Strays

I turn the key and let the truck rumble to life while Owen wrestles with his seatbelt beside me and asks, "Can we get dinner from The Black Dog?"

I shut my eyes, just for a beat, because my body answers before my brain can—a burger with all the fixings. Hot and salty fries dunked straight into Momma Mary, the cook's ridiculously delicious cheddar sauce. Food that feels like a warm hug and costs more than I could spend right now. My stomach twists with equal parts hunger and guilt, because I know exactly how much is in my checking account and exactly how many bills it can't cover right now.

I open my eyes and stare out the windshield, doing the math I never stop doing. Groceries or gas. Heat bill or tires. Wanting one meal at a restaurant shouldn't feel like a luxury, but it does. And somehow that makes me want it even more. Because we

11

deserve better than Sully shaking us down and making me struggle.

But there's fourteen dollars in my bank account. Fourteen doll hairs exactly. And I still need to fill up with gas tomorrow. So, dinner I thankfully thought to put in the Crock Pot at home is what it is. And I'm getting sick of Crock Pot dinners, too.

"We have white chicken chili in the Crock Pot waiting at home," I say as cheerfully as I can manage. But dang, that burger sounds so good after this long day. I'd kill for that burger.

He groans as if I've personally destroyed his dreams. "Not the Crock Pot."

Me too, buddy. Me too. Unfortunately, when he's older, he'll learn the Crock Pot isn't our enemy.

"Come on," I say, ruffling his hair and trying to get him out of his funk. "I'm starving. Let's go home and eat a warm and yummy dinner."

Truth is, I haven't eaten since breakfast. Stress fills me up faster than food ever could. That, and we barely have any groceries right now. Everything goes to Owen first.

As I put the truck in reverse, my eyes land on the photo wedged into the dashboard. Ollie and I were at Wilder Ranch in high school, years ago, both of us holding onto the reins of his old mares. My hair was longer then and my smile brighter. Mom was still alive, and it was a different life. I wasn't fighting for grocery money and working myself to the bone.

We take the quick ride home in silence, and I pull into the driveway. The porch light flickers like it's too tired to do its one basic job.

That porch light will be someone else's problem here soon, it sounds like, I think sadly.

I can tell that Owen is trying to pretend he's not upset after what happened with Sully, but his face is tight, and he keeps wiping at his eyes when he thinks I'm not looking. I crouch in front of him when we get out of the truck. "Hey, look at me."

He does, chin wobbling and eyes glassy.

"It's okay to cry," I tell him. "He makes me cry sometimes, too."

"He told me once that real men don't cry." Owen blinks, looking at me.

"Maybe Sully doesn't cry, but he's also not a real man. A real man doesn't treat their family this way." I tilt my head and add, "Ollie cries sometimes, and he's a real man."

Sully will never be the man that Ollie is. And I hate that he says things like that to Owen. He's not the one to be handing out life lessons. No one should aspire to be like Sully.

Owen nods. "I texted Ollie and told him Sully showed up."

I smile softly. "You can text Ollie, buddy. He's our friend."

He nods through his tears, still fighting them back.

"It's you and me, buddy," I tell him, brushing a tear off his face. "I swear I'll make this life better for us. Whatever comes our way, I'll fix."

He nods, and it kills me to see him trying to put on a brave front. I hug him tight, wishing I could absorb every hurt he's ever felt and make everything better. Only this time, I'm not so sure that I can. I don't think I can save the house and keep paying on the shop, too. It has to be one or the other, and I need the shop to work to make money.

A flash of headlights sweeps across us. I hear the familiar rumble of Ollie's truck as it pulls in. Of course, it's Ollie. The cavalry shows up even when you think you don't need it. But we always need Ollie. He makes everything better. He's like the human equivalent of a golden retriever. Happy, funny, and always making jokes. It's hard to be in a bad mood when Ollie's around.

He hops out of his truck, hair messy, probably from his shift at the firehouse, wearing his Bridger Falls fire jacket that makes women in this town swoon. Not me. I'm not swooning. Nope. Zero swoon. You don't swoon over your best friend. Best friends definitely don't swoon over each other.

"What the hell happened?" he asks the second he sees Owen's face. His body tenses like he's ready to take on the entire world for us.

I stand and shake my head. "I'll fill you in later. It's cold out here and we're heading inside to eat. Want to join us?"

Ollie's eyes flick to the screen door. There's an envelope wedged into it with FORECLOSURE on the front in bright red letters, and my stomach drops. Sully wasn't joking, even though I wish he was.

I stuff the notice into my pocket, but Ollie's brows go tight. I shake my head once, begging him not to bring it up in front of Owen. Owen should never have to concern himself with bills and adult problems. His problems should be which skin he's trying to get in Fortnite, or whether he has basketball practice, and what flavor of Gatorade he's getting at his next practice. That's what I want Owen to have to worry about. The everyday childhood things that I didn't get to enjoy. I'm making damn sure he has what I never had.

"I have bags in the truck," he tells Owen gently. "Want to grab them for me?"

Owen brightens immediately and runs to the truck. He knows that means there are groceries, and it's usually junk food I don't buy. My groceries are ingredients for hearty meals these days. And usually Crock Pot meals he hates, but it's food.

I turn to Ollie. "You didn't have to bring anything."

He shrugs with an easy smile that feels like a warm blanket on a cold day. "It's purely selfish. You feed me, and I want to keep that happening. That means I'm going to bring groceries, so you keep feeding me. I'm like a stray cat who keeps showing up."

I hate that it makes my throat tight. He's saying that to make me feel better and lighten the mood. But I love feeding Owen and Ollie. I wish I had more time to create better meals for them.

"What did Sully do?" he asks quickly, watching for Owen to come in with the bags of food.

I shake my head. "I'll fill you in later. He's upset about it."

"He's a dick, Poppy," Owen calls as he digs through the shopping bags.

"Hey." I laugh softly. "Language. But yeah, he is a dick, buddy."

"You got my favorite cereal?" Owen beams and does a fist pump. "Yes!"

Ollie winks. "I pay attention. You're obsessed with two things right now. That cereal and Fortnite."

Inside, the furnace groans and clicks on, louder than usual. I start to stress and remember I have bigger problems to worry about than the furnace right now.

"You want to play Fortnite after we eat?" Owen asks, excitedly.

"Sure," Ollie says as his eyes reach mine, and it's like he's scanning me for clues to what happened.

"Go wash up," I tell Owen as I put away the groceries. "Dinner will be ready in a few minutes."

I glance around Mom's old kitchen. Faded and peeling wallpaper, a cabinet door that doesn't quite shut, the ghost of a woman who deserved more time. And it kills me that we're going to lose this place that holds what little memories that we do have of her.

"I'm trying, Mom," I whisper to myself, feeling emotional at leaving it all behind and unsure of where we're going to go.

Ollie busies himself unpacking groceries. I move around him to grab bowls, and he puts his hand on my waist as he goes around me. The gesture sends a tingle down my spine.

Get it together, I tell myself. *Best friends don't give each other the tingles.*

Dinner is definitely not burgers from The Black Dog, but it's hot and filling. I pour salt and pepper on it, warm up the biscuits I made yesterday, and set them on the table in our chipped serving bowl.

We sit at our tiny table, missing the fourth chair, with our mismatched bowls and a candle I lit specifically so dinner feels less like poverty and more like ambiance.

'This is amazing, Poppy. We had back-to-back calls today, and it was so cold out. Good night for soup." Ollie leans in and takes a bite.

"At least someone appreciates my Crock Pot cooking." I grin and nudge Owen, who is standing to get his second bowl despite his complaints.

"You ready for basketball tryouts?" I ask him.

"No," he lies.

"You're good," I tell him. "Really good."

He shrugs, but there's something there that's bothering him. "Coach Toddy says he doesn't know if I'll make it."

"What do you mean?" I ask, my spoon pausing in midair. "Of course you'll make it. It's a small town with not that many kids. How can Coach Toddy turn people away?"

"He's just been saying we have to try harder, or some of us aren't gonna make it."

I glance over at Ollie, and his eyes give me a look that says, "we'll talk about it later." We do that a lot. Ollie and I are each other's sounding boards. I listen to his vents about his mom and stuff he has going on at the fire station. He listens to me vent about my dad and crappy customers. Ollie's my person and I am his.

After dinner, we clean up together, and for a little while, life feels almost normal. But the paper crumbled in my pocket reminds me that it's not exactly true.

"Why don't you grab a shower and make sure you wash your hair good," I tell my brother. "Then you can play with Ollie."

"Okay!" he calls as he runs down the hall.

As soon as he's out of earshot, Ollie is on me for the details of what went down.

"Okay, what's going on?" Ollie asks, leaning in and crossing his forearms, thick muscle stretching under his sleeves, and my brain fully checks out for a second.

I pull out the notice I shoved into my pocket when we walked in, and we both read it. "We have thirty days left here."

He shakes his head angrily. "Why hasn't he been paying?"

"I can't even begin to understand Sully anymore," I fume as I load the bowls into the sink just so my hands have something to do. I turn on the water and soap up my dishes. "I'll figure it out."

Ollie leans his hip against the counter. "Move up to the loft with me. You can save money, and I can help you get back on your feet."

I freeze, looking at him like he's nuts. "We're not living in the loft."

"Why not?" he asks, searching my eyes like he's challenging me to give him a valid answer.

"It's like a frat house up there, and that's your space, Ollie," I object, setting the dishes in the dish drain.

"I've been fixing it up," he says with a shrug. "Come on, Poppy. It'd be fun, and we practically spend every day together anyway. What would be different?"

"You need your space to have a life," I remind him. "This isn't your problem, it's mine. And *I* have to figure it out."

He looks at me and says, "I have a life just fine, and you don't have to figure this out by yourself. You have me."

You have me. If only it were that simple, but it's not.

"I'm done, Ollie," I tell him, feeling freakishly calm.

Ollie picks up the dishes, dries them, and says, "What are you going to do then?"

I shrug and begin rinsing out the sink. "If Owen's losing the only home he's ever known, then yeah, I'm done keeping the peace with Sully."

"I agree," Ollie says as he puts the dishes away. "Sully needs to get lost for good."

"I'll figure it out," I say quietly. I always do.

"I don't get why you won't let me help," he murmurs. "You know, I'm here for you guys."

But that's the problem. If I lean on him, he could break me, too. And Ollie's the one person I can't risk losing. How many times does Ollie have to save us before he thinks we're a burden and finally leaves us? I can't even think about how awful that would be.

Owen and Ollie play their game together while I take a much-needed hot shower and relish every last drop of water beating down on my tense shoulders.

In my room, I towel off my hair, and I open my closet door. There it is. A poster of my silly collage of Pinterest dreams. Chickens, wildflowers, a cozy front porch, green pastures, and a tire swing. I can see it when I close my eyes and go to sleep every night. I'm sitting out there on that porch, having a quiet morning with my coffee in my favorite chipped mug that was my mom's. That's the life I dream of when I close my eyes at night. A life where Owen and I have plenty of groceries, and

Sully doesn't come around to take whatever he wants, whenever he wants.

I need to stop wanting this. Because wanting means hoping. And hoping means falling apart when reality hits.

We don't get dreams. We get the Crock Pot.

Chapter 3
Ollie

Pink Skies by Zach Bryan

The firehouse is quiet, just the low hum of the heaters and the bite of strong coffee in the air. I shut my locker with my hip. I've already worked out and showered, and now we're in that waiting stretch. Chores are done, gears checked and checked again. Everything's ready, which usually means it won't stay quiet for long.

My phone buzzes in my pocket. **Owen Murphy.** Worry fills me when I see his name light up on the screen. It's not unusual for Owen to call or text me, although usually it's just texts, and he calls me 'bruh' a lot. But during the school day, this feels off.

I answer instantly. "Owen?"

There's breathing on the other end that's quick and panicked. "Ollie?" Owen whispers, voice shaking. It slices right through me. "I'm in trouble, and I need your help."

My heart practically detonates. "Where are you? What happened?"

"Locker room." He sounds like he's crying or trying not to be heard, and I hear yelling and commotion. "They took my backpack and threw it in the shower. My phone screen got broken, too."

I'm already moving and grabbing my coat. "Who did this?"

He hesitates. "Eighth graders. Coach Toddy told them to teach me a lesson."

Rage floods hot through my veins. "Are you hurt?"

"Yes," he whispers. "My cheek hurts. Please don't tell Poppy. She's already stressed about Sully."

"Owen," I say, voice low and calm. "You never worry about needing somebody. You can call me anytime. I'm on my way."

"Okay... thank you," he whispers, voice cracking.

The call ends, and I swear whoever laid a hand on that kid will wish they hadn't. I'm already grabbing my gear before the call even fully disconnects.

"Gear up, we gotta go to the middle school," I bark out to the guys lounging in the common room. "We need to go. Now."

They all look up fast because I never use that voice unless someone is bleeding out. "We gotta go get Owen," I add. "He called me from the locker room. Eighth graders are beating him up in the locker room, and it sounded like he's hiding. He said Coach Toddy ordered them to do it."

Bucky stands so fast that the recliner slams into the wall. "Oh, hell no."

The rest of the crew echoes it like a war cry. They pull their gear on in seconds, and we haul into the truck and open the bay doors.

Owen's been coming around here since he could talk. He comes by after school, plays Mario Kart on the old Wii with all of us, and eats spaghetti with us on Thursdays, sometimes even when I'm not on shift. Every one of these firefighters would stand up for him because Owen is a great kid. He's *our* kid.

We roll right up to Bridger Falls Middle School like the damn cavalry and haul ass in the front door.

Secretaries stand up, but we stride right past. Bucky murmurs a polite, "Fire department business, ma'am," and then ignores the frantic questions behind us. Teachers freeze, looking around for an emergency they haven't heard about. Principal Masters jogs after us like a confused penguin. "What's wrong?" he pants. "We didn't have an alarm."

Bucky stares him down. "No, but *we* did."

The hallway smells like gym socks and greasy cafeteria pizza. We head straight for the boys' locker room, and I hear kids inside laughing and slamming things around. We push open the door and round the corner to where the stalls are. When I see Owen, red clouds my vision. He's curled up inside the far stall. Knees to his chest, his hoodie stretched tight over his knees like he's trying to disappear. Three eighth-grade punks are leaning over the door and top of the stall, laughing, snapping towels at him, and taunting him. One has a phone out, recording.

Owen sees me, and relief fills his eyes. He gets up and steps out, wiping his face like that will hide the tears.

I point at the three boys crowded around him. "You three. On the wall. Now."

The eighth graders laugh and look at each other like this is a joke. That's their second mistake. The first one is messing with Owen.

Bucky steps forward, and his shadow alone sends them scrambling to the tiled wall. Bucky is also built like an NFL linebacker, and you don't mess with Bucky. He's one of the nicest guys until he isn't. His mean face could make a grown man cry, and I've seen it happen before.

Coach Toddy stands with his arms crossed, smirking like he enjoys the show. "Boys roughhouse. It builds character," he says with a shrug.

The rest of the firefighters behind me get closer and glare at Coach Toddy. His smirk quickly disappears.

I walk up to him until we're toe-to-toe. I'm taller, and I've got about twenty-five pounds of muscle on him. And I'm a whole lot angrier. I went to high school with Jeremy Toddy. And he was an even bigger prick back then. He's one of those guys who peaked in high school and wants to try to be cool with the kids. His social media profile features an old high school football photo from ten years ago. Now, he's still the bully he always was, living out his glory days as if he's hot shit around here. Spoiler alert, he isn't.

"Really?" I growl, low. "Three eighth graders and a sixth grader, and recording it is roughhousing to you?"

He opens his mouth, but I cut him off. "You saw this happening, and you did nothing. Worse, you encouraged it."

"It's just locker room jokes," he tries again.

I laugh, and it's humorless. "Go on. Say that again while I'm right here."

He must hear the danger in my voice, because he looks away and at the other firefighters, as if they're going to help him. We all think Jeremy Toddy is a joke and shouldn't be coaching kids. And after this stunt, he won't be. I guarantee it.

I step back and look at Owen. He's shaking, but he looks relieved. He's still pretty small for his age, and these kids are huge compared to him. He now stands a little taller because his people showed up.

I crouch in front of him until we're eye to eye. The second I really see his face, something hot and sharp detonates in my chest.

His cheek is already swelling. The skin under his eye is

turning an ugly, sickening shade that means it'll be black by morning.

Heat floods my veins. My jaw locks so hard my teeth ache. I force my hands to stay loose at my side instead of balling into fists. I take a slow breath through my nose, but it barely touches the rage burning there.

Easy. Not in front of him.

"Hey, buddy," I say quietly, even though my pulse is pounding in my ears. "Who did this?"

His eyes flick past me, quick and scared, then back again. I don't have to follow his gaze to know where it lands.

Coach Toddy.

My nostrils flare before I can stop it. I swallow the growl climbing up my throat and keep my voice steady, gentle, like everything inside me isn't screaming.

"He tripped and fell," Toddy says defiantly. "You tell him, Murphy." He practically spits when he says Owen's last name.

I help Owen up. "Go out in the hall and wait."

Owen scrambles to pick up his dripping wet backpack and heads to the hall.

The other firefighters close in behind me, not crowding, just enough to be a solid wall at my back.

"Kids," Bucky says firmly, voice carrying. "Against the wall. Now."

They scramble without argument, sneakers squeaking as they press themselves shoulder to shoulder along the cinderblock. I glance their way and feel a grim, cold satisfaction when I see it on their faces. Wide eyes glancing around.

Good. They need to be sorry for this.

They aren't looking at Owen. They're looking at Toddy.

One of them swallows hard and looks around fearful. Another shakes his head, appearing like he wishes he could take something back. A third won't meet Toddy's eyes at all, staring at the floor like it might open up and save him. It won't. Today they're gonna learn.

I clock it all in a second. The way their bodies lean away from him. The way none of them step forward to defend him.

"Stay right there," I tell them, calm and steady.

Toddy shifts behind me. "Look, you can't just come in here like this," he starts.

The kids speak before he can finish.

"He told us to do it," one blurts out, voice cracking.

"He said Owen needed to be taught a lesson," another adds.

"I saw him grab Owen," a third says, barely above a whisper. "He shoved him into the lockers."

The room goes dead silent.

I don't turn around. I don't need to. I already know what my fist is about to do.

My hand slams onto the wall next to Toddy's head, and he flinches. "You wanna put your fuckin' hands on a kid?"

Principal Masters comes up next to Toddy. "We need to gather all the facts first."

I turn and glare at him, eyes narrowed. "I'd be cautious how your next words come out of your mouth."

He opens his mouth and shuts it, looking at Toddy. "If you did that, you're done."

Fucking small towns looking out for their own and not the kids. Perfect. Not on my watch.

"Call it in to Matthews. We're filing a report," I tell Bucky as he picks up his radio and requests law enforcement at Bridger Falls Middle School.

"I don't think we need to go that far," Principal Masters says, looking nervous.

Bucky folds his arms. "A child is hiding in a bathroom stall being abused while an administrator watches and encourages it, and puts their hands on a student, and you worry about optics? Calling the sheriff isn't going far enough. We'll help you out and do the right thing for you since you can't seem to."

Coach Toddy attempts to inch away, and my other hand slaps on the other side of him. "Don't fuckin' move," I bite out.

"I don't know about you, but we're mandated reporters. When we hear about abuse, we call it in. You aren't doing *your* job," Bucky says, glaring at Principal Masters.

"Tell me exactly what happened. Now," I say, eerily quiet. I watch Toddy squirm, and my eyes narrow.

"Kid needs discipline," Toddy mutters.

"Discipline," I repeat quietly. "For what?"

Principal Masters sputters. "Should we call Owen's parents?"

"He doesn't have parents," Toddy says snidely. "Just that sister of his and she can barely take care of him. Look at how he is."

I lean into him and say, "Shut your fuckin' mouth, or you're going to be sweeping up your teeth from the floor of this locker room."

"You can't threaten me like this," Toddy says, but looks around worried.

Bucky examines his fingernails. "We didn't hear anything. And if you know what's best, you didn't either," he says to Principal Masters.

Toddy juts up his chin. "Kid has a smart mouth. He's just as trashy as his old man and sister. He needed to be taken down a peg or two."

Principal Masters closes his eyes and says, "Effective immediately, you're terminated."

The door opens, and Sheriff Matthews rushes in, his eyes taking in the room.

"Thank God you're here! These psychopaths threatened

me!" Toddy yells, looking at our crew and back at Sheriff Matthews.

"Sheriff," I say with a nod. "Jeremy Toddy assaulted Owen Murphy, and we'll be pressing charges. Owen's in the hall and can give a statement."

Sheriff Matthews looks around, and everyone nods, and he gapes at Toddy in disbelief. "You assaulted a student?"

"He tripped!" Toddy says. "You can't listen to them. They're biased. Probably all fucking his sister. That's why they all have that slut's brother's back."

My fist makes contact with Toddy's face, and satisfaction fills me.

Sheriff Matthews pushes himself between us.

I step back. Whatever happens next, that was worth it. For Owen and Poppy. Especially for Poppy. I won't let anyone disrespect her like that.

"You saw that! Arrest him!" Toddy sputters, wiping the blood from his mouth and nose.

"I actually didn't see anything. I was looking at the kid in the hall, whom you just said terrible things about and his family. What happened? Did you trip?" Sheriff Matthews asks, pretending to be concerned.

I laugh as the guys follow me out into the hall. I slip an arm around Owen's shoulders. He leans into me, little fingers gripping my sleeve.

"We need to call his sister," Principal Masters says, looking like he does not want to make that call.

Owen whispers, "Are you sure you want to do that? She's gonna be so mad. She'll probably weld all their truck doors shut."

I chuckle because, honestly, Owen isn't wrong. Poppy's going to be pissed as hell about this. And God help them all when my sister Cami gets wind of this. Toddy might as well change his name and go into witness protection at this point.

"Owen's leaving with us," I tell him, looking at the exhaustion on Owen's face. What Owen needs is a shower, fresh clothes, and a breather from this shithole.

Principal Masters starts to object. "He can't just leave with you. His guardian needs to approve."

"I'm his emergency contact," I remind him. "And you'd better believe he's not staying here after this. He needs a damn minute." I glare at him until he relents with a resigned nod. "You should have kept him safe. Toddy better not have access to kids ever again at this school, or I'm coming for you and your job next."

"And now I have to find a new coach," Principal Masters mutters, shaking his head.

Owen leans in and whispers, "I have basketball tryouts today after school."

I turn and glower at the principal. "He'll be back for tryouts. And there better be no funny business."

Bucky nods toward the exit. "Let's move out."

We leave the school in formation, Owen surrounded by turnout gear and people who love him without question.

Kids peer out from classrooms as we pass.

Owen notices, and his chin lifts.

I catch his eye and smile. "We got you, Buddy."

And the little spark of pride on his face makes my chest feel tight.

Nobody messes with him. Not when he has me. And definitely not when he has us.

* * *

The station felt like a safe house the second we walked through the bay doors, with the smell of beef stew simmering in the kitchen. Owen now has an ice pack pressed to his cheek and a bowl of stew in front of him. The guys made sure he got the biggest piece of cake, too. That alone tells him he belongs here. He looks tired. Sheriff Matthews came, got his statement, and looked madder than a hornet. It's safe to say Toddy isn't going to have a good day today. Asshole.

"Oh, man. Even you guys have the Crock Pot," Owen says with a groan but grins.

But it does feel good to see him smile. I'll take it. "One day you'll learn to love the Crock Pot."

He shakes his head and his bruise looks even redder.

"We have to tell Poppy," I say gently, sitting down beside him.

He nods without looking up. "I know. You know she's going to be so mad."

"Not at you," I tell him. "But Coach Toddy is probably getting a glitter bomb sent to his house by my crazy sister, Cami."

He throws his head back and laughs. "We both have crazy sisters."

"Yeah, we do." I sigh and think about my sister Cami, who on more than one occasion has done crazy shit. She's been compared to Beth Dutton from *Yellowstone*. Combine her with Poppy and it'll be quite the storm. Those two are going to be so mad when they find out that Coach put his hands on Owen and said those things. I don't even know how to begin to tell her any of this.

"Owen." I nudge his shoe. "You can't be scared to call us. We're your family. You always call when you need us no matter what."

His throat bobs as he swallows. "I just don't want to bother

Poppy. She's stressed, Ollie. She isn't doing good with money. I think my dad comes and takes it from her."

My jaw locks so hard it hurts. I'm not sure all of the details of her and Sully's arrangement, but I don't like it one bit. Sully's only done three things right in his life. Marry Grace, and have Poppy and Ollie, and that's it. He doesn't deserve any of them.

"Even when it's stressful, we gotta know what's going on. We can talk to Poppy together."

Owen nods and pulls his knees up in the chair. "Everything has been hard lately. But you help us. And the guys, too. We're lucky to have you."

"Hey." I tilt his chin up, so he sees me. "We're the lucky ones, bud."

The crew pretends not to watch, but they are all listening. That is what we do here. We keep our eyes on our people.

I pull out my phone to text Poppy.

Me: How's your day going?

Poppy: Swamped. Think you could get Owen from tryouts today? He's nervous he won't make the team. I hate that coach.

Oh, I hate him too. And she's going to hate him even more when I tell her tonight what happened.

Me: No problem. Get caught up. I'll get him all set and bring him home after.

Poppy: You're a lifesaver! Thanks!

Later, when my shift ends, I drive Owen back to the school for basketball tryouts. He keeps his head down, but he walks a little taller than this morning.

Principal Masters steps out of the gym the moment he sees us. He looks like a man who has aged five years since lunch.

"Owen," he says carefully. "I'm sorry about earlier. Coach Toddy won't be coming back."

Owen nods, polite but still leery, and I can't say I blame him. I still don't trust Principal Masters either.

"Who's coaching?" I ask, seeing all the boys lined up on the court, practicing free throws. They keep anxiously glancing around, and it dawns on me that they're looking for Toddy. Asshole probably made these kids so nervous.

Masters sighs. "We don't have a coach lined up to replace Toddy, yet."

"I'll do it," I say before I even think. It just comes out.

Masters looks surprised. "You will?"

"Sure." I shrug.

Masters straightens and looks me in the eye. "Thank you. For what it's worth, you'd make a much better coach."

"Listen," I tell him. "Owen's not my kid, but I don't let anyone mess with him—or anyone else's kid, for that matter. I'd commit war crimes to protect any of these kids. I'll keep them all safe. That much is true. That should be your focus. Keeping kids safe."

Masters' eyes widen before he nods hard. "Thank you. I'll email you a few forms I need you to fill out for the district, but you've volunteered for us before, so it shouldn't be a problem as long as you don't punch anyone."

Owen grins up at me like I just promised him the moon.

"You got it," I agree, except for the punching part. I'd do it again if I needed to.

We step closer to the court. Nervous kids dribble basketballs and check over their shoulders. I skim down the roster and see fifteen names—a perfect team. No one needs to be cut. Owen told me Toddy threatened to cut almost all of them. That makes my teeth grind all over again. They should be having fun, not being threatened and bullied by a coach.

I clap my hands loudly, and it echoes.

"All right," I call out. "Listen up. I'm your new coach. Coach Ollie. There will be no cuts. You show up, you work hard, you're on the team."

Heads lift, spines straighten, and hope sparks. Then they cheer and fist-bump each other.

Owen looks happy as he lines up with the other kids.

Okay, I think. *Let's do this.*

This is what it should be like. Someone stepping in and keeping kids safe.

Chapter 4
Poppy

Ruin The Friendship by Taylor Swift

The shop lights buzz overhead, and I'm elbow-deep in another engine again. It's late, and I wish I were at home curled up on the couch after the nearly twelve hours I've put in today. My body hurts in places I didn't know it could hurt.

I'm wiping grease from my forearms when the bell over the front door jingles. Ollie and Owen step inside. And Ollie... *yeah.*

He's in his Bridger Falls Firefighter hoodie and navy cargo pants that sit low on his hips and fit him just right. The sleeves are pushed up, showing off forearms that look like they were carved by a man who lifts heavy things and saves people for a living.

His hair is dark brown, thick, and just long enough to fall into his eyes when he hasn't had time for a cut. Right now, it's messy in that unfair way that looks accidental but absolutely isn't. His eyes are a deep, steady hazel which always make me feel like he's actually listening when I talk, like nothing else exists in the room.

He's tall too. Solid. Easily six foot and then some, filling up my shop doorway.

He looks like a firefighter calendar model who just wandered into my shop.

Which is ridiculous. Best friends don't notice things like strong shoulders and broad chests. They don't clock the way hoodies stretch across muscles or how someone's presence shifts the air in the room. They definitely don't stand there thinking about how unfairly good someone looks in navy cargo pants.

I glance over at Owen and do a double take at his black eye. "Whoa. What happened?" I ask as I cup his jaw gently and turn his face, looking at it.

"I had ice on it." Owen shrugs. "I'm fine."

My stomach flutters with worry. "What happened?"

"You're not going to like it, Pops." Owen grimaces, and my eyes narrow.

"Who did that?" I repeat quietly, trying not to lose it. I grit my teeth.

"Coach Toddy," Owen says, eyeing me cautiously.

"Coach Toddy?" Heat floods my veins as I look at Ollie for confirmation, because surely, I'm not hearing this right. There's no way. No way.

I drop the rag in my hand and grab the nearest wrench, already turning toward the door.

"I will weld his truck to a fucking dumpster. After I smash in his windshield."

Ollie catches me around the waist, laughing even as he hauls me back. "Easy there, Valkyrie."

The warmth of him, his scent, and the solid press of his body slow me down before my brain catches up. His fingers brush mine as he wrestles the wrench from my grip, sparks jumping even as my breathing evens out.

Owen laughs and looks at Ollie. "Told you."

"Don't encourage her, bud." Ollie chuckles, but I detect a hint of concern in his usually playful tone.

"Tell me everything," I demand.

Owen explains what happened with Ollie nodding and clarifying a few things. Then Owen adds, "Ollie punched Coach Toddy square in the nose."

"What?" I side-eye Ollie. I notice a faint graze on his knuckles, obviously from earlier, but it's not the punch that gets me. It's the image of him, storming in like some avenging angel for Owen, that makes my chest twist in a way it shouldn't.

"Everything's fine," Ollie says, giving my little brother a look.

"Are you in trouble?" I ask, eyes wide.

"Nope! Sheriff Matthew says he didn't see nothin'," Owen says proudly.

Oh, thank God. I take a mental note to fix his truck for free next time he brings it in. I've always liked the sheriff. Rumor has it he used to take his vehicle over an hour away to get fixed. But when my dad left, he started coming in, and that isn't lost on me. He didn't trust Sully but trusts me.

"You're still working?" Ollie asks, eyebrows pulling together as he looks around the shop like he's trying to change the subject.

"Yep." I roll my shoulders. "Almost done."

"You eat yet?" he asks, his gaze on me.

I shrug and turn back to the engine. "I ate earlier."

I haven't eaten since this morning, with the two pieces of stale toast I threw in the toaster and put the last bit of peanut butter on, which I make a mental note to replace at the General Store next time I get groceries.

Owen cuts his eyes at him, as if he's telling him I'm lying—little traitor.

Ollie's voice goes serious but firm. "You need to eat."

"Whatever," I mutter, grabbing a ratchet to avoid eye contact.

"Why did the school call you and not me?" I ask, suddenly realizing that I didn't get a call.

Ollie takes a breath like he's prepping for impact. "Owen called me from the locker room."

"But you were on shift?" I ask, confused.

"We all went." Ollie shrugs.

That's great. The Bridger Falls fire department will show up for my kid at the drop of a hat. They'd roll out in full trucks if he called. And Sully can't be bothered even to remember he exists.

The rage tastes bitter on my tongue.

"Thank you," I say softly to Ollie. "For being there."

I want to say thank you for always being there. For being the best friend I could ever ask for. I want to say so much right now, but I'm so exhausted, and there's so much I'd want to say if I could find the words.

He looks at me like he doesn't understand why I'm thanking him at all. "Of course. He called. I'm his emergency contact for a reason. I'll show up for you both anytime and anywhere."

That right there... that hits me too deep.

"Oh, hey, and guess what, Poppy? Guess who's my coach?" Owen smiles proudly.

"Who?" I ask. "And if you say Toddy, I'm gonna throw him off a cliff."

Owen smirks. "Ollie."

I snort and look at my best friend. "You're coaching?"

"Hey! I'm going to be a great coach!" Ollie says.

"Yeah, you will be." I lean into him, and for a moment it's

just a hug, full body contact, arms wrapped tight around each other. "Thank you," I whisper.

Normally, hugging Ollie is casual, friendly, something we do all the time without thinking. But this time... this time is different.

I let myself sink into it, letting the exhaustion from the day, week, years, settle across my shoulders. My head rests just above his steady heartbeat, the rhythm grounding me in a way I didn't know I needed. His arms band around me, strong and warm, holding me closer than usual.

The scent of his firefighting t-shirt, fresh laundry soap mixed with him, fills my senses, comforting and intoxicating. I know I shouldn't feel like this, shouldn't let it make my chest tighten and my thoughts spin. And yet... there it is. That forbidden flicker, the part of me that's always tried to keep him at arm's length, now squirming, alive in the middle of this hug.

"You got it," he says before stepping back.

Owen pulls me in for a hug, which surprises me. He usually acts like I'm trying to murder him when I hug him these days. I know he needs it because he hugs me back, but he usually pretends he's too cool for hugs.

"Thanks, Ollie. For everything," he says as he hugs him next, and my heart clenches a little.

"All right. I'll see you tomorrow at practice, buddy." He waves as he heads up the back stairs to the apartment he lives in above the shop.

"Hey," he calls. "There are some subs on the table there that I picked up at Harvest & Honey. Text me when you guys get home."

"Thank you." I smile gratefully. "I will."

We shrug on our coats, and I turn out the lights. My body aches with every step like I'm carrying too much weight, and I guess I am. Only it's mental weight.

We drive home in my old pickup, and the silence in the cab presses around us until Owen practically falls asleep against the window.

When we walk into the house, I flip on the kitchen light, and the fridge hums loudly like it's mocking me.

A little prayer slips out, quiet and desperate. "Please, God. Just a few more jobs this week. Something. Anything."

Because Owen deserves full plates, a warm home, and a life where people don't bully him. And I'm going to give him all of that. No matter what it takes. I'll work twenty-four seven and forgo sleep and anything else if I need to.

Ollie's earlier words flash through my head. I think about how fast he showed up and how he stood up for Owen and me. And he does it without questioning it.

I'll be calling the school and the sheriff's office tomorrow to follow up and let them know I'm aware. They'd better not let that happen again, and I *will* be following up on what happens to Toddy. This is not okay.

I lean my head against the cold metal fridge door, head throbbing from stress. Then, I take Owen's backpack from his shoulder and set it on the chair. "Why is it all wet?"

He rubs his bruised cheek, embarrassed and tired. "They threw it in the shower."

My chest tightens, and I can feel the prickle of tears gathering behind my eyes. My chin wobbles before I even notice it. How can people not see how precious this kid is? How could anyone treat him like that?

"I'll help you," I tell him, my voice a little shaky as I unzip his backpack and start pulling everything out. My hands shake slightly, not from fear, but from the rush of wanting to protect him from a world that can be so cruel."

"Go on," I say gently. "Go take your shower. I'll get it all cleaned up."

He nods and heads down the hallway, looking so small that I want to keep him in a protective bubble and away from assholes like our dad, Coach Toddy, and those mean kids. He doesn't deserve any of that.

I sigh and stand alone in the kitchen for a long minute, staring at nothing, heart too heavy in the quiet. I clean up and head to the shower, hoping there's still some hot water.

* * *

Three days later, we're at Walker and Violet's house, which smells like rosemary and garlic, and the kind of warmth I dream of a home smelling like. I've called around and asked about rentals, and nothing is available. I'm still looking, and well aware that the clock is ticking. We have to figure out a plan soon. Lights twinkle outside the frosted-over window across their back patio, music hums from the speakers in the living room, and the whole Bridger Falls crew is gathered around Walker and Violet's long wooden table.

Owen sits wedged between Cami and Ollie, telling them some ridiculous basketball story with wild hand gestures while he eats garlic bread. His voice is animated, and he looks happy and safe. And, today, that's good enough for me. Our world is falling apart, but that is what's getting me by.

"Poppy, you need a refill?" Violet taps my arm, breaking me from my wandering thoughts.

"Sure," I say. "This was so good, Violet. Just what we needed. It'll probably put me into a food coma, so I'll finally sleep tonight."

She grins and tops me off with the iced tea pitcher.

Everyone's laughing at something Walker said. Owen's cheeks are pink from the heat of the fireplace and too many dessert samples. And Ollie... he looks stupidly handsome sitting there, relaxed in a faded shirt that fits his shoulders unfairly well, smiling at me.

Maggie raises a brow at the three of us and says to me quietly. "You know... You two look like a family."

I snort. "Whatever, Maggie."

Ollie takes a sip of his soda and says nothing, his eyes meeting mine. I search his face for what he's thinking, and I can't tell. Which is hard, because we usually can have full conversations with just our eyes, and this time I don't know where he's at with his thoughts.

Jack barks out a laugh. "She's not wrong."

Owen beams like someone just handed him a puppy. "We kinda are. Ollie came and rescued me at my school the other day."

"Does it have anything to do with what happened to your face?" Maggie asks.

"Yeah, he kinda helped me with that," Owen says.

My heart does an Olympic-level backflip and lands straight into panic. Oh shit. I haven't told them that story yet.

Ollie grins. "Of course I'm your family, bud."

"We're friends," I say too fast. "He helps because he's... helpful."

Ollie gives me a weird look like, "Are you good?"

"Sure," Violet teases, leaning her chin in her hand. "And when the wedding invitations go out, we'll all act surprised."

Ollie smiles widely, saying nothing. I shoot him a look like *you're leaving me hanging over here.*

Owen squints as if he's picturing said wedding. "At least there'd be cake."

"I could make the cake," Cami says with a smirk.

I shake my head and give her a look that says, "Stop encouraging this."

"We're just doing life," Ollie says, trying to sound casual, but his voice does this little crack at the end that makes me swallow hard. "We're all here for each other."

Doing life is what we're doing. And despite how hard things have been lately, life does feel pretty damn good with Ollie. I don't know what I'd do without him, and I don't want to think about that.

Owen tells them what happened with Coach Toddy and how Ollie is his team's new coach. Cami scowls in my direction, shaking her head. I knew she'd be pissed. We all are. It's not right, and it's so disappointing how they let Owen down. I still haven't decided what I'm going to do about Toddy.

She pats my arm, as if in tune with my thoughts. "We'll plot Toddy's punishment later."

I snort laugh because I can't wait to see what we all come up with. Toddy has bullied so many people in town. He deserves whatever he has coming to him. I haven't had time to deal with him because I've been packing up our house and trying to figure out more pressing things like where we'll be living.

We finish dinner, and Mack and Owen head out to the barn to check on the horses. It's one of Owen's favorite things to do out here at Walker and Violet's.

Walker, Jack, and Ollie head into the barn to see the sheep Walker just got. Cami, Violet, and I are sitting at the kitchen island.

Cami looks at me and says, "You know, I think it's about time Jeremy Toddy gets what's coming to him, don't you?"

Violet nods. "Never liked the guy. He's always rude and arrogant when he comes into The Black Dog."

"He's like the tiniest man. The size of a Polly Pocket. I can't believe he thought he could put his hands on Owen and get away with it," Cami says, shaking her head. "Now it's time for Polly Pocket to pay."

"I don't disagree," I chime in, feeling better that they all know now and I can vent about it.

"I don't know what to do about him, yet," she says, like she's mulling over Toddy's fate. "But this isn't going unpunished. It'll come to me."

"Well, your brother did punch him in the mouth," I add.

Cami shrugs as if that's perfectly normal. "Not enough punishment."

Maggie looks over at us and says, "So, what's going on with you and Ollie? Things appear to be...heating up."

I roll my eyes. "Nothing is heating up."

"So, when are you officially ruining the friendship?" Violet asks as she flutters her eyelashes. "Because that's so hot."

"Eww," Cami says, playfully sticking a finger in her throat and pretending to gag. "That's my brother you're talking about. But I do love him with you and Owen. So, I'll allow it."

"We're not ruining our friendship," I say, more to myself than anyone else. "Ollie and I are best friends. He's my person."

We've been this way forever. Since the day my mom died, and he showed up on my porch with no idea what to say but refusing to leave. Since his house stopped feeling safe and mine became the place he stayed late and left early.

We grew up side by side. Through bad haircuts and bad choices. Through his girlfriends and my dating disasters. Through the years where he dated sweet, normal girls who made sense for a guy like him, and I dated men who never stayed long enough to matter.

Ollie's been my emergency contact for as long as I can remember. The first person I call when something breaks. The one who shows up without asking if I need help. He's the steady thing in my life. The constant. He's my Luke and I'm his Lorelei.

And somewhere along the way, without ever meaning to, my feelings stopped being simple.

That's the problem. Because you don't risk the one person who's always chosen you. You don't gamble your entire world on a feeling that could wreck everything if it goes wrong. So, no. We're not ruining our friendship. I won't let myself want more than this.

"Sure." Cami raises her eyebrows at me in disbelief. "Like, Jack is my support system. And my husband."

"Didn't the guy die at the end of that song? We don't need Ollie to die," Violet calls as we bundle up to head out to the barn to see the new baby sheep.

I shake my head. "Not ruining the friendship!"

Later, we stand by my truck as everyone says goodnight. The cool air wraps around us, and the laughter fades. It's just the two of us for a second, enough space to feel everything too clearly as we wait for Owen to finish saying goodbye to all of the animals.

"I'm gonna help you out," Ollie says quietly, leaning his weight against the tailgate like he's settling in for a battle he's already decided to win.

"You already do too much," I tell him. "I can take care of myself."

His eyes soften. "I know you can. But you're not gonna."

That hits something in me I don't have the tools to fix.

"I don't want to drag you into my mess," I whisper fiercely.

"Poppy." He steps closer, his voice warm enough to melt snow. "You're not a mess. You're the strongest person I know. And Owen... he deserves all of us showing up for him."

I watch his mouth and damn it's a fine mouth. I think about it a lot. What it would be like to kiss it...nope. Can't think about that. Can't think about Ollie like that. Best friends don't think about kissing each other. If I cross this line, I ruin everything. I risk the only steady thing we have. And Ollie's too important to us. I'm selfish for thinking of him this way.

Ollie holds his arms open, and my body doesn't wait for permission. I step into him, and he hugs me like he's been waiting all day for it. His heartbeat is loud under my cheek. His hand rests against my back, steady and warm.

It's not just a hug. It's a temptation. Of something I can't have. Because no matter how much Cami and Violet tease me about ruining our friendship and becoming more, I can't.

We pull apart too soon, both pretending we're fine. He walks around to Owen, who's heading toward the truck, and leans down to him.

"See ya, buddy," Ollie says with a soft ruffle of his hair.

Owen wraps his arms around his waist without hesitation. "I love you, Ollie."

My chest caves in on itself.

Ollie hugs back harder, like he's holding the whole world right there in that small body. "Love you too, buddy."

I look away because I can't handle it. Because Owen can love him so easily. Because Ollie earns that love every time he shows up.

And because somewhere deep inside me...

I already love him, too. And I always have.

But love is a luxury I don't know how to have with Ollie. Because in my world, when you love something, you lose it.

I wave and start the engine. Tell myself I'm fine all the way back to town.

Owen falls asleep halfway home, smiling in his dreams. And I drive through the dark feeling grateful. And more cracked open than I've ever let myself be. Because tonight, we did feel like a family. And that terrifies me.

Chapter 5
Ollie

Days Like These by Luke Combs

Wilder Ranch smells like hay and warm sun cutting through a cold day and feels like every damn dream I ever had about what a safe life could feel like on a ranch. Horses huff contentedly in their stalls. The wind moves softly and easily through the crisp winter air. Somewhere behind me, Owen laughs loud enough that it echoes through the barn, and my chest tightens at the sound.

Wilder Ranch didn't always feel like this. It did back when my grandparents were alive. Back then, this place was steady and happy. After they passed, it stopped being safe for my sister and me. Our parents made sure of that. I couldn't wait to get out, to move into town, to put distance between myself and everything this place had become.

The Wilder Ranch was where all my core childhood memories were magic until I was about thirteen. Then it all changed and my parents ran it into the ground. Jack Jessop's family ran the neighboring ranch, and they were family rivals to my parents. His father was also a criminal who is now in prison for a very long time. Jack, his siblings Weston, Jenna, and Tucker have all worked hard to turn their family's ranch and name around. Jack fell in love with my sister Cami and they're married now.

Jack bought our family's ranch and folded it into his family's land. Brought it back to life in a way I didn't know was possible. Somehow, the magic is creeping back in, quiet and stubborn. And he renamed both ranches Wilder Ranch. Because my grandparents meant something to him and his brothers and sister, too. They were good people who loved this land, this town, and all of the people in it. Seeing it now heals something in me every time I come out here.

It's been a week since the locker room incident. A solid week of practice that actually feels good. A week where Owen's confidence climbs higher every day. He walks taller now, cracking jokes. He looks more like a kid who's having fun playing a sport instead of bracing for the next insult, and that's the way it should be. Sports saved me from my home life, and I want that for any kid there who needs it too.

Toddy coached as if it were his personal mission to break those kids down, and that's not what sports are supposed to be about. It's about showing up and teaching them to work hard without losing their sense of joy. About letting kids be kids. Something Poppy and I are both passionate about.

Watching them have fun feels good. Watching Owen feel safe feels even better.

And damn if isn't the biggest win. Getting to help make a place safe again. A place where kids are protected. A place I needed when I was young, too.

Owen stands beside Jack now, brushing a chestnut mare. Jack gives him pointers, and Owen listens and watches, as if every word is gospel. His cheeks are flushed and happy, and I swear that's all I ever want to see. He reminds me of me with my grandpa Wilder when I was a kid in a barn working with horses. And those are the days and memories that I miss. I know my grandpa Wilder would be so proud of the way Cami and Jack have turned this place around.

On the other side of the barn, Poppy leans into Jack's truck engine, humming off key. It's soft and absentminded, something she does when she's concentrating hard. I don't think she even realizes she does it.

I do.

Her blonde hair is pulled into a messy ponytail at the nape of her neck, strands slipping loose and brushing her cheeks. It's the color of wheat in late summer, darker near the roots where grease has smudged it, lighter at the ends. There's a faint streak of oil along her temple she hasn't noticed yet.

Her eyes are clear, bright blue, sharp and curious, always looking for how things work and how to fix them. Right now, they're narrowed in focus, lashes dark against her skin. She's got freckles scattered across her nose and cheeks, the kind you only see when someone's been outside their whole life. There's a small scar on her knuckle from when we were teenagers and she slipped changing a tire, and another faint one near her collarbone she got long before I met her. I know every one of them.

She's wearing her usual work clothes. Faded overalls smudged with grease. A soft gray long sleeved t-shirt underneath. No makeup. No effort to impress anyone. Just Poppy as she is when she feels safe enough to forget the rest of the world exists.

She looks relaxed here. Peaceful, as if she's finally breathing without carrying the weight of everything on her shoulders.

The shop does that to her. Being around engines and tools and problems she can solve gives her a break from everything else that presses down on her. She needed this. I knew she did.

So, when Jack and Cami invited us out and asked her to look at his truck, she didn't hesitate for a second.

Watching her like this, I feel it again. That quiet, steady certainty that hits me every time I see her in her element.

She's more beautiful like this than anyone dressed up and polished and perfect. Not because she's trying. Because she isn't.

No one else even comes close.

She smiles to herself when she gets a bolt loose, and then reaches for the replacement part.

"You're staring," Cami says beside me, arms crossed, sounding smug. "Big time."

"She's happy out here," I murmur.

"She is," Cami replies. "I think we all are."

My gaze drifts to Owen's small hand running the brushes over the horses, Jack laughing at something he said, then back to Poppy—focused, soft.

Cami nudges me and gives me a more serious expression. "Would you ever want to live out here on the ranch again?"

I keep my eyes on Poppy, and the answer comes easy and undeniable. Home is wherever she stands. But I'm not ready to say that out loud or admit that to Poppy. She's made it clear that I'm friend-zoned. Plus, the ranch isn't my family's anymore. It's complicated, but it's Jack and Cami's now. That ship sailed for me. But I do dream about having a place of my own someday. I don't know where home is anymore except with them.

"You did that thing where you answered in your head, again," she says, rolling her eyes, teasing me.

"I can't afford land or to build out here on a firefighter's salary."

Cami watches me and says nothing. "That's not what I asked."

I huff out a weak laugh.

She tips her head toward the barn. "You two ever gonna get together? Or you just gonna raise Owen together and pretend it's casual?"

Heat crawls up my neck. "We're best friends. She doesn't wanna mess that up."

Cami's voice softens. "You're not messing anything up. You're already family."

You're already family.

Just hearing that is like the air is whooshed out of my lungs. Because I want that. I look at Jack and my sister, and I want what they have. A home, a family to do life with. I want to be needed. And most importantly, I want to be wanted. I want a family. Cami and I didn't exactly have that growing up. Our dad was a con artist. Our mom, Theresa, is a nurse in Bridger Falls, but she's never going to win the Mother of the Year award. She's gotten slightly better lately with Cami, but I still keep her at arm's length. I haven't forgotten how she treated us when we were kids. Both of us worked the original Wilder Ranch as unpaid hands after our grandparents passed. This goes way beyond everyday childhood chores. We ran that ranch full-time for our parents as kids. They ran that ranch into the ground until my dad finally left, and my mom was letting it go back to the bank for unpaid taxes and payments. Jack stepped in and saved it for Cami. He merged it with his family's ranch, The Jessop Ranch, and they rebranded it all Wilder Ranch because the Jessop kids didn't like their family name, either.

Sometimes I wonder if I even deserve to be a part of a family. My dad sure as hell didn't deserve us. What if I turned into the kind of dad he was?

"She doesn't seem to want me," I whisper. "What if she wakes up one day and realizes she can do better?"

Cami's eyes flash. "She already realizes you're the best thing that ever happened to her. And believe me, it scares her, too."

There's a lump in my throat I can't swallow. "She said that?"

"I don't know, bro. I can't tell you what she says. Girl code. You gotta figure it out." She pushes away from the fence. "Go help your girl. She's pretending she's fine, when she's anything but fine."

Jack calls from the barn. "Ollie! You coming to help us out with the horses, or are you just here to stare at Poppy all day?"

I flip him off low by my thigh, so Owen won't see. Cami snickers as I head toward Poppy.

Poppy looks up and smiles. "I think I've finally figured out what's making this stall."

"Of course you did. You're a mechanical genius," I tease.

She smirks and nudges my shoulder lightly. It's an easy gesture, but everything between us is. We've spent years like this—side by side, sharing meals, sharing Owen, sharing life—without calling any of it what it really is. Partners. Without the bravery to cross the line. It's like hanging out by the pool, calling it swimming, but never actually getting wet.

Owen runs by, breathless, waving a soft brush. "Cami says I'm a ranch pro now."

"You are," I say instantly. "You're killing it."

"Have you figured out where you're moving to?" I ask Poppy as we head outside the barn.

"Nope, still working on it," she says, her mouth in a line. I know she's stressed and I wish they'd just move in with me. We'd make it work.

Cami and Jack wrap up for the evening, and Owen insists on helping put away the grooming tools. He takes it very seriously, lining brushes just right and double checking the buckets like he's been promoted to ranch foreman.

When it's finally time to go, he launches himself straight into my side.

"I love you, Ollie," he says.

My chest tightens, sharp and sudden. I don't hesitate and hug him back. "Love you too, bud."

Poppy's standing a few feet away, keys in her hand. Her eyes flick to us, then away just as quickly, like the emotion hits too close to something tender. She swallows and heads for the truck.

I follow.

She's at the rear passenger door when I reach her. Close enough that when she turns, she has to press her back against the door without quite meaning to. She sucks in a sharp breath as if the metal is cool against her spine. I stop in front of her, closer than I need to be, the space between us narrowing until the air feels thick.

Up close, she smells like engine oil and soap, something soft and faintly sweet underneath it. Familiar. Comforting. Dangerous.

Her blue eyes lift to mine, curious and searching, like she's waiting to see what I'll do.

I reach past her and open the door.

It's such a small thing. Something I've never done before. But her breath catches anyway, barely there. She has to slide past me to get in, her arm brushing my chest, her knee grazing my thigh. The contact is brief, innocent, and it hits me harder than it should.

For a second, neither of us moves.

Then she climbs into the seat. I close the door gently and step back as Owen scrambles beside her, already talking about the horses like nothing in the world could ever be wrong.

I stand there under the endless Wyoming sky as the engine turns over. Dust kicks up behind the truck as they pull away, and Poppy glances at me through the window, just once.

I don't look away until they're gone.

I've never been surer of anything. I want to be in their family.

But I don't know if she'll ever let herself believe she deserves me. Or that I deserve them.

But I know one thing for sure. It's always been her.

* * *

It's four in the morning, and I haven't slept at all.

I tried. I laid on the mattress upstairs with the lights off, staring at the ceiling while the building settled and the town went quiet around me. I kept thinking about Poppy standing in my doorway, shaking her head when I offered her the apartment. About the way she said she wasn't ready, like wanting something safe felt dangerous.

So, I got up and got to work.

Now the music is blaring, bass thudding through the old walls, loud enough to drown out my thoughts. The apartment above the shop smells like dust and stale smoke, the kind that's been soaked into carpet for decades. I'm sweating through my shirt as I peel back another strip of disgusting, stained carpet and roll it tight. I drag the roll down the narrow stairs and toss it into the bed of my truck parked below. Murphy's Auto is dark except for the glow spilling from the windows upstairs. Across the alley, the bakery is quiet, ovens cold until dawn. A few blocks over, houses sit dark and still, porch lights flickering like they're half asleep too.

No one's awake but me.

I head back up and grab the pry bar again. The carpet comes up with a sound like it's fighting me, stubborn and angry. I yank harder.

Because even if she said no, even if she isn't ready to move in, I want this place clean. Safe. New. If she ever changes her mind, I want her to know I was serious.

The floorboards beneath are scarred and stained, and the new carpet that's coming in that I ordered will be better. Better than what Poppy and Owen are living with now, with the foreclosure that's looming over her. Better than relying on a man who never actually shows up and does what he says he's going to do.

If they end up here, which is what I'm hoping, I want this place to feel like a home, not a last resort, and I want to surprise her with new carpet and fresh paint. It's the least I can do for them.

I yank up the final corner of the carpet. The room already feels bigger, better, and cleaner without all that grossness. She's going to be surprised.

I think about how blood doesn't always equal family. Life is way too short to give my mom the time of day if she doesn't want to be a mom to Cami and me. Cami still has hope that she will be a mother. She wants to have our mom around, I get it. I wanted that, too. I just don't think she's capable of being who we need. But I also don't want to dampen Cami's joy.

I crack a window to let in fresh cold air. My sweat instantly chills, but I don't stop. I grab the paint can from the hallway and pop the lid. The color is Betsy's Linen that's a creamy white. I picked it because it feels peaceful and fresh. Like a fresh new start.

I start rolling paint onto the wall in long, even strokes. My muscles burn and my back aches. It feels good and purposeful.

By the time the sun starts thinking about waking up, I have both bedrooms painted. I step into the middle of the room and breathe deep. It already feels like a different place.

I rinse paint off my arms in the tiny bathroom sink, then strip out of my clothes and turn on the shower. The pipes rattle to life, and steaming water comes down like a reward. I lean my forehead against the tile.

Cami's words replay in my mind.

"You could live out here."

"You are family."

"She wants you too."

And moving back to the ranch? I lived there before I moved above the shop. I paid my share of rent that my mom required and then some. I took care of everything out there. And every time I handed her money, she would find a new way to suddenly need more. None of it was going to the ranch and we lost it. Seeing Sully do that to Poppy makes me so angry. I remember how Poppy was there for me when that was happening to me. I got through that with her. She gave me this place to live here when I needed it. I'd do anything to repay her, even making this place a home for them. I could always find a place and give them this.

Steam curls around me, and I have to close my eyes because the idea of home keeps turning into her. Poppy in this space. Owen is laughing in the hall. I'm cooking breakfast in the kitchen for them. The kitchen table covered in homework, snacks, and a half-finished puzzle.

A real family. Not one you are born into. One you choose. One that matters and means everything to me.

But what does that even mean? How can you choose your family if they don't choose you back? I need Poppy to want me back.

I turn off the water and towel off fast. My shift starts at seven, and there's still cleanup to finish. I try to get everything done before Poppy gets to the shop. I want to surprise her when it's all done.

I put my gear in my truck and head out just as the first sliver of sun starts to climb over Bridger Falls.

The firehouse smells like strong coffee and aftershave. The guys know I've been working on my place and razz me about it.

"You building a castle up there?" Smith cracks.

"Just fixing a place up," I say, tossing my bag in my locker.

"Fixing a love nest," Mike, one of the opposite shift firefighters, teases under his breath. The station erupts in low whistles.

I ignore them the best I can. I know they mean well. These guys love Poppy and wouldn't disrespect her. They have no idea what I'm doing for Poppy and Owen. I don't even know half the time.

We get called out around dinnertime. Just a transport assist at the retirement apartments. Nothing dramatic. But of course, Mom happens to be the nurse on duty when we get to Bridger Falls Memorial Hospital.

I know before I even see her because my skin crawls. She steps into view, hair pulled back, scrubs wrinkled, eyes sharp as ever.

"Oliver." Her voice drips judgment when I look away. "Still avoiding me, I see."

The guys glance between us like they have ringside seats and don't want them.

I adjust the stretcher position and keep my voice flat. "Been busy working."

She folds her arms. "Are you going to avoid me forever?"

The fact that she's doing this in front of my coworkers and a patient pisses me off.

I meet her eyes. The same eyes that used to look right through me like I didn't matter. "I gotta go."

Her mouth pinches like she wants to say something more. I turn away before she can dig her claws in deeper.

How hard is it to just be a good mom? To show up when your kids need you? To be there?

And then the real question hits like a punch. Is this why I

try so damn hard for Poppy and Owen? So that they don't feel what I felt? Well, I already know they feel it with Sully. But they shouldn't have to. No kid should.

I stare out the window, the whole way, jaw locked tight.

Poppy's dad is a parasite who only shows up to take from her. My mom enjoys wreaking havoc and making herself the center of everything. Neither of them know how to love. But maybe... we aren't cursed with their flaws. Maybe it means we know exactly what not to be.

I think about the fresh paint drying upstairs above Poppy's shop and about Owen's laugh when he brushes the horses and plays basketball with his friends. I think about what it would feel like to come home to them.

I close my eyes and let the thought sit heavy and terrifying in my chest. I want to build something with them that never breaks. I'll work every shift, tear up every carpet, paint every wall, and show up to every call if it keeps them safe.

My family is with them now. And I am going to fight like hell to be worthy of it. I just need Poppy to catch up.

Chapter 6
Poppy

Ends Of The Earth by Ty Myers

Hot water pounds my shoulders, washing grease and dirt down the drain in dark, swirling ribbons. I brace my hands against the tile and let my head tip forward, breathing through the steam as my muscles finally start to loosen.

God, I needed this.

My body's been tight all day. Not just sore but wound up. Like I've been dealing with pent up frustration and I need a release. My shoulders ache. My jaw hurts from clenching. Even now, my stomach feels knotted, restless in a way sleep never fixes.

I slide my fingers through my hair, working the shampoo into my scalp. It's been a disaster all day. Grease stained. Pulled back too tight. My skin reeking of gasoline and oil no matter how many times I scrubbed my hands at the sink.

Now I'm clean and feel human again.

The truth I don't say out loud presses in on me as the water runs. My life's been one worry stacked on top of another for so long I don't even remember what it feels like to relax without guilt tagging along behind it. The shop. Owen. Bills. Calls that never end. Problems that don't stay fixed.

I don't need a vacation or a spa day or some miracle solution. I need relief.

I shut my eyes and let the water hit harder, like it might knock the tension loose if it tries hard enough, but it doesn't.

I turn the water off and I reach for my towel.

Nothing.

I stare at the empty hook as if it personally betrayed me. Of course I forgot to grab one from the dryer. Because the universe clearly decided today wasn't chaotic enough. I rest my forehead against the cool tile and close my eyes. I'm too bone-tired to deal with this.

Owen's over at The Dogwood helping Maggie, which means I'm alone. No witnesses. I can make a quick dash to the dryer like a naked ninja.

I crack the bathroom door and creep down the hallway, every step careful. The last thing I need is to slip, fall, and have to explain to an ER doctor why I'm naked and broken.

I yank open the dryer, grab two towels like I'm pulling off a crime, flip my hair forward, and wrap one around my head. The other goes around my body, tucked tight like my dignity depends on it.

I straighten and look over and lock eyes with Ollie. He's sitting on my couch with his coffee cup halfway to his mouth. Completely still. Like a wildlife documentary moment where the narrator whispers, behold the stunned firefighter encountering a wild, freshly showered Poppy naked in her natural habitat.

I yelp, "Oh my God! I forgot you were coming."

He opens his mouth like he wants to make a smartass comment, then shuts it again. His eyes don't leave me. I feel the weight of his gaze as it drifts downward, slow and deliberate, lingering just a little too long where the towel doesn't quite hide me. My stomach flips, my cheeks burn, and I clutch the towel tighter, partly to cover myself, partly because I can't stop noticing the way he's looking.

"Not a good time for a 'that's what she said' comment, Ollie!" I shriek, and bolt back down the hall, dignity gone.

I dive into the bathroom, tightening the towel to my chest, and scream, "OLLIE, THIS IS SO EMBARASSING!"

All I hear is him saying calmly, "I told you I was coming over to grab you for dinner. You never mentioned I'd be getting a show, too."

"A SHOW?" I practically howl. "OH MY GOD. Why didn't you say something? You just sat there all quiet."

He calls back, "I didn't know what to say. 'Hi Poppy, I can see your naked hot body.' Not ideal."

I cover my face with my palm. I want to die. Actually die. But wait, did he call me hot? Ollie Kendrick called me hot. I mean, sixteen-year-old me would be screaming right now. But twenty-eight-year-old me is now suddenly wide awake with adrenaline.

Then he adds, in the most dramatic voice, "I mean, if you wanted to seduce me, you could've just said so. You didn't need to act out a shampoo commercial."

I huff as I pull on my clothes quickly and towel dry my hair. "I hate you."

He laughs and calls back, "No, you don't."

I head down the hall and flop down next to him. "Did you at least bring me a coffee?"

He smiles and reaches down, picks it up, and hands it to me. His fingers brush mine for just a second as I take the cup.

"Apparently, my sister has jokes."

"She always has jokes," I say, though my voice comes out a little too quick.

I sit on the edge of the couch, closer to him than I planned. Too close. Our knees don't touch, but I'm acutely aware of the space between us. Or the lack of it. I can feel his warmth at my side, solid and steady, like gravity has shifted.

I focus hard on my cup instead of the fact that he's right there. That he just saw me naked not that long ago. That my skin still feels sensitive from the heat of the shower, like it remembers.

The lid is warm under my palm. I turn the cup slowly and spot the note scrawled on the side.

Call me for a good time. Cami.

Of course.

My mouth twitches despite myself. I should say something smart. Or teasing. Or normal. Instead, my thoughts keep snagging on how aware I am of Ollie's shoulder beside mine. The quiet weight of him. The way his attention feels trained on me even when he's pretending it isn't.

I take a sip and stare into the coffee like it might save me.

Best friends are supposed to sit on couches like this without their pulse picking up.

Mine definitely does.

"What exactly is wrong with your sister?" I say with a laugh.

"Like today or in general?" He smirks.

I know he's trying to lighten the mood. I mean, we've gone swimming, done so much life together, seen each other in swimsuits, but not completely naked. Although I really wouldn't mind seeing Ollie naked. But best friends aren't supposed to want to see each other naked. And best friends aren't supposed to like it. And Ollie confuses the hell out of me.

I tilt my head up and groan. "Today has been the worst day ever."

He leans back on my couch, looking far too pleased with himself. "For what it's worth, this is the best day of my life."

I toss a throw pillow at him. "Come on, hot stuff. Let's go grab a burger."

He catches it easily, like he always does, and grins. That slow, knowing one that makes my stomach do something inconvenient.

"Is that an order?" he asks.

"Don't let it go to your head," I say, already grabbing my jacket. "You're just the ride."

"Sure, I am," he mutters, following me out.

The drive is quiet in the comfortable way we've perfected over the years. His truck smells like leather and cold air, with a faint trace of smoke from the firehouse clinging to his jacket. I'm hyper aware of everything. The way his knee brushes mine when he shifts. The way his hand tightens on the steering wheel when I change the radio station without asking.

He glances over once, then back to the road.

"So," he says casually. Too casually. "You feeling human again?"

"Mostly," I answer. "Still thinking about all the things I need to do tomorrow."

"Yeah," he says. "That tracks."

We pull into the burger place on Main. One of those no-frills spots with cracked vinyl booths and a bell over the door that announces your arrival like it's proud of itself.

He holds the door for me. Again.

I clock it immediately.

"Since when do you do that?" I ask.

"Do what?"

"Be polite."

He snorts. "I'm always polite."

"That's a lie."

He laughs, deep and easy, and the sound slides straight under my skin.

We end up in a booth by the window. He sits across from me, forearms braced on the table, hoodie sleeves pushed up. I try not to stare. I fail.

The waitress drops menus and leaves us alone. The air between us feels thicker than it did in the truck. Like we both know something shifted earlier and we're circling it instead of stepping right into it.

"What are you getting?" he asks.

"The usual," I say. "Extra pickles."

"Of course," he says fondly. "God forbid you eat a burger without a mountain of pickles."

"God forbid you comment on my lifestyle choices."

His eyes flick to my mouth. Just for a second. My pulse jumps.

He clears his throat. "You, uh, still humming when you work?"

I blink. "What?"

"Earlier," he says. "At the barn. You were humming."

Heat creeps up my neck. "You noticed that?"

"I always notice that."

Of course he does.

We place our order. Fries to share. Milkshakes because neither of us pretends to be healthy when burgers are involved.

When the food comes, we fall into an easy rhythm that's always been ours. Teasing. Storytelling. Talking about Owen's latest obsession. Complaining about work. Laughing too loud in a mostly empty diner.

But underneath it all, there's a heightened awareness.

Every time his fingers brush mine reaching for fries. Every

time his gaze lingers a beat too long. Every time I catch myself wondering what he's thinking instead of what he's saying.

At one point, he watches me take a bite of my burger, eyes warm and unreadable.

"What?" I ask.

"Nothing," he says quickly. "Just... you look happier tonight."

The words land softly but they hit deep.

"Yeah," I admit. "I am."

And for a moment, it feels like it's just us. No shop. No stress. No walls. Just burgers and shared fries and the quiet realization that being here together feels like relief.

Too much relief.

When we finally stand to leave, he holds the door again. I roll my eyes but I'm smiling.

"Don't get used to it," he says.

"I won't," I promise. But I know he'll always hold the door for me. Always.

But as we step back into the cold night, walking side by side, I already know that something has shifted.

And neither of us is pretending otherwise.

* * *

I wish I had time to dwell on the fact that Ollie saw me naked yesterday, but I have so much work to do right now. I have to get back to the shop and get on my computer. Owen is back from Maggie's and we're hanging out while I make calls and finish up paperwork.

A man in a faded black Carhartt jacket stomps up to the counter at the shop. "I need to speak to the boss. My wife dropped off my truck last week, and whoever worked on it did a crap job."

"I worked on it," I say, wiping my hands on my coveralls. "What's wrong with it?"

He looks at my chest for a long pause, then up at my face in confusion. A laugh bursts out of him. "Yeah, right. Are you the secretary or something? Or just playing dress up for your daddy?"

"Nope. Mechanic and owner too," I say, pulling every last ounce of patience I have to deal with this tool.

"Well, I want a real mechanic. Someone who knows what they are doing," he demands.

Nope, don't like this.

Heat shoots straight up my spine. "If you want it fixed, I'm who you get."

"I don't like your attitude, sweetheart," he hisses, glaring at me.

"I don't like your sexist bullshit attitude, yet here we are," I snap, matching his energy.

Damn. I need money, but not at this cost. Something tells me if I do anything for this guy, he's just going to become an even bigger headache. Nothing will make him happy.

That sets him off. "My wife dropped my truck off and told you to fix two things. Now they're not fixed, and I want a refund, you stupid bitch."

Before I can reply, Owen bursts out of the office, eyes blazing. "Shut up! You don't talk to my sister like that!"

The guy jerks his head back and grits his teeth. "Teach that brat some manners."

"Teach yourself some manners," Owen snaps, fists clenched. "She's the best mechanic in town!"

My chest squeezes as Owen sticks up for me. Not needed, but dang. He's so sweet. He's getting ice cream later. Maybe even his favorite cereal, too.

"Owen," I say softly. "Thank you. Go to the office, please. I've got this."

He stomps away, muttering about grown men being jerks. He isn't wrong.

I stare the guy down. "When your truck was dropped off, I was instructed to change the tension belt. That was it. I have it documented here. That's what I did. And that's what you were charged. Whatever else you have going on, I wasn't made aware of."

He rolls his eyes and says, "Well, you should fix it for free since you wasted my time having to come back down here."

I blink and stare at him, wondering just how many loose screws this guy has. "So, let me get this straight. You want me to fix your vehicle for free because you didn't clearly communicate the things you wanted fixed?"

"That's right, sweetheart." He glares, folding his arms, as if he's trying to look intimidating.

"I think there's probably a mechanic in Jackson who can help you out," I tell him calmly and nod to the door.

"You aren't a real mechanic," he sneers.

"Get out." I point to the door, my eyes on his, not wavering.

"Sully wouldn't have run this place like this," he spits out.

"You're right." I nod. "Sully would have knocked your teeth out if you came in here talking to him like this."

His eyes narrow, and he grits out, "Are you going to fix it or not?"

The audacity that this man has.

I stare him down and grind out, "Not. Get the hell out of my shop. Now."

God, I wish socket wrenches were legal weapons.

He storms out, slamming the door so hard the glass rattles. I turn back to the office and find Owen watching through the window with his arms crossed, shaking his head. He's so damn cute, I just want to squeeze him.

"It's alright, buddy. I'm not working with people like that," I tell him as I pick up my water and take a swig.

My nerves are rattled, but this happens more often than I'd like to think about. Sometimes people suck. They don't appreciate women working in trades. And I've learned that it's a waste of my time to try to educate them on anything. They have their minds made up. Yeah, I need money. But I'm not going to let anyone talk to me or treat me like this. I won't tolerate it, especially when Owen's watching. I'm trying to teach him that we deserve better.

* * *

Later that afternoon, while Owen's at basketball practice with Ollie, I'm elbow deep in the stubborn guts of another truck when the shop door swings open and my besties arrive to save my sanity.

Violet breezes in first, holding a giant brown bag like she's delivering life support. "I'm here to judge your playlist and gossip about everything you haven't told me about the shower incident and that asshole bothering you."

Cami appears right behind her with a giant cake, eyes lighting up. "We got your group text. I heard drama and came running. Please tell me you pulled a Sully and broke their kneecaps."

Before I can respond, Maggie from the Dogwood Inn marches in carrying a pitcher of what looks like margaritas and a stack of cups under her arm. "Girls, I brought drinks. Poppy needs emotional support."

In five seconds, Murphy's Auto Shop becomes a three-ring circus and not the cold and lonely shop it has felt like all day.

68

"Cami, that is a massive cake." I laugh when I see it has the word *congratulations* on it.

"I'm working on test cakes for an upcoming wedding and had extra." She reaches into a paper bag and produces a handful of forks with a grin. "We're not even gonna cut it. Just eat it."

I shrug. "Sounds good to me."

Violet hops up onto the counter and settles in. Cami pushes a straw into her drink and starts talking smack about rude customers. Maggie is already arranging sandwiches as if this were a catered event and muttering, "Anyone insults my girls, they answer to me."

I laugh until my ribs ache, caught up in the joking and the warmth of it, the kind of laughter that sneaks up on you and reminds you that you're not doing life by yourself.

"Okay, so tell me what happened," Violet demands as she takes a forkful of cake. "Mmmm." She nods. "That's good!"

"Thanks," Cami says proudly.

"It was so embarrassing," I admit. "I didn't know he was there and he saw...everything."

Cami shrugs. "And? Maybe it's time you take it to the next level."

I huff. "No! I told you guys. I can't mess up what we have."

Maggie smirks at me. "I think it'd be fun to mess it up."

Cami scrunches her nose. "Well, that's my brother, but I hate to say it. Maggie's right. Maybe you should have a little getaway with Ollie. Like, get stranded in a cabin in the snow. Or break down in the middle of nowhere and have to keep each other warm."

I look at her and say dryly, "No."

"Sounds romantic," Violet says softly.

I shake my head, heart pounding. No getaways. Best friends don't go on romantic getaways.

Because if I do, I won't be able to pretend this is still just friendship.

Chapter 7
Ollie

Worst Way by Riley Green

The bass from the band thumps through my chest as I shoulder my way through the crowd at The Black Dog, dodging swinging elbows and shouting greetings as half the town seems determined to stop and say hello.

"Hey, Ollie!" someone calls out from somewhere in the bar.

I lift a hand in response, weaving past a group clustered near the bar and angling toward the back. The place is packed—all noise and warmth. It's been cold as hell outside, and everyone must have cabin fever and wanted to show up at The Black Dog at the same time.

I spot our booth and aim for it like a man on a mission, smiling and waving, but no longer stopping to chat.

Poppy's laughing so hard at something, she has to grab Violet's arm, cheeks flushed and eyes bright, hair twisted into that messy knot she does when she's exhausted. Cami's midstory, hands flying, clearly thriving off the attention. My sister loves to tell animated stories.

I slow down and take in Poppy in her element with the people she loves and who love her. God, she's beautiful when she forgets to be guarded. And the truth is, I love seeing her relaxed and happy. Lately, these moments have been few and far between due to life repeatedly kicking her butt. I do everything I can to lessen her load, but I know she treasures these moments with our friends when she gets to just be Poppy. And have some fun.

I slide into the booth just as Violet finishes whatever punchline has them all cracking up.

"About time," Cami says. "We were taking bets on whether you'd get stuck talking to half the town."

"I powered through," I say.

Poppy takes a sip of her drink, then sets it down between us. The ice clinks softly, and my eyes track the movement without meaning to. I clock the faint mark her lips leave on the rim before I can stop myself.

I don't hesitate.

I reach for it and lift it, taking a drink from the exact spot she just did. It's instinct. Familiar. Comfortable. And the second the cold hits my mouth, I'm aware of her freezing beside me.

"It was touch and go," I add, like this is nothing. Like my pulse didn't just kick hard in my chest.

I swallow and glance at her over the rim. Her eyes are on me, wide and curious, something warm flickering there that makes my grip tighten just a little.

"You know that's mine, right?" she says.

I nod, calm on the outside. Anything but on the inside.

"Yeah," I say easily. "I know."

I set it back down between us, close enough that our fingers almost touch. Almost.

The space hums. Familiar. Loaded.

I lean back like I didn't just do something that feels a hell of a lot like crossing a line I've spent years pretending doesn't exist.

Poppy furls her eyebrows together. "You look tired. You doing okay?"

"Productively tired," I tell her. "I got a lot done today."

I finished up the paint, and the carpet gets installed in the morning, but I'm not telling her that. I just need to convince her to move in there.

I grab a menu and pretend to read it while my brain does an unhelpful replay of seeing her naked the other morning. That memory isn't going anywhere. Ever. Poppy is gorgeous.

She catches me looking and lifts a brow. "What?"

"Nothing," I say quickly. "You just look... happy."

She smiles, "I am happy." But I don't miss it. Behind the smile there are layers of worry and sadness I wish I could take from her.

The music is live and good, the table shakes as someone dances past, and Poppy's knee bumps mine under the table. Neither of us moves away. In fact, somehow, we end up closer.

"Where's Owen?" I ask.

Her eyes lift to mine, and something in her softens immediately. "He's at Ben's house," she says. "Pizza and Fortnite."

"Good," I say. "He needs that."

She nods and looks away as if she's nervous.

I'm acutely aware how familiar and dangerous it feels all at once. Pure torture to be exact. She smells so good like a clean, faintly soap-like scent and something sweet underneath it. I can feel the tension in her even sitting here, like she's wound too tight and pretending she isn't.

I keep my hands to myself, and I keep my voice easy. But my body knows exactly how close she is.

Every now and then, she glances over at me or pulls me into

the conversation like I've always been there. Like I belong there. It's effortless and natural, just like it always is between us.

I'm very aware of what she's wearing. Loose jeans that sit low on her hips. A soft tight top that hangs easy, not trying to show anything, but now I know better. I know exactly what's underneath. The curves she hides, the gentle dips at her waist. The generous line of her hips that fit my hands far too well in my imagination. A body that's hella strong and sexy from working hard day after day. A body I've memorized in my mind and heart. That knowledge sits heavy in my chest, making every inch of space between us feel charged.

She shifts, and her knee brushes mine again. I don't move away.

I'm out of water before I realize it, too distracted by the way her top pulls up when she reaches for her glass. Without breaking stride, she slides it over to me, smiles, and keeps talking to Cami like she didn't just knock the air out of my lungs.

That's how it's always been with us.

We look out for each other. Quietly and instinctively. I usually know what she needs before she does. And she does the same for me. Always has.

The difference now is that I'm hyper aware of everything I shouldn't be thinking. Everything I am thinking. How easy it would be to lean in. How impossible it would be to take it back if I did.

I pretend my pulse isn't doing something reckless just sitting this close to her.

Jack claps me on the shoulder and slides in across from us. "How's she doing?" he asks, nodding toward her, Poppy not paying attention to either of us.

"Sully's been giving her crap," I tell him, shaking my head.

"Do we need to handle that?" Jack asks, raising his eyebrows.

"We might," I say with a nod. "I hate that he can't just leave them alone. He's making both of our dads look good."

Jack's dad is in federal prison for various white-collar crimes he got busted for a few years back, and he's basically a giant prick like my dad, only my dad isn't as organized with his criminal activity.

Jack laughs. "I wouldn't go that far."

We look up to a guy I've never seen before strolling over, his eyes on Poppy. Mid-twenties, maybe. His smile is too cocky, stretched wide like he's practiced it in a mirror. His cologne hits before he does, sharp and heavy, the kind that tries way too hard to announce itself. He's got on a crisp button down tucked into pressed jeans, boots without a speck of dust on them, like he's wearing a cowboy costume instead of living the life.

He leans against our booth like he owns the place, elbow too close to Poppy, eyes sliding over her in a way that makes my jaw tighten. Not friendly, and more like appraising. Like she's something on a menu. Oh, hell no.

"Hey, sweetheart," he says, voice slick, confidence borrowed instead of earned. "How about a dance?"

Sweetheart. Nope. Absolutely the fuck not.

I don't move. Don't speak. But everything in me goes still and sharp, because this guy is here to take. And I don't like him on sight.

Poppy blinks and looks at Cami in surprise. "Me?"

He grins at her, and it's predatory with all of his teeth showing. "You're the prettiest girl in here. Come on. One dance won't hurt ya."

I'm on my feet before my brain can catch up. "She's not interested," I say, voice low and dangerous.

The guy almost steps back, but Poppy stands too, throwing me a glare fierce enough to take down a man twice my size. "Ollie."

"What?" I ask, my eyes burning into Poppy's, almost daring her to fight me on this. That guy is not good enough for her. Hell, no one in this bar is good enough for Poppy.

She leans into me, brushing my ear with her lips, breath hot as she whispers, "Just because you saw me naked doesn't mean you get to tell me what to do."

My entire bloodstream explodes into flames. Like an explosion, and I go rock hard at her mouth in my ear like that.

The guy waggles his eyebrows, still not getting the memo. "You comin', sugar? You know you want to."

I practically growl at the guy. "Get lost."

"Ollie," Cami grins. "Look at you being all hot and bothered over Poppy."

"You are not dancing with him," I say to Poppy, ignoring my sister. "Not that guy."

She crosses her arms. "You know what, Ollie? I have needs. If I wanted to dance with someone, go on a date, or even go home with someone, you are not the boss of me."

I have needs. The words land hard and ugly in my chest.

I don't actually know how many people Poppy's been with. We've always kept that line clean between us. Best friends. Safe territory. We talk about work and Owen and everything that matters but never details. Never names. Maybe that was on purpose. Maybe we both knew some doors don't open without wreckage we can't undo.

I know she's dated. I know none of it ever stuck. I know no one stayed.

As for me, I stopped trying a long time ago.

It wasn't dramatic. No big decision. Just one date too many where I caught myself comparing. The way she laughed. The way she listened. The way she felt like home instead of effort. Every woman I sat across from came up short, and that wasn't fair to them. Or to me.

So, I quit. Because if it wasn't Poppy, it wasn't right.

The guy still hasn't moved. Still leaning too close. Still looking at her like she's an opportunity.

Something dark coils low in my gut.

No one touches Poppy.

Not on my watch. Not ever.

Because she deserves better than someone who sees her as a moment instead of a whole damn life.

Something ugly and jealous rips out of me before I can stop it. "Maybe I should be."

She stares at me like I just shocked the crap out of her. "What's wrong with you?"

Everything. Everything is wrong with me. I'm so damn in love with her, and she has no idea.

Violet swoops in and smooths the tension like she's putting out a fire. "Here, let's go over to the pool tables," she tells the guy, dragging him away.

Cami says, "Time for more drinks." She gives Jack a look and guides Poppy toward the bar.

Poppy and Cami go up to order drinks, muttering something about men and their stupid egos. But I don't miss how Poppy looks over her shoulder at me as she heads up to the bar, still looking confused by what I said. Hell, I'm confused, too.

"She hates me," I say quietly.

Jack laughs. "No, she doesn't. She's just like Cami. Hyper independent and allergic to asking for help."

I scrub a hand over my face. "She'll never see me as more than a friend. Always keeps me at arm's length."

Jack leans back, studying Cami across the table as she talks to Poppy, animated and fierce. "Yeah. I had one of those."

"You wrangled my sister, though," I say. "How did you do that? She's crazy."

He snorts. "I'm still working on that. But you know how

much I love her and I'd do anything for her. We started out best friends, kind of like you and Poppy."

The words hit me like a punch. "I don't know about that. Poppy and I are legit best friends. You and Cami wanted to kill each other. And for a while, most of us thought you two would."

He laughs and tips his beer at me. "You're not wrong about that. But it always works out. A relationship built on friendship is one that will last a lifetime. A relationship without that will be harder to make last. First and foremost, we love each other's company. We don't get sick of each other. That matters. Hell, I think Cami would crawl into my pocket and let me carry her around all day if I could. We love to be together."

And that makes me think maybe he's onto something here, because it's exactly how I feel about Poppy. She's been my friend since we were teenagers. In high school, I played every sport I could, mainly so I could be away from home as much as possible. If I were off at sports, I wouldn't have to deal with my parents' drama. And Poppy was busy with Owen. When she and I became friends, her mom had just gotten sick. Owen was a newborn, and she stepped up to take care of him. We were barely kids. Not that much older than Owen is now. She and I would hang out, bringing him along in his little carrier everywhere we went. I've known the little dude since he was a baby. I even changed his diapers. And when her mom died, Poppy officially took over raising him, which was hard for her. But she chose him. He was like a piece of her mother that she still had when her dad turned to his biker club and alcohol, and whatever else he was doing back then. God only knows.

I'd do anything for her and Owen. Anything. That's never changed. But my feelings for her *have* changed. I love her so damn much. This isn't best friend level and hasn't been for a long time.

Poppy and Cami come back to set down their drinks and

they are off to dance. I can't take my eyes off her. She looks at Cami and laughs so hard she covers her face. Her eyes shine and her whole body relaxes when she lets herself be happy.

God, I want to be the one who gives her that every day. I want to be her choice. I want to be the one she reaches for, and not just as a friend.

Jack nudges me again. "You gotta give her time, man. She's scared. People leave her. She probably thinks you will too."

"I won't." The words come out of me like a vow. "Never."

"I know," Jack says. "But she hasn't figured that out yet."

I look over at the guy who asked her to dance, who is now dancing with one of my mom's friends, a nurse at the hospital. Good for him.

But I don't want anyone else dancing with Poppy or even looking at her. And most definitely not touching her.

Because I want her, and I want it all with her. Always have, always will. It will always be Poppy. She will always be my choice, and I will choose her, no matter what. I want the three of us to be a family and I'm not sure how long I can pretend I don't.

Across the bar, she glances over, and our eyes lock. Her smile fades into something softer. Something that looks like fear and want and confusion tangled up together.

She looks away first. I swallow hard and realize Jack is watching this whole thing go down with amusement.

Jack taps the table. "That's love, brother."

And deep down, I already know that.

It's always been her.

* * *

Poppy leaves The Black Dog like a tiny furious tornado in boots. I follow a few steps behind, my hands stuffed in my pockets.

Owen got dropped off at her house after hanging out with a friend and she needs to get home to him.

The cold night air slaps my face, but it does nothing to cool the jealousy still boiling in my chest.

She walks fast, and I match her pace. She still doesn't look at me. Finally, she turns on her heels and snaps, "Why are you being so weird?"

I blink. "I'm not being weird."

She points at me. "You practically barked at that guy for wanting to dance with me."

"I didn't bark," I say, offended.

"Okay, you growled, Ollie. It was... aggressive."

I step a little closer. "I didn't like the way he was looking at you."

She crosses her arms. "Maybe I want someone to look at me like that."

My heart tries to jump out of my body. "Someone? Or him?"

She scoffs. "I don't know. Anyone. I have needs, Ollie. I want someone to want me."

God help me. Again, with the needs. The word *needs* ricochets around in my skull like a firecracker. I don't want to think of her with anyone and *needs*. I practically come unglued with even the thought of someone touching her.

She turns and storms off again, boots stomping against the gravel, each step ringing sharp in the quiet lot. The streetlights cast her in a halo of pale gold, and I can't stop staring. She looks impossibly beautiful, every line of her body animated, furious, alive.

I follow, chest tight, hands itching to reach for her. Halfway to my truck, she spins on me, hair catching the light, arms flaring, eyes blazing. "You don't own me. You don't get to choose who I talk to or dance with."

I lift my hands, rubbing the tension from the back of my neck. It's now or never. "I know." I swallow hard. "I just hate watching someone else want what I can't have."

She freezes mid-step, fingers twitching, lips parting, brows knitting, the moonlight catching the curve of her cheek. The air between us thickens, heavy, electric. My own fists clench at my sides, and every nerve in me is awake, wanting, aching.

"What are you saying?" she whispers.

I step closer, letting the tension hang in the moonlit lot, every muscle coiled, every heartbeat loud. "You act like I'm not allowed to want you. Well, I'm sick of it. Because I do want you."

She stares at me, eyes full of shock. "I didn't know. You never said anything..."

I open the truck and she reluctantly climbs in, still looking at me like she doesn't know what to say.

"You never had to," I reply. "You keep me at arm's length, so I never try. It's like you're terrified I'll leave if you let me close."

I climb into the driver's seat and we head to her house in silence, but it's not awkward. It's like she's thinking about what I said.

She looks away but doesn't deny it. We pull into her driveway, and I follow her up to the house.

We reach her porch and she fumbles with her keys. I gently wrap my hand around her wrist before she can unlock the door. "Look at me."

She looks up at me slowly and cautiously. Like, I might ruin her whole life with one word.

"I'm not going anywhere," I tell her. "Not ever."

A tiny, shaky breath escapes her. "Don't say things like that."

"Why not?" I ask.

"Because I'll believe you," she whispers.

My heart physically hurts. I step in, close enough that I feel the heat radiating off her. "I meant it. I want you."

She stares at my mouth, which I consider a good sign.

I tilt her chin up with my fingers, my thumb brushing her jaw. Her lips part on instinct. I bend, noses touching, her breath mixing with mine, every cell in me screaming to close the distance.

We're right there. One inch from everything. Then the front door flies open.

"Are you guys fighting or kissing?" Owen asks, hair sticking up, blanket wrapped around him, a box of cereal tucked under his arm.

Poppy leaps a whole foot away from me like I'm on fire. "Fighting!"

"Kissing," I echo way too fast.

"You're both weird." Ollie squints at us and looks at our empty hands. "I thought you were bringing home chicken strips."

Poppy groans. "Go inside, bud."

He shrugs and disappears like a tiny chaos goblin.

We stand there, staring at each other with freshly scorched souls.

"You almost kissed me," she says.

"You almost kissed me back."

She sucks in a breath. "This is a terrible idea."

"The best terrible idea," I counter.

Despite her panic, despite her armor, despite all the fear she carries like weights strapped to her ribs, she laughs. A soft, helpless little laugh that makes my knees go weak.

She steps backward through the door. "Goodnight, Ollie."

I step forward. "Goodnight, Poppy."

She closes the door before either one of us accidentally decides to be brave.

I stand on her porch, heart pounding, feeling like I just died and survived at the same time.

Inside, I hear Owen say, "You were kissing," and Poppy instantly hissing back, "No, we weren't!"

I grin into the dark. We almost did and almost counts.

Chapter 8
Poppy

Spin You Around by Morgan Wallen

Music thumps through the shop, loud enough to keep my hands moving but not loud enough to quiet my brain. It's supposed to drown out the noise, the worry, the constant *what now* that's been circling my life lately, but it barely makes a dent.

I've only had one customer today. An oil change. One. It's not enough to keep me busy. And definitely not enough to stop my brain from replaying last night over and over, every look and every word stuck on repeat, no matter how hard I try to shake it.

I scrub grease from my hands as if I scrub hard enough, I can erase the memory of almost kissing my best friend on my front porch. It doesn't work. I didn't sleep well. Every time I closed my eyes, Ollie was there. Standing too close. His hand cupping my chin. His voice was low and steady when he told me he wanted me. He wasn't joking about it. He meant it. He was dead serious. The look on his face was real, raw, and terrifying. He wants me, and I'm still trying to figure out what the hell I'm supposed to do with that information.

Because I want to want him, God, I do. But the second I imagine letting him close, really close, it feels like standing on the edge of a cliff with no railing. One bad step and everything falls apart. And things already feel shaky enough in my life.

Loving Ollie means trusting that someone won't leave. And that has never gone well for me.

My mom died, and then my dad somehow became a completely different person and abandoned us in the most vulnerable and horrible moments of our lives. People leave in different ways, and I learned that early. I learned to expect that, and that's what's so hard about this. It's hard to handle good when you're dealing with shit sandwiches.

I hear heavy footsteps overhead. The apartment floor creaks, followed by the unmistakable sound of boots thudding on the stairs. Then Ollie gets to the bottom of the steps, and my brain completely shorts out.

He's shirtless and sweaty. His chest is all muscles and glistening, and my mouth goes dry just looking at him. His hair sticks up like he ran his hands through it too many times.

The full firefighter workout fantasy has entered my workplace. My stomach does an unhelpful swoop. Fantastic. Now I'm going to be weird. Best friends don't think about tracing the outline of their best friend's muscles.

"You doing okay this morning?" he asks, like he hasn't been haunting my every waking thought.

"I'm great," I say way too fast. "Totally great."

He lifts one eyebrow, clearly unconvinced.

He takes a swig from his bottle of water and leans his hip against the workbench, sweat sliding down his neck, and I have to physically force my eyes away.

"Okay," he says. "I'm heading on shift for the next two days. You know where to find me if you need anything."

Ball's in my court. Typical, Ollie. He won't push me. He'll wait for me. But for how long? How many chances will he give me to love him?

Instead, I nod, trying to be casual and normal. Definitely not thinking about how much I already rely on him.

"Still leaving your truck?" I ask. "I want to rotate the tires and check the fluids. It's making that weird noise again."

"Yeah," he says easily. "That'd be great. Thanks."

"Owen has practice tonight," I add. "How do you coach when you're on shift?"

A smile spreads across his face. "The guys have pretty much adopted the team. If we've got practice or a game, we take the truck and stay close. If a call comes in, we roll out, and Principal Masters steps in. But we've made it to everything so far. Even Bucky loves it. The guys even have a dry-erase board in the common room for plays. We're all having fun with it. We are having the team over for spaghetti night every week to build up morale."

My chest tightens. "That's really cool," I say. "Tell them thank you. All of them. I'd love to make you guys dinner sometime soon. Maybe desserts."

Not just Ollie showing up for my brother. The whole damn fire department.

He pushes off the workbench. "You don't have to do that, but we wouldn't turn it down. I gotta go."

He heads up the stairs, then pauses and looks back when he catches me watching him.

He smirks. I immediately regret having eyes. Kill me. Bury me. Friends do not stare at their friends like that.

* * *

Later that afternoon, an older gentleman in a dark brown jacket, button-down shirt and khaki pants walks into the shop. "Poppy Murphy?" he asks with a kind smile.

"That's me," I say, wiping my hands on a rag. "What can I do for you?"

"I'm Jim Fisher," he says. "I've been trying to get ahold of you for over a week now. I've called and left voicemails. I teach automotive tech at the high school. I'm retiring after this year and... well, some of the teachers were talking. They think you'd be great to take over."

I blink. Hard. Oh, wow. I haven't had time to return his calls. I didn't know what he wanted. Okay, now I feel bad.

"Wait," I say. "You want me to teach?"

He nods, like he's been waiting for the moment to explain. "If you'd be interested, we'd have you work with me this year and take over next. It's good pay with benefits."

He pauses, then smiles, softer now. "And honestly, your name's been coming up for a while."

I continue to gape at him in disbelief.

"Mack talks about you at school," he says. "Not in a bragging way. Just matter of fact. My sister also teaches fifth grade and she's mentioned you more than once. Says Owen's proud of you and talks about you all the time. I think she had him last year."

My throat tightens as he continues.

"A couple of the firefighters who help with basketball practice have talked about you too," he adds. "They say when something breaks, you're the one people call. You don't cut corners. You explain things. You treat people right."

He chuckles. "My wife brought her car to your shop last fall when I was out of town for a conference in Tennessee. When I came home, she told me I had to meet you. Said you didn't talk down to her, didn't upsell her, just fixed the problem and sent her on her way. That matters. We need a strong, younger mechanic the kids can all learn from and look up to."

He leans back in his chair. "We want more female students in the trades. We want someone they can see themselves in. Around here, you're kind of a pioneer whether you meant to be or not."

His gaze meets mine, steady and sincere. "I think you'd be a great fit at the school. Really hoping you'll say yes."

The room feels very quiet after that.

And for the first time, it sinks in that this isn't just an opportunity. It's recognition for everything I've been building.

"I don't have a teaching certificate," I say, my mind racing a mile a minute, trying to think of reasons why this won't work. Something I have a bad habit of doing. When you live your life waiting for the other shoe to drop, it's hard to see the good things in front of you when they happen. But all I can think about is that this sounds like a dream.

"We know," he replies easily. "You don't need one for this position. You're a licensed mechanic. And over at the trade school, they still talk about you. You've got quite a reputation for being great to work with. You're very good at what you do. We just have to run a background check and do your fingerprints. Then the school can help you earn certification through its system. We have time to do that before next year."

Wow. I swallow, not trusting my voice to respond. This is wildly unexpected but so cool.

"Just think about it," he says, handing me a card with his email and number on it. "We really want you. It's a good salary, benefits, 401 (k), all of that. I heard that you're raising your brother. He'd be able to hang out with you after school, and you would be on his school schedule. Holidays and summers off."

"Wow, that sounds incredible. Thank you for considering me for this opportunity. I'll definitely think about this and talk it over with my...my family." I almost said my Ollie. Because that's who I want to talk about it with. Immediately, I think of calling him to tell him the news.

I stare at the card long after he leaves. Did this really happen? It would mean a steady paycheck and insurance for Owen and me. I've been paying for everything out of pocket for us, and that has been hard. And a teaching position? This is a dream come true.

I look around my shop. At the lifts. The stains and the memories. Some of the memories are good, but not all. I wouldn't have to take abuse from rude customers. I could teach kids who actually want to learn. I could help girls who don't yet see themselves in these spaces. And that really excites me. I haven't been excited about what I do for a long time. I sit on one of the stools and just stare at the toolbox, its tools missing again. My dad takes what he wants, even though some of them are mine. He thinks he has a right to anything I have here, and I have nothing solid. Everything I have could be taken away by him at any time. He makes sure that we know that, too. This could be something he can't take away from me.

The door opens again, and Maggie comes in wearing her denim coat, denim jeans, and braided leather purse with intricate beading. Maggie is like our very own Dolly Parton here in Bridger Falls, and she has her hand in almost anything that goes on. That's the life of Maggie.

"Hey, sugar. I heard Jim Fisher came to see you."

"You," I say, pointing. "You were behind that."

She shrugs, smiling softly. "You're family, kid. I'm not letting you drown. You deserve room to breathe. And those girls deserve someone badass to show them what's possible down at the school. It was actually Mack's idea. She wanted to take auto shop, but there are no females in there. She mentioned it, and it got me thinking."

"Maggie," I whisper. "You didn't have to do that."

"I did," she says, squeezing my hand. "Because I love you. So shut up and take the win. You are going to do big things, Poppy. We want you to pave the way for other girls here. Plus, they have a welding program there, too. I know you're also a fantastic welder, and they need you badly at the school. Apparently, they're hiring for several positions right now. But that one is perfect for you."

I hug her. She's always been good to Owen and me.

She pats my back. "Don't make me all sappy. I've got a reputation to uphold."

I laugh, wiping my eyes. And for the first time in a long time, something feels possible. And that scares me almost as much as it gives me hope.

She heads out, leaving me to think about Jim's visit and what it could mean.

I pull out my phone and text Ollie. I know he'll be so happy, too.

Poppy: Hey, are you busy?

Ollie: Nope. Just got to the station. Talking to the guys. What's up?

Poppy: Can I come tell you something? It's important.

Ollie: You know you never need an excuse to come see me, right?

Oh my God.

Poppy: Ollie!

> Ollie: Joking. Get your butt down here and tell me.

Only I have a feeling that he's not joking at all. But I'm too excited to unpack that right now.

I slap a *be back in twenty* sign on the door, slide on my coat, and make the five-minute walk down the street to the Bridger Falls Fire Station. The air's cold and sharp, my boots crunching over gravel and frost as I go.

The station doors are lit up like a beacon, a safe place. The way the station has always felt.

When I step inside, warmth hits me immediately. Not just heat, but the smell of coffee that's been sitting too long on the burner, clean soap, and something faintly smoky that never quite leaves a place like this. The floors are scuffed concrete, worn smooth by boots and years of pacing. Gear racks line one wall, turnout coats hanging heavy and ready, helmets perched on top like they're waiting for their owners.

The place hums with low noise. A TV murmuring somewhere in the background. Distant laughter. The clatter of dishes from the kitchen. I smell something cooking and can't quite tell what it is, but it smells good.

I barely make it three steps in before I start scanning the room for him, my pulse picking up like I'm on a mission.

"Hey, Poppy!" Bucky calls from the kitchen area, leaning against the counter with a mug in his hand. He grins like he knows something I don't.

I head over to him and give him a hug, waving at some of the other guys. "Thanks for all of your help with Owen."

"Aww, he's a great kid. You're doing a great job." Bucky says as he pulls a tray of lasagna out of the oven.

"It takes a village, Bucky. I'm thankful for all of you guys. Have you seen Ollie?"

His mouth goes into a line. "His mother just showed up. He's out back talking to her."

"Oh." I grimace.

"Yeah, our thoughts, too." Bucky leans against the counter. He shakes his head with disappointment.

"Should we go save him?" I ask, looking out the window and seeing Ollie stand with his hands on his hips, an expression on his face as if he's trying to find patience. His mom has an angry tone to her voice radiating through the window. She's talking animatedly, her hands flying, and her voice is getting louder as she goes on. Ollie stands there, saying nothing. He looks cold, without a jacket. That's all I can think about is him being cold.

Theresa hasn't been the best mom to Cami or Ollie. She's been coming around more often, but it's hard. They never know what version of her they're going to get. Is she going to be their mother figure or someone who is snarky and manipulative? I've seen both sides, and I'm not a big fan. Ollie used to keep going back to her and doing whatever she needed, and he'd always end up hurt and disappointed, no matter what. In the past few years, he has stopped going around, and he seems happier without her drama.

"Probably a good idea to save him," Bucky says and turns before calling to one of the guys. "Hey, go get Kendrick. Tell him we need him in here."

The newbie cracks the back door and calls out, "Yo, Kendrick. Bucky needs you."

Theresa turns and glares at the interruption. Ollie says something to her and strolls over to the door. She crosses her arms and watches him with narrowed eyes as he heads inside.

He comes in, and his face lights up when he sees me. "Hey, what's up?"

I raise my eyebrows and look out the window at Theresa on

her phone, who's staring at the firehouse as she talks animatedly. "Are you good?"

He rolls his eyes and shakes his head. "Theresa just being Theresa."

"You need help with anything?" Bucky asks.

Ollie shakes his head. "Nope. What do I need to do?"

Bucky shakes his head. "Just a rescue mission."

"Appreciate it," he says. "Come on, Poppy."

I follow him into the garage where the trucks are. The doors are closed because it's a cold Wyoming day. No snow today, but I heard it's coming.

"What did you have to tell me?" he asks, leaning in and giving me all of his attention.

I grin and say, "What would you say if I told you that you were looking at the next auto shop teacher at the Bridger Falls High School?"

He picks me up and spins me around. "What? No way!"

I laugh as he sets me down. "Yes! Jim Fisher from the high school came in and offered me a job!"

"What? Whoa. You'd be perfect for that job. Dang, those kids would be so lucky to have you," he says, just as excited as I am.

"I know, right? Solid paychecks and benefits!"

He smiles. "Amazing. Just amazing."

"What are you going to do about the shop?" he asks, suddenly.

I bite my lip. "I don't know. I can't let it go, but I was thinking of finding a way to make both work. Like maybe run the shop part-time alongside the school. It would be a lot, but I could get caught up. I could definitely make it work until summer and maybe find some help by then."

He nods. "Any chance you could save the house?"

I shake my head. "My dad was so far behind on payments.

And it needs so much work. I think we're better off finding a place in town to rent for a while."

"You know you can move into the garage apartment."

"That's your place," I tell him firmly. "We're not taking your place."

"My place is with you," he tells me, eyes meeting mine.

"I don't know what to say, Ollie. You know you're literally my best friend in the whole world. I can't imagine not having you in my life. And if we didn't work out, so many bad things would happen. Like Owen...and..."

Ollie pulls me close to him. "Poppy."

I sigh. "What?"

"Stop overthinking things."

"I'm not. I'm being logical. I mean, look at us. Neither of us had an idyllic childhood. I don't think I want kids. If I can get my brother raised happy and healthy, that's enough for me," I admit.

Ollie searches my eyes. "And that would be fine. But I love you, Poppy. Both of you."

"I love you, too," I say, looking back. "I love you too much to lose you."

"Then I guess you'll just have to find me," he teases, lightening the mood.

Bucky opens the door. "Hey, you gonna eat?"

"Yeah," Ollie calls back and turns to me, looking hopeful. "You staying?"

I shake my head. "I gotta get back and give Jim a call to tell him yes."

"Make her a to-go container, please!" Ollie says to Bucky.

"You got it!" Bucky calls.

"You don't have to feed me," I say.

Ollie shakes his head. "If I don't feed you, you won't eat."

"Owen's a little snitch," I say with a laugh.

"We need you to have energy and be a badass teacher." He wraps me in a big hug again, and I relax into him, breathing him in.

And how can I argue with that?

"Thank you," I murmur into his chest.

He squeezes me gently. I don't give Ollie hugs often. We don't touch like this in general, but it's getting harder and harder not touch him.

Because Ollie is the one who will wreck me if I let him.

Chapter 9
Ollie

Oklahoma Smokeshow by Zach Bryan

The door opens before I can knock a second time. I immediately slap a hand over my eyes and turn my head like I've walked in on something illegal. "Everybody dressed?"

Owen blinks up at me from the couch, brows pulling together. "Why wouldn't we be dressed?"

Poppy lets out a sharp, nervous laugh. "Really, Ollie?"

I peek through my fingers just enough to see her standing there in a hoodie and jeans, arms crossed, cheeks pink. Very dressed. Annoyed and cute. Bummer. I preferred the naked version.

I lower my hand slowly. "Okay, cool. Just checking."

"Checking what?" Owen asks, sounding confused.

Poppy groans. "You're ridiculous."

I step inside and close the door behind me, toeing off my

boots. "Hey, I knocked. I announced myself. I even covered my eyes. I'm basically a hero."

"You're a weirdo," Owen says.

I set the boxes down carefully like if I'm gentle enough, none of this will be real. I hate that they are losing this house and that this is the nightmare they're living right now. I wish I could make it all better. I wish she'd just move in with me.

She joins me in the living room, helping me with the boxes.

Owen jumps up and says, "Wait till you see how good my free throws have gotten. I've been practicing extra at school. We've had a long-term substitute and she says we can do whatever we want so I just practice extra."

"You're killing it, bud. I can't wait to see," I say as I glance around at the piles of things and trash bags.

"Thank you," she says quietly, her eyes cutting to the boxes. Which is the elephant in the room that no one wants to acknowledge or make real.

I nod.

"Walker said we can store stuff in their pole barn until we figure out the next step."

My mouth tightens. "That helps. We can make trips out."

I glance at Owen who is now setting up his game for us to play and I whisper, "How's he doing with all this?"

She shrugs, but it's tired. "He's not saying much. Which means it's probably bothering him a lot. Maybe you could get him to talk about it."

I nod. I can definitely talk to him.

Owen drops onto the couch and pulls a blanket over him. I hate how he's losing the only home he's ever known.

"I mean it," I say to Poppy. "Come to the shop. Take the apartment. We can make it work."

Her eyes flick up to mine. She looks like she's about to argue, then she doesn't. I hope she's really considering it.

"Maybe," she says. "Even if it's just until we can find something. There's not a lot of rentals right now and I need to save up."

I nod, keeping my voice steady. "I think Owen would like it. It'd be solid. And if you're pulling off two jobs, the high school and the shop, it makes sense to be close for Owen. He could just be right upstairs."

She looks at Owen. "Let's just see," she says.

"Hey, before we get started, let's go grab a few pizzas," I tell Owen and he wastes no time scrambling to get his coat on. "We'll be right back. Any requests?"

She blows out a breath as she opens up one of the boxes and begins to fill it with old photo albums from the entertainment center. "Anything is good. Thanks."

"I got you, Poppy," I tell her as we head out.

Because I will always have them. Even if she isn't ready. I'll be waiting.

* * *

A few days later, everything goes sideways. We've been gone all morning, dropping donations at the thrift store, then hauling a load out to Walker's pole barn. I'm pulling back into the shop with Poppy next to me in the passenger seat and Owen in the back with his headphones on.

"Ollie," she whispers and grabs my arm, and I know immediately something's wrong.

"What are they doing here?" I ask, anger and fear rising in me as I park.

Bikes and trucks I don't recognize are lined up out in front of her shop like a bad memory came back to life. The way the shop used to operate, overrun by drunk druggie bikers who all but practically ran the shop into the ground while Poppy fought to make money and take care of Owen.

My stomach drops.

Poppy gets out, and Owen follows. Her shoulders are squared, and both of them look tense.

"Hey, stay in the truck," I say, and neither of them listen and head inside. Because for them this is their dad. They grew up with this. My dad was a piece of work, but at least he preferred his crimes to be of the white-collar variety and didn't bring menacing bikers home with him.

I don't hear everything at first, but I hear Sully bite out, "Came for my money."

His tone is very much not kind. He's in a mood. I've seen him get like this, and it's never good for the person who is on the receiving end. I don't like this at all. Not one bit.

Poppy doesn't back up, just squares her shoulders and tells him, "I don't have it."

Sully scoffs. "Funny how this keeps happening."

"It's not going to keep happening," she says. "I took a job at the high school. There's benefits and it's solid for Owen."

His face darkens. "Like hell you are. You owe me!"

"What are you gonna do?" she asks, waving at the shop. "You already took our house. You want this too?"

He steps closer. Too close.

Owen presses into her side.

My vision goes red and I sidle up beside her, knowing damn well if I step in front of her, it weakens her and I know she needs to do this. We both know Sully's not going to do anything to her. But the other bikers? I don't know what they'll do. But they'll have to get through me to get to them.

"Call Jack," I whisper in Owen's ear and he nods. I see Owen pull his phone out of his coat pocket and push a few buttons at his side.

I know Jack is in town and he'll get here quick. Plus, this gives Owen something to focus on if this goes south and I have to lay these fuckers out.

Sully sneers. "Who the hell do you think you're talking to? You'd better watch it."

She doesn't move. "What are you gonna do, Dad? Hurt me? Go ahead and try. Spoiler alert, you can't hurt me anymore. I'm a grown adult who is not taking your crap anymore."

"I will get my money," he says in a scary voice. "Or how about Owen comes with me?"

"I'm not going with you." Owen scoffs.

Every biker behind him stiffens and stands up. A few of them look at each other confused as to how they're going to handle this. This looks like more than they signed up for. Worry pulses through me on how this is all going to go down.

"I'll bury you," she says calmly. "All of you. You have no idea who you're messing with. He may not give a shit about his family, but I do. And I will ruin every single one of you if you even remotely try to come for either Owen or me."

She reaches behind the door and pulls out a tire iron. I recognize it instantly. Welded spikes and studs. Weighted. Built with intention. She made that as a weapon. And I hate that she felt like she had to do that. She turns and glares at all of them who look surprised. "A monster fucking raised me. Better rethink what I'm capable of."

One of the bikers steps forward like he's going to do something, and she stares into him with the scariest look I've ever seen on her face. If I didn't know Poppy from the inside out, I'd be literally pissing my pants right now.

Silence.

Owen's eyes are wide. Not scared. Awed. He stares at me and back down at his phone where I can see him recording this.

I hope to God Jack's on his way. I might need backup here. I have no idea what Sully is going to do.

Sully spits on the floor and laughs like he hasn't just lost control. He knows he's got nothing anymore and he's grasping at straws.

"We'll be back," he mutters, then turns and says, "Better keep that firefighter handy. You never know when things will burn down."

She's shaking when I reach her and put my arm around her.

"That's not okay," I say. "He's crazy, Poppy."

She exhales hard. "I know."

"We have to get you out from under him."

"I'm figuring something out."

"Stay away from him," I say. "And his friends. He should be paying you, not the other way around."

She swallows. "If I push too hard, he could try to take Owen. I don't have legal guardianship."

That stops me cold. Like hell he will. No one is taking Owen.

Owen looks at us, totally freaked out.

"Never happening, bud. You hear me?" I tell him. "You did good."

He nods but still wears a terrified expression. "I never want to live with Sully."

"We're calling Weston," I say. "And the sheriff. He can't make threats like that."

She shakes her head. "I don't have the money for a lawyer."

"This is important," I say. "We're doing this. I'll set it up."

I look at both of them. "Nothing is going to happen to either of you when I'm around."

I'll make damn sure of it.

The second I heard Sully make that threat, the way his voice dropped and turned ugly, something in me went cold and sharp. I don't take chances with the people I love. Because saying something like that is halfway to doing something like that.

Hell no.

Owen hands me his phone, his fingers shaking. "I recorded it," he says quietly. "Just in case he said something really bad."

My chest tightens when I hit play. Sully's voice crackles through the speaker, slurred and threatening and way too sure of himself. Every word is another nail in the coffin he's digging for himself. Weston is going to be glad he got this.

"You did good," I remind Owen, keeping my voice steady even though I'm so angry at Sully and his trash friends. "Really good."

Poppy looks pale, eyes bright with that barely holding it together look I know too well.

"I'm staying with you guys tonight," I say, already heading to grab my things. "I'll be right back."

She doesn't argue. She just nods, relief washing over her face like she's been bracing for someone to tell her she's over-reacting.

Sully's gone way too far.

Owen's already in bed when things finally settle. The house is quiet like everyone's holding their breath. Poppy moves through the kitchen on autopilot, locking the back door, turning off lights. I trail behind her, not crowding, just close enough to be there.

She pauses at the sink, toothbrush in hand, then glances at me. "You don't have to stay," she says softly.

"I know," I tell her. "I'm staying anyway."

Something in her shoulders loosens at that. The weight of the world seems to lift some and damn I want that for her. I want to take that from her. The stress of the world.

We brush our teeth side by side at the bathroom sink,

bumping elbows now and then. It's domestic and strange and way more intimate than it should be. She makes a face at the minty foam, and I huff out a quiet laugh. Our eyes meet in the mirror, and the moment stretches, warm and familiar.

When she rinses, a strand of hair slips loose from her ponytail and falls across her cheek. Without thinking, I reach out and tuck it behind her ear. My fingers barely graze her skin, but she stills completely.

For a second, neither of us breathe.

"Goodnight," she whispers, standing in the doorway to her room.

"Goodnight," I murmur back.

She hesitates, then leans in and presses a quick kiss to my cheek. Soft and careful. It lands like a promise I don't dare name. "Thank you," she murmurs.

I take the couch, my boots lined up by the door, my phone on the charger. I don't sleep much. Every creak of the house has me sitting up, listening, every shadow feeling louder in the dark.

In the early hours, I hear small footsteps pad down the hallway. I sit up just as Owen freezes when he sees me.

"You're still here," he whispers.

"Yeah, buddy," I say quietly. "I've got you guys."

He nods, as if he's reassured, and shuffles back to bed.

I don't lie back down after that. I just sit there in the dark, heart steady, senses sharp, knowing that this is where I'm supposed to be. I just need Poppy to feel it, too.

The next morning, we don't waste time.

"Grab your backpack," I tell Owen. "We're taking you to school."

The drive over is tense but determined. Poppy's hands are steady on the wheel this time, jaw set. Owen sits taller in the back seat, phone clutched in his hand.

The school smells like cleaner and pencil shavings and cafeteria pizza. We sit down with the principal, the counselor, and the front office manager. I lay it all out.

"There's an issue with Owen's biological father," I say. "He's made threats. We have them recorded. He is not allowed anywhere near Owen or this campus."

The principal's expression hardens. "We'll flag his file immediately. Teachers, recess monitors, and front desk. If he shows up, we call the police."

Good.

The counselor smiles gently at Owen. "You'll be all right."

Owen glances at me, then Poppy. I nod once. He exhales.

Later that afternoon, we're sitting across from Weston Jessop out at the Wilder lodge, formerly the Jessop lodge. He listens without interrupting, then leans back in his chair.

"I'll help you," he says. "We need to get you solid. Guardianship. Boundaries. Protection orders. I'm on it."

Poppy's shoulders finally sag like she's been carrying the world alone and just set it down.

"Do you think we could force him to give her the shop?" I ask, leaning forward. I want everything we can get for them.

Weston shrugs. "I mean, we can't force Sully to do anything. But that doesn't mean she has to keep paying him. That's extortion."

"Maybe he could be persuaded aggressively," I muse.

Weston snorts. "Well, then you're talking to the wrong brother for that. You and Jack sometimes operate on the other side of the law. I keep you all honest."

"You're no fun," Owen mutters. Then he says, "We could put a skunk in his truck like—"

My eyes narrow. "Hey, how do you know about that?"

Owen and Poppy laugh.

* * *

The court date is a few days later. Weston files everything quickly and we get ready for it. We show up. Sully doesn't. No surprise there. No one really thought he would.

The judge listens to the recording, face unreadable, then grants the restraining orders without hesitation.

Sully can't come near the shop, the house, Owen's school, Wilder Ranch, The Black Dog, the firehouse, and a bunch of other places Weston added to cover us. But most importantly, he can't come near Owen or Poppy.

I stay with them every night that I'm not on shift, just in case. I want to be nearby if they need me. And when I am on shift, I check in all the time.

No one gets to touch what's mine.

* * *

Chapter 10
Poppy

Porch Light by Josh Meloy

"You can't keep your entire life in your head," Maggie says, tapping the colorful planner in front of me. "That's how women snap and end up screaming at strangers in grocery store parking lots."

I'm sitting in the office at the shop with Maggie, surrounded by stacks of paper, notebooks, my laptop, a new planner, and giant wall calendar Maggie insists I need.

"That's never been something I've struggled with," I say with a laugh. "What are you talking about?"

Maggie shrugs. "That happens sometimes."

"Maggie." I snort laugh. "What the heck?"

"Structure, Poppy. Structure keeps us out of jail," she says.

I laugh again and shake my head. "Didn't realize these schedules were that critical."

She slides a printed, color-coded schedule across the desk. Of course it is. I'd expect nothing less from Maggie. She's as organized as all get out, and she loves a good project. And today, apparently, *I'm* her project.

"This is your shop schedule," she says. "This is the school schedule. This is the Owen schedule. And this"—she taps the last page—"is the Maggie makes sure you eat schedule."

"I eat," I protest.

She gives me a look. "You drink coffee and survive on dry toast and whatever you can find. That doesn't count."

I laugh, because it's that or cry. Probably both if I'm being honest.

Maggie sits across from me at the table, planner open, pen tapping thoughtfully as she starts blocking out my days like this is the most natural thing in the world. She doesn't just pencil in work and appointments. She adds reminders to eat. Actual meals. Lunch. Dinner. She even circles one and writes *sit down to eat* next to it.

Something tight lodges in my throat.

I'm not used to this. To someone seeing how much I'm carrying and quietly stepping in instead of telling me I'll figure it out. I've been holding everything together for so long that letting someone else help feels foreign. Heavy. Almost too much.

She tells me she set up a meal train for next week so I can focus on transitioning into the new job and packing up the house. Says it like it's no big deal. Like feeding me and Owen is just another box to check.

I blink hard and stare at the planner, so she doesn't see how close I am to crying.

"Thank you," I manage, even though it feels wildly insufficient.

It's going to be a busy time. Overwhelming. Packing, moving, starting something new. I'm dreading the logistics of it all, the chaos and the unknowns.

But underneath that is something brighter. Lighter.

For the first time in a long while, I'm not doing this alone. And that might be the most exciting part of all.

"I still can't believe I start Monday," I murmur.

"You're gonna be amazing," Maggie says immediately. "Those kids are lucky to have you. And frankly, this town needs more women who don't apologize for knowing their shit."

"I want to help every kid who wants to learn," I say. "This is a dream."

"Yes, well," she says, waving a hand, "we're the lucky ones to have you."

Through the doorway, I can see Mack leaning over Maggie's truck, holding a wrench like she was born with it.

Mack is Walker and Violet's seventeen-year-old. She's a junior in high school and had never been interested in auto class until Maggie told her I would be teaching it. In the words of Maggie, "No crusty dusty boy is going to try to impress Mack with car repairs. Mack can do it herself." And she can. I'll make sure of that. I'll make sure everyone knows the basics. It's important life skills.

"Do I turn this left or right?" Mack calls.

"Lefty loosey," I yell back. "Righty tighty. Words to live by."

Mack grins and twists the wrench. "I love this. I can't wait for auto class."

"That," Maggie says, lowering her voice, "is why this matters. She gets to see women fixing things. Leading things. I'm so proud of you, Poppy. Look at everything you've done. You've really nailed it. I know your momma would be so proud of you."

My chest tightens. "Don't make me cry, Maggie."

"I'm not trying to make you cry, but this matters, sugar. *You* matter," she says as she lays a palm to my cheek. I lean into her hand because her touch is so soothing. A mother's touch. Something I desperately miss. My mom, Grace, was my biggest cheerleader. She would have loved that I was doing this. She always encouraged me to do whatever I wanted.

The glass door to the shop swings open, and a lady comes in, clipboard in hand, a badge clipped to her jacket.

"Poppy Murphy?" she asks.

"Yes," I say, standing. "Can I help you?"

"I'm with Child Protective Services," she says. "We received a report on Owen Murphy and are doing an investigation."

I look at her, confused. "Oh. Is this about what Coach Toddy did to him at school? We already spoke with Sheriff Matthews."

"No, ma'am," the woman says calmly. "This is a new complaint we just received regarding child neglect."

Relief rushes through me so fast it almost knocks me dizzy.

Of course it is. Of course it's about him.

Sully. My mind starts racing ahead, already building defenses, already angry, already tired. And now it's finally catching up to us.

"Okay," I say carefully. "Because his father, Sully, hasn't been involved? There's an open court—"

The woman hesitates. "I'm sorry, I think there's been a misunderstanding. The complaint isn't about the child's father."

The air feels like it's been sucked out of the room.

"It's about you," she continues. "As the child's primary caregiver."

My stomach drops so hard it feels like I might be sick. Me?

Maggie scoffs. "Well, that's absolutely a lie."

The word *lie* cuts sharp through the room.

I stare at her, waiting for the punchline. Waiting for someone to laugh and say this is a mistake. My ears start ringing, and suddenly every sound feels too loud and too far away at the same time.

"That doesn't make sense," I whisper. "I take great care of him."

Maggie steps closer, one hand landing firm and steady on my back.

"Someone filed a report alleging neglect," the woman says gently. "We're required to follow up."

Horror creeps in, cold and heavy. Who would do this? Who would look at my life, at everything I've held together with bare hands and exhaustion, and say that I'm the one failing him?

My chest tightens, disbelief giving way to something darker. Fear. Not for me, but for Owen. Because I can handle being judged. But I will not let anyone take him from me.

He has everything he needs, doesn't he? I mean sure I struggled a bit with groceries there, but he has never missed a meal, and he's had everything he needs. I've made sure of that. I went without before he ever would. I made sure he's had everything.

"So, just to clarify, you are Poppy?" she asks as she looks over her clipboard.

"I am."

"And you don't currently have guardianship over Owen, is that correct? Your father...Sullivan Murphy is his father?"

"I don't have official guardianship, but I have raised him for the past eleven years," I tell her.

We never had a formal guardianship because my dad and I had an understanding and we never had the money to file for things like that, nor could I probably ever get him to agree to it without paying him extra. Until now that Weston is helping.

"I see, and where is Sullivan Murphy?" she asks with her pen poised above the clipboard, waiting for my response.

"He doesn't live here anymore. As I said, I have been Owen's unofficial guardian since he was a baby when our mother died. I'm not sure where he's at but I'm in the process of working with an attorney to get full legal custody."

Thank God for Weston Jessop. I send up a silent prayer for all of his help. And Ollie's. Ugh. I wish he were here.

The woman steps inside and looks around, taking notes. She watches Mack work on the truck in the bay and looks back at Maggie. "Are you any relation to Owen Murphy?"

Maggie grins proudly and protectively. "Well, I'm his stand-in grandma. Been in both their lives since before Poppy here was born. Was good friends with her momma. Did you know Grace Murphy? The woman was an icon in Bridger Falls. She even has her own memorial park bench here on Main Street. Had cancer and died over eleven years ago. Poppy has raised Owen since then, even when she was a kid herself. She's the hardest working woman I know. I can tell you that. There's no child neglect here. We are all here for Poppy and Owen."

"I didn't know that about your mother," the woman says softly, looking at me kindly. "I'm sorry for your loss."

"Thank you," I say nervously. "I'm sorry, what is your name?"

"I'm Monica," she says, reaching out to shake my hand with a gentle handshake. Nothing about this woman screams scary or aggressive. But just knowing that she could have the power to potentially take my little brother from me makes me practically feral. Owen means the world to me. So, I am keeping my distance just in case.

"Nice to meet you," I say. "I'm sorry. I'm just so confused. Who would make a false report like this?"

"We can't say who reported. There are concerns about stability with Owen," she says. "Stable housing, financial support, and possible neglect."

I open my mouth and literally have no words. First, a thought passes through me that maybe I *am* a neglectful sister.

We have been struggling. Maybe this is warranted. Then I shake my head, exhale, and stand straighter. No. I have done my very best. This is bullshit. A lot of people struggle. But Owen is loved and he has everything he needs.

Maggie must sense I'm upset because she reaches out and squeezes my hand then she says what I'm holding back, saying, "Now, honey, you and I both can see that this is horse shit. Owen has everything he needs, wants, and more. Poppy works her butt off. And she has all of us, too. She has a huge support system. Walker and Violet, Jack and Cami, me, and of course, Ollie. You know the saying, 'It takes a village?' Well, Poppy's village is mighty and strong."

Monica glances at Maggie and nods while she writes down more notes.

I give Maggie a look, like 'what do I do?'

Monica's gaze meets mine. "The initial report also indicates your home is in foreclosure."

I swallow. "It is, but that is my father's home, and we're in the middle of moving."

"And where will you and your brother be living?"

I open my mouth, but nothing comes out. Because I don't have the answer to that. I have no clue. And this looks bad. Really bad.

I realize, in that moment, that I can't do this alone. Pride does not protect kids. Paperwork does. I need a plan.

"With Ollie," Maggie says confidently and squeezes my shoulder.

I give her a look, confused and she side eyes me like, 'go along with this.'

"Yeah...yes. We are moving in with my fri...Ollie," I say as Maggie smiles and nods, encouraging me.

Like he's been summoned, footsteps sound on the stairs.

"I heard my name?" Ollie asks as he comes up beside me,

eyes flicking between us and over to the worker. The tension in the room is thick, and he must suspect something is up.

The CPS worker turns and glances over at him. "And you are?"

"Ollie Kendrick," he says, reaching to shake Monica's hand. She looks at him in confusion and back at me. Then she makes a note on her clipboard.

Damn, I wish I could see those notes.

Maggie looks back and forth between us and blurts out, "Ollie and Poppy are engaged. They've practically raised Owen like their child since he was a baby."

Ollie doesn't even hesitate. A brief moment of surprise crosses his face but without missing a beat he says, "That's right. We're engaged."

His eyes give away nothing as if this is the truth, and I'm shocked at how easy he's improvising with this and just going along with it.

He steps beside me and puts his arm around my waist, grinning at me. "What's going on, honey?"

Honey? What the heck? Engaged? They're both insane.

I practically choke on air. "Uh, well. This is Monica. She's a CPS worker investigating me... er... us... for Owen."

He reaches for my hand and squeezes it, firmly, grounding me. "Wow, investigating us for what?"

"Child neglect," Maggie says dryly.

"Whoa, who would make a false report of that? Isn't it illegal to make false allegations like that?" Ollie asks, genuinely confused.

Monica peeks down at her notes and says, "We can't really say who made the complaint."

I see Maggie discreetly peering over her shoulder at her clipboard, her eyes widening. Her mouth opens and closes, her eyes narrowing. The worker pulls the clipboard closer and walks around, taking in my planner and laptop.

Ollie notices this and circles back to us. "Well, I'm sure this is all a misunderstanding," Ollie says confidently. "Poppy and Owen are moving into the apartment above the shop. We were getting the new flooring put in and the walls are freshly painted. It's looking great. You want to see it?"

The worker blinks in surprise and says, "I would."

I would really like to see this, too. Because the last time I was up there, it looked like a frat house full of stale cigarette smoke, stains on the walls, carpet, and a moldy fridge. I rented it to Ollie for practically nothing, and he's been cleaning it up. But I had no idea just how much he was cleaning it up. He made no mention of paint and flooring to me. He makes it sound actually livable. If she walks up there and sees how it was when he first took it over, there's no way that's going to fly with her.

He leads us all up the stairs, talking calmly about the apartment. This is all news to me as well, and I try to play it off like I already know all of this. I haven't been up there. It's his space and when we hang out, we usually hang out at my house, The Black Dog, or at Walker or Jack's.

I stand there stupefied, Maggie and Mack beside me equally in shock, as we take in the upstairs apartment that looks nothing like the shit hole Ollie moved into last year. It's spotless for one and doesn't even seem like the same place. All the walls are painted a creamy white. He has fresh carpet laid throughout and the tile has been redone in the kitchen and bathroom. It's not a big place, by any means, but it's...beautiful. And it smells really clean.

My hand goes to my chest, and I take it all in, trying to blink back tears. I blow out a breath, and Ollie's hand slides in mine. I try to act like I'm not surprised but fail. I've always been a terrible liar.

"I'm sorry. I just get so emotional when I see it," I admit to the worker who is watching me as if I have a test to pass here. "Ollie worked so hard to make this beautiful for Owen and me. Thank you," I say to Ollie and lean my head on his shoulder.

"Of course. Anything for my family," he says naturally, as if this were normal.

But is it? Is it true? Because it feels true and dang I want it to be true. At this point, we have to keep this going. I give Maggie a look, and she's taking all this in and watching us as if she were a proud parent.

"Well," Monica says, making notes on her clipboard. "This is very nice."

"What the hell?" I whisper, looking at Ollie with wide eyes.

He says nothing, kisses my forehead and continues with the charade. "We're going to be so happy here, honey."

We walk Monica back down to the shop, Maggie and Mack following us. Mack seems confused as well but it's like she understood the assignment and isn't saying anything.

"I'll need to come back and speak with Owen. When would be a good time?" Monica asks.

"We could meet you one evening here around six," I offer. "I have to look at his schedule."

She nods. "That'll work. I look forward to meeting him. I might call if I have any follow-up questions in the meantime."

I nod, Ollie's hand sliding into mine protectively. The warmth of it, already relaxing me. "Okay."

She walks out the door, and I wait until I see her get into her car.

I whirl and look at Maggie, who is examining her nails and not meeting my eyes.

Mack sits in my chair at my desk and says, "Wow. You sure have some explaining to do, Maggs."

"What? I was just trying to help," she says with a smirk, pleased with herself.

"We're not together, let alone engaged, Maggie!" I shriek.

Ollie grins. "Hey, I just went with it."

I blow out a breath. "I know. And thank you. What you did upstairs is incredible. I don't even know how to repay you for that."

Ollie shrugs. "I had a buddy from the fire station whose parents own a hardware store. They gave me a great deal at cost, and I just worked on it a little bit at a time. It really wasn't much."

"No. It's amazing. Thank you," I say softly.

"I don't think it was Coach Toddy," Maggie says. "On her notes, it was an anonymous call from a female."

Weird. I thought for sure that it was probably Jeremy Toddy turning us in for him losing his job, but apparently not. I know it wasn't Sully because he's in hot water with abandoning Owen and wouldn't draw attention to that fact. Maybe Toddy had someone else call. A girlfriend maybe? I try to think if he was married but I actually have no clue. Not sure what woman would want to be with someone like Jeremy Toddy.

That night, too upset to even think about packing or cooking, I ride out to the ranch with Ollie and Owen to meet with Weston. He's coming down from Bozeman and meeting us there.

We get to the main Wilder House lodge that Jack and Cami are staying in while their house is being built, and Tessa is there, cooking up a storm.

"Hey, Tessa." I step inside and round the island to give her a hug. "I haven't seen you in a while."

"Poppy, I've missed you! What are you doing here?"

"We came out to visit," I say, my eyes cutting to Owen, who is pleading with me to run down to the barn. "Go."

He scampers off, yelling behind him, "Hi, Tessa! I gotta go see the horses. Bye!"

Tessa smiles. "Have fun!"

"Is Jack in the barn?" I ask, knowing that some of the wranglers will be down there.

"He is, and so is Cami," she says as she pulls a tray of bread out of the oven.

Ollie's quiet and sits at the table. I sit next to him and Tessa says, "Okay, spill. I know something is wrong. What is it?"

"We're waiting to talk to Weston. I'm in a pickle with Owen, and I need him to help me get guardianship of Owen," I say as I slide my hand over Ollie's.

Tessa's eyes watch our hands, and her eyes widen. "Are you two officially a couple or what?"

Panic flashes across my face before I can stop it.

Ollie clears his throat. "It's... complicated."

Tessa snorts. "That's not a no."

I squeeze Ollie's hand a little tighter. "We're figuring things out."

Her smile softens instantly. "Well, it's about damn time."

Chapter 11
Ollie

Your Place by Ashley Cooke

"**S**hould I keep this?" Owen asks, holding up a hoodie that looks like it lost a fight with a lawn mower blade.

"Only if you plan on starting a new trend," I say. "Distressed but not on purpose."

He snorts and tosses it in the not-keeping pile. I make a mental note to take him shopping as soon as we get the time. He has plenty of things that still work but it always feels good to have some new things.

Cardboard scrapes across the worn hardwood floor, and Owen's laughter, bright and unguarded, hits me right in the chest as we talk about basketball and Fortnite. It's hard to remember that he's a kid in all this. Dealt a shitty luck hand he didn't deserve. I know that hand very well.

Cami, Owen, and I all have parents like that. Me and Cami's luck was that we had our grandparents, the Wilder side, to show us what a family is supposed to look like. And when they died, anything that resembled a family was lost. We had to practically claw our way out of our childhoods. Our dad is off in another town, leaving us alone for a while now. Cami tracked him down recently, and she finally realized he was never going to change. Our mom, Theresa, she's...something. Sometimes it seems like she's trying. And other times it looks like she's her usual self again. Selfish, manipulative, and conniving.

Cami has been giving her a chance, but I don't see it. She's not good and only comes around when she wants money or someone to do something for her. And it's hard for me to help her, even though I would naturally help anyone. I think back to our childhood when she never helped us. I remember Jack giving me some of his clothes because mine were threadbare and my parents wouldn't buy me any new ones. They worked us like dogs and neglected us. That's why I was mad as hell when CPS showed up with a child neglect allegation. Because Owen isn't neglected. Not even close. I know what true neglect looks like, and this isn't it. He's happy and thriving. So, getting rid of crappy threadbare clothes and making sure he has every-thing he needs is important. I move a stack of hoodies in great shape, then pile them for trash or donation.

I'm in Owen's room with him, packing boxes, folding shirts, and trying not to think about how things are changing for him. It feels like everything he and Poppy have been carrying is coming to a head. A shift is happening. I can't wait to get them away from here and out from under Sully. Sully has never put them first, and watching how he treats them has been infuriating. That man runs with a dangerous crowd and needs to get gone for good.

Poppy's down the hall packing the kitchen, cabinets opening and closing, her footsteps moving fast like she's trying not to think too hard. I know that pace. It's her, 'I'm fine pace.'

The one that means she's anything but fine. She's stressed to the max.

Yesterday, when Maggie told the CPS worker that Poppy and I were engaged, I just went with it. And I was shocked when she did, too. Then it just fell out of my mouth that they were moving upstairs because that's what I've wanted for a while. I want to take care of them and keep them safe.

Owen pauses, glancing up at me. "Where are we gonna live, Ollie?"

I keep my voice easy even though I know everything is changing fast for them. "We're gonna talk to you about that, buddy. But I think you're gonna like it."

He studies my face like he's checking for lies, then nods once. "Okay."

"Hey," I say, opening my arms and offering him a hug.

Owen hesitates. He's been getting too cool for hugs lately, hovering in that awkward space where he pretends, he doesn't need them, where affection feels embarrassing instead of automatic. I still offer every time, pretending I don't notice the shift, taking what I can get while I can get it.

I don't push. I just wait.

For a second, I think he's going to dodge it like he has before. Then he sighs, dramatic and put upon, like this is a huge favor he's doing for me.

And then he slams into my chest.

His arms wrap around me tight, no half effort, no pretending. I hold him just as firmly, soaking it in, because I know these moments don't last forever. One day he really will be too cool for this. So, I take it now. I love this kid so much.

I rest my chin on his hair and squeeze once, grateful and steady, holding on just a second longer than necessary.

I pat his back, not saying anything, giving him his moment. I know he needs this. Times are uncertain right now, and he needs reassurance.

He pulls back and shrugs his shoulders like he's a big kid when we both know he's not. But I say anyway, "You all right, bud?"

He nods. "Just worried about Poppy. I don't want that CPS lady to take me away from you guys."

"I know. Sometimes things have to fall apart so they can come together the way that they're supposed to. Everything is going to be okay. I won't let anyone take you away. And Weston is working on things."

"Okay," he says as he exhales a deep breath of relief.

That trust guts me, and I hate that he has to second-guess who will be there for him and give him what he needs.

Poppy appears in the doorway and watches us for a second, her expression soft and wrecked and beautiful all at once. Then she jerks her head toward her room.

"Hey," she says. "Can I steal you for a minute?"

I follow her down the hall, and she shuts the door behind us, then pushes me back until I'm sitting on her bed. Which I very much like. Her room smells like soap and something floral and warm. The bed dips beneath me, and I grin before I can stop myself.

"Hey," I say and wiggle my eyebrows.

She crosses her arms, then uncrosses them, then sighs. "We have to talk, Ollie. Like, seriously, talk."

She's wearing tight black leggings and an old, faded, cropped shirt that shows a sliver of skin on her stomach, and my brain immediately forgets every serious thought I've ever had when I'm watching her talk.

"Okay," I say casually, although I'm not feeling remotely serious about anything other than her right now. "Let's talk."

She plants her hands on her hips. "Well, *fiancé*, what are we gonna tell Owen? He's gonna be so confused. I've been rethinking all of this. Maybe we should just come clean with that worker. Surely she'll understand that we just panicked. I can't make things harder right now. And right now, things feel...weird."

I love it when she calls me fiancé. I could get used to this. But I don't say this out loud because that will only freak her out right now.

"Hell no, we're not telling her anything like that. We need to make sure we get things solid for you guys. We have to do whatever it takes, and if being your pretend fiancé and living together for a while is what it takes, we'll do it," I tell her.

"I don't know..." she says, eyebrows pinching. "I'm worried we're going to confuse Owen. He might get his hopes up and then be crushed."

Or more like that is what *she* is afraid of. But I don't say that.

I blink. "Owen isn't confused. He wants to know where we're going and what the plan is. He's good, Poppy. He needs stability and reassurance, which we've always given him. This time it just looks a little different."

"Did you tell him what's going on?" she asks, her eyes widening.

"No." I shake my head. "I thought we'd talk to him about it together."

She exhales hard and rubs her face. "Okay. But do we tell him the truth?"

"Now I'm confused." I meet her eyes. "What's the truth?"

She lightly slaps my shoulder. Not hard. Playful. "Exactly. Everything is a mess, Ollie. Suddenly, we're engaged, without me knowing," she says dryly. "Funny, I don't remember the proposal."

I grab her wrist gently and smile. "I'm just trying to help you."

Her smile falters. "This isn't real."

"Do you want it to be real?" I ask, sucking in a breath, searching her eyes, waiting for her response.

Her eyes shoot to mine, and there's a vulnerability there that makes my heart clench while I wait for her answer.

"Yes. No. I don't know." She smiles weakly and says softly, "I know I can't lose you."

I nod slowly. "So, you think if we're never real, then you can never lose me."

She shrugs and sighs. "I know it's dumb."

"It's not dumb," I say. "You're protecting your heart."

Which makes me angry that Sully did this to them. Made them distrust anyone and unable to be happy. Because both have learned from him that love has to be earned and is never actually attainable. I'd really like to punch Sully right now. They've also been in survival mode, fighting for everything that they have, and that needs to stop, too.

She looks down at the carpet. "I've lost everyone who mattered."

And some who don't matter. That still hurts, too.

"You don't have to protect yourself from me," I say quietly. "I told you I'm here and I always will be. And always have been."

She looks up at me then, *really* looks at me. A whole conversation passes between our eyes. And this is a connection most people never have with another human, yet she and I do. It's pure love. Even when it's not outspoken love, it's always been love for us. It's always been Poppy for me. No matter how bad things have been for either of us, we've always had each other.

Right now, she feels like I'm the one carrying both of them. But she's carried me, too. When I went through the fire academy, it was her and Owen there at my graduation with my sister. When things were bad with my parents, it was Poppy's window I used to sneak into to stay the night. Poppy's been there for me more than she'll ever know. And I would do anything for her. Anything. I need her to understand this.

I don't say it right away.

I reach for her instead, my hands settling lightly on her hips, drawing her in just enough that I have to tilt my head to meet her gaze, just enough that I can read her face. Her palms land softly on my shoulders, her body leaning slightly into me as she steadies herself.

The idea's been brewing for a while now, solid, and right, but it's big. Once I say it, there's no taking it back.

I'm not hesitating because I don't want it. I'm hesitating because I don't know how she'll react.

I take a breath and go for it. "I think we should go down to the courthouse and just get married. Make it official and move in together. That way, we protect Owen. We establish a stable home in the apartment. We get out from under your dad's mess, and the CPS mess, and we live a simple, good life. We can figure out everything later. Let's just do it."

She looks like she's trying to steady herself. "You really mean this?"

"I do," I say, letting her see it in my eyes. "I want this."

She paces the room, still catching herself. "Wow."

I reach for her hands. "Do *you* want this?"

Her eyes meet mine. "I... I do. But what would that even look like? Being married..."

I squeeze her hands, smiling softly. "I love you. I take care of you. You have somewhere and someone warm and safe to come home to at the end of every day. You and Owen. You're my best friend, always. We eat, talk, laugh. Nothing really changes except we sign a legally binding contract to be best friends for life. You, me, Owen... we could be a family. Stable. Loving. *Real*."

Her lips part, eyes glistening. "That... that actually sounds... possible."

"Because it is," I say, my voice quiet but certain. "If you want it, we'll make it real. Together."

"I just feel like you're doing too much for us, Ollie. I don't know how I can ever repay you for this."

"Love isn't transactional, Poppy. We're here for each other, we always have been," I say as I twitch my hands, wanting to reach out and pull her to me.

The room goes quiet. So much isn't being said out loud that probably needs to be.

I take a breath. "I love you," I say quietly. "I always have. And I always will."

It's not a confession. It's a truth we've been standing on for years but afraid to say out loud, instead I showed it through my actions, it's the only way I knew how.

She doesn't speak for a long second. When she finally looks at me, her eyes are bright, like she's holding something fragile together with sheer will.

"I love you so much," she says, her voice cracking. "I couldn't breathe at the thought of losing you."

"You and Owen are my world. My family." The word lands exactly where it's meant to. Family. Not longing. Not want. Not romance, at least not the kind either of us is brave enough to name.

This is the love that shows up. The love that stays. The love that doesn't ask for anything in return.

And that's why neither of us questions it.

And this is what happens when two people who grew up in loveless homes try to find love as adults. We struggle because we were raised with conditions.

I'm still sitting on the edge of the bed while she paces in front of me, hands twisting, shoulders tight. Standing like this, she's taller than me, all restless energy and motion, like she doesn't know where to put herself. I reach out and catch her wrist gently, grounding her just long enough to get her attention.

"Hey," I say softly.

She stops. Looks down at me.

I lean forward and rest my forehead against her stomach, right where she's warm and real and close. It's not dramatic. It's instinct. A quiet anchor.

"I'm gonna meet you where you're at, Poppy," I murmur. "We can figure it all out."

She exhales shakily, one hand coming to my shoulder, fingers curling into my shirt like she's holding on.

And for a moment, the world slows enough for both of us to breathe.

She nods a little and I tug on her to sit down next to me. I pull her to me and give her a big hug. She smells so good and feels so good. God, I love hugging her.

Her voice is small. "Can we just start out fake? Then..."

"You want this to be fake, we'll do fake," I agree. But it kills me. There's nothing fake about my love for Poppy. And I'm going to show her that. But damn if I don't love her so much that I'd do anything for her.

"Pretend," she corrects. "Not fake."

I shrug. "We can pretend."

She nods, tears shining but not falling. She looks relieved and happy.

"So," I say lightly, because if I don't make this funny, I might explode. "Are you gonna marry me, Poppy Grace Murphy, and make me the happiest man in the world?"

She snorts through her tears. "I'd love to get rid of the Murphy last name."

"Me too," I say. "I'm very excited to upgrade you. Although I'm not sure what kind of upgrade Kendrick is."

She laughs, really laughs, and it's my favorite sound in the world. "But I hate to leave Owen behind and not have his be the same as mine."

Ours. I want to correct her, but I don't. We're still pretending, I remind myself.

"Okay, so we're really doing this," she says. "We're getting pretend married."

"We're getting married." I wink. "Don't worry, I'll wear something hot."

"You always do," she mutters.

I grin. "Poppy, are you flirting with your fiancé?"

She scoffs, trying to hide her grin. "No."

"Kinda sounds like it," I say, pulling her in close, loving the warmth of her and feel of her.

"Are you sure you're okay with us moving in with you? That's a big step," she says as she bites her lip.

"Babe, we're getting married. That's a natural step after marriage," I tease.

Her eyes soften when I call her babe, and I make note of that.

"Okay, then. I have to figure out how to get Owen on board. Should we tell him it's pretend?"

"He's on board with whatever," I say. "He just needs to know the plan. We can be straight with him."

She looks at me, worry flickering across her face. "What do we tell our friends?"

"What do you want to tell them?" I say softly, taking her hand in mine.

"I think we should tell them privately what we're doing, but

I think we need to act real with everyone else. We don't know who turned me into CPS. And I think you're right. If Monica gets wind that this isn't real, she's going to think we're even more messed up and take Owen away," she says, shaking her head.

"First off, we're not messed up," I say, cupping her chin. "We're real. And we've always been there for each other and for Owen. That is real."

She nods, her voice dropping. "How do we act in public? Are we supposed to kiss? What if it doesn't look real?"

I smile, slow and knowing, letting my gaze linger on her mouth for a little too long. "Trust me," I say quietly. "When we kiss, no one's going to question whether it's real."

"Well, what if we kiss and it's weird?" she says, quieter now. "Like it looks awkward and they think we're bullshitting."

My gaze drops to her mouth before I catch myself. I lift my eyes back to hers, voice low. "That's what you're worried about?"

She nods, swallowing. "Yeah. I want it to look real."

I lean closer, close enough that the air between us changes. "It would," I say softly. "Nothing about kissing you would be fake."

Before she can think better of it, I kiss her, slowly and deliberate, like I've waited my whole life for this exact second. Because I have. My lips settle against hers, and she exhales into me, melting instantly, like her body's been holding this in just as long as mine has.

She kisses me back, tentative at first, then her fingers curl into my shirt. I deepen the kiss, tilting her just right, my hand sliding to cradle the back of her neck as I take my time learning her. Every breathy soft sound she makes goes straight to my cock, and I have to work damn hard to regulate that because holy shit, I'm kissing Poppy.

I pull her closer until she's straddling my lap, warm and

genuine and exactly where she belongs, my hands framing her face as the kiss turns slow and hungry and impossibly intimate.

My tongue finds hers, and she moves over my cock with her pussy, feeling it and kissing me even harder, making breathier noises. Just like I thought, there's nothing pretend about this. We have it all. The friendship *and* the chemistry.

It steals both of our breath. And I know, without a doubt, that no matter what we call this, pretend or real or somewhere in between, this is the hottest thing I've ever felt in my life. I know she feels it, too.

Her hands grip my hair, pulling me in, riding my cock and moaning softly as I kiss her deeply, my hands gripping her bottom, pulling her onto me, entirely making out now.

She pulls back, breathless, her forehead resting on mine.

"Nothing pretend about that," I whisper.

"We're so fucked," she whispers.

God, I hope so.

Chapter 12
Poppy

High Road by Zach Bryan

We're sitting at the kitchen table surrounded by half-packed boxes. Owen's legs swing under his chair, his face carefully blank in the way that tells me he's bracing for something. Telling Owen is somehow scarier than telling the entire town, which makes sense because how he feels about this is really all that matters.

I clear my throat, nerves skittering everywhere, and Ollie's hand tightens around mine under the table. Just a quiet squeeze. Steady. Reassuring. Like he's saying I'm here without saying anything at all.

My other hand drifts to my face, fingers brushing my mouth. My lips still tingle, like they haven't caught up to the rest of me yet.

Holy shit. That kiss.

It was way too good. Too consuming. The kind that leaves my chest tight and my thoughts scrambled, my body humming like it's been woken up after a long sleep. I'm still a little breathless, still aware of how close he is, how easily he could reach for me again.

And that's the problem.

Because ten minutes ago, Ollie was my best friend and my safe place. The person I trusted more than anyone in the world. Now I've agreed to marry him. To live with him. To share space and mornings and nights and everything in between.

That's not nothing.

Excitement flares low in my belly, hot and undeniable, followed immediately by a spike of panic. How do you go from best friends to this without breaking something? How do you live that close to someone you want without wanting too much?

I swallow hard and force my brain back online.

Focus, Poppy.

I was worried about making this look real, about convincing other people, when my own body clearly didn't get the memo that this was supposed to be pretending. My pulse is still racing, my skin is too aware, my thoughts drifting places I'm not ready to name.

This is going to change everything.

Living together. Sharing a bed eventually. Navigating a closeness that's always been emotional and now feels dangerously physical too. I want it. That's what scares me.

I lace my fingers tighter through his, grounding myself in the familiar feel of him. Best friends. Family. That's what this is supposed to be.

Even if my body is already questioning every rule I've ever made for myself.

"Okay, so there's something we need to talk to you about," I say, carefully watching Owen's reaction.

He sighs and lifts his shoulders like he's bored. "Okay, what?"

I glance at Ollie. He gives me a slight nod like we've got this. We might not, but I appreciate the confidence.

"Owen," I say gently, "Ollie and I are going to get married. It'll be legal and all, but just...pretend."

"And we're all moving into the apartment above the shop together," Ollie adds.

There's a long pause. Then Owen mutters, "I don't know why you two are acting like this isn't real."

"What?" I blurt, caught off guard. "I mean... I don't know how to think about it all yet. It's just... a lot. But we wanted to be straight with you. You deserve to know the truth."

He shrugs. "Yeah, okay. The truth is you make eyes at each other all the time when you think the other one isn't looking. It's gross. Also, very obvious to everyone besides you two bozos that you're obsessed with each other. Grown-ups are weird."

I press my lips together, so I don't laugh. Ollie snorts next to me and covers his mouth, leaning on his elbow as he watches me, waiting for me to respond.

"So, I just have to go along with this?" Owen asks.

"Yeah," Ollie says.

Owen thinks about it, then nods. "Okay. But don't lie to me. Tell me if you two are going to break up or whatever so I can prepare for it."

And there it is. That's why I'm scared shitless about doing this with Ollie for real. Because it's not just my heart at stake here, it's Owen's, too. He doesn't deserve heartbreak, and I can't do that to him. Or to me.

I reach over giving his shoulder a gentle squeeze. "I'll always be honest with you."

Ollie nods. "Same."

His eyes lift, serious now.

"No matter what happens with me and your sister," Ollie

says quietly, steady and sure, "nothing changes between you and me. Ever."

He blinks. "Even if—"

"Even if," Ollie cuts in gently. "I'm not going anywhere. I'm still here. Still showing up. Still on your team."

Something in his shoulders loosens, like he's been holding that question in for a while.

"You don't lose me," Ollie adds. "Not now. Not ever."

He nods again, smaller this time, but it's solid.

"Okay," he says.

And I know he believes him.

"Good," Owen says. "Because if you break up and make things weird, I'm moving in with Jack and Cami."

"Hey," Ollie says with a laugh. "Rude. You want to be closer to the horses."

"Well, duh." Owen grins. "I love the horses."

* * *

That night, we walk into The Black Dog hand in hand, and my heart is beating way too fast for someone who's supposedly pretending. Owen's with his friend at the movies. Hopefully, having a fun time like a normal kid, without thinking about where we're going to live or his fake family, basically things he shouldn't have to worry about.

It's early, and Cami, Jack, and Maggie are sitting at the bar, waiting. Walker and Violet are behind the bar, standing next to each other. I sent out a group text asking everyone to meet us at the bar for an announcement. They all took it seriously because they all showed up. My stomach is a mess with nerves about what we're about to tell them.

Walker looks at our hands and says something first. "What'd I miss?"

All eyes in the bar swivel and stare at us and down at our hands. I take a deep breath.

"This is going to be fun," I murmur.

"Tell me about it." Ollie grins and mutters, "They're going to give us so much shit. Get ready."

I squeeze Ollie's hand. "We've got something to tell everyone."

The Black Dog goes so quiet it's unsettling. No music. No talking. Even the neon sign seems to hum more softly, as if it's an omen. This place is never silent, and now I'm so nervous I feel like my heart is trying to beat right out of my chest.

"We're getting married," I announce. "And we're moving in together above the shop."

The silence stretches like it's being dramatic on purpose.

Walker stops mid-polish of the bar top, the rag frozen in his hand. Someone drops a fork. Another person whispers, "Holy shit."

Violet tilts her head, squinting at us hard. "Okay," she says slowly, "but when do you tell us you're kidding, because I need to prepare emotionally either way."

Jack frowns. "Did I black out? Did she say what I think she said?"

Cami's mouth falls open. "Since when? I don't believe it."

Maggie looks smug. "Prove it."

Before I can answer, Ollie pulls me in and kisses me. His mouth is firm and claiming, the kind of kiss that steals your breath and leaves no room for doubt. I melt into him, heart pounding, because holy shit. This is pure magic.

When we pull back, I'm breathless, eyes wide.

"Since now," Ollie says, looking around the room as if he's challenging anyone to have objections.

Walker stares. "Well hot damn."

Maggie grins and claps. "It's about time."

I give her a playful look with narrowed eyes because she knows this is partly her fault. She doesn't look like she's bothered about any of it at all.

"This is...weird," Cami says as she eyes both of us suspiciously.

I nod to her, and we head to the side of the bar, Violet coming over, too. I whisper to both of them, "Okay, here's the deal. This is pretend to get through all the CPS and legal stuff with Owen. I need you to please go along with this, okay?"

Violet searches my eyes. "Are you sure this is fake? Looks pretty real to me."

"It's pretend," I assure her.

Cami narrows her eyes. "Didn't seem pretend to me either. You both are weirdos. Why can't you call it what it is?"

"Yeah," Violet adds, looking equally confused.

"Well, Maggie told the caseworker we were engaged," I add.

Violet laughs. "Of course she did."

"So, we're going with it. Just until we can get everything solid with Owen, and then we'll figure out what to do after that," I tell them.

"I think we should plan a wedding," Cami says with a smile. "It's not every day our best friend and my brother get married."

"No, we're just going to the courthouse," I say quickly. "It's not a big to-do."

But even as I say it, my chest tightens. Not a big wedding. No engagement ring. Nothing fancy. Just... us. And for some reason, that feels both freeing and terrifying all at once. I've wanted him for so long, buried it under jokes and friendship, pretending like my heart wasn't quietly twisting every time he smiled at someone else. And now, it's all right there, in front of me, undeniable.

Marrying him. My best friend. The person I've always compared everyone else to. Did I ever imagine this? No. I thought marriage was other people's thing. And here I am, about to make it official with him, and part of me is thrilled, part of me is scared out of my mind, and part of me wants to just run and hide.

Violet scoffs. "No. We can have a reception out at the house. It'll be great!"

"I already know just the cake I can make for you guys." Cami smiles dreamily. "Can I surprise you?"

I shrug. "Sure. I'll never turn down an excuse for cake."

"How does Owen feel about all of this?" Violet asks, looking concerned.

"He's okay with it. Glad that we're moving in with Ollie."

Cami smiles. "Owen loves both of you. Pretend or not, he needs both of you."

Yeah, he does.

* * *

Later, I elbow Ollie in the booth. "What the hell was that kiss in front of all of them?"

He grins. "Get used to it. We gotta make it look real. You're gonna be my wife. Besides, you liked it."

My thighs practically squeeze together when he says that because I like the sound of it more than I should, and I loved that kiss even more.

I give him a look. "Well, *husband*, maybe let me in on the plan next time."

His eyes darken instantly. A subtle heat that flares there, sharp and unmistakable, like the word landed somewhere low and dangerous. The corner of his mouth twitches, and my breath catches before I can stop it. There's a jolt that goes straight through me, awareness humming loud under my skin.

Then he leans back, easy and infuriating, like he didn't just do that to me. "Where's the fun in that, *wife?*"

I snort and take a sip of my water, trying to steady my nerves. "At least they're going along with it."

"Yeah," he says, easy confidence in his voice. "I knew they would."

My gaze drifts across the bar and lands on Ollie's mom. Theresa Kendrick sits stiff-backed with her friends, lips pressed thin, eyes sharp as they cut in our direction while she murmurs something under her breath. Whatever she's saying, it doesn't look kind.

My stomach tightens. I glance back at Ollie. "Your mom is here. What are you going to say to her?"

"As little as possible," he says.

"Well, you should probably tell her that you're getting married. That way she doesn't hear it from someone else."

Ollie sighs and stands. I don't envy the conversation he's about to have with her. It never seems to go well with Theresa.

I watch them talk and I can't hear much, but I see her shake her head, her mouth tight. She looks really mad. Ollie stays calm. When he comes back, I already know how it went. It makes me sad to think about how my own mom would have reacted to the news. She was always my biggest cheerleader. Even if it wasn't something she necessarily wanted for me, she always supported me. And if I told her I was getting married, I'd like to think she would have hugged me and been happy for us. Watching Theresa's reaction makes me sad. She has her kids right in front of her, yet she can't do life with them, and she doesn't even appreciate them. My mom would have given anything to be here.

"You okay?" I ask, searching his eyes as he sits next to me.

He nods. "She's not happy. But she'll have to get over it."

He always guards his heart around his mom. Something I do

to him. And that stings because Ollie doesn't deserve that. He deserves to have real support and love. I love Ollie and support him. It makes me second-guess everything we're doing. Could we be real? Could I let him love me and love him the way that both of us, broken people, deserve to be loved?

I squeeze his hand. "I'm proud of you."

He smiles at me like that means more than anything. "I'm proud of you right back, future wife."

And sitting there with him with the bar with his hand in mine, I realize something terrifying and wonderful.

I don't feel like I'm pretending. It feels scary real.

* * *

Moving day is quieter than I expected. I thought it would be hard to leave our home. The only home either of us has ever lived in. But even though I lived there the first sixteen years of my life with my mom and we have memories, the last twelve have been hard. Because they are filled with grief and unpleasant memories of our dad, wiping away any of the good ones that we had with her. Owen has no memories of her because he was just a baby when she died, but I do. I remember everything about her. She was my best friend, and we were very close. It turns out, I just wanted her things. Her clothes that I kept, her recipe cards, and her books. Those are what I need, not the house. The house is just a house. It's not our home. Our home is wherever we are, together. That's what matters.

It was all very anti-climactic. There were no dramatic good-byes. Just boxes, the creak of the worn floorboards, and the strange relief of locking the front door of a house that has felt like it was slipping through my fingers for months.

The apartment above the shop smells clean and new, like

fresh paint. Ollie did a good job. Of course he did. He always does.

Owen drops his backpack by the door and spins in a slow circle. "This is kinda cool."

"Kinda?" Ollie says as he deposits a stack of boxes in the living room. "It's extremely cool."

Owen grins, still in awe. "Okay, yeah. Extremely cool."

This is definitely an upgrade from our worn and weathered home. It feels fresh and new. I set my box down and take it all in. Two bedrooms. One bathroom. A small kitchen. A couch that looks really comfortable.

The business is in both my dad's name and mine. Which means the apartment upstairs is tied to it too. Not a separate lease. Not a safety net. If the shop goes under, if something happens legally, or if the bank decides it wants its pound of flesh, we don't just lose the business, we lose the apartment. That's the part that sits heavy in my chest every time a bill comes in late, or a repair takes longer than expected. I can't afford to make mistakes. I can't afford slow weeks. I can't afford to breathe too easy. If Murphy's Auto fails, everything fails with it.

So no, this place isn't stable. It's conditional and temporary. Always one bad month away from unraveling. And that's why I never fully unpack the tension in my shoulders, why sleep never comes easy, why I keep going even when I'm exhausted. Because survival isn't just about keeping the doors open. It's about keeping a roof over Owen's head.

Moving here doesn't feel as foreign as I thought it might. It's the shop, and Owen and I both grew up here, so it's like a second home to us. I wish we'd have moved here sooner to be honest. It might have been easier on all of us. But I was doing my best to keep us afloat and keep the house. Now...none of that seems to matter. I'm not worried about losing a home. I'm afraid of losing Owen.

For the first time in a long time, my shoulders unclench, and I shake them out. I look over, and Ollie smiles at me as if he knows how I'm feeling right now, and I smile back. No words needed. Because that's just how it is with us, sometimes, we just know.

Dinner is The Black Dog takeout, eaten straight from containers on the counter—burgers and fries with cheddar sauce. I'm living the dream. Walker and Violet sent over a ton of food as a housewarming welcome from our meal train sign up Maggie organized. Owen is setting up the smaller bedroom and immediately starts planning where his posters will go. He's buzzing with excitement. I love seeing him so happy. Neither of us has ever lived in a nice place like this. Our house was deteriorating and needed so much work. There are only so many patches you can put on a sinking ship. Sully never made any repairs, and I could barely keep up with the shop and the house basic needs. Let alone cosmetic fixes.

I pretend right along with him. I'm so nervous every time I see Ollie's arms flex with more boxes. We get everything out of the house and give it a quick vacuum, clean, and wipe down. I can't leave it trashy for whoever gets it next. My mom wouldn't have wanted that.

By ten, Owen's in bed, door cracked, the sound of music playing softly that he listens to when he goes to sleep. I knock softly and peek my head in. "How's the new room?"

"I love it here, Poppy," he says sleepily.

I lean in and kiss his head that smells like Ollie's soap from the shower and grin. "Me, too. Night buddy. Love you."

"Love you, Pops," he murmurs.

I shut his door and head down to Ollie's room to see how

strange it looks with my things in the room. I didn't have much, but it's all here.

Ollie finishes locking up downstairs and comes back up, stretching his arms over his head like today didn't take everything out of him.

"I'll take the couch," he says easily, like it's a settled thing.

I look at him. Then at the couch. Then the bedroom.

He's not exactly a small man. He barely fits on that thing sitting up, let alone trying to sleep on it. And more than that, this isn't some favor he's crashing for. This is his home. He lives here. He's lived here long before all of this blew up.

The thought settles heavy in my chest.

I can't kick him out onto a couch like he's a guest or an inconvenience. Not when he's doing all of this for me. For Owen. Not when he spent the entire day hauling boxes, lifting furniture, sweating and grunting and never complaining.

He didn't hesitate. He just stepped in and made space for us.

The least I can do is not pretend he doesn't belong in his own bed.

And that realization hits harder than I expect, because it's not just about where he sleeps tonight.

It's about the fact that he's already given us more than I know how to repay.

"It's a big bed," I say. "Just don't try to cuddle me, Ollie."

He grins like he's been waiting for that. "You can cuddle me if you want."

"I don't cuddle," I say with a smirk.

Ollie laughs, shakes his head, and goes to the dresser, grabbing clothes. "I'm going to take a normal shower. Because I know you're going to take longer than me."

I snort, because honestly, he's not wrong. I love my long hot showers, and today I earned one. "Okay."

Then I hear the shower turn on. The sound of running water carries down the hall, and my brain immediately conjures images I do not need. Strong and broad shoulders. That sexy, unfair body that is rippled with muscles that he wears proudly.

I grab my clothes and lay them out, trying to stay busy and keep my brain from drifting to places it shouldn't. Pretend fiancées shouldn't think of their pretend fiancés naked and wet. Nope. I'm going to hell.

When he finally comes in wearing gray sweatpants and a Bridger Falls Fire Department t-shirt that fits him criminally well, hair damp, I refuse to look directly at him because I value my sanity.

"Want to start a new show?" he asks, as he settles into what is his side of the bed and grabs the remote. "I found a few new ones we can start when we're done with the one we're watching. I think we have just a few episodes left."

How is he acting so casual? Why is this so hard for me?

"Yes, that's fine," I say too fast. "I'll hurry."

But now I need space between Ollie, who smells amazing, lying next to me on his bed. We've slept in the same bed countless times over the years. But now things have changed. We definitely aren't looking at each other like we did back then.

"Take your time," he says as he watches me, probably trying to figure out why I'm acting so weird.

I head to the shower and take a quick one, washing the day off me. I lean my head back and try to practice taking normal breaths. I towel off and dry my hair, braiding it in its usual nighttime braid.

I head back to the room and step in, just the glow of the TV lighting up the room.

I prop pillows against the headboard and put on the familiar opening credits of the show we've been watching for months. It's comfortable, familiar, and safe.

Ollie's on his side of the bed, and I'm on mine. I set up a very clear line of pillows between us like a peace treaty.

"See," I say. "Plenty of space."

"Thrilling," he says, watching the TV. "I've always dreamed of sharing a bed with a pillow wall."

Halfway through the episode, my eyes start to close. I fight to keep my eyes open and lose.

The next thing I know, low morning light is spilling through the curtain, and something warm is wrapped around me.

I freeze, and very carefully, I look down.

I'm curled into Ollie's chest, my arm draped over his waist, my leg hooked over his as it belongs there. And his very hard cock is pressing into me. Morning wood. And it feels so freaking hot. Damn.

He's still asleep, one arm around my back, hand resting at my hip like it's the most natural thing in the world.

I pull back slightly. "Ollie."

He hums but doesn't wake.

"I told you not to cuddle me."

He opens one eye and then the other, clearly confused. "You're cuddling me, Poppy."

I scoff. "That's not true."

He glances down at our limbs, then back at me. "You're literally wrapped around me like a koala."

I sit up fast, cheeks burning. "I move in my sleep."

"I can tell," he says as he stretches, entirely too comfortable for a man who just got caught in a cuddle crime. "You snore a little, too."

"I do not." I scoff.

"You do," he says. "It's cute."

"I hate you."

He smiles. "No, you don't."

"I have to get ready," I say finally. "First day is today."

The words spark something bright in my chest. Excitement, sharp and buzzing, the kind I haven't felt in a long time. I woke up before my alarm, heart already racing, mind jumping ahead to lesson plans and classrooms and the smell of oil and metal in a place that isn't mine to keep afloat.

For once, the day ahead doesn't feel like a list of things that could go wrong.

It feels like possibility.

I can't wait to get started. To walk into that building knowing I belong there. Knowing I earned this. Knowing this job is mine because people saw me and trusted me and believed I could do it.

Hope feels strange in my body, light and unfamiliar, like a muscle I haven't used in years. I almost don't trust it.

But it's there all the same, humming under my skin, pulling me forward.

And for once, I let myself feel it.

He nods. "You're gonna crush it. It'll be nice to have a solid job."

"I'm still keeping the shop open Wednesdays and Saturdays," I remind him. "I need to. Those will be long days."

"I know," he says. "We'll make it work."

We'll.

The word catches on something inside me and tugs harder than it should.

It's small, and casual. Ollie probably doesn't even realize he said it. But it lands heavy in my chest all the same, warm and terrifying all at once. I'm so used to everything being *I* that hearing him include himself without hesitation makes my breath hitch.

We'll figure it out. *We'll* make it work. *We'll* handle it.

The idea of not doing this alone feels unreal. Like stepping onto solid ground after years of bracing for the drop. I want to lean into it, let it settle, let myself believe in the safety of that word.

At the same time, it scares me.

Because getting used to *we* means trusting that he's not going anywhere. Means letting go of the instinct to do everything myself and accepting that this isn't just pretend in the ways that matter.

I swallow and nod like it's nothing. But inside, that one little word keeps echoing, reshaping the edges of my world in quiet, dangerous ways

I swing my legs out of bed and head for the bathroom, pausing at the door.

"Hey," I say.

"Yeah?"

"Thanks. For this. For all of it."

He looks at me like it's the easiest thing in the world. "Always you."

I shut the door and lean against it, heart pounding. "Always you," I repeat back. Something we've said to each other since we were teens, when life got hard. We are each other's ride-or-die. Always you.

This isn't fake. Not really. Not all of it can be fake when we're always that for each other.

And that thought both terrifies me and makes me smile as I get ready to start the rest of my life.

Chapter 13
Ollie

Burning House by Kameron Marlowe

"You're nervous," I say casually as I wander into the kitchen, pour myself a cup of coffee, and lean back against the counter like I don't feel it buzzing off her in waves.

She's puttering around the kitchen, overfocused in that way that always gives her away. Breakfast burritos are lined up on the counter, foil-wrapped and warm. Next to them sit three packed lunches, neat and ready.

She rolls her eyes at me, but there's a smile there, too. "I made us all lunches."

I follow her gaze to the counter, then back to her. "You made me lunch?"

She shrugs like it's nothing, her cheeks pink. "I figured you needed to eat."

I take a sip of coffee to hide my grin, because suddenly this feels like the best part of my day. Well, that and waking up with her in my arms. This day is off to a good start.

She's not wrong. But it's not the lunch I want to eat. Her pretend bullshit feels anything but pretend. The way she's all the sudden acting nervous and looking at me just like I've always looked at her.

She's so damn beautiful in this kitchen, her hair in that long braid down her back. And this is what I've dreamed of. Everyday moments with her. Coffee in the kitchen, lunches together, and waking up beside each other. But I can't say any of this to her. Not yet anyways.

Instead, I make a joke because that is easier than lusting after my pretend fiancée. "That's really sweet of you," I tell her.

She shrugs and gives me a dry look. "Don't make it weird."

Owen wanders out of his room, rubbing his eyes. "Is today your first day of school, Pops?"

"It is," she says, handing him a lunch bag. "High school mechanic extraordinaire."

He grins. "Don't drop the wrench."

She laughs, but her hands shake just a little as she takes her coffee mug. "What the heck, Owen? Who taught you that? It won't be bad. It's just high school."

He shrugs. "High school sounds scary. You should see middle school. It's even worse."

I snort laugh, shaking my head, and lean in to kiss her temple. "You're gonna crush it."

She looks up at me, eyes soft and unsure, and says softly, "I hope so."

I hope so, too, because she deserves stability, respect, and a room full of kids excited to learn from her. Not the crappy customers she's been getting who don't appreciate her. Or her sleazebag dad coming around and stealing from her. That shit is done. He's not getting anything from her ever again.

"Whoa," Owen says, eyeing all the food laid out. "What's all this?"

"First day fuel," Poppy says. "Eat."

He sits, immediately digging in.

I watch her fuss over him, making sure he's got his homework folder, his jacket, and his lunch.

"You all set for practice today?" I ask, taking a sip from my mug.

"Heck yeah. Basketball has been so fun with you and the guys," he says, swinging his legs in his chair.

I don't miss Poppy's expression as she watches him, seeing her happy when he's happy.

Owen grabs his things and runs down to the truck that's parked down in one of the bays. "Bye, Ollie! See you at practice!"

"Bye, buddy."

When Poppy grabs her bag, she pauses by the door. "Okay," she says. "I'm nervous."

"I know," I say. "You're gonna do great. I'm off today, so I'll be here if you need anything."

She bites her lip. "You think we're doing the right thing?"

"Definitely."

She exhales, then leans in and presses a quick kiss to my cheek. It lands somewhere between friendly and something else entirely. Now that I've kissed her and shown her the buzz between us, the sexual tension is almost palpable.

"Wish me luck," she says.

"Good luck," I say, grabbing her arm and pulling her back to my chest. I kiss her lips, and she kisses me back, melting into me. We kiss until she pulls back breathless.

"Go show them how it's done," I murmur, and she smiles as she heads to the door, face red.

She leaves, and the apartment feels quieter without them.

* * *

That night after basketball practice, Poppy and I sit at the table while Owen gives the CPS worker a full tour of the apartment and his room, like he's showing off a mansion on an old episode of MTV's *Cribs*.

I haven't had a chance to ask Poppy a single real question yet, and it's killing me.

When she came home earlier, she looked different. Lighter. Like she was floating a few inches off the floor and didn't even realize it. Her hair was coming loose from its clip, her cheeks flushed, eyes bright in a way I haven't seen in a long time. She was tired, yeah, but it was the good kind. The kind that comes from doing something that matters instead of surviving another day.

She grinned at me when she walked in, wide and unguarded, like she couldn't quite hold it in. I caught the words tumbling out of her in pieces as she kicked off her shoes. Names. Stories. A laugh that bubbled up and surprised even her. And then Owen needed help with homework, and dinner happened, and time slipped away.

Now she sits across from me at the table, hands folded tight in her lap, that earlier glow dimmed by nerves. She meets my eyes for a second, and there's so much there I want to ask. *Did you love it? Did it feel right? Did they see how good you are?*

I'll hear all of it later. I have to. But for now, this matters more.

I watch Owen proudly point out his posters and his bedspread and the corner where he keeps his basketball, and I keep my attention where it needs to be. Still, I tuck that image of Poppy coming home happy into my chest like a promise.

This interview won't last forever.

And when it's over, I'm going to sit with her and hear every single detail.

He even opened the fridge and shows her all of the food that I bought today. And overbought if I'm being honest. Because I never want them to go without anything they want or need ever again.

"This is where my bed is," he says proudly. "And that shelf is for my trophies. And Ollie helped me hang my posters." He points to posters hung beside his bed.

The worker smiles and takes notes. "Do you like living here?" she asks, smiling at Owen's enthusiasm.

"Yes," Owen says immediately. "Our old house was okay, too. But I love my new room."

Poppy's hand clenches in mine under the table, and I squeeze back.

The interview is calm and straightforward. Owen answers honestly, and Poppy and I are quiet, just here to support him. He talks about school and basketball. He tells her that he loves going out to Jack and Cami's and Walker and Violet's. He tells her he loves Maggie, and she lets him come to the community bingo sometimes. And then she asks him if he feels safe, and he says, "I always feel safe with Poppy and Ollie. They're my family."

My heart squeezes when he says that.

When it's over, the worker closes her folder and looks at us. "So, let me get this straight. You both have been essentially raising him since he was a baby after your mom passed away?"

We both nod.

"And you're just now engaged and getting married?" she asks, looking confused.

I shrug. "Yeah."

She nods, and what feels like a full minute passes as she

looks us over and nods. "Seems coincidental that you're engaged and getting married when this complaint came up."

"Honestly? I've had my heart set on Poppy for years," I say, leaning back like I'm just going along with our little act. "I was planning to ask her a long time ago, just hadn't found the right ring. But then I thought... if I wait for everything to be perfect, we could be waiting forever. So, here we are. All part of the plan, of course." I glance at the CPS worker. "The complaint was a false allegation. And I wasn't about to let someone else's bitterness stop me from asking the love of my life to marry me."

She looks at us for a moment and smiles. "I see no reason not to recommend you both as permanent guardians if you're married. You're both doing a fantastic job with Owen, and you should be so proud of yourselves. Really, strong and amazing young people here. Owen is fortunate to have you both."

Poppy's breath catches. I feel it, too. "Thank you," she says quietly, her eyes shining.

"Just one thing," she adds, "If you aren't being honest in this process, it could reflect negatively. Just something to keep in mind."

I tilt my head at her. "Nothing to be dishonest about here. I love Poppy and Owen."

She glances between us and looks hesitant. "Okay. Do either of you have any questions?"

"What's going to happen with Sully?" Poppy asks.

"The state is filing charges for parental abandonment. The state recognizes that a minor took over the parental obligations, and we want to make note of that."

"What does that mean?" I ask.

"It means he may owe restitution and have that on his record," she says.

After she leaves, Poppy calls Weston and puts him on

speaker. We quickly fill him in on everything Monica said when she was here.

"That's great," Weston says. "I'm working on some paperwork on my end, too. We're getting there."

We thank him profusely before hanging up.

Owen crashes hard that night, exhausted in the way only happy kids get. I watch him sleep for a second longer than necessary before closing his door, thankful that they're both here and safe.

Poppy's exhausted, too. She's in the shower, and I close my eyes and plop down on the couch, trying not to picture her in the shower. This is killing me.

She steps out, wrapped in a towel, and the image hits me anyway of the other morning. The split second where there was no towel, no warning, no space to look away fast enough. I remember everything. The smooth pale line of her skin. The curves she hides under denim and grease and layers meant to keep the world at arm's length. The way my brain short circuited while my body very much did not.

I know what's under there.

That knowledge sits heavy and relentless in my chest now, makes my pulse jump, makes the air feel thicker than it has any right to be. I drag my eyes up, force myself to focus on her face instead of the towel clutched tight at her middle.

I inwardly groan, because this is torture of the highest order.

So, I keep my hands to myself. I keep my expression neutral.

And I pretend the memory isn't burning a hole straight through my self-control.

"Sorry, I forgot my clothes," she murmurs as she steps into the bedroom and closes the door.

A few minutes later, the door opens and she comes back out wearing an off the shoulder T-shirt, the fabric slipping low on one side and baring a hint of collarbone. Soft gray sweats hang loose on her hips, worn thin and comfortable, like she didn't bother changing for anyone but herself. Socks pad quietly across the floor as she crosses the room.

She looks beautiful and relaxed in a way she rarely lets herself be.

She sits next to me on the couch, close enough that our knees touch, and we turn toward each other like this is exactly where we're meant to be.

"Tell me everything about your first day," I say softly.

I reach for her feet and tug them gently into my lap. She doesn't hesitate. Just lets me. I peel her socks off one by one, slowly and carefully, setting them aside before grabbing the lotion from the table next to us.

Her skin is warm under my hands as I start rubbing her feet, thumbs pressing into tired arches, working out the ache she's been carrying since morning. She exhales, a quiet sound that tells me how long it's been since anyone took care of her like this.

I keep my eyes on her face, the way her shoulders slowly drop, the tension easing bit by bit.

"Start at the beginning," I murmur.

And as she does, talking softly, smiling more than she realizes, I think about how easy this feels. How natural. How dangerous that is.

She leans back and moans a little, which makes my cock go hard against her foot, and I know she has to feel it.

"I can't tell you that while you're doing this," she says, leaning back, relaxed.

"Were you on your feet all day?" I ask, rubbing stronger.

"Yes, and I'm so tired," she says with a deep sigh. "But a good tired. It was a really good day."

"How was it overall?" I ask.

"The truth is...I love it. I love the kids, the projects, the vibes...all of it. I feel like I somehow won the lottery in life."

I smile. "It all just gets better from here."

The silence stretches between us and she finally says, "I have to tell you something."

Her tone makes me pause.

"What?"

"I have a bigger reason why this can't be real. I don't want a family," she says softly. "Not like the white picket fence, matching Christmas pajamas, and all that. I'm just not built for that life. I don't think I want it. I like how things are with me and Owen. And you."

I stay quiet and listen.

"I just want a good life for Owen," she continues. "I want to make sure he's okay. That he's safe. And I want you with us. But I don't know if I can do more than that."

I continue massaging her feet, gazing at her, waiting for her to finish.

She looks over at me. "And I can't imagine you not here with us. But if you want more than that, I wouldn't blame you. You deserve a picket fence and matching pajamas. You deserve everything, Ollie."

I say nothing because I know she's not finished and needs to get whatever this is off her chest.

"I'm scared," she admits. "Of promising something I can't ever give you. I'm just not sure I'm built to be a wife and a mom like that, to have babies."

I pull her into me and hold her to my chest.

"I'm here for whatever," I say. "I'm not asking for anything with you, Poppy."

She rests her head against my chest. "I don't want to disappoint you."

"You won't," I promise. "Not now or ever."

She breathes me in like she's memorizing the feeling.

"Matching pajamas are so lame anyway," I say, and I feel her shaking with laughter.

"Right?"

"I don't even like pajamas. Before you, I just slept naked."

She snorts. "You can sleep however you want to be comfortable, Ollie. I'll adjust the pillow wall accordingly."

I laugh. "I don't think your pillow wall held up. And I'm comfortable with you here, Poppy. I love having you both here."

"Thanks," she says softly. "I'm happy here, too."

I stare at the wall over her head and think the quiet thought I don't say out loud.

I love her so damn much. I'll take whatever she'll give me.

Chapter 14
Poppy

Quit You by Karley Scott Collins

It's been a week since the CPS interview and things are finally settling down. I'm hefting up the door to the shop bay when a big, brand-new-looking black SUV that I don't recognize pulls up like it owns the street right in front of my garage bay.

The windows all roll down, and Violet's smiling face leans out the tinted window. Maggie's in the passenger seat, waving excitedly, Mack's wedged behind her, peeking out, and Cami's grinning, leaning over like she knows something I don't.

"Hey," Violet calls excitedly with a big smile. "Get in, we're going shopping."

I blink. "What?"

Ollie steps up beside me and gives a casual nod, as if this is all completely normal, and calls out, "Hey."

"Hey," Mack and Maggie say in unison, waving.

"Hey, little bro. I'm taking my future sister-in-law wedding shopping," Cami announces. "It's time to pamper Poppy."

My brain short circuits. Pamper me? I don't even know what that really entails, and my first instinct isn't excitement. It's math. Numbers lining up automatically in my head. What it costs. What that money could cover instead. Groceries. Gas. Owen's shoes when he outgrows the ones he has, which will be any minute now.

Old habits die hard.

For so long, I've been the one who goes without. Skipping meals without thinking. Puts everything extra toward making sure Owen has what he needs. Comfort always felt optional. Indulgence felt irresponsible.

I hesitate, the word *pamper* hovering in the air like it belongs to someone else's life, not mine.

"I don't know," I start, already pulling back. "That sounds... expensive."

Maggie gives me a look. Not sharp. Just knowing. "Poppy."

Cami leans in, softer. "You just worked your first week at a new job. You're exhausted. You've earned this."

"And," Maggie adds, tapping the planner, "this is our treat, so sit back and enjoy it."

I swallow, the resistance still there, but weaker. Because the truth is, it does sound divine. After the week I've had. After the years I've had. My body aches in that deep, bone-tired way, and the idea of someone else taking care of me for once makes my chest feel tight.

Wanting things still feels dangerous. But maybe it doesn't have to be.

I let out a slow breath and nod, tentative but real. "Okay," I say quietly. "Maybe just this once."

And even as I say it, I can feel how badly I need it.

"No idea what that means, but I'm in." I grin. "Thank you so much."

Owen walks out and looks from the SUV to Ollie, eyes wide. "That sounds terrible."

"Yes, it does," Ollie says, smiling way too big as he agrees. "That's why your sister's going, and you and I are gonna go do guy stuff."

"Yes!" Owen says, pumping his fist in the air, looking relieved. Then he pauses and looks at me. "Oh. Have fun, Poppy."

I laugh as Violet hops out, wraps me in a hug, and pulls me toward the SUV. "Come on. Trust us. We're going to have a blast."

I glance at Ollie. He squeezes my shoulder once, soft and grounding. "We'll see you later. Have fun."

I grab my purse and coat from the office and climb in, and the door shuts behind me with a final *thunk* that feels like crossing into another world.

The SUV smells like coffee, Maggie's perfume, and excitement. Music's already playing, something upbeat and loud, and by the time we're out of town, everyone's talking at once, singing along to the music, and passing around road trip snacks that they packed in a big cooler. It's a long drive to the big town where we're going shopping, and they seem to have a great plan.

An hour later, I'm laughing so hard my cheeks hurt.

We talk about the reception they're all planning, which is in two weeks, on a Saturday. Walker and Violet have heated tents coming in. A real catering company from Jackson. Cami's making the cake because, of course, she is. I wouldn't want to have any other cake. Maggie's already planning flowers like she's running a military operation. I can't believe they're doing this for us.

"Oh," Violet says casually, like she's not dropping a bomb. "And Riley Blue and Mandy Moran are coming to play."

I nearly choke on my iced coffee. "How the heck did you manage that?"

Violet shrugs, trying not to smile. "Walker's idea. He knows some people."

Of course, he does. Walker and Violet are both amazing country musicians. Walker is a country music legend who retired here in Bridger Falls. He was a songwriter for a long time until Violet came along to stay with her Aunt Maggie. Those two fell in love, and the rest is history. They started their own recording studio, hosting artists and musicians, and producing songs. It's really fun to meet everyone who comes through town. A little surreal sometimes, but really cool. It's not surprising that Walker convinced two of the top country music legends to sing for us at our reception. Ollie isn't even going to believe it when I tell him tonight.

I shake my head in disbelief. "I can't believe it."

She leans closer. "Don't you dare tell him I told you this, but we're writing you guys a song. Just for you. It'll probably eventually go on an album but know it's your song."

I press my hand to my chest. "Aww, Violet. I can't wait to hear it. No one has ever written me a song before."

My eyes burn a little, but it's the good kind. I love that they are excited for us, regardless of whether this is real or not. I'm beginning to feel sad that this is a pretend marriage. And a pang of sadness hits me that it isn't real. Because it's starting to feel real.

At the first store, they don't even let me protest how they're fawning over me. When we open the door, there's a table set up with a charcuterie board, champagne, and cider waiting. There are even iced cookies that read "yes to the dress" and are in the shape of wedding dresses.

"This doesn't feel like shopping," I say, looking in awe at everything. "This is a party."

"Yes," Cami agrees, grinning. "This is a Poppy party. It's not every day my brother and best friend get married."

They pull dresses I'd never pick for myself. Things that fit and look amazing instead of hiding my curves. Maggie cries over the first one I try on, which is dramatic and unnecessary but somehow perfect. She clasps her hands and says, "My baby is getting married."

And somehow, that heals something in me I didn't know I needed. I pictured my mom being with me on a day like today but having Maggie and all my friends with me is as close to that as I could ask for.

When I step out in the dress that ends up being the one, they all go quiet.

Cami whistles. "Well. Damn. I hope Ollie keeps the fire department on standby. Because you're a smoke show, Poppy."

Mack grins. "Ollie's gonna pass out when he sees you. They better have the paramedics handy, too."

My stomach flips at the thought of what Ollie's going to think when he sees me. Then I picture him standing there in a tux and my heart clenches. I bet he'll look so freaking good. I've only seen him in a tux at Violet's wedding and prom. And he looked so good. I remember seriously lusting after that man that night and thinking I shouldn't have been thinking of my best friend like that. And now here I am marrying him. Pretend marrying him. But, still.

Later, when my hair's washed, cut, and blown out, and my makeup actually looks like me, just brighter, we sit on velvet chairs in a little boutique with champagne flutes in our hands. I glance around and realize that Violet and Mack are drinking cider.

"What if it stops being pretend?" I ask suddenly.

They all look at me, then they laugh.

Okay, not the reaction I was expecting.

"What?" I laugh, along with them, because honestly, this whole thing is absurd.

"Nobody really thinks this is pretend, but you, Poppy. My brother is head over heels in love with you. Everyone can see it," Cami says as she sips her glass. "And you better not break his heart because he's the best."

I would never hurt Ollie. I love him was my immediate thought. I love him. Shit, I do. I really love him so much.

Violet looks over at me. "Girlllll, what kind of friendship do you think this is? This is a whole relationship. Ollie's been waiting for you to catch up."

I stare into my drink. "I don't think I want a traditional marriage. I don't want a white picket fence. Ollie deserves more than that."

What I'm really thinking is that maybe I don't deserve that. It's not that I don't want it. I just don't think it's possible for me. I've never had that life and don't know if it even really exists.

Cami reaches over and takes my hand. "What if all he wants is you, Poppy?"

Maggie hums. "I love you, sweetheart, but I think you're both being ridiculous. I've never heard Ollie say he wants some traditional fantasy life that you seem to have worked up in your mind that is superior to the life you're living right now. Life isn't like that. It's not always picket fences like that. Sometimes it's just like this. Friends that become family. And best friends who become your life partner. You getting to do life with your best friend sounds like a pretty good life to me. No matter where you live. And picket fences are ugly. Sometimes you need barbed wire like the ranches have. Keep people like Sully out."

I laugh at that last part, because she's not wrong. Our life is more like barbed wire than a picket fence. And I thought that was a bad thing, but maybe it's not.

Violet smiles softly. "Some people don't want the picture-perfect life. They want the right one. And the right one is right for you."

Lunch turns into cocktails, with Mack agreeing to be the designated driver, and when Violet orders a lemonade, the table goes silent.

Everyone looks at her. She looks anywhere but at us.

"Violet," Cami says slowly. "Anything you want to share with the class?"

She sighs. "Okay. Fine. I'm pregnant. I didn't want to tell you during Poppy's special time."

I'm out of my seat in seconds, hugging her. "Violet, no. I'm so happy for you guys. This is big."

We celebrate her right there, clinking glasses and laughing and crying all over again.

When Violet drops me off at home later, my arms are full of bags.

A dress for the reception, new makeup, and several sets of lingerie I swore I'd never wear, but they bought them for me anyway. I've never had fancy lingerie, and honestly, I couldn't stop looking at all of the pretty things in every color imaginable. I may be a mechanic, but I am a girly girl at heart. I love feeling pretty and having nice clothes. When I'm not working and wearing my usual navy coveralls, I love to dress up. Of course, I haven't had the money for cute clothes for a while, but I also love thrifting and finding pieces to pair with what I already have.

But the lingerie? Cute panty-and-bra sets have always been Violet's thing. She told me she pretty much has a rainbow-colored collection of every color and style possible, and she loves to feel pretty and sexy. She told me that when she met Walker, and he found out she wore those every day, it practically made him feral. I think about adding more to my collection, because I want to feel like that, too. And maybe I'd love to see Ollie be feral, too.

I unlock the door and step into the apartment, smiling so hard my face aches. I've never felt so full. And for the first time, I let myself wonder if maybe what I want and what Ollie wants don't have to be so different after all.

The apartment is dim and peaceful, a candle lit on the coffee table, which surprises me because Ollie is usually anti-candles as a firefighter. He only lights them for special occasions. And today's been a very special day, I guess you could say.

Ollie's on the couch, sprawled out, arm behind his head. He looks tired in that good way, like his body earned it. And damn it's a nice body.

"Hey," he says softly, sitting up and coming to the door to help me with my bags.

"Hey," I whisper back, smiling, kissing him softly, his warm lips gentle on mine.

"How was your day? Owen already asleep?" I ask, glancing around at the spotless apartment that smells amazing, like a yummy dinner that was made here.

He perks up. "Yeah, he's out like a light. It was such a good day. You should've seen him today. Jack took us out to the back pasture on a ride to check some cattle. Owen rode like he'd been doing it his whole life. Didn't complain once and asked a million questions. I swear, I've never been prouder. He's a natural at ranch life, Poppy."

My chest warms. "Sounds like you both had the best time. You haven't been out on the ranch in a while, either."

Ollie grew up on Wilder Ranch and loved it when his grandpa Wilder was running it. Then, after he passed away, it became like a violation of child labor laws out there instead of fun. It has taken him a while to enjoy it out there again. With Jack home now, running both Wilder Ranch and The Jessop Ranch together, he's made Ollie's visits more fun.

Ollie grins. "I didn't realize how much I missed it. It was a great day. How was yours? What did you get?"

I set my bags on the table. "Shopping was really fun. I got so many pretty things."

He tucks a long lock of my blonde hair behind my shoulder and murmurs, while his eyes scan me in the candlelight. "You look so beautiful. I love your hair like this."

"Thanks. I had a blowout, and my makeup done. Got some things for the reception," I say shyly.

He's already digging through the bags like a kid on Christmas morning. "You got a lot of cool makeup."

"Don't you dare look at the dress," I warn as I hang up my coat. "You're not supposed to see me in it before the reception Violet said."

He freezes, holding up a piece of light pink lingerie, mouth hanging open like his brain just shut off.

I snatch it out of his hands, forgetting about the lingerie. "Violet insisted," I say quickly, tucking it back into the bag.

"Well, hold on, now. I think you should model the lingerie at least," he says, grinning.

"Not a chance." I smirk. "I do like the lingerie, though. I've never owned any pretty bra-and-panty sets. I might start wearing them regularly."

"You're going to give me a permanent hard-on," he groans. "I can't go through my day knowing that's what you're wearing."

"That's going to be painful for you," I tease.

He laughs, eyes bright, and he gets more serious. "You're getting into this. I love it."

"Yeah," I admit, smiling. "I kinda do too."

He pulls me in, slow and warm, and kisses me. One kiss turns into several, soft and unhurried. I end up straddling him without even thinking about it, my hands in his hair, his hands steady at my waist.

Eventually, I pull back, breathless. "We should probably go to bed."

"Yeah," he says, forehead pressed to mine. "But, I like kissing you."

"I love kissing you," I say, and I mean it.

I grab my pajamas and head for the bathroom. He follows, leaning in the doorway.

"It'd be faster if we showered together," he says lightly.

I smirk. "Best friends don't shower together."

"Pretend fiancés do," he replies and shrugs. "Haven't you heard? Apparently, it's a new thing."

He steps closer, brushing his thumb over my lips. "And if you like what I do with my mouth here, you should see what else I can do with it."

Holy shit. I want to see.

I grab his shirt and pull him into the bathroom before I can overthink it and push the door shut quietly. I turn the water on to cover up any sounds, and he backs me gently against the wall, kissing me until my knees forget how to work. I drop my clothes on the floor. Ollie watches me with eyes that are nothing short of wanting to devour me.

He strips off his shirt with one easy motion, reaching back and tugging it free at the back of his neck. The sight of him always makes my breath hitch. His body is all hard lines and strength, a solid wall of muscle across his chest, broad shoulders tapering down to a narrow waist with that deep V pulls my gaze lower, my pulse skidding.

He slides his shorts and boxer down, making his cock spring

free, and my mouth practically waters for it. It's definitely not an average cock, that's for sure. My best friend has been packing a massive cock, and you're telling me I've held back on this? I shake my head, thinking that I have been crazy to deny this all along.

"Okay, ground rules. What if we just got this out of our system one time?" I ask nervously.

He laughs. "You think one time would cure you from wanting it more?"

His hands trail down my breasts, and I moan. "Ollie, I need an orgasm so bad. I need this. It's been so long. I can't even take care of it because we share a bed."

God, I hate how I'm begging, but I need this. So badly. I haven't been with anyone in an embarrassing amount of time.

Ollie nips at my ear and says, "You might be pretending about marrying me. But there isn't anything pretend about what I'm going to do to you with this mouth. And all you had to do was ask. I'll give you what you need tonight, baby."

His dirty words send a shiver through me, heat curling low in my belly, leaving me dizzy and undone.

We step into the warm water, and he backs me up until the tile is cold against my spine, his body all heat and pressure, trapping me there like he means to keep me forever.

Steam curls around us, thick and clinging, fogging the edges of the world until it's just us. Ollie drops to his knees in front of me, so suddenly it steals my breath. The sight of him there sends a jolt straight through me.

He looks up at me, dark eyes locked on mine, hot and intent and unflinching. Like he's exactly where he wants to be.

His hands slide firmly over my thighs, spreading them, anchoring me in place. The confidence of it makes my knees go weak. My body reacts before my brain can catch up, heat pooling low and urgent, my pulse hammering everywhere at once.

I gasp as his mouth finds me, skilled and relentless, and my head falls back against the tile. Sensation builds fast, rolling and sharp and overwhelming. My thighs start to tremble, betraying me completely.

One of my hands dives into his hair, fingers threading through the dark strands, gripping just enough to guide him, to tell him exactly where I need him. The other arm flies up, pressing across my mouth as a broken sound tears out of me anyway.

He doesn't rush it.

Just when I feel myself tipping too close, he eases back, drawing it out until I'm breathless and aching and desperate. Then he takes me right back there again, slow and sure, over and over, until my whole body is shaking and I can barely stay upright.

I'm so close it hurts.

And he knows it.

"Oh my God," I gasp, the sound barely holding together.

His grip tightens, grounding me, owning me, and when his hand comes up to cover my mouth, it's gentle but commanding, like he knows exactly how close I am to unraveling.

"Ollie," I moan, his name breaking apart on my tongue again and again until it's all I can say, all I can think about, until pleasure crashes through me so hard that I shake, clinging to him as I come undone against his mouth.

He rises slowly, water streaming down his chest, eyes dark and locked on mine. The hunger in his expression steals my breath. Every inch of him is tight with restraint, with want. I swallow hard.

"Ollie," I pant, breathless.

He murmurs, mouth at my ear now, voice low. "Told you I could do things with that mouth."

I laugh softly, shaky and breathless. "Showers together are absolutely dangerous with you."

He smiles against me, wicked and warm. "Worth the risk."

My hand drops to him without thinking, fingers curling, and the sound he makes is rough and unfiltered, like I've touched something raw. He presses his forehead to mine, both of us breathing hard, bodies slick and flushed and aching.

He grabs my hand. "I can't," he says quietly, steady even though I can feel how hard this is for him. "Not like that."

I look at him, confused, breath still uneven.

"It's not about wanting you," he continues, voice low and honest. "God, Poppy, that's not the problem."

He swallows, eyes holding mine. "I don't want you giving me pieces of yourself like this if your heart isn't all the way in. I don't want something that's half real. I don't want comfort or relief or a moment that we pretend doesn't mean anything tomorrow."

His thumb brushes my hand, grounding, reverent. "If this was just about sex, I'd do it. But it's not."

He exhales slowly. "I only want you like this if you're choosing me. All of me, for real. No pretend. Not because you're lonely."

His gaze softens and he continues, fierce and gentle at the same time. "I don't want your body unless your heart is ready to come with it."

Wow. I didn't expect that from him. But I respect the hell out of that.

"I'm terrified you'll wake up one day and realize I'm too much," I admit.

He lets out a shaky laugh. "Poppy, I've already built my

whole life around you. Waking up and choosing you is the easy part."

He cups my face. "I'm not going anywhere. Not tomorrow, and not when things get hard. I'm right here. It's always you."

"Always you," I whisper as he kisses me.

I've spent so long believing love had to hurt to be real. But standing here with him, wrapped in warmth and promise, I realize maybe real love feels like safe and chosen.

Chapter 15
Ollie

Fix You Too by Megan Moroney and Kameron Marlowe

I peel off my gear when we get back to the station, heat and sweat clinging to my body. My body is running on muscle memory after that call. Just another shift, another fire, another reminder that I know how to step into chaos and come out steadily with everything in my life, except Poppy. It's been a few days since I tasted her and now, I can't stop replaying it in my head. She's the only fire I've never been able to extinguish. Because she's the fire of my heart. The one person I think about at any given point of my day. She's everywhere. In my heart, a photo on my dashboard, a photo in my locker. I even have a picture of her in my helmet. Poppy means the world to me. I want everything with her.

I stow my gear and open my locker, hands moving automatically, when the memory hits me when I see it.

A photo of us at the lake, our senior year. A bonfire burns low in the background behind us, our cheeks pressed together while music thumps out of someone's truck. If I close my eyes, I can practically still hear it. Laughter drifting over the water. And Poppy by my side.

Her hair's pulled up messy on the top of her head, cheeks flushed from the night and the noise and the way I'm looking at her like I don't know how not to. I can still smell that night, like smoke and summer. The way she laughs when I said something stupid to hear her laugh. I did that a lot back then, trying to get her to laugh. I craved her laughter. I think we all did everything we could to save Poppy back then. She had it rough raising Owen practically on her own, so making her happy was important. She deserved that after all the hurt she had been through losing her mom.

I remember sneaking away from the crowd with her, our toes in the sand, moonlight cutting a silver line across the lake. I leaned in before I could talk myself out of it and kissed her. She let me, just for a second. Her mouth was soft and warm and perfect against mine.

Then she pulled back.

"Ollie," she says, breathless and scared all at once. "We can't."

I remember the way my chest tightens, and the hurt I felt. "Why not?"

She looks at me like she's holding something fragile. "Because I can't lose you. I can't ruin our friendship. You're my best friend."

And that's it. That's where it ended. Her best friend. Period. That's all I was. Friend zoned and that's all I allowed myself to be.

I didn't push her or beg her to see me. I had just nodded, swallowed it down, and told myself that loving her quietly was better than losing her completely. I said to myself that night on the beach that friendship with Poppy would be enough.

For ten years, I've tried so hard to believe that lie, but being her friend will never be enough.

I shut my locker harder than I mean to, the clang echoing through the bay. One of the guys glances up but doesn't say anything. They're used to me being in my head.

Years of birthdays and holidays and late-night phone calls. Years of watching her shoulder more responsibility than anyone should. Watching her become the strongest person I know. Watching her love fiercely and protectively, and never once asking for help.

If I'd had her back then, I probably would've lost her. We were kids. Messy and impulsive, and still figuring out who we were. I would've loved her wrong and probably messed it all up. She would've burned herself out trying to hold us both together with everything else she had on her plate. Friendship saved us.

But now?

Now she's admitting the fears and feelings both of us have wrapped up in layers for years. And those layers are stripping off one by one, and our hearts are laid bare now.

I drag a hand down my face and blow out a breath.

I meant what I said. I can't fuck her unless she's really mine. Not because I don't want her. God, I want her so bad it hurts. But because I know myself. I know once I cross that line, there's no going back. I give everything. I don't know how not to. But that's the one piece of me I can't give unless it means something with her. And I can't risk it if she's still halfway out the door.

I don't want to be the guy she's with when she's lonely. I don't want to be the mistake she regrets, the one that changed things. I don't want her to wake up one day and realize she needed comfort, not me.

I want her to choose me the way I've been silently choosing her for years as a best friend, secretly always wanting more. Only I don't want to be silent anymore. I want us to be loud and proud.

And if it took Maggie making up some bullshit lie to get us there, then fine. I'll do whatever it takes to get the woman I love to love me back and finally see me as more than her best friend. I want to be everything with her. Fuck her stupid picket fences. I'm not even a picket fence kind of guy. I'm a guy who is hopelessly in love with Poppy Grace Murphy—head over goddamn heels.

I want her. Not just the way she fits against me like she was always meant to. I want her mornings, her bad days, and her responsibilities. I want Owen's basketball practices and games, late dinners, and fixing things that break together. I want the life she already has. I want to be in it.

The station quiets as the shift settles back into routine. Someone starts a pot of coffee. Someone else flips on the TV in the common room. Normal life resumes with ordinary day-to-day noise. Meanwhile, my heart's still a mess from last night in the shower when I ate her until I felt like I would come just hearing her moan my name.

I think about the way she looked at me when I said I couldn't do this unless it were real. The fear in her eyes. The want. The way she didn't break things off then and there. She's getting closer.

That's what's different now.

* * *

The gym smells like smelly middle school boy sweat and the sharp bite of disinfectant they never quite get rid of. I clap my hands a few times, and the boys hustle back into line, sneakers squeaking, faces flushed and happy.

"Free throws," I call. "Same rules. Miss it, and you cheer louder for the next guy."

Groans and playful laughing. Owen grins at me like this is

the best part of his day. Because here no one is going to mess with him. He can just be happy, have fun, and play a sport. The way it should be. That alone makes it worth it. Principal Masters has checked in and thanked me profusely for stepping in to coach at the last minute. I haven't even seen Toddy around and wonder if he left town. Good riddance. Because he's still facing legal trouble for hitting Owen and I'm seeing that through, making sure he gets what's coming to him.

I'm watching Owen square his shoulders to make a free throw when Walker steps in through the side door. He leans against the wall for a second, taking it all in, then makes his way towards me, his black cowboy hat pulled low.

He walks over and claps me on the back. "Hey."

"Hey," I say quietly.

"Just checking in. Poppy said I could find you here. I'm waiting on Mack to finish up band practice next door at the high school and figured I'd come say hi."

"Good to see you. Just coaching these boys and working. What's new with you?"

Before Walker can respond, Owen sinks his shot and pumps his fist. I point at him. "That's how it's done."

Walker smiles. "You're a natural at this. I remember when that was you out there."

"Those were the days," I say. "I played every sport that would keep me out of the house."

One of the boys trips over his own feet and pops back up laughing. Another kid makes his shot, and everyone cheers like he won a championship. The energy in the gym is good and fun. This was how it was for me as a kid. This gym and this school were a safe haven for me when home wasn't a good place anymore. I want this to be a fun escape for these kids if they need it. A place to have fun and blow off steam. A bully-free environment. So far, we haven't had any issues, and we're going to keep it that way.

Walker watches me for a minute. "You look happy, man."

I nod. "I am."

The boys start a dribbling drill, balls pounding the floor in uneven rhythm. Owen glances over at me between reps, checking in like he always does. I give him a thumbs up.

Walker lowers his voice. "So how are all the wedding plans coming along?"

"I heard you and Violet have been doing a lot for us, and I wanted to thank you. Really, I think you're doing so much, and I really appreciate you guys."

He shrugs. "It's what family does, Ollie."

What family does. That means more to me than he'll know. Walker is a stand-up guy. He's always been there for me. Front row seat with Mack at my graduation from the fire academy. At my high school graduation. He's always been there.

I exhale. "I want to convince her to make it real by the reception."

His eyebrows lift, but he doesn't look surprised.

"I want that night to be special for her," I say. "I want it to be incredible. I want her to feel like it's real. Like it's all for her. Because it is, I love her so much."

Walker's gaze softens as he watches Owen laugh when another kid loses control of the ball. "You gotta get to work, Ollie. It's time to unravel all those years of friendship and finally make her your wife."

I swallow. "I'm up for the challenge."

And I am. I have been for years now.

He nods. "It's gonna be the most important thing you ever do."

The boys rotate stations. Free throws again. Owen wipes his forehead with his sleeve and sinks another one. He gives a high five to another teammate. Pride hits me hard and fast in the chest. I'm not just fighting for her, I'm fighting for him, too, because life without them isn't a life.

Walker's quiet for a beat. Then he says, "I remember when Grace Murphy died. It left a crater-sized hole in this town. Mack was three. And we all went to her funeral, the whole town."

My chest tightens at the memory. Grace Murphy was a woman Sully never deserved. She fought cancer alone with a baby and a teenage daughter. She was the mother any kid would have been lucky to have. I loved Grace Murphy, too. My mother was friends with her because Grace was friends with everyone. She baked you banana bread and brought you a meal if you had a baby. She cheered for me at my middle school and high school games. She was the heartbeat of this town. I know when she died, I was thinking what a lot of other people were probably thinking as well. Why couldn't it have been Sully, instead? Sully did nothing for anyone, and he was a real jerk. Everyone knew it then and knows it now. Why do good people have to die? It's not fair.

"You know who didn't go?" he asks, igniting anger that lives deep down.

I close my eyes for half a second. "Sully."

I see it like it's happening again. The front row of the church. Poppy was holding Owen, sobbing so hard her shoulders shook. Owen was only a baby and slept through the whole thing. She refused to put him down. Maggie on one side. Walker and me right there on the other side of her. The pews were packed. People standing in the back and around the front entrance to the church. The gravesite burial was the saddest thing I've ever seen. I remember there was a double rainbow when we left the cemetery. Poppy said it was a sign that everything would be okay.

The town showed up, and from that day forward, we all sat with her. No matter where she went, what she did. Her and Owen became our family. We absorbed them into ours because that's what you do when you love people. You take care of them.

Walker exhales. "She didn't just lose her mom. She lost her safety net. And you've been part of what caught her. You've always been there, Ollie. They need you, and I think you need them."

My breath catches, and I nod, eyes on Owen as he laughs at something and makes another free throw, high-fiving another player. I do need them—more than they know.

Walker claps my shoulder. "You've got this."

The whistle blows. Practice wraps up in a mess of high fives and noise. Owen runs over and gives me a high five.

"Did you see that shot?" he asks.

"I saw all of them," I say. "You all crushed it. We have a great team this year."

"Hi, Walker," Owen says as he grabs his water bottle.

"Looking good out there," Walker calls as he watches us, grinning.

I look down at Owen, then back at the court, the town, the life we've built piece by piece.

This isn't pretend. It has never been.

And before that reception night is over, she's gonna know it too.

Chapter 16
Poppy

No Horse To Ride by Luke Grimes

This is the biggest day of my life, and I'm nervous. It's almost time for us to meet at City Hall and get married. I stand in front of the mirror at Boots & Bangs and smooth my hands down the front of my dress, still in disbelief that it's me looking back in the mirror.

Cami, Violet, Maggie, and Mack helped me change into my dress. It looks like it belongs in a fairy tale. It's what dreams are made of, a long, bustling skirt and a laced top with long sleeves covered in lace. It makes my boobs look fantastic with amazing cleavage. This is the dress that I tried on with them that made me feel like a beautiful princess. My white heels have red bottoms, a little secret splash of bold that feels just like me. I have no idea what kind of shoes they are, but Violet surprised me with them, and they fit me like a glove and feel like the best shoes I've ever worn. Butter soft. So pretty, I'll keep them where I can see them to remember this day. Maggie drapes a fake white fur stole around my shoulders earlier, fussing until it sat just right.

Cami places light blue teardrop pearl earrings in my ears that belonged to her grandma Wilder for something borrowed and blue. "So many people here with all of us today watching in spirit. I know Grandma Wilder would have loved you both together."

"Don't make me cry," I tell her, pulling her in for a hug. She leans back and looks at me with her long hair curled around her shoulders, looking stunning as ever.

"Thanks for becoming my sister," she says, smiling back tears.

"I've always been your sister," I tell her proudly.

I'm wearing lingerie too. The light pink set Violet insisted on. Ollie probably won't see it and might not even know I have it on. But I do. I've never felt prettier. He says he won't take it there with me unless we're real. I want that so badly, but I have no idea how to tell him.

We're still finding our footing and still learning how to say what we mean without getting scared. He still looks at me sometimes like he's waiting for me to change my mind. Like he can't quite believe I want him the way he wants me.

I love Ollie, and I'm nervous. I don't know how to say it so he'll believe it. But I do want this to be real.

The stylists from Boots & Bangs move around me, curling and pinning, brushing and blending. Soft music plays. The mirror fogs slightly from hairspray and nerves. When they step back, I finally really look at myself.

My hair is half pulled up and braided around my crown, with loose tendrils around my face. My blond hair curls into lovely waves around my shoulders and down my back.

I've never felt more beautiful in my entire life. And there's one person that I always thought would be here on the day I got married. My mom. And that stings. But I won't cry and ruin my makeup, I remind myself.

Maggie stands behind me, her hands clasped together. When our eyes meet in the mirror, hers shine with tears.

"Oh, Poppy," she says softly.

I turn toward her. "What?"

She steps closer and cups my cheek. "I know your momma has to be looking down at you right now. So proud of you. Of the beautiful woman you've become. I love you so much, sugar."

My throat tightens instantly, and she knew why I was upset. Every girl dreams about their wedding day and pictures their mom there. I've always known that my mom wouldn't be there, and today that became real, and I hate it even more.

"I wish she were here," I whisper, my lip quivering and my nose starting to run with emotion.

"I know," Maggie says. She pulls me into a warm, solid hug. "But she's with you. Always has been."

I breathe her in and let myself have the moment. The ache, love, and missing her.

When we finally head to City Hall, my heart starts beating faster with every step. I keep my stole pulled close, my heels clicking softly against the floor. Maggie squeezes my hand once before letting go.

They're already there. Owen is the first person I see. He's in a tux that fits him perfectly, black and crisp and handsome. He spots me, and his face lights up. He pulls at his collar like it's strangling him, clearly not a fan.

"Poppy." He waves, turning to show me his tux proudly.

"You look so handsome," I tell him, and I mean it with my whole heart.

Ollie quietly walks up and stands beside him, and my breath hitches when I see him. He looks devastatingly handsome with a fresh haircut, his tux is sharp and tailored, his shoulders broad, his posture proud and steady. His eyes meet mine, and something flickers there. A hint of awe, relief, and love fills his face as his eyes meet mine and shine with pride.

I choke up instantly as I put my arms around him and pull him in for a hug. His arms tighten around me. "You look so beautiful, baby," he whispers in my ear and then kisses my forehead.

Owen tugs at his collar again, and Maggie gives him a look, one eyebrow lifting in silent warning. Owen grins mischievously and freezes in place like he's being perfectly behaved.

I smile through the tears. And this time they're happy tears. Owen stands next to us, proudly, belonging and happy.

I love the way Ollie loves us. The quiet guidance and humor. The steadiness in the way Owen watches him, like he's learning how to be a good man just like Ollie.

If there ever was a man I could dream of marrying, it's Ollie. He's the only person I could ever see fitting into our world, sliding in like he was always meant to be here.

We stand together before the clerk. The words are simple. The vows are quiet and sincere. When Ollie says my name, it sounds like a promise.

When he slides the basic gold wedding band onto my finger, my hands shake. We picked them out online, and they're not real, just something we could get quick. Just like our wedding, I try to remind myself. But it doesn't feel pretend. This feels very real to me, anyways.

When it's time to kiss, he pulls me in slowly, one hand settling at my waist like he's steadying us both. His other hand comes up to tip my face, thumb warm at my jaw, giving me a second to breathe him in. Then his mouth meets mine, unhurried and sure, the kiss deepening a fraction at a time. It's soft and deliberate, like he's memorizing the feel of me, like he has nowhere else to be. I feel it everywhere, the quiet intensity of it, the promise in the way he stays, and I know I'll remember this kiss for the rest of my life.

He leans in and presses his forehead to mine. "You okay?"

I nod. "Yeah." I'm more than okay.

Later, before the reception, I step away for a moment. I find a quiet corner and let myself feel it again. The missing. The wishing.

I close my eyes. *I wish you were here, Mom. I wish you could see him. See Owen. See us. I know you'd love Ollie. He's the best.*

Maggie finds me like she always does.

She doesn't say anything at first. Just wraps an arm around me and lets me lean into her. "Ready, sugar?"

My makeup and hair are touched up, and Maggie smiles proudly as she leads me to our reception that already has soft music playing.

"Hey, all that sappy yappy is gross," Owen complains from the doorway. "Are we almost ready? I'm hungry."

"Come here, bozo," I tell him and pull him in for a hug.

"You look pretty, Pops," he says in my ear.

"And you look so handsome, buddy. Are you ready to have fun tonight?" I pat his back and pull back.

"Yeah, you should see all the food! Walker said I can have as much as I want!"

I laugh. "Okay."

"Are you missing Mom?" he asks wistfully.

"Yeah, I am. But I feel like she's here with us," I tell him.

He nods. "It feels like a good day. I'm glad you're marrying Ollie. We need him, and he needs us. Did you know that today was his grandma and grandpa Wilder's anniversary? Kinda cool you guys got married on their anniversary."

I bite my lip and admit. "I didn't know that was today."

"I had a weird idea," he says, and looks around. "What if I

changed my name to Kendrick, too? I don't want to be a Murphy anymore, Poppy."

My stomach twists because I don't either and I can't blame him. Sully tainted our family name and no one respects it.

He nods. "Can I be like you guys?"

I pull him in for a hug. "We'll figure it out, buddy."

* * *

I step out into Walker's backyard and feel like I've crossed into another world.

Soft lights glow everywhere, warm and golden, strung through the trees and wrapped around posts like something out of a storybook. Lanterns flicker along the paths, their light dancing over petals scattered across the grass. The air smells like flowers and champagne. Maybe hope.

An acoustic version of *Today Was a Fairytale* drifts through the space, gentle and dreamy, the kind of music that settles right into your chest. It mixes with the sound of laughter and low conversation, the clink of glasses, the soft hush of people moving carefully like they don't want to break the magic.

I stop walking without meaning to.

Everything feels hazy and unreal, like I'm inside a dream I didn't know I was allowed to have. The night air brushes against my skin, cool and light, carrying the warmth of bodies and joy and celebration. Even the ground under my feet feels softer somehow, like it's cushioning every step.

It really does look like a fairytale.

I'm still taking it all in when Violet appears in front of me, eyes shining. She doesn't say a word. She just smiles and pulls me into a hug, tight and warm and grounding, like she knows I need a second to believe this is real.

I wrap my arms around her and breathe it in.

For once, the world feels beautiful instead of heavy.

And for a moment, I let myself believe in the magic of it all.

"You deserve your fairytale, Poppy. Now, before we go in, Ollie wants to have a moment alone with you before we formally announce you as a couple."

I nod and look around, nervously. "Where is he?"

She turns and points. He's in the gazebo with his back to us, looking out at the frozen lake. Heaters are everywhere, keeping it warm out here, not making it feel like Wyoming in January.

I make my way to the gazebo, and he turns when I get close, wearing his emotion on his face. Our eyes lock on each other as I make my way up the steps and he reaches out for me. "Wife."

"Husband."

We stand looking at each other as if we're not real. Finally, he says, "I have something for you."

My eyes widen in surprise as he pulls out a velvet box from his pocket. "Tucker brought this back from Jackson for me this afternoon, and it almost didn't make it in time. I had it resized for you, and it wasn't ready before the wedding. But I have it for you now."

I cover my mouth. "Ollie…"

He nods. "Only the best for you, Poppy. I love you. I know we agreed to pretend. And if that's all you can give me, I'll take it. But I'm not pretending with my love for you. I love you and I always will, Poppy Grace Kendrick."

He opens the box, and it's a beautiful gold ring set in an antique-style band, its large diamond sparkling. I freeze when I realize it is his grandma Wilder's ring.

"Is that?" My hand goes to my mouth in surprise.

He nods. "It was my grandma's. Cami and I both agreed that it would be perfect for you."

"It's exquisite," I tell him, as he slides it on my finger. "And on their anniversary."

He leans down and kisses me softly, like he's savoring it. Like he already knows this moment matters.

"Yes," he murmurs. "It's a very special day."

My heart is pounding so hard I'm not sure how it hasn't given me away already. It thuds against my ribs, loud and frantic, like it's trying to escape. My throat tightens, heat rushing up my neck, my eyes burning suddenly and I have to say it. I have to.

It just spills out of me, driven by nerves and adrenaline and the dizzying feeling that I'm standing on the edge of something that could change everything.

"I don't want to pretend, Ollie," I blurt.

The words hang there, terrifying and fragile.

My breath comes out shaky. My nose stings. My vision blurs just enough that I have to blink hard to keep it together. I feel exposed, like I just cracked my chest open and handed him my heart without a second thought.

"I love you."

Saying it aloud is like stepping off a cliff and finding solid ground instead of air. Fear and giddiness crash together in my chest, followed by a rush of relief so strong it almost makes my knees weak.

Whatever happens after this, whatever comes next, I don't have to carry it alone anymore.

And for the first time, that feels more hopeful than terrifying.

Relief fills his face, and he kisses me again, holding me close as if he's afraid to let me go. "I love you so much, Poppy," he says as he peppers my face with kisses, and I laugh.

"Today is real," I tell him, our hands still together.

He smiles. "I love you. Always you."

"Always you," I repeat.

"Are you ready to go to our reception, Mrs. Kendrick?" he asks as he rests his forehead on mine.

"Let's do this," I tell him. "If we don't hurry, Owen is going to start a riot because he can't eat yet."

"This is gorgeous," Ollie says in awe as we walk over to the arch, where Violet stands, microphone in hand.

"Are the bride and groom ready?" she asks.

"We are," we say as he holds my hand. I keep holding my hand out and looking at the ring and grinning at Ollie.

"All right, ladies and gentlemen. I have a very special couple to announce to you. A whole family, to be exact. Let me be the first to introduce you to Mr. and Mrs. Kendrick!"

Everyone stands and claps and cheers as we make our way down a faux candlelit walkway.

We stop at the end, and he reaches down under my bottom, picks me up effortlessly, and spins me before sitting me down to kiss me in front of everyone as they cheer.

"That doesn't look pretend," Cami whispers smugly.

"Hey," Ollie says with a look. "That's my real wife you're talking about."

Cami smiles and nods with approval. "I love you guys."

Theresa is standing off to the side, looking into the distance, more like a distant relative or friend than the groom's mother. She doesn't even look happy, which confuses me. She glares at everyone and shakes her head, her arms folded across her chest. She clearly doesn't want to be here.

"Hi, Theresa," I call as she looks at us, her eyes narrowing.

"Congratulations," she says coldly.

If it bothers Ollie, I can't tell because he doesn't show a reaction. He says, "Thanks."

We make our way down the receiving line, talking and hugging everyone as we get to the tent and find our seats at the front of the tent, which is decorated in cozy twinkle lights, hearts everywhere, and a heated floor to dance on, which is impressive. The temperature feels perfect, even though we're next to a lake in the middle of winter.

Violet and Walker really outdid themselves.

Owen sits with Maggie at the table in front of us and waves. "Can we eat now?" he mouths and points to the buffet line.

I laugh and wave to him to go, and he scrambles to the front of the line.

Ollie glances over and squeezes my hand, and I squeeze back.

We both look over when we hear something and see Cami and their mom talking in the corner. I can't see Cami's face because her back is to us, but I see Jack go to Cami and put his arm around her. Whatever is said must not make Theresa happy because she turns and leaves, and I watch her walk out as if she's going home. Cami turns, and her face is neutral. Jack slides his hand in hers protectively and pulls her close, kissing her forehead. I don't know what just happened, but it didn't look good.

"Hey, baby," Ollie whispers.

"Yeah," I whisper back.

"You got that lingerie on?" he says in my ear, and warmth pools in my core.

"Yes, you want to take it off later?" I whisper back, and his eyes darken when he smirks.

"You can count on it," he says and kisses me. "Be careful, or we'll leave right now."

I playfully swat him. "We're not leaving our reception."

We eat excellent steak, every delicious side dish you can imagine, and then the best cake I've ever had in my mouth. It's a traditional vanilla cake with buttercream icing, which she knows Ollie and I love. It's a special day I'll never forget, surrounded by the people we love.

Chapter 17
Ollie

Sleeping On The Blacktop by Colter Wall

Music thumps through the heated tents, bass humming. Laughter and singing spill into the cold night air, glasses clinking as people crowd together, dancing shoulder to shoulder like this is exactly where we're all supposed to be.

I scan the space out of habit, and my chest loosens when I spot Owen.

The guys from the station have him completely surrounded. Bucky's pretending to lose at some dumb game just to make him laugh. Someone else spins him around until he's breathless, his laugh cutting through the noise, loud and wild and unguarded. Another lifts him onto his shoulders so he can see everything, like he belongs right at the center of it all.

Owen's having the time of his life.

They watch him without hovering. Always within reach.

Always circling back. Like it's instinct now. Like protecting him is just part of the job.

I feel it settle deep in my chest. That familiar swell of gratitude I never quite know what to do with.

This is my family. The one I chose. The one that showed up and stayed. And somehow, without ever asking, they wrapped their arms around Owen too.

I glance back toward Poppy, watching her watch him, and I see it on her face. That soft ache. That realization.

I gave her my life without thinking twice. But tonight, standing here with music pounding and my people keeping her kid safe and happy, it hits me that I didn't just bring her into my world.

I brought her home.

Walker and Violet did something for us I'll never forget. Pulling this off as quickly as they did was a miracle. Me and Poppy's moment before the reception was everything to me. It's what I needed. I always said that when we got older, I'd marry my best friend someday. We're older, and she's right here now. And she's my wife. How we got here doesn't matter. We got here.

I watched my parents fight and have a horrible marriage. But I also watched my grandpa and grandma Wilder have an awesome marriage. And they were best friends. They loved being together, doing life together, and they made everything fun. That's the kind of life I want to have with Poppy. I want to do everything with her and have the best life possible for Owen. That's why I wanted her to have my grandma's ring. Cami agreed, saying Jack had already wanted to buy her a ring, and she wanted a bigger diamond. Poppy has always loved older things, so this is perfect. Getting married on their anniversary is something special that just so happened to work out. I want to think it was a part of them watching over us from up above and making things happen.

If she doesn't want kids or whatever picket fence bullshit she thinks about, I'm good with that. Not sure how great a father I'd be anyway. I like kids, and I especially love Owen, but I just want her. Poppy is my endgame in life and always has been.

I keep catching myself looking across the room to make sure Poppy's still there.

She's laughing with Maggie and glowing in a way that makes my chest ache when I think about us and our life together now.

I still can't believe she told me she wanted it to be real. I practically cried like a little baby with relief when she admitted that to me.

Someone bumps my shoulder, and I turn to see Cami grinning at me. "Dance with me," she says.

I blink and tease her as a brother should. "Like... actually dance? Do you know how?"

She nods. "Like a sister-brother dance. Because our mom is lame and she bailed."

I glance around instinctively. "What happened with her? I saw you two talking."

Cami shrugs. "I don't want to ruin your night."

I snort. "Cami."

She sighs. "Basically, if something isn't about her, you know she's gonna ruin it for everyone."

I nod in agreement. "Yeah, that sounds about right."

"We didn't exactly luck out in the mom department," she says lightly, like she's talking about bad weather instead of something that still hurts.

I don't argue. There's no point pretending otherwise. "Pretty much the parent department."

She grabs my hand and drags me onto the dance floor. The

song shifts into something upbeat and ridiculous, and we immediately start dancing like idiots, laughing, and being silly.

Not smooth. Not cool. Just flailing arms, exaggerated spins, and Cami pretending to dip me so hard I almost lose my balance.

People around us laugh and cheer. I catch Maggie wiping at her eyes, crying, laughing at us being silly. Jack's watching us with that look he gets when he pretends he's not soft.

"We're terrible," I say, laughing.

"That's the whole point," Cami says.

I smile big and real. Because this night isn't about what we didn't get growing up. It's about what we built anyway, without our shitbag parents here to ruin our day.

Cami bumps into my chest and then looks up at me, suddenly serious.

"You know I would take a bullet for you, Ollie," she says.

I laugh. "Cami, you'd be the reason we were getting shot at in the first place."

She bursts out laughing and throws her arms around my neck, hugging me tight. "Rude. But honestly, probably fair."

"I love you, Cami," I say, meaning every word.

"Love you too, Ol," she says back.

We stay like that for a second longer than necessary, swaying in the middle of the dance floor while everything else keeps moving around us.

I think about how many years it's been just us against the world. We learned early that family isn't always the people who give birth to you. Sometimes it's the people who choose you and show up for you when they have nothing to gain from it.

When the song ends, Cami kisses my cheek and playfully shoves me. "Go," she says softly. "Your wife's looking for you."

Wife. The word hits me right in the chest.

I turn and see Poppy standing near the edge of the floor, her second dress flowing around her legs, eyes locked on me like she's checking to make sure I'm still hers, too.

I cross the room without thinking. She smiles when she sees me, that soft, knowing smile that still feels unreal. I slide my hand into hers, and she squeezes like she's grounding both of us at once.

"You okay?" she asks.

"Yeah," I say honestly. "I'm more than okay now that I have you."

She leans into me, head against my chest, and for the first time all night, I stop scanning the room. Stop waiting for something to go wrong.

This is it. We may not have started like a traditional couple. But if there's one thing I've learned, it's that life doesn't always go like that. It's messy, and sometimes we do things out of order.

The music swells again. Someone shouts. Someone laughs. The town keeps celebrating around us.

And right here, holding Poppy while my sister watches my back from across the floor, I know something deep and steady.

We didn't get everything we deserved growing up, but now we have everything that we need.

And tonight, that feels like more than enough.

* * *

Walker's driveway is still buzzing when we finally make our escape. Everyone's waving glowsticks in the air like we're leaving a concert instead of our own wedding reception. Laughter fills the air and I give Walker a big hug, "Thank you for everything."

"Absolutely our pleasure," he says as he looks at me proudly. "Happy for you both."

Owen stands at the front of the crowd with Maggie, a glow-stick looped around his neck like a medal. He's grinning so hard his cheeks look sore.

"I get a sleepover at the Dogwood Inn," he announces proudly. "Maggie promised chocolate chip pancakes at Harvest and Honey in the morning."

"Extra chocolate chips," Maggie adds, wagging a finger at him.

I laugh. "Of course she did."

I pull him in for a hug after Poppy hugs him. "Love you, Owen."

The crowd starts cheering as Poppy and I head toward my truck. Cami whoops. Jack whistles. Violet throws her arms around Walker's waist, glow stick waving.

"Go," someone yells. "Get outta here and have smoochy smoochy time!"

I laugh as I open the door for Poppy, and she slides in, laughing and waving back at everyone. I climb in and start the engine. The cheers get louder.

"That was absolutely amazing." Poppy sighs, leaning back against her headrest.

I reach for Poppy's hand as we head back toward town, fingers lacing together like this is exactly where they're meant to be. "It was incredible."

We're almost home. Home. The place we're starting our lives together. For real now. How we got here doesn't matter.

We pull into one of the bays and park, closing the door and locking up. She turns to me before we head upstairs, looking nervous, wearing my suit jacket over her dress.

"Hi," she says.

"Hi," I answer, and it feels like the most important word I've ever said.

I pick her up and throw her over my shoulder in a fireman carry and run up the stairs, kicking it shut behind me and locking it after I set her down, her breath heaving from laughing.

"Ollie!" she squeals.

"What? I'm excited to get my wife home. Sue me."

She grins, leans in, and kisses me softly. "Okay, husband. No suing needed. I'll allow it."

I take her coat off slowly, like there's no rush now, like I want to remember every second of this. My hands linger at her shoulders, my thumbs brushing her collarbone, and she lets out a breath that sounds like relief. Like she's finally letting herself have this. Whatever invisible battles she's been fighting.

We kiss again, softer this time. Deeper. Not the kind of kiss meant to convince anyone. This one is just for us. I feel her melt into me, feel her fingers curl into my shirt like she's afraid I might disappear if she lets go.

"We're real," I murmur against her mouth.

"I know," she whispers. "I just... I need a second. I'm nervous."

I rest my forehead against hers. "Take all the seconds you need."

When she finally nods, it's like a door opening. She presses her palm to my chest, right over my heart, and the look she gives me wrecks me. Open. Certain. Brave.

We move together without talking, shedding layers, finding each other by instinct. Every touch is careful and reverent, like we're learning each other all over again. I kiss her jaw, her neck, the place beneath her ear that makes her shiver. She laughs softly when I murmur her name, like she can't believe this is real either.

When I lay her down, I take my time. I want her to feel chosen, cherished, safe. I want her to know I'm not going anywhere.

She reaches for me, pulling me closer, and when I finally

sink into her warmth, the world narrows to the sound of our breathing and the way she fits against me, as if she always belonged there. We move slowly at first, finding a rhythm that feels like trust. Like home.

She wraps her legs around me, forehead pressed to mine, whispering my name like a prayer. I kiss her through it—through the way she opens and gives and finally lets herself have this. The intensity builds quietly and deeply, not rushed, not frantic. Just inevitable.

When she comes undone in my arms, it feels like fireworks under my skin. Like everything I've ever held back, finally has somewhere to go. I follow her, holding her close, grounding us both through it, through the way we fall apart together and come back whole.

After, I don't move. I keep her tucked against me, her head on my chest, my hand tracing slow circles along her back. She's warm and genuine and mine in a way that feels sacred.

"I didn't think it would feel like this," she says quietly.

I kiss the top of her head. "Me neither."

But I think I did. I think I always knew it would with Poppy.

I hold her a little tighter and close my eyes, already certain of one thing.

This isn't the end of something. It's the beginning.

Chapter 18
Poppy

House Again by Hudson Westbrook

I'm sitting at my desk in the little office off the auto shop, and I still can't believe this is my life. Last weekend I married my best friend, and this week I'm having fun teaching kids. And Mr. Fisher has been fun to work with, too. You can tell he's tired and done. He's ready to retire. But he seems like a good man who genuinely enjoys what he does and is happy to pass on the torch.

The high school smells like oil and metal and floor cleaner, and the windows on the bay doors let sunlight spill across concrete floors that have already seen better days. The kids are loud and curious and actually listening. I love it here. I love the hum of engines and the way my hands feel after a morning of teaching, rather than just fixing things in a rush.

Ollie's on speaker phone, static crackling softly from the firehouse. "How's your day going?" he asks as I finish my lunch. Some of the teachers asked me to go in on takeout, but I'm still trying to catch up on bills. But it feels great to have co-workers finally and to be included. Someday.

"Great," I say, smiling at nothing. "I think I might actually love my job."

"That makes me ridiculously happy for you, baby," he says. "I'm on shift but keep me on. I want to hear everything."

I'm just about to tell him more when Mack pops her head in the doorway, eyes bright.

"Hey," she says. "I talked to the counselor. I'm officially switching to auto tech."

"Hey, Mack!" Ollie calls through the speaker like he's announcing a celebrity sighting.

"Hey, Ollie!" she shoots back, equally serious about it.

"That's amazing," I say. "I'm proud of you. You're going to have a lot of fun."

She grins, rocking back on her heels. "Yeah. I wanna learn from you. A bunch of my friends are trying to switch, too."

My chest does that warm, expanding thing again, the one that sneaks up on me when I'm not paying attention. "I'd love that."

"See?" Ollie says smugly through the speaker. "Absolute legend."

I snort. "I don't know about that."

"I didn't think us girls were really allowed out here. I mean...I guess we were. But it didn't feel very welcome. We're glad you're here. One of my friends Emily and I are thinking about getting an old car to restore. My dad even said he'd try to help us find one to work on."

I smile at this because this is exactly what I wanted it to be like for the kids. I never took shop class when I went there. Mostly because my whole life was a shop class outside of school. School was the one place I could go to escape the shop under my dad's thumb. But the fact that kids are excited about this and choosing it makes me feel good. Kinda like what Ollie's doing coaching basketball. Making places safe for kids that need them.

Mack beams. And just like that, the shop feels exactly like it's supposed to.

A knock taps against the doorframe, and a woman steps inside with a clipboard tucked against her chest. She's young, probably not much older than me, with black rimmed glasses and a friendly smile.

"Hey, gotta run," I tell him. "I'll call you later when I'm off."

"Bye," he says and disconnects.

"Hi, I'm Elena," she says, shaking my hand. "The guidance counselor."

"Poppy," I say, offering my hand. "Nice to meet you."

She glances past me at the shop floor, where a group of girls is crowded around an engine in the bay. "You're becoming quite popular, Miss Murphy."

I laugh. "Thanks. I'm having a lot of fun, and I'm really glad to be here. And actually it's Mrs. Kendrick now."

Elena smiles wider. "I heard. Congratulations! We've had a ton of requests for kids to switch into auto class. Mainly female students. They're very excited."

I smile. "That means a lot."

"It should," she says. "You're doing something special. The kids are all really enjoying the class. Of course, everyone loves Jim, but it's fun to have someone new around who gets more kids excited."

We chat for a while, and after she leaves, I sit there for a second and let it sink in.

I eat my lunch at my desk, answering emails and jotting notes for tomorrow. I catch myself smiling again, like my face doesn't know how to stop.

I'm teaching. I'm helping kids. I'm building something solid.

For the first time in a long time, my life feels like it's moving forward instead of just holding steady.

And I love it.

Owen wanders in like he does every afternoon after basketball practice, backpack slung low, already mid-conversation with a few of the kids. They're bent over an engine bay, heads together.

"No, see," Owen says, pointing. "If you listen when it turns over, you can hear it hesitate right there."

The older kid looks impressed. "You know a lot."

He shrugs, trying to play it cool. "I've been around my sister a lot. She's the teacher here."

I watch from my desk, smiling and aching all at once.

Owen shows a couple of the kids how to check a belt, confident and careful, not bossy. He belongs here in a way that makes my chest swell, and he's not even in high school yet. And then it hits me how different this is from when I was his age.

I wasn't hanging out after school, having fun. I was working at my dad's shop. Doing the jobs my dad wasn't keeping up with to make sure our bills got paid and learning that my value came from what I could do for someone else. Back then my dad treated me differently. Extended praise and encouragement. But was it genuine? I think he just wanted me to work for him like a slave and take care of Owen. He never seemed to care what I wanted. I blink and wonder would I have chosen this life if I had a chance?

I shake it off and think it doesn't matter now. I want this life I've made. It's a pretty great life, actually.

I don't want what I had for Owen. I want him to be a kid. To chase whatever makes him happy. Basketball, or engines, or something we haven't even imagined yet. Lately, he really seems to enjoy the horses out at the Wilder Ranch, so there's also that. Life is too short not to do what we love.

Ollie wants that for him, too. We've talked about it. Neither of us had a childhood that felt soft. We worked hard and were expected to be grateful for it.

Owen deserves better than Sully. Hell, I deserved better than Sully.

When we leave the school, it's already getting dark. We swing by the general store for groceries. I grab a basket and fill it without doing the math in my head. Chicken, pasta, vegetables, and a brownie mix.

The relief is huge. I can grab groceries without counting out the total beforehand. Having a solid paycheck is everything right now.

Then I see him. Sully stands near the coolers, eyes sharp and cold when they land on us. On Owen. Then they move to me.

I lift my chin and keep my shoulders back, even though my pulse is hammering.

He glares at me for a long, ugly second before his mouth twists into something mean. "Looks like you still owe me money."

Owen turns, brows knitting. "What's your problem?"

"My problem is I want what's mine," Sully snaps, voice sharp and slurred at the edges. "You don't get to just cut me off. Half of that business is mine."

I don't flinch. I don't raise my voice.

"That's not true," I say evenly. "And you know it. You stole all the tools and sold them off. Even some that were mine. And you took half the money for the past ten years. I'd say we're pretty even on the business if you ask me. You also never supported Owen. You owe us, if anything."

He steps closer, too close, and grips the front of my cart hard enough that it jerks to a stop. The metal rattles, loud in the aisle. A couple people glance over.

"You think you can just walk away from me now?" he sneers. "Heard you got yourself a husband. You think that fixes this?"

Owen stiffens beside me.

I feel something settle in my chest. Cold. Solid.

"There's a court order," I say clearly. "You're required to stay away from me and from Owen. You're not supposed to be here talking to us at all."

His eyes flash, wild and unfocused. "That paper doesn't mean anything."

"It does," I say. "And every word you say right now is another violation."

His grip tightens on the cart. His jaw works like he's chewing on rage. "You're going to give me my money," he growls. "You don't get to decide this."

"I already did," I shove the cart forward, breaking his hold, and step past him without waiting to see his face. I don't give him another second of me.

I look down at Owen, keep my voice calm, normal. "Do we need milk?"

He blinks, then nods like he's taking his cue from me. "Probably."

He reaches into the cooler and grabs a gallon like this is any other grocery run.

Behind us, something crashes. I hear cans clatter and a cart slam into a display. Someone curses under their breath. I hear Sully shouting, angry and unhinged, the sound of him storming off echoing down the aisle.

I don't turn around.

I keep walking. One hand steady on the cart. The other brushing Owen's sleeve, grounding both of us.

For the first time, I don't feel like I'm running. I feel like I'm done.

"Hey, let's go pick out your favorite cereal, too," I say as we move through the store.

"What do you think he's going to do?" Owen whispers nervously when we make it to the cereal aisle.

"I don't know, buddy." I shake my head. But I know one thing for sure, I'm not letting him intimidate us anymore. This has to stop.

Back at the apartment, I tie my hair up and get to work. Cooking feels like love when I get to do it like this. I get the brownies and cookies baking, and I make dinner. I pack everything up while Owen sets the table and sneaks chocolate chip cookies when he thinks I'm not looking.

Ollie's on shift, so we load up the truck and head to the station.

Laughter spills out the front door when we walk in. The guys light up like we're expected.

"Well, if it isn't our favorite people," someone calls.

I set the food down, and they swarm it, teasing and groaning and already asking for seconds.

"Man," one of them says to Ollie, not knowing I can hear. "We love her."

I pause, pretending to rearrange containers.

Ollie looks at me and smiles. "Get in line. I love her, too."

My heart flips. I love him. And the way he looks at me tells me he feels it too.

We eat together, crowded around the mismatched tables and chairs, Owen in the middle, laughing too loudly and having a good time with the guys. It feels like a family dinner, the kind I always wanted.

When it's time to go, Ollie walks us out. He pulls me in, arm snug around my shoulders, and kisses me.

"Thanks for this," he says softly.

"Always," I say.

"Yuck," Owen adds immediately, wrinkling his nose up at me kissing him.

The whole place erupts in laughter.

Ollie grins and ruffles Owen's hair. "Night, buddy."

On the drive home, I watch the lights of Bridger Falls roll past and feel something settle deep in my chest.

This life we're building, It's not perfect. But it's ours. Maybe those white picket fences aren't what they're supposed to be.

And for the first time, I have hope. But still, a slight uneasy feeling settles in my chest. I need to make sure my dad leaves us alone. I can't keep living my life under his thumb. He contributes nothing to this business, and he's stripped away any assets he brought to the table, which wasn't much.

I have an idea, but I can't take Owen with me.

I pull into the shop and park at the front, as I usually do. "If you take your shower now, you can play your game until bedtime." I nod toward the direction of the bathroom.

He wastes no time and scrambles up the stairs and does just that. I pull out my phone and call Maggie. She picks up and says, "Hey, there, sugar."

"Hey, Maggie. Are you busy?"

"That entirely depends on the rest of the information you're about to give me."

"Would you sit with Owen for an hour or so? I need to run an errand," I say, hoping she won't ask me too many details.

"Sure, let me get my shoes on, and I'll head on over. See you in a bit."

I close my eyes and lean my head back against my headrest. Either this is the dumbest idea I've ever had, or the best. Time will tell. Either way, Ollie is not going to be happy about this, and neither is my dad.

But sometimes when you fuck around, you find out. And

my dad is about to find out. Or me. Probably both. I might be making a huge mistake, but here goes nothing.

* * *

Twenty minutes out of town. That's how far my dad's biker buddies like to be from town. I pull off the highway and keep driving until the road turns to dirt and bad decisions. Ollie's probably going to be so pissed that I'm doing this.

I park down the road where my truck won't be obvious and sit there for a second with my hands on the wheel. I reach down and grab the tire-iron creation I welded myself. It's heavy and spiked. A thing of beauty, really. I tuck it into the side cargo pocket of my coveralls, where I can reach it fast if I need to. And hopefully I won't need to.

My hair's yanked up in a messy bun with a red bandana knotted across my forehead as a headband. No makeup. Clean face. When I catch my reflection in the rearview mirror, I look younger than I should. Like, I belong in a classroom, not walking toward a biker compound.

I could be walking into my death. But I need help. And calling my dad's bluff feels like the only card I have left to play.

I move through the trees, keeping low, counting cameras, and checking out the fence. There's a chain link fence around the compound, and I find a gap in it. Lazy maintenance. I climb it easily and drop down on the other side.

That's when the dog comes out growling, hunched down, teeth flashing in a snarl.

Black and brown, looks like a pitbull mix. Before I can stop myself, I kneel slowly and whisper in a sweet voice, "Hey, baby. Come here."

The dog freezes, looking confused. Then leans in and sniffs

me once, sneezes, then starts wagging his tail like we're old friends, his whole-body wiggling.

"Of course, I knew it," I mutter sweetly. "You're just a good boy, aren't you? Just look at you. You're perfect."

I scratch behind his ears, and he presses closer, his whole body continuing to wiggle as he kisses my cheek. He drops to the ground and rolls onto his back like he's auditioning for a commercial. Sidetracked, I'm on my knees petting him, and telling him how handsome he is. I can't help it, he *is* a good boy. He didn't eat me after all. That definitely makes him the best boy in all the land.

That's when I hear the unmistakable click of a gun and a gravelly voice that rasps, "Don't fuckin' move."

"I wasn't planning on it," I say, slowly lifting my hands while the dog licks my chin and growls at the gun wielder. "But you might want to lower the gun. You're upsetting your dog."

"Bandit," the biker snaps. "You're a worthless guard dog. Oughta beat your ass."

I turn my body toward the voice. "Hey, don't talk to that baby like that. And if you lay a finger on him, you and I are gonna have big problems."

I crouch fully and rub Bandit's belly. He groans happily and rolls more in the dirt.

"You're just a baby, aren't you?" I coo. "Yes, you are. He didn't mean to talk to you that way. You're a good boy."

The biker stares at me like he doesn't know what dimension he's in.

"Are you gonna shoot me or what?" I huff. "Just don't scare the dog."

"Get up," he growls, yanking me to my feet, shoving me toward a metal door against the brick wall I hadn't noticed before. It bangs open, and the smell hits me like a brick to the face. The smell that filled Murphy's Auto during my childhood, before I took it over, and Sully stopped working there.

Smoke, marijuana, booze, sweat, and oil. I glance around through the haze, and it looks like a bar for all intents and purposes. But then I look more closely and realize it's also a garage, with a truck parked there, the hood propped open.

The dog that scary guy called Bandit stands at my side, wagging his tail and looking at the bikers like I'm a prize he's found. The scary guy is looking at me like he's not sure whether I'm going to live to see tomorrow or not.

The room is full of bikers in leather cuts, their tattoos visible, some on their necks. Beards and flannel. Every single head turns toward me at once. The rock music keeps playing, but the room itself goes dead quiet. I count at least twenty of them. Some are clustered around a table playing cards. A few are behind a make-shift bar.

I raise a hand, smile, and wave. "Hi."

"Jesus," one of them says. "Pint, where'd you find the chick?"

"Climbing our fence and using sorcery on our piece of shit dog," Pint bites out.

I glare at him. "You don't deserve the dog, *Pint*."

"Oh, shit," someone grumbles.

Another guy squints at me like I've just ordered a death wish.

"Where's Grave?" the scary guy whose name I now know as Pint asks the group.

"He ain't back yet," someone says, blowing smoke rings. "This ain't gonna be good for the chick."

My stomach flips. What the heck does that mean?

Okay, maybe this was a huge mistake. I didn't think this through. Ollie's going to kill me. Well, they might kill me first, technically. Then Ollie can kill whatever's left of me. And rightfully so.

Then I think of Owen, without another mother figure. And I think, no way. This isn't happening. I didn't come here to chicken out. I came here to handle business. I also was staring at the open truck engine and noticed one of these dumbasses put the oil filter on upside down.

I yank my arm free from Pint, who had a tight hold on it. "Hands off, motherfucker."

That gets their attention. I decide to run with it and use my best teacher voice on them. Maybe it'll work. Heck, I escaped death with the guard dog. I can handle a few dozen bikers.

"Who's in charge here?" I ask, planting my hands on my hips, looking around. "Well? Is it the Grave man?"

They all stare at me, and no one answers. They all wear the same black leather coats, some more worn than others, some newer looking. The pint next to me looks like it's new. He must be a new addition, a recruit, or whatever. I grew up around bikers, but I don't recognize any of these guys. Not a single one of them. But it's been a long time since my dad was at the shop with his biker friends. Maybe they don't have very long lifespans. Kind of like raccoons in the wild have an averaged two-year lifespan. If domesticated they can live up to seven to ten years. Maybe bikers are like wild racoons.

Pint swears under his breath and grabs me again. "You're done."

"Wait!" I hold up my hands and Pint stops.

I shrug out of his grip and walk ten feet to the truck engine. I reach in, pull out the filter and reset it. "Someone doesn't even know how to put on the freaking oil filter," I mutter as I finish tightening a few of the screws. I turn and they're all still watching me, some of them looking confused, a few shooting glances at each other.

Pint grips my shoulder and shoves me. I'm hauled down a hallway and manhandled into a back room that smells like mold and regret. I hit my head when I land and I rub my head. "Ow."

I regret coming here. The door slams shut behind me, and the lock clicks. Oh, shit. This just got really, real. And I don't like it. It's dark, with concrete walls. No windows. I reach for my phone. No signal in my concrete jungle.

I lean back against the wall and blow out a breath. "Cool. I'm in a concrete coffin. Great."

At least if Maggie doesn't hear from me in like an hour or so, hopefully she'll call someone. If I'm still alive until then. But they'll probably have no way to know where I went. I regret not taking someone with me. I should have brought Cami or Violet with me. Wait, scratch Violet, she's pregnant. And Cami would probably have gotten us shot already. Probably should have brought Maggie. She'd have charmed them all and I definitely wouldn't have been kidnapped. Anywho, I wouldn't want to drag any of them into my mess. Keep them all safe.

I slide down to sit on the floor, hand brushing the tire iron tucked in my side.

If this is how I go out, at least I'll go out swinging.

Chapter 19
Poppy

Dancing In The Sky by Sam Barber

I wake up convinced of three things. One, my head hurts from Pint pushing me in here and my head hitting the wall. Two, I am absolutely being kidnapped. Three, my tire iron is still in my hands, clutched to my chest like a baby. That's my lifeline that will be absolutely used on Pint's kneecap when he comes back, Nancy Kerrigan style. Asshole. I'm getting a goose egg, and he's going to pay for that. And for threatening the innocent dog. Because who does that? A freak that's who.

I have a weapon if I need one. I can take care of myself. Well, I thought I could anyway, but here I am trapped in a concrete room that apparently lulled me to sleep by the buzzing sound of a bug zapper or something.

I blink a few times, and the room swims into focus. Concrete walls. Low light from a single bulb buzzing overhead like it's debating its life choices. *Same, lightbulb. Same.*

And two men are watching me.

One of them is the pint. I recognize him instantly. Same greasy scowl, he looks like he's barely older than some of my students at the school. Same confused expression, as if he didn't order this level of chaos. Yeah, he definitely needs a tire iron to the kneecap. But I don't necessarily want to provoke someone with a gun, either, so there's that.

The other one stops my brain completely.

He's tall, broad, and scary in a quiet way where you can't read what he's thinking. Dark hair pulled back and a dark beard neatly trimmed. Tattoos peek out from under his sleeves, and his eyes are sharp and unreadable. He has massive forearms and a very foreboding presence. Unlike the pint. Douchebag. I narrow my eyes at the pint. I think I'm going to call him the prick from now on.

But the other guy is hot in a terrifying way. I'm a married woman now, but I know a good-looking dude when I see one.

They're both staring at me like I'm an unsolved mystery or potentially about to become my own Dateline episode.

I tighten my grip on the tire iron when I think of the last option.

"Jesus, Pint," the hot, scary one says. "What the fuck?"

Pint huffs. "She's alive."

Something nudges my boot, and I yelp, curling around my tire iron protectively.

"If you're gonna kill me," I say quickly, "can I at least say goodbye to the dog first? I would really like to pet him while you take me out. It feels rude not to let me have a last dying wish."

The older guy snorts before he can stop himself. He turns his head away and shakes it once like I'm a headache. "Get up," he says.

Pint tries to grab me, and I slam the tire iron into his kneecap. "That's for hitting my head on that wall." Then I kick him in the nuts when he falls to his knees. "And that's for threatening Bandit." The hot scary dude watches all this with fascination and then reaches out and hauls me to my feet like I weigh nothing, which I resent deeply. He marches me down the hall while I drag my boots and glare over his shoulder at the pint who is yelling back to me and grunting.

"You know," I say, "this is not how you treat a guest."

He doesn't respond, shoves me into an office and pushes me into a chair in front of a desk.

I look around in surprise. Wow. It smells like leather, smoke, and pine. The hot, scary guy sits down in a chair behind the desk and leans back in his chair like he owns every breath in the room. He slips a toothpick into his mouth and tilts his head, studying me. I'm guessing he's the boss around here.

I cross my legs and tuck my tire iron into my lap, taking in the room. It isn't really how I pictured a biker's office to look.

He looks down at my coveralls. "Murphy's," he says slowly and then looks back up at me curiously.

I swallow. This guy is not the guy I need to provoke with a tire iron. He is the human equivalent of big dick energy, while the prick is needle dick energy. Pint's mean to dogs, and that's all I needed to see to know he's a bad dude. Anyone who means harm to animals is never good. I should have hit him in both kneecaps.

Then, the man before me widens his eyes slightly in recognition. "You're Sully's daughter?"

My jaw tightens, and I look away. "I don't like being associated with him."

That finally gets his full attention. He straightens a little, toothpick shifting. I can see the wheels turning. Measuring. Connecting dots.

"Why?" he asks quietly.

The room goes very still.

Finally, I say, "You want the long version or the short answer?"

He says nothing, the silence stretches, and I decide he's getting the long version. If he's associating with my dad, he should know what kind of shitbag he's dealing with. Maybe he cares, maybe he doesn't. But he should know. I wish I had known and had a chance.

My hands curl tighter around the tire iron, knuckles aching. "Because he's a really bad man," I say quietly. "The kind of man who abandons and steals from his own kids. He's a bully who only picks fights he knows he can win with smaller people he thinks he can manipulate. He stole my tools, my money, and ruined my childhood. He hurt me any chance he could and called it 'teaching me how the real world works'."

My throat burns, but I keep going because once I start, I can't stop. Hot tears prick my eyes, and I don't know why I'm confessing all of this to a scary stranger, but it feels right in this moment, and I feel like I can't stop now. I have to get it all out.

"He drinks, gambles, and steals. He looks at me like I owe him just for existing. Like I'm his property. Like my shop, my work, my life is his, and he can show up whenever he wants and ruin my life over and over again."

I glance down at the tire iron in my hands, then back up.

"He's a scumbag," I say, softer now. "And the saddest part is I spent a long time believing that because I'm his daughter, I was scum, too."

I sniff and shake my head. "So yeah. That's why I don't like being associated with Sully. Because I'm not a scumbag. I pay my bills, do honest work, and take care of my brother. So, by the way, if you plan on killing me, he'll be without a sister, and without a mother, so consider that before you murder me, scary hot guy."

His mouth twitches at the last part and he watches me for

another long moment, then leans back again, eyes never leaving my face. "Well," he says calmly, "this just got interesting."

I swallow and wait for him to talk.

He watches me for a long second after I finish speaking. He doesn't rush it. He leans back in his chair, leather cut shifting, the edge of a black T-shirt showing underneath. The toothpick moves to the other side of his mouth.

"So, what do you want?" he asks.

My throat tightens. This is the part where pride is supposed to stop me. Or fear is supposed to tell me to run or not have come in the first place. It's too late. If I'm going to get my dad to leave us alone, I'm going to have to go to someone bigger than him. Not the law, but someone who can make him stop. The law is slow and won't protect me. I want to be able to take my little brother to the grocery store without worrying about him showing up and trying to intimidate us. We deserve better than that.

"I want you to make him leave us alone," I say. "I came here to beg you to make him stop."

His eyes stay on mine, and I swear I can see his thoughts churning in there.

I keep going. "I don't care if I owe your club. I don't care what it costs. I can save up and pay you back. I just need help. I need you to make him stay away."

The words come out smaller at the end, and I hate that. I hate how asking for help always feels like shrinking.

His eyes flick down to my hands. To the tire iron I'm still gripping like it's a security blanket.

"How old's your brother?" he asks.

"Eleven." I tilt my chin up. "He's a good kid."

That changes something in his expression. Not softer exactly. Sharper. Focused.

"You know what you're asking?" he says. "This isn't a favor you pay back with cookies."

I huff a weak laugh. "Yeah, but I bake really good cookies."

That gets another brief twitch at the corner of his mouth. It's gone just as fast.

"This kind of protection comes with rules," he says. "No lies. No half-truths. If Sully comes around again, you call us first. Not after."

I nod fast. "I can do that."

"And you don't owe my club," he adds. "You owe me."

"I'm married. Honestly, he's probably going to kill me when he finds out I came here."

Another twitch of his mouth. "Who's your husband?"

"Ollie. He's a firefighter in Bridger Falls."

"Kendrick? Know his dad." His eyes narrow.

Nope. Don't like that. Damn it. Why do we both have to have asshole dads?

"Ollie's nothing like his dad. His dad is as useless as mine."

Grave nods in agreement.

I swallow. "You'll make him stop?"

Grave leans forward then, elbows on the desk, eyes locking onto mine. "Something you should know is that Sully Murphy is no longer affiliated with my club."

My pulse pounds in my ears. "So, that's a no?"

He stands, and the room feels smaller immediately.

"You came out here alone," he says. "That tells me two things. You're either reckless or desperate."

"Or brave," I say quietly, tightening my grip on the tire iron.

His eyes darken. "Yeah," he says after a beat. "That too."

I stare at him, wondering what he's going to do.

He turns toward the door. "I'll handle Sully."

Relief hits so hard, I practically drop my tire iron.

"You shouldn't have had to raise yourself or your brother,"

he adds over his shoulder. But, for what it's worth, you're doing a helluva job and you're better off without him."

The door opens and light spills in.

"And no one touches you or your brother," he assures me. "Consider yourself club property now."

For the first time since I got here, I let myself breathe. I don't know what that means and that might sound equally scary, but Sully staying away sounds better. I can handle some cookies.

I stare at him for a second, not sure what to do with the relief pounding through me. My hands shake. My chest feels too full.

Something in me moves anyway. I step forward and wrap my arms around him, before I can overthink it. "Thank you, Mr. Grave."

He stiffens like no one ever hugs him. Then he pulls back gently, steadying me by the shoulders.

"Just Grave," he says. "This motorcycle club is under new management. We took out a lot of the trash. Your dad was trash."

My stomach flips, like something awful is finally over.

"Thank you," I say again, and I mean it with my whole soul.

"Don't thank me. Be ready to pay up someday. You owe me."

I turn and head for the door, and bend down when Bandit trots over. His tail thumps like he's been waiting for me.

"Bye, buddy," I whisper, scratching his ears. "Be good. And feel free to bite the pint."

That makes a few of the guys behind me laugh.

I kiss the top of his head and stand, walking back toward my truck. I can feel Grave watching me as I go. When I glance back, he's shaking his head slowly, like he still can't believe any of this actually happened.

Neither can I. I think I probably just escaped being murdered.

The drive home is a blur. By the time I pull up to the apartment, my hands are still trembling as I park my truck in one of the empty bays.

The truck door flies open before I even shut the truck off.

Ollie's there, pacing like a caged animal. His radio's clipped to his cargo pants, boots still on, hair messed up like he's been running his fingers through it.

"Where have you been, Poppy?" he demands, panic written all over his face.

"I'm sorry," I say quickly. "I went to the biker club."

His face drains of color. "Did they hurt you? What happened. Was it your dad?"

"I'm okay," I rush out, stepping toward him. "I swear, I'm okay."

He grabs my arms, checking me like he doesn't believe his eyes. "Did anyone touch you? Why do you have a tire iron tucked in your pants?"

"No," I say firmly. "Ollie, listen to me, this is a good thing."

He's breathing hard, eyes wild. "What the hell, Poppy?"

"I went there on my own," I say. "I talked to the president. I told him everything about Sully. He's going to help us by keeping Sully away from us."

His jaw clenches. "Why would you go there alone at night?"

"Because I had to. He's not going to leave us alone."

He squeezes his eyes shut as if he might scream. "You could've been killed."

I whisper, "But he's done now. We're under protection, now."

That stops him cold.

He opens his eyes slowly. "Protection?"

"They're done with him," I say. "They'll make sure he leaves us alone."

Ollie stares at me, shock and fear and something else battling across his face. Then he pulls me into his chest so hard my feet almost lift off the floor.

"Don't ever do that again," he says, voice rough. "Don't ever scare me like that."

I bury my face against him. "I didn't know what else to do. I wanted him to leave us alone."

He holds me tighter, one hand cradling the back of my head, like he's grounding both of us.

"You don't have to do everything alone," he says quietly. "Not anymore."

I nod against his shirt, tears finally spilling.

And for the first time, I believe him.

Chapter 20
Ollie

I find Jack out at the ranch just as the sun starts dropping. He's leaning against the fence when I pull up, arms crossed, jaw tight like he already knows this isn't a casual visit.

"You look like hell," he says. "I thought the honeymoon period was supposed to make you glow and shit."

"I thought so, too," I tell him, shutting the truck door harder than I need to. "We need to talk."

That gets his attention. He straightens. "What's going on?"

I scrub a hand over my face. "Poppy went to the biker compound and confronted them about her dad."

It's been a few days now and I still can't get over her doing that. I've been so worried.

Jack blows out a slow breath, eyes dropping to his boots. "Shit."

"I didn't know until after," I say quickly. "She didn't tell me. She went alone."

Jack's head snaps up. "She did what?"

"I know," I say, sharply. "Her dad wasn't there. They told her he's been kicked out of the club with a bunch of others. So, whoever Sully's running with isn't affiliated with them anymore."

He shakes his head once, like he's trying to reset his brain. "I've heard they're overhauling that club. Cleaning house. Got away from drugs and trafficking. Still doesn't make them safe. I don't trust 'em."

"The guy running it goes by Grave," I say. "Real name's Silas Knox. Supposedly, his dad ran the club. His lieutenant is a guy named Jonesy. I've been doing some digging to find out what we're dealing with since she went there, and we're now on their radar."

Jack's expression tightens. "Yeah. I know who Grave is."

"I don't like this." I crack my knuckles, feeling all sorts of emotion. Overwhelm, nervousness, anger that she did that.

"They call him Grave because he's not afraid to take it to the grave," Jack says. "And Poppy confronted him?"

I nod and add dryly. "With a tire iron."

Jack's eyes widen. He actually looks rattled. "Jesus, Ollie."

"I know," I snap. "I'm terrified about the deal she made with them."

Jack frowns. "Hold up. What deal?"

"I don't know," I say, my stomach already sinking as the words leave my mouth. "She said we're under club protection now."

Jack goes still. Then he shakes his head slowly. "That's bad, dude."

My chest tightens. "I know."

"Clubs don't do that without wanting something in return," he says. "There's always a hook."

My stomach drops hard. Worse than it was with Sully making threats. Worse than the CPS meetings.

"Yeah," I say quietly. "This feels worse than worrying about Sully."

Jack thinks for a second, then nods. "We could go talk to them. I know some people who could set it up. Neutral ground."

"I don't know," I say, pacing now. "Maybe. We need to know what we're dealing with first. What if this messes things up with CPS? What if it makes things look worse instead of better?"

Jack nods slowly. "Yeah. You're right. Gotta lay low, man."

I stop pacing and look at him. "I just want my family safe. And I don't like not knowing who thinks they've got a claim on them."

Jack meets my eyes, serious now. "Then we move smart. No panic. No big moves. We watch. We listen. And if we have to step in, we do it the right way."

I nod, even though every instinct in me wants to kick down doors and demand answers.

Jack claps a hand on my shoulder. "We'll handle it. But we do it clean. We're not doing things the way our fathers did."

I take a breath, slow and steady, and nod again.

Because whatever Grave thinks he bought, he didn't buy her.

That's *my* family. *Mine.*

* * *

By the time I get back to town, I'm calmer. We're in a good place now, and I'll be damned if someone is going to try to take that from us. But I'm still so mad at her for doing that. I pull up, park in the back, and head upstairs first, checking in on Owen. I unlock the door, and he's got his headphones on, working on homework at the table, his head bobbing to his music.

He looks up and grins. "Hey, Ollie."

I smile. "Hey, bud. Is she down in the shop?"

"Yeah, her and Cami are down there. It's her night to do the shop thing. She didn't get her work done this week."

Yeah, your sister was off threatening bikers, but I don't tell him that. I just nod.

"All right, get your homework done and we'll figure out dinner when I come back up," I say, heading to the entrance of the shop. I hear voices and listen at the top of the stairs.

Cami sounds mad, and that can't be good. I look down, expecting to see bikers, but it's Randy Garvin, looking like a giant turd, his arms crossed, throwing a fit.

I don't like that guy. I've seen him be rude in The Black Dog. And honestly, my sister's wrath directed at this guy might make me feel a little better after the day I've had.

He stomps in, boots loud on the concrete. "This thing's still making a noise," he says. "I told you last time it wasn't fixed right."

Poppy keeps her voice even. "Garvin, I replaced what was failing. What you're describing now is a different issue."

"Well, it needs to be fixed right now," he says, leaning an elbow on the counter as he owns it. "Seems like you should just fix it for free since I had to come back again."

I step closer, just enough to see her face. She looks irritated.

"I can take another look," she says. "But there are no discounts."

Garvin snorts. "Figures. Guess customer service isn't your strong suit. Your dad would be so disappointed in you."

Poppy shrugs. "Probably. I'm pretty unimpressed with how he turned out, too."

That's when I notice Cami leaning against the tool chest near the bay door, arms crossed, expression flat and unimpressed. She's been watching, clocking everything. She already doesn't like Garvin. He's banned from Steamy Sips, her coffee trailer, for being rude. He's known around town for being entitled and a selfish jerk.

Garvin turns slightly and notices her for the first time. "What's your problem?" he asks. "Oh yeah, you're the one who makes shit coffee."

Cami pushes off the chair and walks up beside Poppy, close but casual. Protective without making a show of it.

"I was just wondering," Cami says, voice calm as hell, "if it ever bothers you that the greatest thing you'll do with your life is to exist as a warning to women."

Garvin blinks. "What?"

"He's so stupid," Cami says to Poppy as she shakes her head.

"What did you call me?" he asks again, trying to intimidate her, and I laugh quietly because my sister is about to eviscerate him. And I can't wait to watch. He has it coming.

Cami tilts her head. "I called you stupid. I'm sorry. I just assumed you already knew."

Poppy sucks in a breath, trying not to laugh. I don't even try to hide my smile.

Garvin's face goes red. "You can't talk to me like that."

Poppy doesn't raise her voice or step back. "You're done here. Get out. You can add this place to the list of places you're already banned from. At some point, you might want to move to another town."

He looks at Poppy as if she expects her to fix this, to smooth it over like she always does. She doesn't. She stands a little straighter instead.

"Don't come back," Poppy says.

I sidle up behind the counter then, just enough to be seen.

Garvin clocks me and hesitates. He mutters something under his breath and turns for the door. The bell jingles when he leaves.

Cami smirks at Poppy. "Anytime you want me on standby, I'm happy to ruin a man's day."

Poppy laughs, soft but real as she shuts the hood to the car she's working on.

I don't even think about it. I cross the shop in three long strides, slide a hand to her waist, and lean in.

"Hey, baby," I murmur before I kiss her.

It's soft and grounding and just for us. The kind of kiss that says I'm here and I've got you without needing to spell it out. I pull back slowly, my forehead brushing hers, and I can feel the last of the tension bleed out of her body.

Cami scoots back on a stool to give us space, grinning like she's proud of herself. "Hey, Ollie. You missed me trying to make Garvin cry."

Poppy snorts, her hands landing on my chest like she needs to make sure I'm real. "It was beautiful," she says. "Truly inspirational."

"I heard some of it," I say, my thumb brushing her hip. "Sounded like you had it handled."

Cami shrugs. "I like to give back to the community."

Poppy laughs then, real and full, and it hits me straight in the chest God, I love that sound. The way she finally looks relaxed in her own space again. But I look closer and think maybe this isn't what she wants. The shop feels more like a means to an end now.

I dip my head closer to her ear. "You okay?"

She nods. "Yeah. I am now."

Good.

I press another quick kiss to her temple and keep my hand

right where it is, solid and obvious. Let anyone watching understand exactly where I stand.

Because if Garvin or anyone else gets confused again, I'm more than happy to clear it up. Including that motorcycle club.

* * *

The Black Dog is loud with good music and laughter tonight. Owen studies the menu like it's an official contract, eyes wide, finger tracing every option.

"Get whatever you want," I tell him.

"Yeah," Poppy adds, smiling. "Whatever you want. Or we could go home and I could make a Crock Pot dinner."

"No." Owen rolls his eyes at her comment. "For real? Even a milkshake?"

"Even a milkshake," I say, laughing at the Crock Pot honorable mention. I love her dinners. But I think Owen got a little sick of them on repeat. I'm making sure we have balance. I make dinners, too, and we go out sometimes.

I look at our table, we're here as our first official dinner out as a family. It's a celebration. I reach over and slide my hand over Poppy's. Her eyes meet mine. She feels it, too.

Owen grins like he just unlocked a cheat code. "Okay, then I want a burger, fries, and a milkshake."

"Dream big," I tell him.

He laughs, waving to Walker across the room. "Can I pick a song?"

Poppy nods, watches him with that soft, stunned look she gets when life is behaving for once. I catch her eye, and she smiles back, like she's filing this moment away, too.

We put our orders in, and Owen takes his time picking out music on the retro jukebox in the corner.

Momma Mary brings over a tray of complimentary appetizers and gives each of us a hug. "Congratulations, newlyweds."

"Thank you, Momma Mary," I tell her, patting her back. "Thank you for the goodies."

Cami and Jack are holding hands, and she leans in and whispers something and kisses him. I love seeing them happy.

Walker taps his glass a few minutes later, the sound cutting through the noise. Violet steps in beside him, fingers laced together, her other hand resting over her stomach.

"So," Walker says, grinning, "we figured it was time to make this official and tell our family."

Violet beams. "We're having a baby."

The place erupts. Chairs scrape back, people cheer, and someone whistles. Cami gasps and launches herself at Walker, laughing and crying at the same time. Jack pulls them both into a hug, looking like he might burst with pride. Cami already knew but that doesn't make this any less exciting. I love this new chapter of life for them.

Maggie hugs Walker, patting him on the back, wiping her eyes. "I'm so happy for you both."

Owen sneaks up to the bar, having Cash, the bar manager, refill his soda, and dancing to the music, happy alongside everyone else.

I glance at Poppy, and she's glowing, eyes bright. Good things. Real things. It feels like the universe finally cut us some slack. Things are going to settle down finally, and we're going to have the good times. We made it through the bullshit, and life is good.

For a minute, everything feels easy. No drama, just us celebrating happy things with our friends. The good life.

Chapter 21
Poppy

Weight Of Your World by Chris Stapleton

After we get back from The Black Dog, Owen's asleep upstairs and the apartment is quiet in that late-night way that makes everything feel closer. I'm downstairs in my office, finishing the last of the paperwork I couldn't leave undone, when I look up. Ollie leans against the doorway, watching me like he's been there a while. He's wearing a T-shirt and gray sweatpants that hang low on his hips.

Merry Christmas to me.

My pulse stutters. "You gonna keep staring," I say lightly, "or are you gonna come say hi?"

His eyes darken as he steps inside, slow and deliberate, and says casually, "You know I've always wanted to fuck you on this desk."

Okay, I really like dirty Ollie. Like, really *like him.*

Who knew that underneath that golden retriever-ness was a dirty man who does dirty things? I'm not complaining at all.

Heat floods me instantly, sharp and delicious. I lean back in my chair, tilting my head. "That's funny," I say. "Because I've always wanted you to fuck me on my desk."

Something flashes across his face. Want, but underneath it, something deeper.

"You really scared me the other night," he says, low and honest. "I feel like I just got everything good with us. We're together, married, and Owen is safe with us. We don't need chaos."

The room shifts. I stand and close the space between us. "I know," I whisper. "I'm sorry. I was trying to eliminate chaos, not make more."

"Don't do it again," he says as he comes closer and pulls me up against him, my chest slamming into his, my nipples immediately pebbling at his proximity. He smells good like pine and sandalwood from his shower.

His hand comes down on my ass, firm and possessive, not playful at all. My golden retriever just turned into a guard dog, and holy fuck it's hot.

"I'm gonna remind you," he murmurs, mouth close to my ear, voice rough and controlled, "that you don't ever do that again."

My knees threaten to give out. God, I love dirty-talking Ollie. Love the way he sounds when he's all promise and restraint.

He leans in closer, his breath warm against my skin. "*I* protect my family," he whispers. "Not bikers. *Me.*"

My hands curl into his shirt. "Okay."

He pulls back just enough to meet my eyes. "Say it, Poppy."

"You protect me," I breathe. "You protect us, Ollie."

That's all it takes.

He kisses me deep and sure, like he's staking a claim he's had for years, and when he lifts me onto the desk, the paperwork scatters, and I don't care. His hands are everywhere I need them, grounding me, reminding me exactly who I belong to and who belongs to me.

He reaches down and pulls my shirt up, revealing a hot pink lace bra that he has gone in seconds. He palms my breasts and leans his head back and groans. "I love these."

He reaches down and slides my jeans and hot pink panties down. I kick off my shoes, pants, and am fully naked in front of him. He groans when he looks down at the panties.

"Knowing you're wearing those bra and panties drives me crazy, Poppy."

"Oh, yeah? What are you going to do about it?" I tease.

He looks down and back up at me. "I'm going to worship this body. This body is mine."

Holy shit. I used to be so self-conscious of my body with Ollie. But he makes me feel so sexy.

He reaches down and runs his fingers through my pussy. "You're so wet and ready for me, baby."

I moan as he kisses me, not giving me a chance to respond as his hand works my clit in fast circles, making me work up faster and faster as I clutch his T-shirt and moan softly into his mouth.

He pauses. "You're going to come on my hand, and then you're going to come on my cock. I'm going to fuck you on your desk, baby. I'm gonna ruin that pussy right here."

"Yes," I pant as he moves his fingers over my clit faster and faster, and my head rolls back. He watches me, and when I come apart, he slides his sweatpants down, revealing his big cock ready for me. I want it so bad.

He holds me in place as he slams into me, and my breath hitches, and I work up fast, him pounding me hard until I'm close. He pulls out, flips me around, and takes me from behind. He goes hard and fast, and it's the best feeling and the best fucking I've ever been given.

"Ollie!" I yell as he is deep inside of me. "More!" I bite my lip as he somehow goes deeper, making me clench up and come, and it feels so good. So good. He goes harder and longer, and moments later I'm coming again.

I moan and clutch the edge of my desk, and he finally pulses into me, coming hard.

"Poppy," he says softly, panting over me.

"Why haven't we been doing this more?" I pant.

I wrap myself around him, heart pounding, body humming, and the world narrows to heat and trust and the way he stays.

And when everything finally fades, I know this isn't just what I want anymore. This is what I need. I needed him.

With him, I'm home. He's my safe place and my everything.

$$* * *$$

The next morning, Ollie is up and at the station before my alarm goes off. I wake up and turn it off, sad that his side of the bed is cold. We no longer have a pillow wall, thank God. It's like a sex marathon over here now, and Ollie's the best.

I pad to the kitchen to start the coffee, only to find it's already made. There's a fresh pot on.

I am still sore from last night, but damn if I don't want him again. And again. I'll never look at my desk the same.

I carry a mug of coffee back to bed and sit for a minute before I have to get ready for school and get Owen up.

My phone gets a new text:

Ollie: Hey, Wife. Good morning.

I smile and text him back.

Me: Morning, Husband. Thanks for the coffee.

Ollie: I wish I didn't have to be on shift today. I didn't want to leave you.

Me: Me, too. I want you so bad.

Ollie: You get me tonight.

Me: Can't wait. Love you, have a good day.

Ollie: Love you, too. Have a good day, baby.

I smile, get ready for school, and wake Owen up, making us quick bagel sandwiches to go. It's going to be a great day.

* * *

Owen and I pull up to the apartment after school. I'm in desperate need of a snack, a shower, and a nap before I figure out what we're scrounging up for dinner when I notice three bikes parked out front. My stomach sinks until I see Grave standing by the front door, his hands in his pockets, dark sunglasses on, watching us, his arms crossed.

Owen freezes. "Is Dad here?"

I shake my head. "Dad can't come around anymore, buddy. And he's not affiliated with these guys anymore. These guys are going to make sure of that."

I hope, I think to myself. Grave said I owed him, and now I wonder if he's coming to collect.

We get out, and I throw my bag over my shoulder. We walk up, and Grave nods at us.

"Hi," I say quietly.

He nods to me, and I notice the other bikers that I don't know. I look at their patches, and their names are Bear and

Axel. I nod to them. Relieved to see the pint isn't with them. I hate that guy.

"Owen, go ahead and get started on your homework. I'll be up in a minute," I tell him quietly.

He looks at me reluctantly and heads up the stairs. Ollie's going to hate that they're here.

"What's up?" I ask them as they follow me into the bay.

"Sully been around?" Grave asks.

I shake my head. "No."

He nods thoughtfully. "Good." He looks around the shop, then back at me. "We have a proposition."

I close my eyes. Here it comes. They want me to do something illegal. "What's that?"

"We need a good mechanic we can trust to work on club vehicles and bikes," he says.

Relief fills me. "That's your favor?" I ask, hesitantly. "But I thought your club was a garage."

He nods. "It was, but we're not equipped, and we want somebody good."

"How do you know I'm good?" I ask with a laugh.

He cocks his head. "You know you're good."

"What's the catch?" I ask, setting my bag down on the tool bench.

"No catch. We drop our stuff off, you tell us how much, and we pay and pick it up when it's done."

I bite my lip. "Okay, I could do that."

He nods. "We have a bike we need to leave here."

I glance around and notice the bike out in front. "Okay."

Grave looks up and nods. One of them opens the bay, and a bike rolls in and parks, making a noise I recognize instantly.

"How do you want me to get ahold of you when it's done?" I ask.

"We'll be around," Grave says as he turns and leaves, shutting the door behind him. I guess we're done.

Okay, that was weird.

The bay door rattles shut as they pull out, engines roaring to life before the sound fades down the road. Two bikes. One truck is following close behind. I watch until they disappear, then turn back to the shop.

The bike they left behind sits quietly and innocently, like it didn't just arrive with a whole lot of baggage. I jot down the part I'll need to order and add it to my list, then wipe my hands on a rag and head upstairs.

Owen's at the table with a bowl of cereal and his math spread out like it personally offended him.

"What did they want?" he asks, spoon hovering midair.

"They dropped off a bike to get fixed," I say, grabbing a bowl and pouring myself cereal—dinner of champions. I sit across from him and eat while I watch him stare at his worksheet.

He chews, thinking hard. "Not all bikers are bad."

I take a bite. "No, probably not. These guys don't like Sully and are going to make sure he leaves us alone."

He nods, satisfied, then squints at the paper. "But some of them definitely look like they'd punch a guy for looking at them wrong."

"That's fair," I say. "That's a solid observation."

He sighs dramatically and pushes his bowl aside. "Can you help me with number seven? I don't get why there are letters in math anyway. That feels like a trap."

I lean over and glance at it. "It's not a trap. It's just algebra."

He groans. "See. That's exactly what a trap would say."

I laugh, nudging his knee with mine. "You'll survive. I promise."

He eyes me over his cereal spoon. "You always say that."

"Because it's always true."

He goes back to his math, muttering under his breath, and I sit there with him, spoon clinking against the bowl, thinking how moments like this feel normal in the best way. He shouldn't be worried about our safety. He should be worried about algebra.

* * *

The shop door rattles open, and I don't even have to look up to know it's Ollie. I feel him the second he steps inside, that shift in the air that always happens when he's near. I wipe my hands on a rag and turn just in time to see his eyes lock on the bike sitting in the bay.

The temperature in the room drops.

"What's that?" he asks, already sounding pissed.

I walk toward him, keeping my voice calm. "They dropped it off this afternoon. Said they needed some work done. Just business."

His jaw tightens as he looks back at the bike, then at me. "Poppy, we live here."

"I know."

"I don't want them coming where we live," he says, stepping closer now. "With Owen here."

"I trust them," I say, softer but firm. "They're bringing me business. They're keeping us safe."

He lets out a sharp breath. "At what price?"

I open my mouth, but he keeps going, voice low and intense. "The guy goes by the name Grave. He literally isn't afraid to put people in the grave, Poppy. And that's who you chose to bring around here and do business with?"

My chest tightens. I hate that I hear fear under the anger. "I didn't *choose* him," I say. "I chose not to let Sully scare us anymore."

We're both quiet for a second, the bike looming between us like a third person in the argument.

Then Owen appears at the top of the stairs, cereal bowl in hand, eyebrows knit together. "Are you guys fighting?"

Ollie and I both freeze.

"No," I say at the same time Ollie clips, "We're talking."

Owen squints. "You sound like you're fighting."

Ollie rubs a hand over his face and exhales. "We're not fighting, buddy. We're just... being loud adults."

Owen nods slowly. "Okay. If you are fighting, can you not break up? I like our family."

I bite back a laugh. Ollie snorts despite himself.

"We're not breaking up," he says. "Families have disagreements."

Owen looks between us, then back at Ollie. "Also, we need to leave soon for my basketball game."

"Yep, let's get ready," Ollie says, finally smiling as he pulls him into a side hug. "You're going to do great. I've seen how much you've been practicing."

The tension eases just enough for me to breathe again. Ollie looks back at me, concern still there, but softer now.

"We'll talk about this later," he says quietly. "Together."

I nod.

Owen calls back to us. "Can we order pizza later?"

Ollie chuckles. "Yeah, kid. We can order pizza."

I sigh with relief. Because he's right. Families have disagreements. I don't want Ollie or Owen to think I'm like Sully bringing bikers around. I'm not here to BBQ with them and sing Kumbaya. I like Sully gone, and I wouldn't mind a little business. I do like working on bikes.

Chapter 22
Ollie

I think I'm In Love With You by Chris Stapleton

It's my day off, which means I'm trying to relax. Life is finally slowing down and I'm here for it. I'm halfway through my first cup of coffee, standing in the kitchen in gym clothes, already running through my mental checklist for the day. Gym first. Text Maggie to see what she needs help with over at The Dogwood. Swing by the store and grab some groceries. Normal stuff. Easy stuff. I like easy. Because after living in chaos for so long, I need easy. We all do.

My phone starts vibrating on the counter.

I ignore it at first, take another sip, and tell myself if it's important, they'll leave a message. The buzzing doesn't stop. I reach for it, thumb hovering, and that's when I see it.

Seven missed calls. Same unknown number.

My chest tightens, sharp and familiar, like my body already knows something my brain hasn't caught up to yet. Then the voicemail notification pops up. Bridger Falls Memorial Hospital. Whatever this is, it isn't routine. It isn't nothing. My hands go cold as I hit play on the voicemail.

"Mr. Kendrick, please call us back as soon as possible at this number."

I hit redial, already pacing back and forth in the kitchen. All those missed calls and a voicemail from the hospital can never mean anything good.

"This is Ollie Kendrick returning a call," I say, trying to keep my voice steady.

The receptionist pauses. "Hold please."

I pace the kitchen, unable to stand still. I know Owen's at school, and Poppy's at the high school. And Cami is out at the ranch with Jack. I'm guessing it has nothing to do with them, or I would have a lot of text messages.

There's a pause. Then, "Ollie?"

I jerk back in confusion. "Mom? Are you okay?"

"You need to come down to the hospital right away," she says. Her voice is clipped, professional in that way that means something's wrong. "Come up to the fourth floor. I'll meet you there and explain everything."

"Is Cami okay?" I blurt. "Is she hurt?"

"Everyone's fine," my mom says quickly in a hushed tone. "Just get down here."

That's not comforting. Not even a little. I don't like this.

I'm in my truck two minutes later, and every red light feels like a personal attack. By the time I pull into the hospital lot, my hands are shaking. I take the elevator and don't even notice where I'm going until I step out onto the fourth floor.

Labor and Delivery. The freaking maternity ward.

I stop short. "What the hell?" I mutter.

My mom stands at the nursing station, scrubs on, hair pulled back, eyes locked on me the second she sees me. She doesn't smile and looks serious, and it's freaking me out.

"Come with me," she says. "I have to show you something."

My pulse roars in my ears as she leads me down the hall and into a room. It smells clean and warm and quiet. Too quiet.

There's a bassinet by the hospital bed with a baby in it. I glance around the room, waiting for someone to explain what the hell is going on. It's just my mom and another nurse, and they're watching me intently.

I freeze in the doorway, backing out into the hall, running into my mom. "Mom," I say slowly. "Whose baby is that?"

She turns to me, expression unreadable. "Apparently yours now. The mother said it was your father's, but she told the hospital to call you. This is your sibling."

The room tilts. I jerk back as if this is a joke that isn't even remotely funny. "That's not funny."

"The mother gave birth and left," my mom continues. "She told the staff to call Ollie Kendrick. They paged me because I was on shift, and they know you're my son. What are you going to do, Ollie?"

I stare at the tiny baby swaddled tightly in a white blanket. Pink little face sleeping peacefully. No bigger than a loaf of bread. So tiny. I'm glued to the floor in the doorway, unable to pass through. Because if I step inside that room, that baby becomes very real.

"Did you know about her?" my mom asks softly. "Did your dad mention anyone?"

"No," I say, my voice hoarse. "Who is she?"

My brain scrambles, searching, and nothing comes to me. I haven't talked to my dad in a very long time.

My mom steps aside. "Do you want to hold her?"

Her. She's a girl. My heart squeezes when I look at her. A rush of emotions overcomes me. Emotions, I can't even place a name on right now.

I move toward the bassinet like I'm underwater. The card clipped to the edge catches my eye.

Baby girl Kendrick.

Holy shit. This is freaking REAL.

I stare at her for probably a full minute, her little pink lips moving. What kind of joke is this? This feels like a sick joke.

She starts to cry, and her eyes open, searching the room. My mom watches, her hand to her mouth, unsure what to do. She doesn't make a move to get her, and I look around for the adult in the room and realize...it's me. She needs someone.

I reach without thinking and lift her carefully, my hands shaking, and the second she's against my chest, something cracks wide open inside me. She's warm and smells like clean skin and something soft and new that I already know I won't forget. The weight of her settles right over my heart, like she found her place. It's a feeling I could never fully describe or forget.

"Hi there," I whisper, because anything louder feels wrong.

The blanket slips and her tiny fingers curl around my thumb, warm and sure, like she knows exactly what she's doing. Like she already decided I'm hers.

"Oh," I breathe. "Oh, hey."

My legs finally give out, and I sit down hard in the chair, my pulse roaring in my ears. I stare at her face, the soft curve of her cheek, the way her lips twitch like she's working through something important. Fear hits first, sharp and immediate. I don't know how to do this. I don't know how you keep something this small safe when the world keeps proving it isn't gentle.

Then awe follows right behind it, just as strong because she's here. And because somehow, impossibly, she's family.

My mom's voice echoes in my head, careful and tight when she said the word baby. The nurse saying my name like she wasn't sure I'd stay. Like she wouldn't blame me if I didn't. The idea that someone looked at this tiny human and decided I was the answer makes my chest ache.

And then Poppy's voice slides in, uninvited and unavoidable. I don't really want a family, Ollie—Owen's enough for me.

The words land heavier now than they did then. At the time, I told myself I understood. I told her it made sense. She's spent her whole life carrying more than her share. Wanting less feels like survival, not selfishness. And we finally come together and reach a place where we can live, not just survive.

But this changes things. This complicates everything.

What does this look like to her? Me walking out of the hospital with a baby she never asked for. A responsibility she never wanted. A future that doesn't match the one she imagined. Panic curls low in my stomach. What if Poppy decides it's too much? What if she sees me with this baby and walks away from everything we've just put together?

The thought of losing her hits hard but the thought of this baby alone in the world without parents makes my stomach turn. I look down at the baby in my arms, and my grip tightens without meaning to. The idea of putting her down makes my chest seize. I didn't ask for this, and I didn't plan for it. But the truth settles in fast and unmovable. Neither did her mother it sounds like. But how she could walk away from her is beyond me.

I'm not walking away from this baby. That doesn't mean I'm walking away from Poppy either, because Poppy has never left when things got hard. Not once. She stayed when my mom made things messy. She stayed when life felt heavy, uncertain, and unfair. She stayed when I needed her and didn't know how to ask.

And I've stayed too. We've always shown up for each other. Even when it was inconvenient. Even when it cost us something. Especially then. We've always been there for each other.

Always you. That echoes in my head, something we've always said to each other. And we mean it.

The baby shifts against my chest, a soft sound barely there, and my body responds before my brain catches up. I think of the memory of Poppy holding Owen when he was smaller, the way she looked exhausted and completely determined all at once. I think of how she didn't plan for that life either, but she took it on anyway because someone needed her.

She understands this kind of choice better than anyone. She'll understand. Will she? Yeah, she has to. She loves me and I love her. And if this baby is part of my family, she'll love it. I hope.

The baby's tiny fingers tighten around my thumb, her grip small but fierce, and something in my chest steadies.

"I've got you," I whisper, my voice breaking just enough to scare me. "I don't know how yet. But I've got you."

"What are you going to do, Ollie?" Mom asks from the doorway and I realize I'd forgotten she was there.

"I'm going to call my wife," I say and I pull my phone out of my pocket.

"Wait," my mom says. "Do you think you should find your father? I heard he's in a lot of trouble with drugs these days."

I glare at her. "Can you leave?"

She scoffs. "I'm only trying to help. The mother might be scared and she left because she didn't..."

"Out," I clip, glaring at her.

She stands there gaping at me.

I call Poppy.

She answers on the first ring. "Hey, what's up?"

"Poppy, I need you," I say, voice breaking. "I'm at the hospital."

There's a pause. "What happened? Are you okay?"

"I'm okay. I need you," I say. "Can you come?"

"Is it Owen? Are either of you hurt?" she asks, frantic, and I can hear movement on the other line.

"No one's hurt," I say softly. "Just please come right now. I'll explain everything when you get here."

"Okay," she says immediately. "I'm on my way."

I look down at the baby again, my sister, and swallow hard.

Everything just changed between us.

And somehow, even terrified, I know exactly who I want beside me when I figure it out. I need my wife and my best friend.

I'm sitting in the chair by the window, the baby tucked against my chest, when my mom finally breaks the silence.

"So," she says. "You're not even going to consider what I have to say?"

My heart is still trying to catch up to the news that just shocked me and I don't understand why she's still here ruining my moment with this baby.

"I don't know why you're still here," I say honestly.

She pulls a chair closer. Too close. "Why can't you let me voice my opinions?"

I look down at the baby and then back at her. "Because you've never helped me. You've never been the mother I needed you to be. And I'd like for you to leave."

The words hit harder than I expected. My chest tightens, and my thoughts start racing, overlapping, piling up too fast. CPS. Poppy. Owen. The shop. Money. The way my life just split open without warning. And Mom's here adding to the chaos. I don't need her. I need Poppy. I've always needed Poppy.

I want my mother away from me. I want to be left alone.

She studies my face, then huffs out a breath. "Fine," she says. "I'm leaving."

The door closes behind her, and the room finally goes quiet, and I look down at the baby in my arms.

She's beautiful in a way that makes my chest ache. I lift the tiny knit hat and find soft, dark hair underneath, already curling a little, already familiar. Her nose is small and perfect, her mouth a delicate bow.

I ease the blanket back just enough to check on her, careful not to break her. Tiny toes flex, pink and wrinkled, her legs tucked in close. A little diaper on her, looking comically large. I wonder how much she weighs. It can't be much. Her arms are small and strong, fists opening and closing like she's testing the world.

She looks healthy and solid. But so tiny.

I check her fingers next, slow and careful. She wraps one around mine like she's got a grip on me already. Like she's saying, please don't drop me.

"Hey," I whisper. "I'm kinda freaking out, just so you know. Our other sister is a lot bigger and scarier than you. But you'll love her, too. She's pretty great."

She makes a soft sound, something between a sigh and a hum, and my chest aches so hard it almost hurts.

I have no idea what I'm doing. I can't see what the future could even look like now, but I know one thing. I can't leave this baby here all alone like Madison did. That's the kind of stuff my parents did. And I will never be like them. But I look at her again, and one thing settles, deep and steady. Whatever happens next, I'm not walking away.

I press a careful kiss to the top of her head and hold her a little closer, waiting for Poppy, waiting for my world to catch up to this moment.

Chapter 23
Poppy

I'm Gonna Love You by Cody Johnson

I'm standing at the whiteboard with Mr. Fisher, walking the kids through the worksheet, when my phone vibrates in my pocket.

I ignore it at first but then get a bad feeling, especially when I pull it out and see it's Ollie calling. He never calls when I'm teaching. He texts, knowing I'll see it on my break, and I'll call him then. My pulse starts to race, and my goosebumps cover my skin. Something is definitely wrong.

"I'm so sorry," I murmur to Mr. Fisher. "I need to take this. I think it's an emergency."

He frowns and nods, concern covering his face. "Sure."

I step into the hallway and answer. "Hey, what's up?"

His breath comes through the line unevenly. "Poppy, I need you. I'm at the hospital."

I don't remember much of the conversation because my head is swimming with fear and possibilities and I always go

247

back to the day Maggie came and got me at the school and told me that my mom died.

We hang up, and I realize I'm breathing heavily.

Nope, I silently tell myself. No one died. He would have said. I can't let my head go there. I pull it together.

I poke my head back into the classroom. "Mr. Fisher, I'm so sorry. There's an emergency. I have to go to the hospital."

His expression shifts instantly. "Go. We've got this."

I grab my coat and purse and head for the parking lot, my hands shaking as I dig out my keys. The drive feels endless. My mind spirals in every direction at once.

Everything feels like a blur after that. Getting a call from your husband that he's at the hospital and needs you is never something you prepare for. Was he hurt at work? No, that can't be right, he's off today. Was he in a wreck? Was it his mom? I am just flooded with worry. What if he's hurt more than he's letting on? What if he was trying to be strong but it's bad. Or what if one of the other firefighters got hurt?

I grip the steering wheel tighter and push the speed limit just enough. By the time the hospital comes into view, my heart is in my throat. Whatever it is, I know one thing for sure. He didn't sound like my Ollie, who is cool, calm, and collected. He sounded shocked, upset, and like he needed me.

I pull into the hospital parking lot way too fast and slam the car into park with my heart already racing. My phone buzzes before I can even grab my bag.

Ollie: Come up to the fourth floor.

That's it—no other explanation.

I jog inside, shoes squeaking against the polished floor, and hit the elevator button harder than necessary. My thoughts are already spiraling as the doors slide shut when I look at the sign and realize the fourth floor is Labor and Delivery.

Confusion slams into me hard. Oh my God, did something

happen to Violet? She just found out she's pregnant. I replay every recent conversation in my head, searching for something I missed. I don't know anyone else who's pregnant. Not one person, and I don't think Ollie does either. At least no one he's mentioned.

The elevator dings and the doors open. The hallway is quiet and bright and calm in a way that makes my skin prickle. Nurses move with purpose. Somewhere a baby cries softly, and my chest tightens at the sound. It's sweet.

I take a few steps forward, focused on the nurses at the nurses' station, and nearly collide with Theresa Kendrick.

What is going on? I thought she worked in the emergency room.

She stops short, takes one look at me, and sighs, looking irritated and rolling her eyes. "Of course *you* came."

I don't even slow down. I don't have the energy to argue with and I don't have the patience. I want to get to Ollie.

"Where is he?" I ask, already scanning the hallway behind her.

"He's in room 393 down the hall," she says. "Poppy, you should probably—"

I'm already moving past her, ignoring her. I'm used to Theresa Kendrick dismissing me. She has for years. All I know is that Ollie asked me to come, and nothing else matters.

My pulse pounds in my ears as I walk faster, my steps turning into a near run as I get to the room. Whatever this is, whatever happened, I need to go to him. And the longer I walk down this hallway, the more I know one thing for sure. My life is about to change. I don't know how yet. But something feels different. I stop dead in the doorway.

Ollie's sitting in the chair by the window, his arms wrapped around a tiny bundle. A baby. A real one. Pink hat and small against his chest.

My breath leaves me all at once. "Ollie," I whisper, surprised. "Whose baby is this?"

He looks up at me, and his face crumples. "My dad's," he says. "The mom left her here."

The word hits me hard and soft at the same time. My heart swells so fast it almost hurts. Confusion riddles my body. I step into the room on instinct, like my body already knows where it belongs.

"What?" I stare at him, my pulse hammering. "Why?"

"I just found out," he says, voice shaking. "I didn't know. My dad had gotten someone pregnant. Apparently, he's into drugs now and has nothing to do with the mother who left."

My chest tightens when I really look at him. He's wrecked. Like the ground dropped out from under him, and he's still falling. No wonder he called me freaking out.

"Did you call Cami?" I ask.

He shakes his head. "Not yet. I needed you first. To help me figure out what to do."

Neither of us says anything for a while. The room feels too small, too quiet. He looks terrified. He wipes at his eyes and rocks her like he's afraid to stop moving, afraid she'll disappear if he does.

"I'm sorry," he whispers.

That's what breaks me. I don't think. I don't weigh it or talk myself out of it. I step closer and put my hand over his, steadying the rocking, grounding him.

"Why are you sorry?" I say softly. "We'll figure it out."

Relief fills his eyes, and he leans into me.

My eyes flick down to the baby in his arms. She's so pretty. My stomach twists, fear and something else tangling together so tight it steals my breath. This isn't what I wanted or planned. But neither was Owen. And I have had the best life with him and don't regret him one bit.

I look back up at Ollie and force myself to be honest, even though my heart is pounding. But dang she is a cute baby. Seeing him hold this baby is doing something to me that I can't explain or put into words.

I move closer. "Can I hold her?" I ask gently, like I'm afraid the question might break something.

He nods immediately, stands, and carefully passes her to me, hands lingering like he's afraid to let go.

The second she's in my arms, something in me shifts. She's warm and light and real. I settle into the chair and rock her without thinking, my finger brushing over her tiny hand. She curls her fingers around me like she already trusts me.

"Oh," I breathe. "She's naked, Ollie. She needs clothes."

He seems so overwhelmed that he lets out a broken laugh, more like a sob. "Yeah. I know. I didn't even think about that. I don't know what to do, Poppy."

"Okay," I say quietly, because it's the only word that fits yet. "Okay. Tell me what happened. Where's her mom?"

He lets out a frustrated sigh. "She left her here and told them to call me." He drops into the chair across from me, elbows on his knees, face in his hands for a second before he looks up again. "She needs us, Poppy," he says. "And I know I'm just springing this on you. I don't even know what to do. If you want to leave me, I'd understand. I know Cami and Jack will help, too. But I can't risk her being left again. That bothers me so much."

But when he says the last part, he looks at me as if that would destroy him if I left. That thought was never in my mind.

"Don't be silly." I stroke her cheek, soft as air. "You're right. She needs us."

My chest aches as I look at him, really look at him. The fear. The love was already there for this unexpected baby. The way he's trying to hold it together for everyone else, like he always does. Only now he needs to be loved and doesn't know how to let anyone in.

"You have always been there for me and Owen," I say quietly. "You didn't hesitate. You just jumped right in with me. And I needed you. I tried to pretend that I didn't, but I did."

"I know. And I love you both," he says firmly.

I look down at her again and rock her gently. "I'm not leaving you alone with a baby, Ollie. We'll figure it out."

His eyes fill again. "You're not?"

I shake my head. "I have about a million questions. I'm terrified and confused, and my heart is doing something really weird right now." I meet his eyes. "But this is your sibling, Ollie. And we're in this together."

He stares at me like he's afraid to believe it. "You're sure?"

I nod, firm and steady. "I'm sure."

"I love you, Poppy."

"I love you, Ollie, always you."

"Always you," he repeats with a sigh of relief. Because that's how it's always been. No matter how hard life has been for us, we've always had each other. Ollie has been there for me through it all. And now I'm going to be here for him.

The baby squirms and lets out the tiniest sound, and Ollie reaches for her automatically, his hand brushing mine. Our fingers tangle for a second, and neither of us pulls away. My heart is all over the place. I feel scared, overwhelmed, and in awe. But one thing is clear as I hold her close. This is messy and terrifying and nothing like the plan.

And somehow, I'm exactly where we're supposed to be.

Chapter 24
Ollie

A Lot More Free by Max McNown

"What do you want to name her?" Poppy asks softly as we settle into the hospital bed side by side together, careful and awkward, curling around her as we're figuring out this whole new person. We hold her between us, this tiny, warm weight settling into us like she's always belonged.

I look down at the tiny bundle between us and shake my head. "I don't know. What do you think?"

She smiles and coos at her. "Well, we can get to know her and think of a name."

Something in my chest loosens at that thought. *We.* I want to be angry, but mostly I'm just sad for the baby. Her mother left her here at the hospital. I know she was safe here with the nurses, but I can't imagine leaving a helpless baby behind and just walking away. I don't have that in me. Now that I know she exists, I can't fathom it.

A nurse knocks on the door and steps in holding a bottle. "Hey there," she calls gently, "It's about time for her to eat."

I nod.

The nurse smiles. "You're doing great."

I fumble a little, hands shaking as I take the bottle and feed her, watching her mouth work, her tiny fingers curling and uncurling against my skin. My throat tightens so hard it almost hurts.

Poppy watches me, eyes soft, her head resting on my shoulder like she's treasuring this very moment. I'm in awe of this baby. Because what does someone even do in a moment like this? This baby was just born and abandoned by her mom. She needs someone. She needs us.

The door cracks open, and my mom's head appears. "Ollie?"

I stiffen instantly.

She lingers for a second too long, eyes darting to the baby, to Poppy, to me without my shirt on. I meet her gaze and glare at her. I don't want her here.

She must have gotten the message, because she clears her throat. "I'll come back later."

I sigh. "Please don't."

After she leaves, Poppy shifts closer. "What's up with your mom?"

I keep my voice low. "I don't want her in here."

"We can keep visitors out if you want," the nurse offers.

"This is like our first moments with her," I say to both of them. "And I don't want her in here."

Poppy doesn't argue or question it. She nods once and leans her head against my shoulder. "Okay," she says quietly.

And that's why I love Poppy. She doesn't question things. She just gets it.

"I will make note of it and tell her to go ahead and take off," the nurse replies and updates something on the dry-erase board on the wall. "No problem."

I look down at the baby again, her cheek warm against my chest, her breathing slow and steady. My whole world feels as if it has narrowed to this bed. This room. This tiny life between us. Only Owen is missing. He's at school, which feels strange without him here with us.

After I feed her, the nurse shows me how to burp her. I feel ridiculous at first, patting her back like she's made of glass, but then she lets out the tiniest little sound and relaxes against my chest.

"There you go," the nurse says softly. "You've got it."

We change her diaper together after that. Poppy's careful and gentle, talking to her like she already knows her. I clean her up, hands steadier now, and when we're done, she settles in, content.

The nurse leaves us alone again, and the quiet settles back in.

I glance at Poppy, and something tightens in my chest. I know she has questions. A million of them. She's holding herself together, but I can see it in her eyes.

"We have so many questions," I say with a sigh.

She nods, but her smile doesn't quite reach her eyes. She hesitates, then asks the question I knew was coming.

"Who is her mom?"

I take a breath. "Apparently someone my father had a one night stand with."

I watch her face closely, hating that I'm the one putting that look there. She must realize I'm waiting for her to freak out and her face softens.

"I'm not upset, just confused and want to know what happened, and to try to understand it all," she admits.

"I don't know how to get a hold of her. The nurse said she just left."

Poppy shakes her head. "I don't understand how that can happen. How can she just leave this sweet baby?"

I sigh, relieved that Poppy gets it. But of course she does, I don't know why I ever thought she wouldn't.

She bites her lip, emotion flickering across her face. "Are you worried she might not be your dad's? I hate to say it, but it's a valid question, given that she just left like she did."

I scrub a hand down my face. "No. I mean, we'll find out for sure. But I'm going to take care of her and love her until I know. No matter what. She needs someone in her corner. She needs us. I'll be there. And I know when I tell Cami she will be, too."

Poppy nods her head. "We'll all be there." She looks down at the baby, then back at me. "Can I tell you something?"

"Yeah," I say immediately.

"I'm going to be devastated if she's not your sister," she says, the words tumbling out too fast, like she didn't mean to admit them yet. She shakes her head, a breathless little laugh escaping, half disbelief, half panic. "This is ridiculous. I barely know her. I know that." Her fingers twist together in her lap, nerves written all over her. "But I already care," she admits softly. "Like, a lot. And that scares me."

She finally looks at me, eyes bright and conflicted. "I don't know what that means yet, Ollie. I don't know where it goes or what I'm supposed to do with it. I just know the thought of her not being okay feels... unbearable."

She swallows. "I'm not saying I have it figured out. I don't. I just—" She exhales. "I already love her. And I don't know how that happened so fast."

My chest aches in the best and worst way all at once. I nod, voice rough. "I know, me too. I don't understand how, but it's true. She's pretty amazing."

I look at the baby between us, this tiny person who changed everything in an instant, and then back at Poppy. Whatever happens next, I already know one thing. We're in this together.

I lean in and kiss her softly. "I love you."

"I love you, too. Now let me get some pictures of you both," she says, pulling out her phone. "This is a special moment."

* * *

I refuse to leave her now, and we have to wait for the social worker to come in and talk to us this afternoon before we can take her home. I'm freaked out about taking her home, so I know exactly who I can call. Walker. Walker's daughter is seventeen now. But he was a single dad before he met his wife, Violet, and I know he can give me some pointers.

Poppy leaves to check in with Mr. Fisher and get Owen to bring him back to meet the baby. I have no idea what he's going to think.

I pick up the phone and call Walker.

He answers saying, "What's up, Ollie?" I hear noise in the background and realize he must be at The Black Dog.

"Hey, I don't know how else to say this, so I am just gonna say it. I need your help, man."

"Sure, what do you need?" he asks casually, as if this wasn't a monumental, strange ask.

"Can you, by chance, swing by the hospital right now? And don't tell anyone."

"Uhh, yeah. Are you okay?" he asks, sounding worried.

"Everyone is okay. I need your help. I'll owe you big, man."

"No worries. Cash just got here, so I'll head that way. Be right there."

"Fourth floor."

"Got it," he says and disconnects.

About twenty minutes later, Walker walks in the door and stops when he sees me holding the baby, laying on the bed. "Whoa."

"Yeah," I nod. "Apparently, me and Cami have a baby sister."

"Uhhh." His eyes widen. "When did this happen?"

"We just found out today, and I'm freaking out. I don't know what to do. I don't even have clothes for her or a name. I'm..."

"Hey, hey, hey," he says softly, going to the sink and washing his hands. "One thing at a time."

He dries his hands and comes over and takes her from me. Then, he settles into the chair. "Where's Poppy?"

"She went to get Owen."

"So, how did this happen?" he asks, rocking her with the confidence of a dad, staring at her, examining her little fingers.

"A woman had a one-night stand with my dad. He wanted nothing to do with it. Apparently, she gave birth and left her here for me to come pick up," I say quietly, and hearing it out loud doesn't make it any more real. This whole thing feels wild.

Walker whistles softly. "You're in a pickle. How does Poppy feel?"

"Tell me about it. And she's been great, shocked but understanding. But I don't know what to do. I mean, what do I do? If I take her home, I don't know what to do."

He laughs a little. "Well, I hope you're taking her home. She's beautiful, Ollie. And it's all gonna work out. Just relax."

I nod. "Okay, I knew you'd know what to do."

"It's been a long time, but I needed a refresher because we're about to be in the same boat in about six months."

"Hey, your baby and my sister can be friends." I smile at the thought, then try to picture what that'll look like years from now. I can't even see past today.

"Yeah, absolutely," he says, rocking her gently and adjusting her hat.

"Were you scared when you had Makayla?"

"Of course. I was even more scared when her mom left us in a similar boat as you are right now. You lucked out, Ollie. You have a great woman by your side. Not to mention a huge group of friends who will shower you with support."

I smile. "Yeah, I do."

The door creaks open, and Poppy and Owen walk in. Owen looks so confused. "Walker, did you have your baby already? Where's Violet?"

Walker chuckles. "This one's not mine, kiddo."

"Hey, Walker," Poppy says as she comes in and settles in next to me.

"She's already a good baby, I can tell," Walker says softly, his eyes still on the baby.

"Do the parents know you have it?" Owen asks, stepping closer like the baby might disappear if he looks too hard.

"Well, buddy, she's ours," I say.

He squints at me. "What?"

Poppy clears her throat gently. I shift closer to her and squeeze her hand without thinking.

"We're her family," I correct.

Owen's eyebrows shoot up. He looks between us, then back down at the baby, who is sleeping peacefully and utterly unaware that she just flipped our entire lives upside down.

"So," he says carefully, "like... another sister?"

There's hope in his voice. Real, fragile hope. I knew he would be into this. Owen loves being a part of a family. He lights up around Mack, Walker, and Violet.

He leans in, inspecting her tiny fingers and her scrunched little nose like he's evaluating a very important project. "She's kinda cute," he adds. "Really small though. Kinda has an egg head."

Poppy watches him, her expression soft and a little nervous. "Would that be okay?" she asks. "If you had another sister, I mean."

Owen looks up at her like the answer is obvious.

Then he grins. "I mean," he says, shrugging, "we already have a weird family. Why not make it weirder?"

I laugh, the sound surprising me, and something in my chest finally loosens. Poppy laughs too, wiping at her eyes, and Owen steps closer, reaching out one careful finger.

The baby curls her hand around it.

Owen goes very still. "Oh," he whispers. "She likes me."

I glance over at Poppy, and she looks back at me, and for the first time since this all started, the fear quiets just enough to let something else through.

"Of course she does, buddy," I say softly. "You want to hold her?"

He nods and steps closer, careful and serious. Once he's seated, Walker helps settle her into his arms.

She sighs and relaxes like she knows exactly where she is.

I watch them, my chest tight and steady all at once, and realize I'm not scared of what this looks like anymore.

Chapter 25
Poppy

Hold On by Luke Grimes

"Can I tell Violet?" Walker asks, half grinning. "Because if I don't, she's gonna know something's up and assume the worst. She has my location on her phone and will wonder why I'm at the hospital."

Ollie shakes his head quickly. "Let me tell my sister first, or she'll lose her damn mind."

Walker laughs. "Yeah. That's true. Carry on. But just so you know, her and Violet were at the bar when I left, and it's only a matter of time before they realize where I am."

Before anyone can say anything else, there's noise in the hallway. Fast footsteps and voices. Then a sharp knock that barely waits for permission. The door swings open, and Violet barrels in first, Cami right behind her. They stop short and stare at all of us.

"So much for the no visitors sign," the nurse says with a sigh.

"These visitors are welcome," I tell her.

"There you are," Violet says, breathless. Then she sees the baby. "Oh my God, Asher Walker. My ovaries hurt so bad right now seeing that baby, honey. Whose baby is this?"

Walker smirks. "Well, good thing you're already pregnant."

Violet fans herself dramatically. "I might just get pregnant again."

"I don't think that's how that works," Owen mutters.

Cami squints at Ollie. Then the baby. Then back at Ollie again. "Whose baby is this?" she asks, looking confused. "Are you guys okay? What are you doing here?"

Ollie runs a nervous hand down his face. "I was just about to call you."

Cami shrugs. "Mom called me. Told me to come down, and then Violet realized Walker was here. What's going on?"

Not a HIPAA violation at all, I think sarcastically. God, Theresa is the worst.

Ollie sighs. "Well…" He looks as if he's struggling to tell her, and overwhelmed.

Owen answers around a mouthful of snacks he definitely did not have five minutes ago. "It's their baby."

The room goes silent.

"Whose baby?" Cami clarifies, her mouth dropping.

"I said," Owen repeats patiently, "it's *their* baby."

Cami looks at me. Then Ollie. Then the baby. "I'm sorry," she says. "I feel like I skipped a couple of chapters."

Before anyone can explain, the door opens again, and Maggie comes bustling in, purse on her shoulder, slightly out of breath.

"I had to park practically a mile away," she announces. Then she stops and stares. "Where did y'all get a baby?"

Owen looks up from my purse, grabs another snack, and shrugs. "Probably the stork."

That kid is always hungry and apparently funny. But he's taking this better than I could have imagined so there's that.

Maggie stares at him and says playfully, "That probably checks out."

Violet starts laughing, and Walker's shoulders shake. Cami drops into a chair, rubbing her temples.

"Walker leaves the bar for thirty minutes," she mutters, "and y'all acquire a whole human."

Ollie looks down at the baby, then up at all of us, helpless and overwhelmed and smiling despite himself. I slide my hand into his and squeeze.

"Cami, this is our sister," he says softly.

Cami opens her mouth and closes it again, just as shocked as I was. "I'm sorry?"

Ollie says, "Apparently our dad had a baby and then abandoned it. The mother left my name for some reason and Mom called me down here."

Welcome to the weird family, I think. Apparently, we all just got a little weirder, and I wouldn't have it any other way because we're all here for each other. Weird, good or bad. It should be a wedding vow at this point. For better or worse. For weird or whatever.

Ollie gives them the basic version of what happens, and Cami looks like she still doesn't believe it. "Are you messing with me right now?"

He shakes his head.

"Holy shit, you're serious?" she asks, her eyes bugging. "We have a sister?"

Owen leans back in the hospital bed and messes with the buttons.

"Can I hold her?" she asks.

"Of course," Ollie murmurs, picks her up, brings her to Cami, before laying her gently in her arms.

"She kind of looks like a potato." Owen grins, looking over at her. "We can call her tator tot."

I snort. "Well, she does need a name, but I'm not sure it'll be tator tot."

Cami reaches out, lays her hand on Ollie, and says, "Hey, are you okay?"

He nods. "Just shocked. Didn't have this on the agenda for the day or my bingo card for this year."

"And how do you feel about all this?" Cami asks, looking at me with a worried expression.

"I'm shocked. But here for Ollie," I say firmly, sliding my arm around him.

Maggie looks emotional and fans herself. She whispers to Violet, "I just can't..."

The knock on the hospital door comes way too soon. Again. I'm expecting Theresa, who has been dying to come in here, but for some reason, Ollie isn't having it. I don't know what she said or did before I got here, but he is not happy with her. Well, unhappier than usual, we'll just put it that way.

I look up from where I'm perched on the edge of the bed, and Ollie looks up from the baby at the same time. Owen's on the couch in the corner, legs dangling, working through his bag of pretzels like it's his job.

The door opens, and in walks the hospital social worker wearing a badge, and a familiar face is right behind her, the CPS worker, Monica.

Owen squints. "Wow," he says, looking at Monica. "Do we get a punch card or something? Like every five visits, we win a prize?"

I press my lips together. Ollie chokes back a laugh.

"Can we have a moment with Mr. and Mrs. Kendrick?" the hospital social worker gently asks the room.

"Can you stay, Cami?" Ollie asks.

"Of course," she murmurs.

Owen shrugs. "Sure. I'll just be over here mentally preparing for my free footlong sandwich for the next visit."

Neither of their faces give anything away, and neither of them laughs.

Walker, Violet, and Maggie all file out to the waiting room, looking back at us and waving.

The hospital social worker explains that they can't discharge us until CPS conducts an interview, given the circumstances and that this is standard protocol in situations like these.

But it all sounds like noise. It makes me swallow and look around, fear creeping in. I hate that CPS is involved, and I don't want them around Owen—or this baby.

It makes me wonder how often things like this happen. How often do mothers abandon their babies and leave a note for the father to come, who had no idea there was even a baby in the first place?

I wish I knew what she was thinking and why she did this. Is she going to come back and take her from us? Are we going to fall unbelievably hard for this brand-new tiny human, only to have to fight for her, too? Because, I'm getting tired of fighting for everything that I have.

Monica stands there the whole time, face unreadable, eyes moving from Ollie to me to the baby and back again like she's trying to solve a highly complex puzzle. *Me, too, Monica. Me, too.*

"I didn't expect to see you again so soon," she finally says. "I haven't even completed my first investigation."

"Yeah," I say with a smile. "It's weird. That seems to be our word of the day."

She nods slowly and looks at me cautiously. "We've received recent additional information that your marriage may not be legitimate."

I blink. "I'm sorry, what?"

Okay, now I'm getting pissed. Who does this lady think she is?

"There's concern that some of these recent choices were made to influence an open CPS case," she continues carefully.

I stare at her for a beat, then laugh. I can't help it. Laughter just pours out of me, and Owen and Ollie look at me like they aren't quite sure what to do.

"Who would fake this?" I say, gesturing vaguely at everything. "Literally, this is our life. It's messy, wild, unplanned, and absolutely not something anyone would choose for appearances. Wouldn't you agree?"

Ollie tightens his arm around the baby. "We're not pretending," he says calmly.

I continue, "Look, we are both good people. We stepped up and we're doing it again. We want to be where we are, as strange as it may look to someone on the outside, so you can put that down in your little notebook, too. Because if anyone tries to come between me or either of these kids, I'll fight them. I'll spend every dollar, I'll go to court, I'll do anything. Do you understand me, Monica?"

Monica looks surprised and still holds her expression blank. "Understood, Poppy. Understood."

"Good. Because I mean it, whoever is feeding you bullcrap information needs to stop. It should be a crime to make false allegations," I add, shaking my head, so angry now.

Ollie doesn't look overwhelmed so much as frustrated by what she's saying.

Monica studies us long and hard.

"And you're happy about this baby?" she asks. "It's my understanding that neither of you knew about her. You didn't mention anything in our previous interviews about a baby."

"I'm happy." Ollie nods. "And we didn't know. Otherwise,

we would have said something. We've been forthcoming on everything. This isn't something we could have predicted."

I don't even hesitate. "I'm happy. It's a surprise, but this is our family. We stick together and support each other through it all. I love my husband, and this baby is our family. The circumstances about how she got here really don't matter. She's here, and she needs us. And our family sticks together."

"We'll have a discussion and be back," the hospital social worker says.

She makes a note and leaves with Monica without another word.

The door shuts, and the room goes quiet.

Ollie and I look at each other and have an entire conversation without speaking. Both of us are scared and worried.

I lean in and whisper, "We'll do whatever it takes."

He nods and squeezes my hand and agrees. "Whatever it takes."

My lips find his, and it's soft and grounding, like sealing our plan with the kiss. We hold the baby together like she's the center of gravity, keeping us from floating apart.

"I already love her so much, Poppy," he says softly, cradling her in his big hands.

"I know, me too," I say, leaning into him.

"No one is taking her from us," Cami agrees. "I'll call Jack. We'll be here. Whatever it takes."

A few minutes later, the door opens again. Monica steps back in and pauses. "The waiting room down the hall is full of people who seem to love and support you. You weren't kidding when you said you had a great village. It's a rather large village. And they're all supporting you more than I've ever seen people pull for someone."

Monica glances back down the hall and then back at us. Her

expression doesn't soften, but something shifts. "I'll be in touch," she says.

When she leaves for good, Owen grins. "Do you think the prize is still on the table?"

I laugh and pull him into a side hug. "If it is, you're definitely winning it."

"Who would have it out for us to call CPS?" Ollie says, shaking his head.

"I thought maybe it was Jeremy Toddy. Or a disgruntled customer." I shrug.

"You think it could be your dad or the motorcycle club?" Ollie asks.

I shake my head. "Motorcycle clubs aren't calling CPS for complaints. They handle their own business. And my dad is in hot water with CPS, so he's not making complaints. He's probably lying low."

"We'll figure it out," Ollie says, kissing the top of my head, and I press closer to him, heart racing but steady.

This is chaotic, but this is us.

And no one is taking any of it away.

Chapter 26
Ollie

You For A Reason by Warren Zeiders

The nurse comes in, smiling, with paperwork, and says the words I didn't realize I'd been holding out on and was scared to hear. "You're cleared to take your baby home."

My chest loosens all at once. "Home," I repeat, like I need to hear it again. She gets to come home with us. Having the social worker and the CPS worker here made it seem as if that might not be possible. And I'll be damned if I'm leaving her here.

"We still haven't figured out a name," I admit. Something so important takes time. Most people have their entire pregnancy to decide, and I had just a few hours. I double checked, and the nurse said Madison didn't give the baby a name.

"You've got time to decide on a name," she says. "For now, she's still Baby Kendrick in the system. Here are instructions on what to do when you have a name."

I look down at our baby, swaddled and sleepy in my arms. Baby Kendrick. Holy hell. This feels so real. I feel like I've been in a fever dream all day.

"Do you have a carseat?" the nurse asks.

I don't have anything, but I don't tell her that because I want to take her home, and I assumed I'd figure out the rest later. I completely forgot the carseat.

"Yes," Violet says from across the room. "We have a brand new one in the box that they can have. I'll order another one. One perk of early nesting is that I have a nursery started and supplies to get you by until you get whatever you want."

Walker's already on his phone. "I'm calling Mack," he says. "She and her friends are at the house and can bring things."

"I'll text her exactly what to bring." Violet is texting, and her fingers are flying across her phone.

Walker ends his call and says, "Violet went a little wild buying baby stuff early. There's a whole nursery sitting there doing nothing. I told them to load up everything and bring it here."

I laugh, the sound shaky but real. "Thank you. I appreciate it. I can replace everything or pay you back."

"I won't hear of it," Violet says proudly and shakes it off. "Consider it your first baby gift. I'm so excited for you guys."

True to her word, Mack shows up not even forty-five minutes later. I head downstairs to help and stop short when I see the back of her truck.

It's packed full of boxes and bags. A bassinet wedged in sideways, still in the box. Diaper boxes stacked like a game of Tetris. Stuffed animals and toys peeking out of bags in the backseat.

"Wow," I say. "It looks like you guys robbed a baby store."

Mack beams. "Violet told us to grab everything that would fit in the truck."

"I think we accidentally grabbed a lamp that wasn't supposed to be in there," one of her friends adds.

"Thank you, guys. I have no words. This is so amazing," I say, gratitude and overwhelm filling me at the same time. I don't know why I thought I couldn't do this. We do have a pretty amazing village.

I grab the carseat box and haul it upstairs to the hospital room, my arms full and my heart pounding. Walker helps me set it up, showing me how everything clicks into place. I nod like I know what I'm doing. I absolutely do not and I'm still scared as hell I'm going to mess this up.

Violet hovers the whole time, bouncing on her toes. "I can't believe this," she says. "I mean, I can, but also I can't. Look at her. She's perfect."

Poppy's standing close to me, hand warm on my back, steady and grounding. I glance at her, and she smiles as she cradles the baby.

"We're really doing this," I say quietly.

She nods. "Yeah, we are."

When everything's finally ready, the nurse wheels us toward the exit. I buckle Baby Kendrick into the car seat with shaking hands, double-checking every strap like my life depends on it. She looks obnoxiously small in the carseat.

Violet claps her hands. "Okay. If you need anything, literally anything, I will buy it. I love baby shopping."

Walker nods. "She's serious."

"I'm so serious," she says. "I've been waiting for someone to have a baby for me to spoil."

I look down at the baby one more time, her tiny chest rising and falling, and something settles deep in me.

We're taking her home. I don't know her name yet. I don't know what tomorrow looks like. But I know that she's ours.

"Alright, let me get the hot dad walk on video," Violet says, holding up her phone as I pick up the carrier to head downstairs to the warm truck.

"What's a hot dad walk?" I say, wrinkling my nose.

"Just carry her down to the car." Violet winks, and Poppy laughs.

"I am not thinking of my brother like a hot dad," Cami grunts.

"I think he's a hot dad." Poppy grins.

I wink at her.

"DILF," she mouths and winks back.

"Gross." Cami pretends to throw up.

Poppy follows as I hook the carrier under my arm, and we walk to the elevator. My mom is at the nurses' station watching, and she narrows her eyes at us. I turn and look straight ahead. She's not ruining our day. She gets no attention.

We get home, and everything is hauled up to our tiny apartment, which is comical. It's a lot of stuff and covers the entire space. Diaper boxes are stacked in the hallway, baby gear all over the living room, and piled up in the corner of our room next to the bassinet Walker has put together. Jack meets us there and helps unpack. "Man, I was in meetings all day, and when I finally check my phone, you have a whole ass kid?"

I shrug. "Apparently. She's pretty darn cute, though."

Jack stares down at her. "Yeah, she sure is."

Poppy and Owen are sitting on the couch, and there's a knock at the door. Maggie opens it and says, "Dinner's here!"

Cash, the manager from The Black Dog, brings in bags and takes out carriers of food end sets it on the kitchen counters.

"Congrats, man," he says, clapping my back. "I gotta get back to the bar, but Walker wanted me to drop off dinner."

I stare at the Army-level spread of food and try not to laugh. It looks like we're feeding a small army, not two exhausted adults, a hungry middle school boy, and a baby the size of a loaf of bread.

"You've already done so much for us," Poppy says. "But thank you."

"Not a problem," Walker tells her, deadly serious. "You've added a whole new human to your household. You need fuel."

Everyone filters out, giving us space, and suddenly it's just us at the table. The baby is asleep in the middle, like she called a board meeting, and we attended like her faithful peasants.

We start eating. Then we... stare at her.

Poppy murmurs, "I don't remember Owen being that small."

I nod. "Yeah, she could fit in a bread basket."

"She hasn't moved," Owen observes, chewing his pasta.

My chest tightens for half a second. "She's breathing."

Poppy leans closer. "Her hands are fists like she's ready to knock someone out."

"Already mad about something," I say. "Probably not having a name yet."

We take a few more bites, still watching her like she might do something wild.

"She looks like a grumpy old man," Owen says and then squints. "She looks like she's judging my chewing."

"I already love her," I say quietly.

Poppy nods. "Same."

Owen shrugs, "I love her, too. But I'm not changing her diapers."

I laugh and glance back at the tiny human who just rewired my entire life. "Also," I add, "I've never wanted a nap more."

"Same," we all groan.

* * *

Weston schedules the DNA test like he's booking a dentist appointment, which is how I end up sitting in a sterile office holding a baby while a nurse swabs her cheek and tells me to relax.

"I am relaxed," I lie to her face. There's been nothing relaxed in me since I got to the hospital and held my sister in my arms for the first time.

Weston was great about filing emergency custody paperwork immediately in case Madison tried to show back up and take her. I don't think she will, but then again, Madison just left her there. I don't know what she's capable of at this point, and we're not taking any chances.

The baby makes a tiny, offended noise, as if she knows something suspicious just happened. I immediately apologize to her because she doesn't deserve this. I try to think about how we'll have to explain this to her someday, and it'll break her heart.

Welcome to the broken parents club. You're an official member, too. You fit right in with all of us.

"I'm sorry," I whisper. "I promise I'll never let anyone bother you again. Except doctors. And your Aunt Cami. She'll definitely bother you."

Poppy squeezes my knee. "You're doing great."

I don't believe her, but I nod anyway.

The doctor tells us the results will come back in a few weeks, maybe sooner, and then waves us out like this is all very routine. Nothing about this is routine. It makes no sense, and our whole world has been turned upside down in the past forty-eight hours.

We take her out to Cami and Jack's and tell everyone to meet us there. By the time we pull into the driveway, it looks like a town event. Cars everywhere. Lights on. People are already inside and baby decorations are everywhere.

Maggie opens the door before we even knock and lets out a shriek. "Oh my God," she says, clutching her chest. "They're here everybody!"

The house explodes into noise. Violet squeals. Walker laughs. Jack claps me on the back hard enough to knock the breath out of me. Owen parks himself next to the carrier like a bouncer.

"Okay," Maggie says, leaning in dangerously close. "What's her name?"

My heart starts pounding. I look at Poppy and lean in, whispering it to her first because that feels right. It only counts if she says yes. We've gone over every name we could think of for the past few days and we landed on the perfect one.

Her face softens instantly. She nods and kisses my cheek. "I love it."

I clear my throat. "Eleanor Grace."

The room goes quiet.

"Eleanor," I say, my voice shaking just a little. "After my grandma Wilder. Grace after Poppy. And her mom."

Poppy squeezes my hand. "We're calling her Ellie."

Violet melts completely. "Ellie Kendrick," she says. "You are going to be ridiculously loved by everyone."

Maggie wipes at her eyes. "I knew this family needed more chaos."

I laugh. "No, we don't. But she's worth it."

Jack grins at me. "You look terrified."

"I am," I say honestly. "But I'm also really happy."

Cami nods. "I'm so happy we get her."

Ellie makes a soft sound, as if she's contributing to the conversation. Owen beams. "She agrees."

Poppy slides her hand into mine without thinking, and I don't pull away. I lace my fingers through hers like it's the most natural thing in the world. Like whatever line we were pretending to stand on before quietly disappeared.

I look around at the people filling the room. The noise. The laughter. The way no one questioned this for even a second.

I'm freaked out, exhausted, and overwhelmed. I'm also so in love it's terrifying.

This is my family.

Chapter 27
Poppy

Life With You by Kelsey Hart

I wake up to an empty, cold bed beside me. My hand slides across the sheets and finds nothing but cool cotton. My heart gives a slight, stupid lurch when I hear the soft crying down the hall.

I sit up and pad into the living room, blinking against the low light of the table lamp. Ollie's standing there in yesterday's clothes, hair a mess, eyes glassy and looking overwhelmed. Ellie's tucked against his chest, wiggling and fussing.

"I can't get her to settle," he whispers frantically. "I fed her, checked her diaper, and walked her around. I think I broke her."

I smile gently and step closer. "You didn't break her."

I take Ellie from him. The second she's in my arms, she quiets, blinking up at me like she's reassessing the situation. Ollie exhales hard, his shoulders sagging with relief. I look at the clock, and it's two am.

"You're on shift tomorrow," I say softly. "Or today. Go back to bed. I got her."

He hesitates. "I don't want to leave you."

I guide him down the hall and toward the bed. "You're not leaving us. You're right here. And I'm off tomorrow. There's no school."

He sits, then immediately tips sideways and rests his head against the pillow like his body finally gave up pretending it could stay upright. I rub my hand along his arm, slow and steady.

"You take care of us," I murmur. "Let us take care of you, Ollie."

His eyes flutter. "Okay," he whispers.

He's asleep in seconds.

I gently tuck a blanket around his shoulders and press a quiet kiss to his hair. Then I carry Ellie into the living room and sink into the couch, pulling a blanket around us.

She studies me seriously, tiny brow furrowed like she's trying to figure me out. I brush my thumb along her cheek, and she relaxes, warm and trusting in my arms.

"I love you, sweet girl," I whisper. "I know you already have a momma out there somewhere. But I hope it's okay that I love you, too."

I kiss the top of her head, breathing her in, and rock us both as the house settles into quiet.

This baby is the best and most confusing thing to happen to us, and yet, I love her so much.

* * *

The next morning, I've got Ollie's truck pulled into the bay, and my coffee is balanced closely on the workbench like a lifeline. He took my truck to work so I could finally fix his with the part that just arrived. Owen's in the office with Ellie playing a game on my computer while he keeps an eye on her for me. She's got her days and nights mixed up, it seems. She's sleeping most of the day and up at night. So, that's fun. If I play my cards right, it should just take me under an hour to fix, and we can all go upstairs and take a nap. Unfortunately for Ollie, he's working, but if he has a slow day, maybe he can catch a nap. It's a day off from school for training that I didn't have to attend, so I'm glad to be home and catch up.

Ellie's asleep in her carrier in the office, tiny chest rising and falling, completely unaware she's already spending quality time in a mechanic's shop just like Owen did as a baby. I keep the door cracked, wiping my hands on a rag between steps, checking on her more than necessary. Owen gives me a thumbs up when he sees me and rolls his eyes the next few times I peek in.

I'm halfway under the hood when the bell over the front door rings. I have the closed sign up so I can focus on this, but this person must not have seen it.

I straighten and wipe my hands on a rag before turning around.

A woman stands just inside the doorway.

She's about my age, maybe a little younger. Slim, but not in a polished way. More like she's been running on fumes for a while. Her dark hair is pulled into a low, messy knot that looks like it's been redone too many times. She's wearing an oversized hoodie and leggings, the fabric stretched thin at the elbows, like comfort won out over everything else this morning. Her arms are wrapped tight around herself, shoulders hunched, eyes darting around the shop like she might bolt at any second.

Then her gaze lands on the truck in the bay.

And sticks.

"I'm looking for Ollie Kendrick," she says quietly.

My stomach drops hard enough that I have to brace myself against the workbench.

Of course you are.

A flash of heat goes through me before I can stop it. Something sharp and protective that makes my spine straighten. This is my space. My shop. Ollie's truck. Ollie's life. And suddenly there's a stranger standing in the middle of it.

I keep my voice steady. "He's not here right now."

Her eyes flick to me, sharp despite the nerves, like she's weighing whether I'm lying. "Isn't that his truck?"

"Yeah," I say. "That's his."

She swallows, glancing around again, fingers tightening in her sleeves. When her eyes meet mine, they're glossy and frantic, like she's been holding it together by sheer will.

I hesitate.

Then I ask, softly, "Are you Madison?"

Her face crumples just a little at the sound of her name. She nods.

Fear flashes across her expression, raw and unguarded, like she's bracing for bad news. "Do you know if she's okay?"

That's the moment something inside me shifts.

I really look at her then. The dark circles under her eyes. The way her hands are trembling just slightly. The exhaustion that clings to her like she hasn't slept properly in days. She's not confident or smug or trying to stake a claim.

She's terrified.

"She's okay," I say gently. "Are you okay?"

Her shoulders sag, the question hitting harder than anything else so far. Like no one's thought to ask her that.

"She is?" she whispers.

"She's beautiful," I say. "She's sleeping right now."

Tears spill instantly, fast and uncontained. She presses a hand to her mouth, breath hitching. "Can I... can I see her?"

I hesitate.

Not because I don't feel for her. But because this is complicated. Because a dozen thoughts collide at once. How much this changes things. How protective I already feel.

But underneath all of that is something quieter and undeniable. If that were my baby, I'd burn the world down to see her.

"Yeah," I say finally. "You can."

Relief floods her face so fast it almost knocks her sideways. She nods quickly, tears still falling. "Thank you."

This woman isn't a villain. She's a mother who looks wrecked and overwhelmed and desperate to know her baby is okay.

I lead her to the office and gently open the door wider. Owen looks up from my chair and Ellie sleeps on top of the desk in her carrier, peaceful and perfect with a blanket tucked around her. Madison steps closer, hands trembling, tears sliding silently down her cheeks.

"Oh," she whispers. "She really is okay."

I don't say anything, firing off a text to Ollie that she's here. I don't know her, and I don't know what her intentions are with Ellie. Weston said she can't come and take her, but I don't want to risk anything, especially without Ollie here.

> **Me:** Madison is here at the shop. Do you want to come talk to her?

> **Ollie:** On my way. Don't let her leave.

"She's very loved," I say quietly, sliding my phone back in my pocket.

Madison nods, wiping at her face. "I didn't know what else to do. I couldn't keep her."

Owen watches all of this curiously and asks her, "Is that your baby?"

She nods, blinking back tears. "I can't keep her, though."

"It's okay," I say, because honestly, I have no idea what to say. I want Ollie to get here. He'll know what to say.

She looks at me for a while. "Wait, you're Poppy. I've seen you around."

I nod. "Yeah."

Madison exhales, a shaky sound that feels like relief and grief all tangled together. And I know, standing there in the quiet of the shop, that this moment was always coming. And that nothing about this is going to be simple.

I close the office door behind us to keep the heat in and keep my voice gentle. "What happened, Madison?"

She stares at Ellie for a long second, as if looking away will let the courage leave her. "I don't want kids," she says, words tumbling out now. "Not now or ever. I can't be a mom. I was scared. I didn't know what to do."

Her voice breaks, and she presses a hand to her mouth, shoulders shaking. "I didn't know how to do this. I was afraid. Then at the hospital, I freaked out. I had to get out of there."

I nod slowly, letting her talk. But I don't understand. And I'm not sure I ever will. But this woman brought Ellie to us, so for that I am grateful.

"I just needed to know she's okay," she says through tears. "That she's safe. That I didn't ruin her life before it even started."

"She's okay," I say softly. "She's fed and warm and loved. She's going to be just fine. Ollie's a good brother and Cami is a great sister. She's my best friend."

Madison's knees buckle a little, and I step forward without thinking, wrapping my arms around her. She cries into my shoulder, quiet and wrecked and human.

Owen looks at us with concern. He mouths to me, "Is she taking her?" and glances at Ellie, nervously.

I shake my head gently at him.

"You guys must think I'm a monster," she says as she sobs.

"We don't think that," I whisper.

She nods against me, crying harder for a moment, then slowly pulls herself together. I keep my arms around her until her breathing steadies.

"I'm glad you came to check on her," I say. "She's okay. I promise."

Madison wipes her face and looks back at Ellie one more time, love and grief tangled together in her eyes.

"Thank you," she says.

I squeeze her once more. "Sure."

I glance toward the bay door just as the firetruck pulls up out front. A couple of the guys hang back, pretending not to stare, giving space in that quiet, respectful way they do when they know something big is happening.

Ollie comes through the door a second later, eyes already searching. He stops the second he sees Madison kneeling down by the carrier, Owen watching over them as if he's Ellie's personal bodyguard.

She stiffens, and her face crumples when she sees Ollie standing there. "I'm sorry," she says, the words breaking apart as they come out. "I didn't know how what to do. I tried to tell your dad, but he said he wanted nothing to do with her. I knew you were his son, and I just told the hospital to call you."

Ollie takes a deep breath. He looks steady, grounded, like he's holding himself together when I know he's angry that she didn't tell him, and he had to find out as he did.

"We're keeping her," he says firmly.

Madison nods immediately, tears sliding down her cheeks. "Okay." She wipes at her face. "Can I... can I check in from time to time? To know she's okay?"

Ollie doesn't hesitate. "Yeah. But we need to do this the

right way. I need to know how to reach you so we can handle everything legally. I have a friend who can help us, and we'll take care of everything. You just need to sign."

She nods again. "Okay."

Relief fills me that she's not going to fight us on any of this. I can see it in Ollie's eyes, too.

Then she hesitates, voice dropping. "What's her name?"

Ollie smiles, soft and proud. "Ellie."

He glances over at Owen, who's perched on a stool guarding, then at me. He checks us both, as he always does, to make sure we're okay.

I give him a small smile and nod.

Madison hands him her contact information, fingers shaking. He takes it, nods once, and that's it. She takes one last look toward Ellie, then turns and leaves. She looks relieved and exhausted.

Ollie crosses the shop in three long steps and pulls me into his arms. He holds me tight, forehead pressed to mine.

"I'm sorry," he says quietly. "Were you guys freaked out?"

I shrug a little, honest. "Yes and no. I was worried she would change her mind and try to take her."

"Weston says she can't," he says firmly. "But hopefully she signs everything and moves on. No hard feelings. I just don't want Ellie to be confused growing up. I will keep her updated, but she's not going to be in her life."

I nod against his chest, relieved.

He kisses my hair and holds on a second longer, like he's grounding himself again. "She's ours."

Out in the bay, the guys pretend very hard not to notice. Owen hops down from the stool and wanders over, waving at the guys.

"So," he says casually, "is it spaghetti night?"

Ollie smiles and squeezes my hand. "Yeah, buddy. We came to see if you guys wanted to come down and eat with us."

"Yes!" he says, excited.

"Obviously," I say, because this is my life now. Surprise babies, CPS pop-ins, bikers, firefighters, and spaghetti night like it's the most sacred tradition we have.

And I wouldn't have it any other way.

Chapter 28
Ollie

Backseat Driver by Kane Brown

The Bridger Falls middle school gymnasium smells like popcorn and varnish that they use on the floors like they're trying to cover up the smell of stinky middle school boys. Because there's plenty of that smell, too. The bleachers are half full of families yelling and cheering. The energy in here is jittery, chaotic, and fun—the way a middle school basketball game is supposed to be.

I've watched the boys we've been coaching for the past few weeks grow into a team and encourage one another. I've watched them improve, smile, and be happy. And that's something Principal Masters says didn't happen when Coach Toddy was coaching.

Ellie's tucked into the baby carrier on my chest, warm and perfect in her tiny baby way, completely unbothered by the noise. Her little head rests against my chest like she was meant to be there all along. And she has, I just didn't know it.

Poppy's sitting in the bleachers with Cami, Violet, Mack, and Maggie as Owen's team runs onto the court. She's trying to act casual, but she's beaming with pride. She wanted to hold Ellie, but I couldn't let her go, she was sleeping so well. The second Owen spots all of us, his whole face breaks open into the biggest grin I've ever seen. Not a middle school trying-to-play-it-cool grin. A full, unfiltered, *that's my people and they showed up for me* grin.

And I swear, in that moment, standing there with a baby on my chest and the woman I love watching that kid light up because we showed up...

I've never felt more exactly where I'm supposed to be.

Not just a smile. A full-on, heart-bursting grin. He points at us, at Ellie, and pumps his fist before scrambling into position.

My chest tightens.

"That look," Poppy says softly as she comes up beside me. "He's so happy."

I nod, not trusting my voice. "Yeah."

We cheer like maniacs. I clap one-handed, careful not to jostle Ellie, and Poppy yells Owen's name. He plays better because we're all here. Like knowing we're here makes him more confident.

Poppy leans in closer, her mouth brushing my ear. "You know you look ridiculously sexy right now, right?"

I blink. "Oh, yeah?"

She grins, eyes flicking to the baby carrier. "Oh, yeah. Holding a baby and coaching a basketball game. It's unfair how sexy you look right now."

"Good to know," I say with a smirk.

"Yeah, just wait until later." She grins and gives me a look.

I huff a laugh. "What's going to happen later?"

She shrugs. "You'll find out."

I roll my head back and look up at the ceiling, "You can't whisper this to me right in the middle of a game."

"Just keeping you on your toes. I can't help it that you look like a walking, talking sex dream."

I laugh, then say softly, "I thought you didn't want this life."

She looks at me then, softer than I've ever seen her. "Maybe I just want you," she says quietly. "And whatever comes with you. I just want you, Ollie Kendrick."

My heart clenches at her words. Because deep down, hearing it means everything to me.

"Because I love you, Ollie," she continues. "Ridiculously, obsessed, in love with you. I want to be your wife, mother to your baby, and do life with you. Because it's a pretty great life."

The gym noise fades into the background like someone turned the volume down on the world. I tip my forehead to hers without thinking, my hand finding hers automatically.

She's right. It is a pretty great life.

* * *

The house is quiet, and the kids are finally asleep. And if you'd tell me that I'd be saying that very sentence just a few months ago, I wouldn't have believed it. I shut the door softly behind me and peel out of my clothes, dropping them in a trail on the floor like I've been waiting all day to do this, because I have.

"I need my wife," I tell her, low and urgent.

Her smile is slow and sexy. "I need my husband."

She tilts her head toward the baby sleeping in her bassinet next to the bed. "She just had a bottle. If my predictions are right, we've got a two-to-three-hour window."

"I'm going to need every minute of that for you," I say softly, like it's a promise instead of a threat.

I catch her legs and draw her closer, easing her to the edge of the bed with unhurried care. She lets me, trusting, watching me with that open look that always knocks the breath out of me. I settle between her knees, grounding myself there like this is home. Because it is, I could live here. I could live anywhere as long as she's with me.

My smile turns slow and reverent. She squirms under the weight of my attention, already flushed, already undone, and I don't rush it. I never want to rush this part. I want her to feel how seen she is. Needed. I hit the jackpot with Poppy. I'm going to worship this body.

"I need you," I murmur, lowering my mouth to her.

I breathe her in as I move closer, the familiar scent of her wrapping around me, steadying me in a way nothing else ever has. My lips brush her skin, slow and reverent, like I'm reminding myself that this moment is real.

"I've needed you all day."

Her hands slide into my hair, not frantic, not unsure. Certain. Like she knows exactly where I belong. Her fingers tighten just enough to make my breath hitch, grounding me, claiming me back in the quietest way.

"I need you more," she says, her voice soft but unshaking.

I pause, pressing my forehead to hers, eyes closing for a beat. My chest feels too full, like if I open my eyes too soon, I might lose this. Like I need one second to absorb the fact that she's here, that she's choosing me, that we're standing on the other side of everything.

I kiss her again, slower this time. Deeper. Not rushing anywhere. Pouring everything I can't put into words into the way my mouth moves against hers. Gratitude. Want. Relief. Love that's been stretched thin and survived anyway.

She sighs into me, a soft sound that loosens something in my chest, and I pull her closer, hands fitting to her like they always have. Like they always will. I trace her back, her sides, memorizing her again, not because I've forgotten, but because touching her like this feels sacred.

We fall back onto the bed together, not breaking contact, not wanting to. Knees hit the mattress, and she goes with me willingly, pulling me down with her, laughter and breath mingling between kisses. The dark closes in around us, warm and safe and private.

I hover over her for a moment, just looking. The way her eyes shine. The way her chest rises and falls. The way her hands rest on me like I'm home.

"Hey," I whisper, brushing my thumb along her jaw.

She smiles, small and real. "Hey."

That's all it takes.

I kiss her again, unhurried, letting the world fall away until there's only us and the bed and the steady rhythm we find together. The way we fit. The way we always seem to come back to each other when it matters most.

Nothing else exists. Nothing else needs to.

Everything else can wait.

Chapter 29
Poppy

You Look Like You Love Me by Ella Langley

School's out, and Owen and I got home not too long ago. The shop's closed tonight, and it's time to finally just breathe. I just got out of the shower, hair still damp and curling at the ends, skin warm and loose in that way that only happens when you're finally done for the day. I'm in soft pants and a worn T-shirt, curled up on the couch like I don't have anywhere else to be. Because I don't.

Ollie's beside me, stretched out with Ellie tucked against his chest. She's swaddled tight, tiny and warm, her cheek pressed into his shirt like that's exactly where she belongs. His hand rests on her back, steady and absentminded, like he doesn't even have to think about it anymore.

Below us, the shop is alive with music thumping through the floorboards, bass-heavy and loud enough that I can feel it in my chest. I hear Mack's laugh echo up the stairs, loud and easy, followed by Owen's higher voice, excited and proud and talking

293

a mile a minute. They've been downstairs working on an old go-kart in one of the empty bays, taking advantage of us only being open two days a week and working on their own fun projects on the off days. This is what I wanted for him. For us. A place that feels safe and normal.

I stare at the ceiling, brain half-on, drifting. What do we want to make for dinner? Something easy. Pasta, maybe. Or breakfast for dinner. Eggs and toast and whatever's left in the fridge. I should probably ask Owen what he wants. He'll say something ridiculous but then end up eating seconds of whatever we put in front of him anyway. It's just what he does—pretend to complain but he secretly loves anything.

Ellie makes a soft noise, and Ollie adjusts her automatically, murmuring something under his breath that sounds like it's just for her. It makes my chest ache in that quiet, full way I'm starting to recognize.

Footsteps hit the stairs. I look over and wait for either Mack or Owen to open the door to the apartment, asking what's for dinner.

Owen appears in the doorway, and the look on his face pulls me upright instantly. His brows are drawn together, mouth set, eyes darting behind him like he already wishes he wasn't the one delivering the news.

"Poppy," he says, out of breath. "Bikers are here."

My stomach drops. "Is it Sully?" I ask, sliding on my shoes.

"I didn't see him." He shakes his head. "One of them is asking for you."

Ollie stands, going tense beside me, every muscle locking into place. His arm tightens around Ellie without even realizing it. The calm is gone. And I know whatever dinner plan I was thinking about doesn't matter anymore.

"Wait for us," Ollie tells Owen, calm and firm. "Stick with Mack. Don't leave her side."

Owen hesitates, looking at me. "They don't look mad or anything."

"I'll see what they want," I say. "It's okay."

Owen nods and disappears down the stairs.

Ollie adjusts Ellie higher on his chest. She lets out a tiny sigh, completely unbothered by the tension wrapping tight around the room.

"I'd tell you to stay up here, but I know you won't," he says to me.

"No," I say immediately. "I'm dealing with them."

He looks at me, and I know he wants to argue. Instead, he exhales through his nose and shakes his head, looking pissed. "Fine," he says. "But you stay right next to me."

We head down the stairs together.

The music cuts off the second we step into the bay.

Mack's standing by the go-kart, hands on her hips, posture casual but eyes sharp. Owen's beside her, arms crossed, trying to look menacing and not succeeding.

The front bay door is open, and it shouldn't be. They were supposed to be tinkering with the closed sign on the door.

Three bikes are parked just outside next to a truck with tinted windows. Three of the men are leaning against their bikes. One has his helmet tucked under his arm. The other's arms are crossed, expression unreadable. The third is standing a little apart, hands loose at his sides, eyes scanning the shop.

I don't miss the way Ollie shifts Ellie.

"What do you want?" Ollie asks. His voice is calm, but there's something sharp underneath it, something that makes the hair on my arms stand up.

I give him a look that says chill, but he ignores me.

Grave flicks his gaze curiously to the baby for half a second before returning to Ollie.

"Easy," Grave says. "We're not here for trouble. We brought you something."

"I fixed the bike you dropped off. Someone already came to get it," I say, stepping forward despite Ollie's hand tightening behind me.

Grave's eyes slide to me. "I have two things for you."

Mack moves closer to Owen without making it obvious. Owen leans into her instinctively, like he knows exactly where he's safest.

"We don't need anything from you," Ollie clips.

Grave nods. "It's not from me."

"Who is it from?" I say.

Grave's mouth twitches. "Sully."

The word hits like a punch. Ollie's body goes rigid. His arm flexes around Ellie protectively.

"We don't want anything from him, either." I shake my head.

Grave's gaze hardens just a little. "That's too bad, because you're getting it anyway until we say otherwise."

"Anything Sully gives comes with expectations or strings attached," I say. "And we don't want him around. You promised."

Grave nods again. "I keep my promises. He won't be coming around anymore."

"Then what is it?" Ollie asks, voice easy but eyes cold.

Graves holds his gaze for a long moment. Then he nods to a guy in the truck who gets out. I watch as the dog from the biker compound jumps down from the car after him and looks around, then runs to me, his tail wagging.

Without thinking, I lean down and pet him. "Hi, Bandit. How are you doing, good buddy?"

Owen gasps. "A dog! Cool!" The dog turns and runs to him next, hunched, tail wagging, excitedly.

Ollie looks at me, confused. "Whose dog is this?"

"Bandit belongs with a family," Grave says. "He's yours now. Figure he'd make a good shop dog."

Ummm, okay? I mean, life just handed me a baby and a husband, what's a dog, too?

Bandit doesn't look bothered at all, and his tongue is out, tail wagging as he circles Owen, excitedly. And judging by Owen's reaction, it's a good match.

Grave hands me a thick envelope, then walks back over and swings a leg over his bike. The others follow without a word.

Engines roar to life and take off, the truck following them. When they pull away, the silence they leave behind feels heavier than the noise of their bikes did.

I exhale shakily. "Did we just get a dog?"

Ollie doesn't move. He stands there, just as confused as me, Ellie tucked tight against him, eyes locked on the open door long after the bikes disappear.

Ollie finally look down and Ellie blinks up at him, completely content, one tiny fist gripping his shirt. He presses a kiss to the top of her head.

"How do you know this dog?" he murmurs. "And why did they leave him here?"

"I think he was supposed to be the guard dog at their club, but he wasn't doing his job very well." I shrug. "He's a good boy."

I step into Ollie, sliding my hands around his waist, pressing my face into his chest. "I don't know, but Owen looks pretty happy."

Owen is laughing with Mack and playing with Bandit, who didn't look the least bit bothered that his owners left him in a strange place.

I shut the doors and make sure the front door to the shop is locked. "Don't open the bay doors," I tell them, and they nod, playing with the dog.

"Let's get him a water bowl," I hear Owen say. "Oh, they left his food and bowls."

We shut ourselves into the office, the door clicking closed behind us. The hum of the shop fades, replaced by the small, contained quiet of paperwork and old coffee and motor oil that never quite leaves the walls.

Ollie dumps the envelope onto the desk.

Bills of various amounts fall out. Mostly twenties. Holy crap.

I stare at it for a second before I start counting, fingers steady even though my chest feels tight. One hundred. Two. Five. I stack them into neat piles, the way I always do, like order makes things easier to swallow.

"There's a couple grand here," I say finally.

The words feel strange in my mouth. Unreal.

Ollie lets out a low whistle. "Damn."

I stare at the cash for a second longer than necessary. Not counting it. Just looking at it. My stomach twists, old instincts kicking in fast and hard.

"They must be shaking down Sully," I say. "I wonder if he likes how it feels."

His mouth pulls into a hard line. "He owes you. For everything he took. And for never supporting Owen."

I shrug, forcing casual even though my chest feels tight. "I'm probably never going to see the rest."

That part still hurts. Not the money itself, but what it represents. Years of scraping by. Of skipping meals without thinking twice so Owen could eat. Of pretending hunger was normal. Of telling myself I didn't need much anyway.

I look down at the bills again, really seeing them this time.

Because my life doesn't look like that anymore. I've got

steady work now. A paycheck I can count on. Full benefits. A job where people respect me. I'm helping Owen in ways I never could before, and there's money coming in from the bikers too. Money they're insisting I take. Money that doesn't feel like it's going to vanish the second I breathe wrong.

Ollie's voice pulls me back. "Maybe," he says. "But save this. Just in case. We can start a savings account for Owen if you want."

Something warm and overwhelming swells in my chest.

An account. Savings. A future that isn't built on panic and crossed fingers.

I nod slowly, the amazement settling in deep. "Yeah," I say softly. "I'd like that."

I gather the cash and tuck it away carefully, like it's fragile.

Not because I'm afraid to lose it.

But because it feels like proof that my life is changing.

And for the first time, I don't feel guilty for letting myself believe it.

I nod and slide the money back into the envelope, and the office door creaks open.

Owen peers in, eyes immediately locking on the desk. "Cool," he says, grinning. "We're rich. Can we go out to eat?"

I laugh, sharply and tired, and shake my head. "Nope. I'm not going anywhere tonight. I've had enough people interacting."

I lean into Ollie, resting my head against his shoulder. He tips his head slightly, resting his cheek against my hair like it's instinct.

I stand and flip off the lights in the bay. "I'm going to start dinner. Don't talk to strangers or let them in."

"Got it," Mack says.

"Can we at least keep the dog?" Owen asks.

He's already kneeling, Bandit losing his mind, kissing his

face, spinning in tight circles like he's won the lottery. Owen's laughter fills the shop, bright and free.

I look at Ollie.

Something in him softens. I can see it happen in real time.

"Yeah, bud," he says quietly. "You can keep the dog."

"Yes," Owen squeals.

Mack laughs and drops down to pet Bandit, who accepts the attention like this is exactly where he's always belonged.

Later that night, the shop is dark and quiet. Ollie's doing one last check of the doors. Ellie's already down, snuggled into her bassinet, arms tucked in tight, breathing slow and even.

I poke my head into Owen's room and nearly jump when Bandit's head pops up from the bed. His tail thumps hard against the frame.

"Oh," I whisper. I forgot you were here now. I crouch and scratch behind his ears, his whole body leaning into my hand.

"Take good care of my brother," I murmur, kissing his head.

He licks my hand as if he understands the assignment.

Gifts come in many forms. This one was meant for Owen. They were inseparable all night. Bandit followed him everywhere, even lying outside the bathroom while Owen showered, waiting like it was his job.

When I finally crawl into bed, Ollie pulls me close, his arm solid around my waist.

"Maybe the bikers aren't that bad," I murmur, half asleep. "They bring presents. Like fairy godmothers on motorcycles."

Ollie exhales slowly. "I'm just afraid of what they'll want in return. And how it'll look if they're hanging around with CPS watching."

All valid concerns. I sigh and drift off to sleep in Ollie's arms.

Chapter 30
Ollie

Run Your Mouth by Gavin Adcock

I haven't been to work in five days, and it's the longest stretch I've taken off since I joined the department. I love my job and didn't really take much vacation. But now I love every moment just soaking up time with Ellie and our new little family. Every single guy at the station made a big deal out of me getting Ellie. And the support, encouragement, and love I've received have blown me away.

They covered my shifts without complaint. High fives and back slaps. A couple of jokes about me having a baby now. Someone taped a handwritten sign to my locker that says "CONGRATS" in red marker, and I left it there because I love it.

They dropped off a tiny firefighter onesie that looks like turnout gear and a baby fire helmet that's so small it makes my chest ache. I stare at it for a minute longer than I should. It's the cutest thing I've ever seen.

I tuck it into the bag and grin. Can't wait to show Poppy. This is everything I never knew I wanted at the most inconvenient but most perfect moment in my life. But isn't that how life works? It happens, and you roll with it. Celebrate the good and survive the bad. This time it's feeling pretty good.

Poppy laughs when I pull the little firefighter outfit out later. Ellie's on the bed between us, freshly changed and blinking up at the ceiling like she's trying to figure out how all of this happened. *Me, too, kid. Me too.*

"Oh my God," Poppy says. "That's ridiculously cute. I need a picture of you wearing your gear, holding her in that."

"I know," I say. "She's wearing it."

Ellie's a good baby. It's like she's already decided we're her people and this is just what life looks like now.

We take her to her well-baby appointment together. I hold the diaper bag and Ellie. Poppy handles the paperwork. Ellie sleeps through most of it, only fussing when the doctor checks her reflexes.

"She's perfect," the doctor says. "Good job, Mom and Dad."

Poppy looks at me and softens, and neither of us corrects her. Because we're both loving this even though it's been exhausting and hard.

After the doctor's appointment, we meet Weston at Harvest and Honey for lunch and to catch up. The place smells like espresso and pastries and something sweet baking in the back. Weston stands up the second he sees Ellie, eyes softening in a way I've never seen before.

"Hey," he says quietly, like he doesn't want to spook her.

"Do you want to hold her?" Poppy asks. "She won't break."

Weston grins. "Sure, I don't think I've ever held a baby, but okay."

Weston takes her, and I show him how to hold her neck, and he holds her, softening. "She's perfect," he tells us.

He peers at her. "She's smaller than I expected."

Poppy peers over his shoulder. "She looks like she's thinking about something."

Weston reaches out one finger, and Ellie curls her hand around it instantly.

His breath leaves him in a rush.

"Oh," he says. "Oh wow."

Poppy laughs. "You're done. You're gonna need one of your own."

Weston clears his throat. "I'm fine."

He's not fine. None of us are. Ellie has brought more joy to all of us than we ever could have imagined.

We sit together, pulled together at one of the long tables. Ellie sleeps through most of it, tucked against my chest in the carrier, her weight warm and steady.

Poppy keeps glancing at her like she's afraid she'll disappear.

Weston raises his coffee. "To Ollie and Poppy. That baby and Owen are lucky to have you two as parents."

The conversation drifts, as it always does, to ranch stuff. Music stuff with Walker and Violet, and firehouse gossip. Weston updates us on all the legal things with Owen and Ellie. Ellie starts to fuss and I check her over.

"She's good," Poppy says, stroking her back.

I check anyway, and she's fine.

Weston watches me and smiles. "You're different now."

"Am I?" I ask.

"Yeah," he says. "You're more serious."

I snort. "That's not true."

Weston tilts his head. "You are, though. Like you've got something to be happy about now. Being a family man looks good on you."

I look down at Ellie, at the way her cheek presses into my shirt, her tiny breaths puffing against my skin. Then I look over at Poppy, who is just as present with me, by my side. Taking on an additional motherhood role without even hesitating.

"Yeah," I admit. "It feels pretty good."

Poppy's hand reaches mine, and she squeezes.

Weston shifts in his seat. He watches Poppy for a second, the way she leans in to kiss Ellie's head without thinking.

Then he looks back at me. "You're kinda making me want one," he says.

I choke on my drink.

Poppy loses it. "Oh my gosh, really?"

Weston smirks. "I didn't say now. Just someday."

Ellie stirs and opens her eyes, blinking up at all of us.

By the time we stand to leave, Weston's hovering when I lift Ellie back into the carrier.

"If you need anything," he says. "Anything at all, I've got you."

"I know," I tell him. "Thanks, man."

As we walk out into the bold but bright afternoon sun, Ellie tucked into her car seat, Poppy's hand warm in mine, it hits me all at once.

I'm off work. The world can wait. I've got everything I need right here. My family. Poppy, Owen, and Ellie.

*** * ***

The Black Dog is loud in a good way. It's what we needed tonight. No chaos, just life. Music from the speakers, the sound of pool balls cracking together, laughter, and happy chatter bouncing off the walls. It smells like beer, fried food, and something sweet Momma Mary, the cook, baked earlier that she swears is to test, but always ends up on our table.

Poppy and I haven't been out like this in weeks. We've been

getting to know Ellie, newly married life, and our new home together. Life really said, "Hold my beer," and put us on a roller coaster.

Mack's got Owen and Ellie back at the apartment. Ellie went down easily and will probably sleep for 2-3 hours. Owen's perfectly happy and already sent me a picture of a Minecraft castle he's building while eating pizza, like he's living his best life with Mack. We're only a few blocks away, yet close enough if they need us. We could be there in five minutes. Poppy and I needed this night out together.

I keep checking my phone anyway.

"She's still asleep," Poppy murmurs, leaning into my side. "You've checked four times."

"Five," I correct. But who's counting? Mack's been a great babysitter, and she knows what she's doing, but Ellie's just so new.

Poppy smiles and presses her cheek into my shoulder, warm and solid and exactly where she belongs. It feels good to be here like this. Eating dinner. Having a drink. Doing grown-up things with her tucked into me like it's the most natural thing in the world.

Violet slides a basket of cheese fries onto the table. "Eat," she orders. "You look like you forgot how."

"I know how," I say, snatching a fry, taking a bite. "These are good."

"You forget how to be a human when you live with babies," Maggie says, sipping her drink. "You get so consumed with everything they need, you forget what you need."

Walker's at the pool table with Jack and Cami. Jack lines up a shot and laughs at something Cami says. Jack's talking trash like it's his job. Cami leans against the table, beer in hand, laughing every time Walker misses on purpose.

Violet catches my eye. "You ever need a weekend away, we'll keep Ellie. We've been thinking about going on a baby moon to Coconut Beach."

I don't disagree. I would love a weekend away with Poppy. Just not now with Ellie, so new. "Well, if you want us to look after Mack, just let us know."

She smiles. "We might just take you up on that. Look at us trading babysitting."

Jack looks over and laughs. "You have the babysitter, Violet."

I laugh. "She is a good babysitter. She sends updates every twenty minutes because I think she's tired of me asking."

Poppy chokes on her drink. "I'm guilty of it too, now."

"I don't mean to," I mutter. "I just miss them."

Walker raises his glass. "To Ollie and Poppy. New helicopter parents."

Jack nods solemnly. "It's happening."

Violet smiles at me, genuine and warm. "It's sweet."

That quiets me faster than anything else. "It'll be your turn here, soon."

We eat and drink. Someone puts on a song everyone knows, and Maggie turns it up just enough. Walker and Jack argue over pool rules. Violet beats both of them without trying. Cami steals Jack's fries, and he lets her.

At some point, Poppy shifts and curls closer, her arm sliding around my waist. I kiss the top of her head without thinking.

This is what it's supposed to feel like.

I check my phone again. A picture pops up. Owen grinning, controller in hand, Bandit curled up next to him. Ellie's bassinet in the background still sleeping.

Mack texts: All good here. She's still snoozing.

I exhale with relief.

Poppy tilts her face up. "See. Everything's fine."

"Yeah," I say.

And for once, I actually believe it.

I glance around, and Maggie is laughing with someone at the bar with Violet. Walker is lining up another shot. Jack is leaning in to my sister and grinning like the lovesick idiots they are.

Real family right here.

Poppy squeezes my hand. "You happy?"

I don't hesitate. "Yeah." I really am. "Are you happy, baby?"

She leans her head onto my shoulder. "Very happy. But very tired."

I spot him the second he walks up to the bar, and my stomach tightens. Poppy stiffens beside me, her shoulder brushing mine like she's grounding herself without even thinking about it. I set my beer down slowly and keep my eyes on him. Toddy has lain low since he got charges and trouble. I have kept an eye out for him, but Weston told us that he got fired and has been looking at out-of-town jobs. I pity the town that hires him, but I wouldn't mind seeing him gone.

Violet's behind the bar. She's calm and professional and not in the mood for bullshit. None of us are. The night has been going so well, no one wants him here to ruin it. Because there's no way he's here to do anything but stir up shit.

Toddy plants himself on a barstool and leans forward. "What? Can't even smile?"

Violet doesn't blink, just looks at him like he's a bug she'd like to squish. "What can I get you?"

He chuckles like he thinks that's charming. "Wow. That bad of a day, huh. You can't even be friendly."

Her voice stays cool. "Nope."

He turns his head and locks eyes with Poppy. "Can't even say hello?"

Before I can move, Cami straightens from her stool like she's been activated by divine rage.

"Oh my God," she says brightly. "Forgive us, Captain Shit Muffin. None of us realized we were in the presence of such royalty."

The bar goes quiet in that slow, delicious way. Oh, this is going to be good.

"The balls on you," Cami continues. "She doesn't owe you shit. No woman does. Why do you assume everyone owes you anything? No one owes you shit, and you don't deserve shit."

Toddy scoffs. "Excuse me?"

"You know what person responding to you would be good for you?" Cami says, tilting her head. "A therapist. Book an appointment. Learn how to treat people. Stop abusing children."

Toddy's face turns red. "It's COACH Toddy. And I don't abuse anyone."

Violet finally looks up, eyes sharp. "Coach Toddler, let me tell you a little something about our bar." She sets the glass down with care. "It's ours, which means we can do whatever we want. And we don't serve child abusers or people who enjoy humiliating kids. Or people who push others around. And that's what you do."

"I don't do that," Toddy snaps. "And you don't know what you're talking about."

Cami gasps dramatically and drops her voice into the most exaggerated baby tone I've ever heard. "Look how consistent you are, Coach Tooty," she coos. "Always condescending, always in denial."

Violet doesn't miss a beat. She smiles sweetly, voice dropping to a baby voice, too. "Coach Tooty, you're so passionate. So loud. It must be so exhausting."

I bite my lip. Hard. My chest shakes with laughter.

Walker has both hands over his mouth, shoulders shaking. Jack's bent over the pool table like he might pass out from holding in laughter. I'm not doing much better.

Toddy looks like he's about to explode with rage.

"Stop talking to me like that," he snaps as he looks back and forth between them in shock.

Cami nods seriously. "Aww. He doesn't like it, guys."

Violet tilts her head again. "Funny how that works."

Toddy's fists clench. He looks around like he's waiting for backup. He finds none. Half the bar is watching and holding back laughter, some not holding it back at all. Maggie appeared at the counter with her arms crossed, looking amused. Poppy's tucked into my side, steady and strong.

"This place is a joke," he spits.

"No," Violet says. "You are. Move away. You're not welcome here in Bridger Falls."

That's all it takes. Toddy turns and storms for the door, muttering under his breath, shoulders tight with rage. The door slams behind him hard enough to rattle the windows.

There's a beat of silence. Then I lose it. "Oh my God." I practically wheeze with laughter. "Captain Shit Muffin. I'm stealing that one, Cami."

Jack wipes his eyes, shaking with laughter. "Coach Tooty."

I shake my head, laughing despite myself. "I can't believe none of us went to jail just now. We all hate that guy."

Cami grins and lifts her drink. "No one messes with Owen. He's going to love this story."

Violet clinks her glass with Cami's. "Especially when men are being assholes."

Poppy leans into me, her mouth at my ear. "Thank you for not throwing a punch."

I kiss her temple. "I didn't have to. They handled it."

"Thank you for not welding his truck door shut." I grin.

"Who says I haven't?"

"You haven't had time," I say with a laugh.

She shrugs. "You're right."

I've never been prouder to be surrounded by these people.

Chapter 31
Poppy

Feathered Indians by Tyler Childers

We've been settling into a semi-normal routine. As normal as it can get, when life drops big surprises on you, one right after the other. School just got out, and we just got home and pulled into the bay.

Ollie's standing in the bay, holding Ellie up in the air like Mufasa holding Simba, when I pull into the bay to park, and the way he's smiling so proudly makes me laugh.

Owen's talking a mile a minute beside me, with Bandit perched between us in the cab of the truck, words tumbling over each other, backpack half unzipped, hoodie sleeves pulled over his hands. I park and cut the engine, heart already racing and excited to see Ollie and Ellie. Owen's out of the truck before I can say anything, sprinting towards Ollie and jumping up and down, telling him something exciting. Bandit is next to him, tail wagging wildly, just as excited for whatever is happening in this moment. Those two have basketball practice tonight, and Owen is very excited, to say the least. For a kid who went from living alone with his older sister to having two parental figures and a little sister in a month, I'd say he hit the jackpot. A month ago, everything felt uncertain, and now? Now, it's exciting and full of hope.

Ollie watches him like he's just as excited as Owen is. While Owen is yammering, Ollie is intently listening, focused on him, nodding and grinning. Ellie's comfortable in his arms and sleeping, her little face scrunched, not a care in the world.

And I think...damn. This is my whole world right here in this auto shop bay, where memories here feel like bad ones, not the good ones standing in front of me right now. I mocked that white picket fence life, but life sure has a way of laughing and handing me something that looks an awful lot like it. Two kids and a dog, a home, and Ollie? Yeah, maybe that picket fence life isn't so bad after all because it feels strangely like it fits on us anyway.

Ollie's smiling so big, and he's practically bouncing on his heels, hands shoved into his pockets like he doesn't know what to do with them. His eyes are bright and shiny and fixed on me like I'm the only thing in the room.

"What?" I say, breathless. "What happened?"

Lately, I've been really trying to stop waiting for the other shoe to drop. And right now, I have a feeling something big has happened. And judging by his face, it looks like it's good.

He crosses the space between us in three long steps. "We got the paternity results back. She's biologically my half sibling," he says, voice thick. "She's ours."

My knees go weak with emotion. Hearing this definitely brings us some closure while we move forward and build this life together.

"I didn't doubt it," he keeps going, words tumbling over each other. "I never doubted it. But Weston wanted everything clean with no loose ends. He crossed every t, dotted every i. I swear, he doesn't miss a damn thing."

I laugh and cry at the same time, covering my mouth with one hand. "No, he doesn't. This is great news!"

Ollie lets out a shaky breath and nods. "He called a little bit ago. Confirmed it all. Madison signed everything. She officially gave up her parental rights to us, so we don't need anything else. He's handling my dad."

I feel it then, the shift. The weight lifted off my chest that I didn't even realize I'd been carrying. "She's yours," I whisper.

"She's ours," he repeats, softer now, like he's afraid saying it too loud might break something between us.

His smile wobbles. He scrubs a hand over his face, blinking hard. "I'm relieved that this is confirmed and everything is going to be done."

I wrap my arms around his waist and press my face into his chest. God, he feels good.

"I knew it," I say into his shirt. "Somehow she was meant to be."

He laughs. "Yeah. Me too. I didn't doubt it."

"Well, she's kinda cute, for a baby, I guess. I'm glad we're keeping her," Owen says as he scratches Bandit's ears. "Although she does poop a lot, which is gross, but she can work on that."

We laugh, and I take Ellie from Ollie and kiss her head, holding her to me, breathing her sweet baby scent of baby lotion.

Ollie hugs Owen. "You okay with all this?"

Owen nods immediately. "Yeah. That makes us an even weirder, cooler family."

Ollie looks at both of us and says, "He did update us on Sully. He's been trying to find him to get him to sign some papers, but no luck yet."

"What about the club? Do you think they could find him?" I

ask with a shrug. "They must know where he is if they're getting money from him."

Ollie sighs. "I don't want to ask them for anything. But speaking of, somehow another envelope appeared on your desk today."

Ohhh, interesting. I don't even know how they got in here and I probably don't want to know. I make a mental note to rekey the locks.

"But they did give us this super cool dog." Owen grins as Bandit wags his tail, happily watching all of us.

That they did, and Sully hasn't been around. I'll take those wins.

* * *

A few days later, Ollie refuses to tell us where we're going. He just told us to dress very warmly and bring warm blankets. Which didn't give me a lot to go on, but I did what he asked.

Which automatically means Owen is vibrating with excitement in the backseat, next to Ellie in her car seat, with a million questions.

"Is it snow stuff?" Owen asks for the fourth time, nose practically pressed to the window. "Because I brought my gloves. And my backup gloves. And my extra socks just in case it does involve snow."

Ollie grins over at him, one hand on the wheel. "Probably a good idea. You'll see."

I narrow my eyes at him. "You're being very secretive. Are you sure it's going to be warm enough for Ellie?"

He just smiles wider and shrugs. "I guess you'll see."

When the gates to Wilder Ranch come into view, Owen practically loses his mind when he looks over and sees a sleigh with horses attached to it.

"No way," he says, excitedly. "NO WAY."

Jack and Cami are out front waiting for us, bundled up. Maggie's there too, bundled up and waving. She's wearing a massive puffer coat that looks comically oversized on her small frame. Walker's truck pulls in and parks next to us.

We get out, and the air smells like pine and cold and something clean and quiet that makes my shoulders drop the second I step out of the truck. It's been snowing for a few days straight, and the snow is beautiful and perfect for a sleigh ride, which sounds amazing.

"Ollie, this is so amazing!" I say as I wave to Violet and Mack.

We get out, and Ollie comes to my side, kissing me softly. "I knew you'd love it."

"It's stunning," I say, breathless, looking at the massive white sleigh that's decorated in pine and lights.

Walker, Violet, and Mack get out of the truck, and they're in awe, too. "Where did you get a sleigh, Jack?" Mack asks as she finds Owen, and they both are practically jumping with excitement.

Jack smiles and says, "Tucker found it at an auction and brought it home. He restored it for the past few months, and it's finally ready for its maiden voyage."

We laugh and bundle up in layers until Ellie looks even more like a marshmallow, snug in her carrier, with only her pink cheeks peeking out.

Jack hands Owen a pair of snowshoes like he's presenting a crown. "These are also for you to try out later with your dad and me...I mean Ollie," he says and shakes his head like he made a Freudian slip.

"Sorry," he says.

Owen laughs and shrugs. "Well, he's kinda like my dad."

Ollie and my eyes lock, and he grins as he squeezes Owen's shoulder. "I definitely am, bud."

Owen looks down and back up at us, bashful. I put my arm around him and pull him in for a squeeze.

"You ready?" Jack asks. "We'll do some snowshoeing and take turns with the sleigh."

Owen nods so hard his hat slips down over his eyes. "Yes!"

"Wait for me!" Mack calls as she scrambles to grab her snow shoes from the truck.

"This is so magical! Also, I bought you something," Violet says as she motions for me to come to the backseat of their truck. "I got Maggie and Cami one, too."

I walk over, pulling Ellie in tighter. She's bundled up and sleeping soundly. "It is magical! Did you know about all this?"

She shrugs with a grin. "Kinda. That's how I knew to buy you this!"

She pulls out a white coat and squeals. "It's like mine, and it's heated!"

I laugh, and she helps me put it on over the baby carrier. "How is it so big and perfect?"

She laughs. "I got them big to go over our belly and babies!"

If you'd have told me that a few months ago, Violet and I would be standing here talking about holding babies, I wouldn't have believed you. But here we are, and I realize I love it. It's kind of crazy that I thought I didn't want something I now can't imagine not having.

"Thank you," I say, hugging her. "Ellie thanks you, too."

We spend the next hour laughing ourselves breathless sledding and snowshoeing through the trees. Owen wiping out and popping right back up like it's the funniest thing that's ever happened to him. Sledding down a gentle hill while Jack pretends not to be competitive and Ollie absolutely is. Both of them crash and laugh.

Ellie's bundled up and tucked against my chest, blinking up at the sky like she's trying to memorize it. She's probably going to sleep so well with all of this fresh air, we all are.

Eventually, Maggie clucks her tongue and reaches for her. "All right. That's enough winter wonder for you, my girl. I'm taking her inside the lodge to watch you guys from the window while I drink my hot cocoa."

I gently hand her over, and Maggie beams as if she just won a prize.

"I'll keep her warm," Maggie says. "You all go play."

She heads inside like a woman delighted to be on grandma duty. I smile as she closes the door. I wonder what life would be like sometimes if my mom were here. Where would she be? Would she still be married to my dad? I hope not. She deserved so much better than Sully. We all did.

Ollie joins me, arm around me as we watch Mack, Owen, and Cami sled down the hill, laughing.

Tucker appears, grinning as if he's just walked into Disneyland. "Hey, everyone."

"Hey! I love your sleigh!" I call.

He waves. "Isn't it great? I found it at an auction last year, and it took me a long time to get her restored and ready to go again."

Jack calls out to us. "All right, it's you two lovebirds' turn on the sleigh."

Ollie takes my hand and helps me into the sleigh like a gentleman and tucks the blanket in around us, his arm sliding around me.

"Are you warm enough?" he asks, his eyes searching over me.

"Yeah, I am after Violet bought me this heated coat," I say with a laugh.

He leans in and kisses me softly. "Good."

"Are you warm enough?" I ask, pulling the blankets over him and fussing over him a bit.

"I am now that you're here, snuggled in next to me."

Tucker drives the sleigh, and we settle in, the world feeling hushed as we head off on a sleigh ride. Just snow and trees and the sound of hooves.

Ollie pulls me closer. "I wanted a chance to talk to you."

"Okay," I say softly, unsure of where he's going with this.

He squeezes my hand through my gloves. "I want to make sure you're okay with all of this. I know it's all happened so fast. I want to see where your head's at."

"It's been a lot all at once," I admit.

And that feels like the understatement of the year.

Nothing is the same. Not my job. Not us. Not Owen. Not the shape of my days or the way I wake up in the morning. My life used to be hunger and exhaustion and counting dollars in my head while pretending everything was fine. It was going without so Owen didn't have to. It was surviving on fumes and telling myself this was just how it was.

Now I'm tired in a different way.

It's the good kind that comes from doing work that matters and coming home to people who need me and love me. From having stability under my feet instead of quicksand. From Bandit's muddy paws at the door and Ellie's soft weight in my arms. From knowing Owen is safe and laughing and growing instead of bracing himself like I did as a teenager.

"My job, us, Owen, Bandit, and Ellie," I say, smiling a little as I list it out. "Nothing is the same." I swallow, emotion pressing thick in my chest. "But it's also been the most amazing time of my life. I wouldn't trade it for the world."

Ollie's gaze stays steady on me, warm and sure. "I wouldn't either," he says. "We got here in the most unconventional way, but we're here. That's all that matters."

Something settles in me at that.

Overwhelmed sometimes, sure. Exhausted often. But happy in a way I didn't know how to imagine before.

And for the first time, I don't feel like I'm waiting for it all to fall apart.

I nod. "I love you, Ollie."

He dips his forehead to mine. "I love you so much, Poppy."

"Are you good with everything? Are we too much…"

"No," he says, shaking his head. "You and Owen have been my family for a long time. It's just official now. I wanted to talk to you about something. Do you think we could adopt Owen? Make him officially ours?"

I suck in my breath, hot tears pricking my eyes. "Yes, I think that would mean a lot to him, too."

"What do you want, Poppy?" he asks quietly, like it's just between us.

I stare out at the trees sliding past, my breath puffing white in the air.

"I want a little home someday that's ours," I say softly. "With a yard that Owen and Ellie can play in. And maybe more animals. I want to go on family trips and see fun places. I think road trips would be fun. I want to have dinners together at our little house, with our friends and family over. I want to take Owen and Ellie to baseball games. Maybe someday have more kids. I don't know." I swallow. "But, honestly, I just want you, Ollie."

He doesn't answer right away. I worry he might not want that, either. And then worry fills me. "But if you don't…"

Then he turns his head, presses his forehead to mine, and smiles in that steady way that makes me feel like nothing's impossible.

"I want to give you the world, Poppy," he says. "I'm going to give you every single thing on that list and more. You should have what you want, and I'm going to do everything to make that happen."

He cups my chin and pulls me to him, his lips warm and solid on mine. He kisses me so tenderly and softly like he's sealing it with a kiss like a promise. And I love it. I love him.

The sleigh keeps moving. Snow falls slowly and quietly around us.

And for the first time, the future doesn't scare me. It feels like something I can reach for and be excited for. Not waiting for the other shoe to drop. Because even if something else comes our way, we've proven we can make it through anything.

Chapter 32
Ollie

Buy Dirt by Jordan Davis, Luke Bryan

The day starts like any other shift, which means it doesn't start calm at all. Lately, we've had a lot of calls. Mostly tourists driving through that don't know how to drive in snowy weather, and they underestimate Wyoming winds.

"You're smiling again," Bucky says. "That baby's got you soft."

I don't bother denying it. I just grin like an idiot and nod. "She's perfect, man."

Bucky nods. "Yeah, she is."

Ellie's picture is still open on my phone from earlier. Poppy sent it while I was resetting all the equipment. Ellie's swaddled in Poppy's arms, blinking at the camera, and Owen's arm is slung protectively around her like it's his job. Because it is, since he's her big brother. Even the dog was next to them for the picture. Everything I care about fits on one screen now.

"I'm not going to lie, it's been exhausting, but in the best possible way," I say.

Bucky snorts. "You were made for this role, Ollie. I don't know anyone more of a family man than you."

Those words mean more than anything anyone has ever told me. Because I didn't think I could have this or want this. I thought family was something that other people had. Or something you make with people you choose or who choose you. And here I am, making my own most unconventionally, yet making it right beside the woman I love.

Before I can respond, the bay doors start rattling. Not the usual sound either, like a truck rolling by too fast. This is heavier and deeper. Noises that aren't supposed to be here.

The room stills and every head turns toward the doors.

I feel it in my chest before I see them. Bikes. Several of them, big and loud. Parked right out front in the parking spaces like they're daring someone to come outside and say something. The kind of presence that doesn't belong at a firehouse.

"What the hell?" someone mutters.

My jaw locks because I already know why they're here. "I'll handle it," I say as I shrug on my hat and coat, pulling on my gloves.

Bucky steps closer. "Ollie."

"I've got it," I repeat and walk out before anyone can stop me.

Cold air hits my face. One of the men steps forward, older than the rest, gray in his beard and eyes sharp but not cruel.

"Ollie Kendrick," he says with a wave. "We're looking for you."

"You shouldn't be here. This is my work," I say and nod down the street to the shop. "And that's my home."

The older guy lifts his hands slightly. "Name's Jonesy.

Grave sent me to talk. I think you might have us misunderstood."

I laugh without humor. "That's not possible."

He studies me for a second, then nods. "Fair enough."

The other bikers hang back. Jonesy keeps his voice calm. "I want you to know something up front. We have no problem with you or your wife."

My stomach twists when he mentions Poppy.

"We don't like your dad," he continues. "Don't like hers either. Men like that cause damage wherever they go. But you and her. You're good people. No one messes with your family."

I take a step closer. "Why are you doing this?"

Jonesy doesn't blink. "The minute your woman came on club property asking for protection, she got it. For whatever reason, Grave likes you folks, and he wants to make sure nothing happens to you. The club used to be something good. I was around when it first began and my dad was in the original club. Sully got involved, and it went to shit not long after. Grave has been cleaning it up. He also grew up with a dad who tore that club apart. So, you can see we appreciate when kids of these bastards don't have to shoulder their parents' consequences. Those consequences aren't ours."

My teeth clench. "What do you want in return? I know there has to be something."

He nods once. "That's a fair question. You need to understand that we're not your enemy."

"Everyone has a price," I say, giving him a shrug like I didn't just get emotionally blackmailed by a biker with a mustache.

"The price is being a decent human and accepting the friendship," Jonesy says, shrugging right back. "Also, just so you know, no one has ever been able to crack Bandit. We figured that dog was broken until your woman showed up. Then he kept trying to run away back to town, and we figured out he was looking for her. When the bike came back smelling like her, he went nuts."

I snort before I can stop myself.

"Turns out," he continues, "he just wanted to live with you guys."

"I thought he was supposed to be a mean guard dog," I say.

Jonesy grins. "Oh, he can be mean as hell. Just not to you guys. But if anyone tries to come near your family, Bandit's gonna give them hell."

I shake my head. "Great. So, the toughest guy in your club is a dog who emotionally ghosted everyone until he found Poppy."

I do like the dog.

"How do I know you won't come back asking for something?" I shake my head, still not sure I believe them. I watched my dad hang around people like this and they always came around and threatened him or stole from us.

"You don't owe us anything," Jonesy says. "Poppy doesn't either."

I scoff. "Then why are you involved? It doesn't make any sense."

"Because Sully owes her," he says. "And we're making damn sure he pays her back."

I don't disagree, because he does owe her. But we also don't want any of his bullshit, so we'd rather have nothing to do with him. It's not worth it.

I stare at him. "You shake him down?"

"We collect what he stole and return it," Jonesy says. "That money goes to her. Clean, no strings attached."

"And then what?" I ask.

Jonesy tilts his head. "We'll take her skills if she has availability. She's a damn good mechanic, and we need to take our vehicles and bikes to someone we can trust."

That surprises me more than anything else. He's right, she is the best mechanic. I'm so damn proud of her.

I study his face. "No contact with the kids. No intimidation ever. If you ever threaten my family, I'll remind you that I'm still a Kendrick and whatever my father did will look like fuckin' child's play compared to what I'd do to protect my family."

"Agreed," he says immediately with a grin. "Damn, Ollie. I didn't know you had that in ya."

I just stare at him and he stares back for a beat.

"Okay," I say finally. "When you see Sully, can you get him to go to Weston Jessop to sign away his rights so that Poppy and I can adopt Owen?"

Jonesy watches me for a beat and nods. "I'll see what I can do."

I sigh with relief. "Thanks."

Jonesy exhales. "There's one more thing we need to talk about with you."

My shoulders tense.

"You're not going to like it," he adds.

"Try me." Because I don't really like any of this.

"We did some digging," he says carefully. "It's about the CPS report that started all this."

My jaw locks, bracing for what he's about to say. I have a feeling it's just going to piss me off.

"Like I said, you all are under club protection. Someone messes with you, we're going to be on it."

"Who was it?" I ask, bracing myself for Jeremy Toddy or some customer with a beef against Poppy.

"It was your mom," he finally says.

I stare at him, waiting for the punchline that doesn't come. "You're serious?"

Because there's no way. She's a shit mom. But I didn't think she would hurt Poppy and Owen. Two innocent people doing the best they can. She's a nurse. She's supposed to help people. What the actual hell? This is unbelievable.

Jonesy nods his head. "We know for a fact."

The engines start up again. Jonesy says, "Sorry man. We'll be in touch on Sully." The bikes roll out. The firehouse doors loom behind me like a sanctuary I didn't realize I needed. Betrayal feels pretty heavy right now.

When I walk back inside, every single guy is staring at me from the doorway with arms crossed. They saw and heard the whole thing. Great.

"What the hell was that?" someone asks. "Do we need to go and handle something?"

I don't answer. I barely hear them. Because now, I'm freaking livid. There's like a roar of heat in my ears.

All I hear is my mother's voice about Poppy. Judgmental, always watching, and disappointed. She acts like she's tried to warn me about Poppy and her family. About her being unstable. As if our family was any better than Poppy's. My family is shit just like Poppy's. Even worse now.

I always thought my mom was just being cruel. Something I came to expect from her. Turns out she was also dangerous. Because she's willing to hurt her own family. If she can hurt them, then she can hurt me. She has no moral compass whatsoever.

Unfortunately, I have a shift to finish, so I need to focus on that. I don't have the luxury of going and finding my mom and ripping her apart.

We stay busy with calls, even end up at the hospital on a transport, and, luckily, I don't see her. I need to call my sister and tell Cami what happened. If our mom can do this to Poppy and me, there's no telling what she would do to Jack and Cami. She's vile.

The drive home is quiet. I rehearse the words a hundred

times, and none of them feel right. How do I tell Poppy this without coming unglued? I'm still livid and it's been hours.

Poppy's at the counter when I walk in, Owen on the couch playing a game, Ellie sleeping in her bassinet. The sight of them makes me not want to tell them at all. It feels peaceful here and I'm sick of my mother stealing my peace from me.

She takes one look at my face and sets her mug down.

"What happened?" she asks as she cups my jaw, looking me over. "Are you hurt?"

I don't sit or take off my jacket. "Let's talk for a minute," I say as I guide her down the hall to our room.

"The bikers came to the firehouse," I say as I close the door behind us.

Her eyes widen. "What did they want?"

"I think you were right. They might not be that bad," I say quietly.

She blinks. "Okay. So, why do you seem upset?"

"There's more." I blow out a breath and pace the room.

She steps closer. "Ollie, you're freaking me out."

"It was my mom," I grit out. "She's the one who called CPS."

Silence.

Poppy's face doesn't crumple. It hardens to stone.

"What are we going to do?" she asks. "Have you told Cami?"

I shake my head. "I had to tell you first."

That question wrecks me. Because I know what I want to do. And I hate that I have to do it. I just don't want to bring that ugliness around my family. They've been through enough.

I drag a hand through my hair. "I'm so mad I can't see straight."

She steps into me and wraps her arms around my waist. I cling to her like I might fall apart if I don't.

"I don't know what we did to get this shit luck with parents," she murmurs. "Besides my mom."

Her hand rubs slow, comforting circles on my back.

"But we're not them," she continues. "We do things differently. We fight together."

I press my forehead to hers. "You and me. Always you."

She smiles softly. "Always you. We can fight anything together, Ollie."

Owen knocks on the door. "Everything okay?" he asks, stepping in with a curious expression.

I look at him. At her. At the life we're building.

"Yeah," I say. "It will be."

And for the first time today, I believe it, now that I'm with them.

Chapter 33
Poppy

Wanna Be Loved by The Red Clay Strays

I've had a few days to sit with it and to let the shock wear off. And now the anger is just settled deep inside of me, and I'm not sure what to do with it. I want to find Theresa and go off on her. I want to take out over eleven years of rage of my mom dying, our dad abandoning us, me raising Owen on my own, and barely scraping by. Because this is just the cherry on the top of the bullshit. And I went through all of that while some people made it harder for me than it needed to be. Like Theresa Kendrick calling CPS on my brother and me. And for what? Because she didn't want me to be with her son, and she thought that if she made it harder for us, maybe he'd leave us? That's the only reason I can think of. Because what kind of person does that? Not a mother, that's for sure.

That she could do this to her own son and hurt an innocent little kid, who did nothing wrong, she risked my little brother because of her own spite. And that's just beyond not okay.

I'm not even crying about it anymore. I ugly cried the first night Ollie told me while he was in the shower. Mostly for Ollie and Cami, basically losing a mother, just like I did. Only their mother is still alive but she's just evil. I can't imagine what she was thinking when she made that call to intentionally hurt us. False allegations meant to destroy.

Now I feel... done. Sad for Ollie but done with her. Like if I saw her on the street, I'd pretend I don't even know her. Because I don't. I never did. None of us did.

Parents don't always turn into the people you need them to be. Sometimes they don't change. Sometimes they don't show up. Sometimes they stay selfish, brittle, and toxic right to the end when you have to call it and cut them out. And that never hurts them as severely as it does you. Having to cut them out because people like Theresa and my dad don't care about their families.

That truth hurts. I'm sick of the way Cami and Ollie are feeling right now, but I'm glad they know now before she does more damage to them. She can't be trusted with my family. And Ollie and Cami are my family.

I'm in the bay with Owen and a bunch of bikers, watching him zip his little go-kart back and forth in the lot outside the shop doors. He's got his helmet on, and his tongue poked out in concentration, like he's auditioning for a very serious car race movie that only exists in his head. He's been working on getting the thing up and running with Mack, and I love seeing them have fun with it. Ellie's with Maggie while I get shop work done and catch up on paperwork.

Inside the shop, the vibe's different these days. It still smells like oil, metal, and gasoline. But it looks different now that I'm teaching at the school and only working part-time in the shop to keep it going until I figure out what we're doing. We can't live in the apartment forever. And sometimes living here feels like living with ghosts.

Jonesy's here with Grave and a few others. I haven't seen Pint around, and I think he got the memo that I didn't like him or want him here. Bandit growled at him when he came around, so I told him off one day. But I like having the rest of them around. They've been working in one of the bays, and they don't bother anyone. One of their guys has a bike up on a stand in the bay, fiddling with it while Jonesy helps him. Everyone's relaxed but alert, like a room full of big dogs pretending not to notice each other. Biker energy is strange. Bandit follows Owen throughout the parking lot, even riding next to him in the go-kart. It's just about the cutest thing ever. Grave looks at him and shakes his head, but his mouth turns up in a smile. He doesn't say much to anyone really, just walks around looking hot and being quiet, but Jonesy is friendly and shoots the shit with me. They're comfortable enough that they leave beer in my office fridge and hang out here sometimes. At this point, I'm not even sure how they get in, but they clean up after themselves, and they never bother us. And mysterious stacks of cash end up in my top desk drawer every week. Ollie and I opened an account for Owen and started putting everything in it. That money is for him.

My guard will probably always be up around the bikers. But they pay, they're respectful, and they treat my shop like a business. And whatever happened between them and Ollie, he's more relaxed about it, too.

It is what it is. This is our new normal. Biker protection, living together, and being a family. I love it.

Jonesy wipes his hands on a rag and leans back against the workbench. "You ever think about hiring help around here?"

I glance up from the invoice I'm working on. "Help for what?"

He shrugs. "I'm a mechanic. Just not working right now. Don't love sitting around. Grave and I were tossing the idea around of what if we became partners, got this place up and going together with you."

I consider what he's saying. He's older with gray at his temples. I've watched him for a while now, and he knows his way around the shop. Knows not to treat me less than because I'm a female mechanic. That alone puts him above a lot of men I've dealt with.

"I'd have to think about it," I say. "But maybe."

It's funny, the thing I hated about my dad was him and his bikers around growing up. I steered clear of them all. Now these guys are here, and we're doing okay. Better than okay.

His mouth tilts like he knew that was the answer he'd get. "Fair enough."

The shop door bangs open hard enough to rattle the glass, and Cami storms in like she's about to commit a felony. She just might.

Her cheeks are flushed, her long dark ponytail's coming loose, and her eyes are wild in that way that usually precedes Jack Jessop doing damage control after whatever it is she's about to do. He's literally the only person on the planet who can tame Cami, especially when she's mad. And right now, she looks really mad. She doesn't even seem to notice that the shop is full of bikers.

"Ollie called me," she announces to no one in particular. "I know what our mother did."

The shop goes quiet in that way that only happens when everyone is pretending not to listen.

I swivel on my stool. "Let's chat in the office."

She follows me without argument. I don't bother shutting the door or offering her a chair, because she's pacing like an angry lioness anyway.

"I can't even with her," Cami says, throwing her hands up. "She's been included in dinners with us, and she's been acting like a human being, and then she goes and does this. Why, Poppy? Why?"

I lean back against the desk. "Sometimes parents just suck."

She stops pacing and looks at me. "You're not wrong," she says flatly.

I wait, letting her get everything out and vent. Because this isn't a good feeling, figuring out the people who are supposed to protect you are the ones who hurt you.

"My husband told me to calm down," she continues. "Which is brave of him. It's like he wants his own Dateline episode."

There's a snort from outside the office. I'm pretty sure that's Jonesy. He's the nosey one. And they've been following along with the Theresa saga.

Cami rubs her face. "I had to come here because I want to go find her and rip her a new one."

"You have every right to be angry," I agree. But she's furious. And sad. I know these feelings well.

She exhales hard. "What are you guys going to do about her?"

I don't answer right away, because this isn't fully my call. But I know Ollie, and I know myself. This isn't going to continue. We can never trust her again. Because one thing is for sure about Ollie and me is that we don't tolerate people trying to hurt us or the people we love anymore. We're raising our own kids now. We're not doing that or putting up with that.

Cami answers her own question anyway. "There are about three people in this town who should probably call the cops when they see me coming. And my mother can now be added to that list."

I smile sadly because this is literally Cami trying to joke about it, even though she is hurt and angry.

Cami sinks into the chair across from me at last. "We're obviously done with her, and that hurts. But what hurts more is that she thinks nothing of hurting us and the people we love to get what she wants." She looks up at me, eyes bright and fierce. "So, I'm going to show her that I'm crazier."

I blink. "Wait, what?"

"Because that's what you do, Poppy," she continues, still angry. "You show the people who want to hurt you that the only reason you're not in an insane asylum is that you're functioning. Screws loose and all."

Okay, angry Cami has officially entered the chat. Scary for Theresa.

Then Jonesy's voice floats in through the doorway as he talks to one of the bikers. "Bridger Falls women are built different that's for sure."

I snort and look at Cami, who isn't even paying attention to her audience. She's lost in her thoughts, which are now alarming.

Cami straightens in her chair like she's done throwing grenades for the moment. She glances at me and softens. "I used to be a strong and independent woman," she says. "Until Jack."

I raise an eyebrow because we both know damn well she's still a strong, independent woman.

"Now I'd live in his pocket if I could. I love him so much," she admits, with a dreamy look on her face.

I laugh at that because I know the feeling. It's that feeling of loving someone so much. I get it.

Cami laughs. "And I know you're the same with my brother. You both have been like that for as long as I can remember. I used to think it was weird until I had it with Jack."

I nod.

"So, you understand that I'd do anything to protect that man and my family at all costs. And Theresa isn't our family anymore."

She rises to her feet, and I hug her. "It's going to be okay."

And standing there, in my messy office with bikers in my shop and my sister-in-law plotting emotional war crimes against her mother, I realize something settles in my chest.

Things aren't perfect. They'll probably never be easy, but now we at least know and can figure it out together.

Owen zooms past the shop doors again, laughing like the world hasn't tried to take pieces out of him yet.

I watch him and think about chosen family. About how sometimes love means walking away instead of begging someone to change.

Cami heads for the door. "I love you, Pops."

"I love you, too."

"And Poppy?"

"Yeah."

She grins. "She's going to pay for this."

"I'm legit scared for her." I grimace.

She leaves like a storm, the same way she came in.

Jonesy watches her go, wiping his hands on a rag. "She's intense."

I smile but am legit worried for Theresa. "You have no idea."

* * *

Ellie's warm little body is tucked against my chest, her cheek pressed into my neck. Owen's curled up on the other end of the couch, one sock missing, eyes glued to the TV. Some animated movie that has him sucked in.

The house smells like popcorn and clean laundry. Ollie's

hoodie is draped over the arm of the couch, and I pretend that's normal and not something that makes my chest ache. I miss him when he's at the firehouse. We were lucky that he got to take time off, but now we're trying to find a new normal. We Face-Timed earlier at dinner, and he said it had been a slow night. The guys gave him crap for saying that because they said if he says that, it gets busy. And he's been quiet for a while, so it probably did.

My phone rings and Maggie's name flashes across the screen.

"Hey, Maggie, what's up?" I ask quietly, not to wake up Ellie.

"Sugar," Maggie says, her voice tight. "There's been a bad fire."

The room tilts, nausea fills me at the words she just said.

All the blood drains from my face so fast I feel lightheaded, like I might pass out where I'm sitting. My stomach twists hard, sharp and nauseating, and my hands start to shake before I even know why.

I sit up too fast. The world blurs.

Ellie lets out a startled squeak in my arms, her little body jolting with me.

"Is Ollie okay?" I hear myself ask, but the words feel far away, like they're coming from underwater.

There's a pause on the other end. Too long.

"He was hurt on the call," Maggie says carefully. "They're taking him to the hospital."

My heart slams into my throat, loud and frantic, like it's trying to escape my chest. Adrenaline floods my system in a hot, dizzy rush. I can hear my own breathing, shallow and uneven, like I forgot how to do it properly.

Hurt. Hospital. Ollie. Everything inside me explodes into motion at once.

Owen's already up, standing in the doorway, eyes wide and scared. He looks at my face and knows something's wrong before I say a word.

"I'm on my way," I say, forcing the words out, forcing my legs to work as I stand.

Owen doesn't ask questions. He just runs. A minute later he's back with both our coats and Ellie's car seat, moving on pure instinct like I taught him to do in emergencies. That thought almost breaks me.

I pace the living room, hands useless at my sides, heart racing so fast it hurts. Oh my God. Oh my God. He has to be okay. He has to be okay.

We move in fragments. Buckling Ellie in with fingers that won't stop shaking. Grabbing my purse without checking what's inside. Slamming the door behind us.

We sprint downstairs to the truck.

The drive is a blur of streetlights and red lights and me gripping the steering wheel so hard my hands ache. Owen asks questions from the passenger seat, his voice tight, and I don't have answers to give him.

Ellie starts crying, sharp and distressed, like she can feel the fear pouring off us in waves.

"I know, baby," I whisper, even though I don't know what I'm reassuring her about. "I know."

I pull into the hospital lot too fast, tires crunching hard against the pavement, like I'm chasing something instead of arriving somewhere.

Like if I move fast enough, I can outrun the worst of it.

Like if I don't stop moving, he'll still be okay.

Inside, the lights are too bright. The air smells like disinfectant and cold. Maggie waits inside for us, and she pulls Owen in for a hug.

"Is Ollie okay?" he stammers.

I hand Ellie to her automatically. "Hold her for me. Please."

She nods, jaw tight, eyes shiny. "Of course, honey."

"Where is he? Is he okay?" I ask, my eyes wild and darting around.

"They took him back for tests. He fell through a barn floor," Maggie says. "That's all I know."

"I need him," I say to the woman at the desk, my voice cracking. "My husband is here. Ollie Kendrick."

She doesn't even flinch. "He's okay. He's getting checked out. I'll take you back."

Okay is not a word that means anything to me right now. I need to see him for myself.

I spot him on a bed and everything inside me lurches.

My eyes race over him from head to toe, scanning for damage like it's instinct, like it's survival. His turnout gear is half on, half peeled away, blackened and streaked with soot. There's dried blood along his hairline, dark against his skin, and a smear on his cheek that makes my chest seize until I realize it's not still bleeding.

Bruising is already blooming along his jaw. His hands are scraped, knuckles raw and angry looking. His jacket hangs open, collar askew, like it was torn off in a hurry.

His hair is mussed, wild in that way it only gets after a rough call. His brow is furrowed, mouth pulled tight, irritation written all over him. He looks uncomfortable. Annoyed. Like he wants to be anywhere but here.

Not broken.

The realization hits me so hard my knees almost give out.

He's breathing. He's conscious. He's glaring at the ceiling like he's mad about being stuck in a hospital bed instead of out there doing his job.

Relief crashes through me, hot and dizzy, and I have to press a hand to my chest to keep myself upright.

Oh, thank God.

He turns his head then, eyes finding mine, and something in his expression softens immediately.

And that's when I know, down to my bones, that we're going to be okay.

"Poppy," he murmurs, like he didn't just take years off my life.

I rush to him and kiss his face, relieved to see him. "What happened?"

"I'm fine," he says immediately.

The nurse snorts. "No, he's not. He has a concussion."

Ollie rolls his eyes. "It's mild."

She raises an eyebrow. "You blacked out."

"I'm fine."

I hug him hard, pressing my face into his neck, breathing him in, the smell of smoke, sweat, and him.

"I'm so glad you're okay," I whisper. "Ollie, we need you to be safe."

His arms wrap around me, solid and warm. "I know. I'm okay."

"We're taking him for another test. We'll be right back. You can wait here," the nurse tells as she wheels his bed away.

His helmet is on the chair beside the bed. I notice it because something's sticking out of it. I reach for it and pull out the pictures tucked inside. One of us together at The Black Dog posing for a selfie. It's from before we got together but the way his arm is around me, we look like a couple. I can't believe I missed all the clues that he was mine long before he was. One of him and Owen fishing, both of them grinning while Ollie leans down next to him. Another one of newborn baby Ellie sleeping on me, Owen next to me on the couch, napping as well. I didn't even know he took that one.

My throat closes as hot tears stream down my cheeks.

Ollie's wheeled back in and he looks okay but tired.

"I'm so glad you're okay. I love you so much."

Theresa's voice cuts through the hall like a knife, ruining the moment. "I have a right to see my son."

"Please don't let my mom in here," he says to the nurse.

She nods. "Got it."

Three firefighters step in front of the door like a wall.

"Nope," one says. "Not happening, Theresa."

"I want to see my son," she snaps. "Get out of my way."

I step into the hall and slip around them before they can say another word.

"This woman is not to come near my husband's room," I say loudly. "If she does, I will call the police. Do you hear me?"

Two nurses at the nurses' station freeze and nod. One stands and comes to get Theresa. Another murmurs something about calling security.

Theresa's face twists. "You have no right. That's my son."

I laugh—a sharp, humorless sound.

"No, Theresa. I have every right. That's my husband. And he doesn't want you here. You need to leave."

She opens her mouth, but I'm not done.

"And that call you made to CPS?" I continue. "Yeah, we know you made the false allegations, and we will be reporting you for that too."

The hallway goes dead silent.

Then she says, "That was supposed to be anonymous. That's not your business who reported you."

"Keep throwing bricks," I step closer. "I'm building a fucking house with them. You will never be a part of my family's life. You're done. We'll be filing restraining orders. You will never come around any of us again. What you did was unforgiveable."

Theresa's eyes dart down the hall, and I notice Cami heading this way. I'm the least of her problems now.

Theresa looks scared and turns before heading the opposite way. I doubt she'll be back. I breathe a big sigh of relief and lean back against the wall.

Cami storms over. "What did I miss?"

I tell her everything and that Ollie's okay.

Her jaw tightens. Her eyes go cold, and she turns to follow her mom. "Go be with Ollie," she says. "I'll handle it."

And I know she will. This won't be good for Theresa, but that's not my problem. Making sure my husband is okay is my focus.

I go back into the room and sit carefully on the bed beside my husband, pressing my forehead to his. "You're okay," I whisper.

He kisses my hair. "Yeah, we are."

Outside the door, our people stand guard.

Chapter 34
Ollie

Tennessee Orange by Megan Moroney

I'm home recuperating from a stupid fall. The floor gave way, and I fell, and it pissed me off. Because number one, it was a mistake, and I knew better than to trust that floor of that barn, but I did it anyway, and I'm not taking risks like that again. Lesson learned. I can't risk anything happening to me. My family needs me.

The Crock Pot in the kitchen smells amazing from whatever it is Poppy threw in there this morning. I have the week off from work while I recover, and I don't mind our little family hunkered down on this cold day, with movies and the smell of good food.

Owen works on his math at the coffee table in front of us. And he informs us, "I see the Crock Pot made the move with us. Great."

Poppy doesn't look up but laughs. "It absolutely did. I wasn't leaving it behind."

I nod. "Hey, I love the Crock Pot. I don't know why you don't."

Owen squints at me. "Because it doesn't taste like The Black Dog?"

"It's even better," I say proudly.

He sighs. "If you say so."

Poppy looks between us. "Why do you hate it?"

"Because Crock Pot food is for old people," Owen says.

I snort before I can stop myself. "No, it's not."

Ellie sighs contently in her sleep next to me on the couch.

Poppy presses her lips together. "Okay, first of all, rude. We are not old."

Owen points. "See? Ellie even agrees."

I laugh because this is what life is about—just being together, laughing, and doing life.

Poppy's hovering, straightening the throw blanket that doesn't need straightening. She touches my shoulder, my arm, my knee, like she's checking me to make sure I'm okay.

"You good?" she asks for the third time.

"I'm good," I insist, chuckling.

She doesn't look like she believes me, but she smiles anyway. I know I scared the hell out of her, and I hate that I did but that's the job and she knows it. I've had close calls before and I'll have close calls again.

Owen's pencil keeps rolling onto the floor. Poppy's kneeling beside him, humming under her breath without realizing it.

She only hums when she's worried.

The Crock Pot bubbles from the kitchen with the roast and potatoes that Owen pretends he hates but will have three helpings. The smell makes me feel like everything's going to be okay.

Owen climbs onto the couch beside me, careful not to jostle the baby. He leans into my side like it's the most natural thing in the world. He watches Ellie for a moment, then looks up at me.

"Ollie?"

"Yeah, bud?"

He hesitates, chewing on his lip, and something in me goes still. I know this moment. I know not to rush it.

"Do you think," he blurts, "you'd ever want to be like a dad to me, too?"

Everything freezes in the room—the sound of the Crock Pot bubbling, the hum of the heater in the apartment.

I look at him and over at Poppy. My chest squeezes with a hug. Emotion grips me and fills me as I've never felt before. Because this is a hell yes question, and hell, yes, I'd love to be like a dad to Owen. I already feel like I am. I hope that he feels it, too.

Poppy's frozen, emotions tangled in her eyes.

I choose my words carefully because this vulnerability didn't come easily to Owen. It couldn't have. I remember feeling a similar way when I was his age. Not having parents who cared and wondering who would show up for me and be there. I'll make it my mission in life to make sure he never feels that way ever again.

"If you want me," I say slowly, "I'd be honored to be a dad to you, Owen."

Owen doesn't hesitate. He launches himself into me, wrapping his arms around my middle.

I pull him in, tucking him close, my arm around him, Ellie still asleep next to me, my whole world right here.

I look up and meet Poppy's eyes over the couch as she stands in the kitchen.

We both silently freak out.

Then she turns away, wiping at her eyes like she's just checking the roast.

I press my cheek to Owen's hair and breathe.

* * *

Weston knocks and smiles when we let him in. His expression tells me something's going on. "You're not going to believe this."

My chest tightens on instinct. Poppy's hand slides into mine, warm and steady. Because normally, these types of meetings and hearing things like that haven't been good for us lately.

"Sully came to see me," Weston continues. "He signed away all his rights. Full guardianship to you and Poppy. He's not fighting you on anything. He also signed the shop over to you. I don't know what got into him, but he did the right thing here."

The room is still, and my brain tries to catch up with what I'm hearing. The bikers made this happen. I'll be damned.

"He didn't seem happy," Weston adds. "And he grumbled a lot, but he did it."

"What did he say?" Poppy asks.

"Mostly complained about you messing things up for him with the club."

I huff out a breath. "Shocking." Everything has always been about Sully. He doesn't care about anyone but himself, and he never has.

"I pretended I had no idea what he was talking about," Weston says dryly. "I just focused on getting the papers signed. I had my eye on the prize, and we got it."

Relief crashes into me so hard I have to sit down. Months of waiting for the other shoe to drop, and suddenly there isn't one. It's all over.

Poppy squeezes my hand, her eyes bright and wet. She feels it, too. She laughs once, a shaky sound that turns into a breath.

"So," I say, voice rough. "Does this mean everything is over?"

Weston smiles and nods. "It means you're Owen's legal

guardians. Permanently. And if you want, you could pursue adoption. Make him a Kendrick."

He pauses, then adds, "I've also checked with CPS. The case against you is closed. You should be getting paperwork confirming that any day now to keep for your record."

I bite my lip, words rising before I can overthink them. "What if we changed our name?"

Poppy turns toward me, surprised. Weston's brows lift.

"To what?" she asks softly.

"Wilder," I say. The word feels solid. Right. "What if we became Wilders? What if we made a new line of Wilders and a new legacy with Owen?"

The room goes quiet again, but this time it's the good kind, like the wheels are turning and they're all considering it. The only Wilder who wasn't worth a damn is Theresa, but she's not in our lives anymore.

Poppy's face breaks into a smile that wrecks me. "I love it, and I think Owen would love it too."

"No one wants to be a Murphy or a Kendrick," I say quietly.

Weston nods, his voice gentle. "I think your grandparents would be so proud of you both."

My throat tightens. I squeeze Poppy's hand and finally let myself breathe.

"Let's do it," I say.

The future feels like something we're building and can be proud of.

Chapter 35
Poppy

Pieces by Muscadine Bloodline, Lainey Wilson

Wilder Ranch glows in the late afternoon light. It's bitterly cold outside, the kind that bites straight through your jeans, but the lodge feels warm and welcoming. The fireplace roars, and the whole place hums with that quiet, rare magic that exists here in Bridger Falls. Cami hosts book club the same way she hosts literally everything else. Big. Cozy. Slightly unhinged in the best possible way.

Cami's outdone herself, which surprises absolutely no one. She's turned Wilder Lodge, the former Jessop Lodge, into a welcoming space, and it's the perfect spot for a book club.

There's a long table set up in the lodge that looks like it belongs on a baking show finale. Cookies, bars, and homemade breads, and something dusted in powdered sugar that I don't recognize but immediately want to eat. And of course, the coffee station. Not just coffee. Fancy coffee with syrups and frothy things. Labels written in Cami's neat handwriting, like this, are a pop-up cafe and not the family's lodge. She and Jack built a home not far from here, between the old Wilder land and the Jessop Lodge. But Weston stays here when he comes, and Tucker still lives here and works the ranch. It's essentially the family meeting place.

Maggie's planted herself near the couch with a basket full of paperbacks, calling it her mobile free library like she's running some underground romance ring. She's got everything in there. Old school bodice rippers with scandalous covers. Cute illustrated romcoms. A couple thrillers she swears count as book club material because they involve relationships *and* murder.

It's been a long time since I've had the luxury of reading just for fun. It's been a while since I could focus without working sixteen hours a day, or a stack of bills sitting on the counter that I have to read instead of a book for fun. But lately, the teachers at the high school have been passing around books and talking about them in the lounge, laughing and debating endings like it's normal to enjoy something again. And I decided I want that.

I wrap my hands around a warm mug and smile to myself, realizing I'm actually excited. Not just to be here, but to read. To sit on a couch with friends and talk about fictional people making bad choices while everything else in my life gets to be quiet for a little while.

That feels like magic, too. I'm leaning into the peaceful quiet these days. I'm living out my own fictional romance fairy tale with Ollie, and it's pretty great.

Violet's balancing a drink and a book in her hand. Mack's stretched out on her stomach on the plush rug, flipping pages and pretending she's not listening to everyone else as she reads one of the thrillers. I love that everyone is welcome at book club, from Maggie, who is seventy, to Mack, who is seventeen, and a baby. Cami's whipping up coffees for everyone.

There's a new face today.

Sutton sits cross legged beside Maggie, her little boy, Crew, balanced easily on her lap. She looks late twenties, maybe early thirties, young but a little worn in the way motherhood does that to you with a baby that keeps you busy. Petite, but not fragile. Sturdy and strong.

Her hair is blonde, pale and soft, pulled into a loose braid that slips over one shoulder, wisps escaping around her face no matter how many times she tucks them back. Her eyes are a clear blue, bright and observant, the kind that miss nothing even when she's smiling. There's a faint dimple in her cheek when she laughs at something Maggie says, and a tiny scar near her eyebrow that gives her face character instead of perfection.

She wears leggings and an oversized sweater, one sleeve pushed up so Crew can gnaw happily on her wrist. She doesn't even flinch. Just steadies him with one arm and keeps listening, fully present, like this room and these people already matter to her.

Something about her feels gentle but grounded. Like she's been through things and came out softer instead of harder.

I clock all of it in a second and understand why Maggie has already claimed her.

Her baby's about nine months old, chubby and curious, drool shining on his chin. Maggie has already fully adopted both of them into the book club circle.

"This is Sutton," Maggie announces proudly. "She loves books, and she's brave enough to show up to book club with this wild group."

Sutton laughs. "I needed adult conversation, or I was going to go stir crazy cooped up in the house. This winter has been brutal."

We all nod. We get it.

"It's nice to meet you, Sutton. Crew is adorable," I say as I sit next to her.

"Thanks," she says shyly. "How old are your kids?"

I smile proudly when they're called my kids. "Owen is eleven, and Ellie is almost six weeks old."

"Wow, you look so young," she says, surprised.

"Owen's actually my little brother, but my husband and I are adopting him," I say before I realize I haven't told them all that, yet.

Cami gasps, and the room goes quiet.

Maggie says softly, "Really? Oh, sugar…"

I nod, excited. "Weston's helping us make it official. We're all changing our last name, too."

Cami softens and says, "You're all going to be Kendricks."

"Nope," I say, smiling so hard my cheeks hurt. "We're going to be Wilders."

For a second, there's silence. Then the room explodes.

Maggie gasps and presses a hand to her chest. "Oh, my heart."

Violet claps. "That's perfect."

Cami lunges over and hugs me. "I love that so much. Because yeah…fuck that Kendrick name."

Maggie smiles softly. "That's really beautiful. I love that we have Wilders around again."

I swallow around the lump in my throat. "It feels like a fresh start. Like we get to choose what comes next."

Mack looks up. "Wilder is a way cooler name than Murphy or Kendrick."

"Exactly," I agree.

"Congratulations." Sutton smiles.

We pivot to the book like we always do, because the book club never stays serious for long.

"Did everyone read the new one?" Violet asks. "Just Another Summer Escape?"

Maggie fans herself. "All those cocktails and beach vibes. I need a vacation immediately."

"It made me want sand, sunshine, and a drink with an umbrella," Sutton says. "I love all the books by that author. The Wisteria Cove series was my favorite. I want to live there and go to the bookstore and apothecary shop."

Violet grins. "Funny, you say that. Walker and I are going to Coconut Beach for our baby moon. Our music manager, Will Maren, has a sister who owns a cottage there. We're stealing it for a week."

Sutton sighs. "That sounds so romantic."

"A week of waves and sunshine," Violet says dreamily. "And my hot husband all to myself. We might never even leave the cottage."

Mack makes a dramatic gagging noise. "Yuck. And I'm staying here with Cami and Jack."

Cami laughs. "Yeah, but we're going to have fun, aren't we?"

"Heck yeah," Mack says. "I'll take that over your baby moon vibes."

Cami tilts her head at Mack. "Are you excited to have a baby sister or brother?"

Mack smiles, softer this time. "I am. I love babysitting. Also, if you ever need one, Sutton, give me a call. Crew is adorable."

Sutton's eyes light up. "I may just take you up on that. I'd love a night out sometime if you ladies ever get together. My social life has been on life support."

"Do you have a significant other, sugar?" Maggie asks.

"Nah, I prefer my men fictional these days. I'm good." Sutton shakes her head with a laugh.

We all laugh because Maggie is the town meddler and loves

to play matchmaker. And knowing her, she probably already has someone in mind for poor Sutton.

Crew lets out a happy squeal and bangs his hands together like he's applauding us.

I lean back in my chair, the sound of laughter and pages turning and babies babbling around me and think about names and legacies and how none of this looks like the life I planned. But it looks exactly like the life I needed.

Cami clears her throat, and the energy shifts. Not heavy, exactly, but real.

"So," she says, picking at the edge of her book. "My mom listed her house. Looks like she's moving out of town."

Everyone stills. I never asked Cami what happened at the hospital that day with Theresa. I know that she sent Ollie a long letter, and she hasn't tried to reach out since. And he hasn't had a lot to say. He doesn't seem sad, just finished like I am. And that's sad but necessary. She caused a lot of unnecessary chaos in all our lives.

"She also got fired from the hospital," Cami continues.

"Ohhhh." Violet cringes. "She definitely messed around and found out."

"She got the memo," Cami says, her voice steady even if her eyes aren't. "She's not to come around any of us anymore. We're done. As done as we are with our dad."

Maggie exhales slowly and reaches for Cami's hand.

Mack's jaw tightens in that quiet, protective way she has. "My mom sucks, too. My dad raised me since I was a baby. It all works out."

"We're making new futures and families," Cami says.

I don't even think about it. I stand and pull her into a hug, holding her tight.

"I'm sorry," I say into her hair. "But I'm also so damn proud of both of you."

She hugs me back just as hard. "Thank you."

For a moment, no one talks. Crew babbles softly on Sutton's lap.

"What do you do for work?" Cami asks Sutton.

"I'm actually a freelance editor. I mostly edit romance books for indie authors."

Violet grins. "That is so cool!"

"Ohhh, so you can help us pick our next one!" Maggie smiles.

"I have so many recommendations," Sutton says, adjusting Crew. "Say the word, and I'll give you a list."

Love these people and sitting here at the Wilder Ranch, surrounded by chosen family and second chances, it feels like we're all doing the bravest thing we've ever done. We're choosing ourselves and building our own family.

* * *

I sit at the beat-up folding table in the back of the shop, the one that smells like old coffee and the lemon cleaner I used this morning. Ollie sits beside me, close enough that our knees touch. Jonesy leans back in his chair like he owns the place, boots crossed at the ankles, weathered hands wrapped around a beer. Grave sits across from me, elbows on the table, calm eyes taking everything in.

No one says anything for a moment.

The shop hums around us. A fan rattles. Somewhere out front, a radio plays low. This place has always been loud and chaotic, but right now it feels like the quiet before a storm, or maybe the quiet after one.

Grave lifts his bottle. "Like I told you before, Poppy, we're restructuring. Making things new."

I nod slowly, keeping my eyes on his face. Ollie's hand rests on my thigh, warm and steady. I can feel his thumb move just once, grounding me.

"We took out the trash," Grave continues. "And we're creating something legit. Above board. Different from what it was."

Something tightens in my chest. I glance at Jonesy, who's wearing a faint, amused smile like he already knows what I'm about to ask.

I clear my throat. "What does taking out the trash mean?"

Jonesy tips his head back and laughs. "That's a dangerous question, sweetheart, that you might not want to hear the answer to."

Grave raises an eyebrow at me. "Do you really want to know?"

I hold his gaze, then shake my head. "No, I probably don't." I pause, choosing my words carefully. "But what I want is no violence or anything illegal anywhere near this shop. This is a place where people feel safe. They trust us. I won't have that trust ruined. We do things right, or we won't work with you."

Ollie squeezes my knee, just a little. These are all the things we've talked about together before we agreed to the partnership and set up this meeting. I'll walk away if it's not above board.

Grave nods, slow and deliberate. "I agree. That's what we want too. But you have to know that this partnership and the club are separate. We don't talk club business outside of the club. We keep things separate. You two will never be a part of our club and you'll never know club business."

Jonesy's smile fades into something more serious. "We're done with the old way."

"So," Grave says, lifting his beer slightly, "we're on the same page?"

I nod. "Okay."

I hesitate, then ask the question that's been sitting heavy in my chest, but I need to know. "Have you heard from Sully?"

The air changes. Ollie goes still beside me. Jonesy looks down at his bottle. Grave clears his throat.

"He's working out of state," Grave says. "And he knows he's not to come to Bridger Falls under any circumstances."

I nod, relieved.

"He'll be paying you back for a long time," Grave says evenly. "He won't be bothering you anymore."

I nod, swallowing hard. "But he's safe?"

Grave meets my eyes. "He's alive."

I study his face, searching for anything that tells me otherwise. I don't find it.

"This club runs differently now," he continues. "And I mean that."

Silence settles again, thicker this time.

Grave leans back in his chair. "Sometimes we get a shit hand when it comes to parents. That doesn't define us or reflect on who we are as people."

My throat tightens.

"But when you have the opportunity to break a generational curse," he says, voice steady and sure, "that's what you do."

He looks at me, really looks at me. "And that's exactly what you're doing with your brother."

Something in my chest cracks open. I blink hard, refusing to let the tears fall in front of them. Ollie's hand slides into mine, our fingers lacing together.

"Thanks," I say quietly.

Jonesy nods at me, expression soft. "You're doing good, kid."

I stand, pushing my chair back. "I appreciate that."

Grave stands too.

I walk toward the door, my boots echoing against the concrete floor. Before I step outside, I glance back once. Ollie's watching me with that look he gets when he's proud and worried and in love all at once.

I give him a small smile.

Then I head out into the afternoon light, the shop door swinging shut behind me, feeling lighter than I have in a long time.

Chapter 36
Ollie

Holy Smokes by Bailey Zimmerman

I've been summoned to the Wilder Ranch by Cami and Jack. I don't know what they need my help with, but they know they've got it. Jack's truck is parked by the barn, and the side-by-side is parked beside it. It's cold today, so whatever it is, I hope we take the truck with the heat on full blast.

I kill the engine to my truck and climb out, shoving my hands deep into my coat pockets. I'm expecting Jack to have a fence down, cows loose, a horse acting stupid, or a tractor that probably needs Poppy more than it needs me. But Poppy's working today, and Maggie's got Ellie and Owen. Jack told me to come out alone. So, yeah. I'm curious as to what they want.

I look around, and Cami steps out of the barn and smiles like she has a secret and is about to spill. Jack follows behind her, one hand on her lower back, the other holding a thermos like he's trying to keep this casual. Like, he didn't summon me out here, being ominous.

"Hey," I say, nodding at them. "What's up? Somebody die?"

Jack snorts. "Not yet."

Cami rolls her eyes. "Ignore him and come on. We're taking the truck."

Thank God.

My brows pull together. "What's going on?"

"We want to show you something," Jack says, already climbing into the driver's seat, "Hop in." That's Jack's version of subtle.

I climb in behind Cami, and the engine coughs to life. The seat's cold through my jeans. Cami pulls her beanie down and tucks her hair behind her ear, and I watch her hands for a second. She's fidgety and gets that way when she's nervous. And that's not very often.

Jack drives us past the main barn and out toward the back of his property, the land opening up and stretching wide like it could swallow you whole—fence lines cut through fields packed with snow, with the ridges of the mountains snow-capped and mapping out the sky in front of us. Snow sits in shallow drifts in the shade, but the sun has melted the rest down to brown grass and exposed dirt on the road we're on.

I do miss the Wilder Ranch in some ways. But I made peace with letting it go years ago. We ride in silence for a minute, the engine rumbling beneath our feet. Jack keeps his eyes forward. Cami keeps looking at me like she wants to say something.

My stomach tightens. "Okay," I finally say. "You're freaking me out. What's going on?"

Cami exhales, a shaky breath, and then she reaches over and grabs Jack's hand. "It's good," she says quietly. "You'll see."

Relief fills me because I can handle good. I can't handle anything that isn't good right now. What I have right now with Poppy, Owen, and Ellie is so much better than good. I won't take anything less than good for my family and me anymore.

Jack slows the truck and stops next to a field. The engine clicks and then goes quiet. The world goes still except for the wind.

Cami turns toward me fully, eyes bright. "You've always been there for me," she says, her voice cracking a little. "You're the best brother I could've asked for."

I blink hard, caught off guard by the emotion in her voice. I look away, out at the field, because I don't want to cry.

"I don't deserve you," she keeps going, and her laugh is wet. "And somehow I get you anyway."

I swallow. "Cami. You deserve me."

"Let me finish," she says quickly, shaking her head. "I need to say this."

Jack hangs his head and listens. I can tell he's emotional, too.

"Our parents are shit," she says, blunt as always. "They're selfish and broken, and they hurt us, and I hate that we got that."

I soften as she lets it all out. I know she's upset.

"But I have you," she says, voice softening. "And you'll always have me. You always have. And now you have Jack. You've always had him, but you have him as an official brother now."

Jack shifts in his seat, glancing at her, then at me, his throat working like he's swallowing something down, too.

"I don't know how we turned out the way that we did with what we had." I shake my head, trying to shake off the emotion that is pouring over me.

Cami's eyes shine harder. "I want you here, Ollie," she says. "I want us to raise our kids together, be there for each other. I want Owen riding horses and doing everything that he loves. I want Ellie growing up knowing she's loved by more people than she can count."

My chest aches. "Kids?"

"Someday we'll have them." She grins, squeezing Jack's hand, and he nods.

"And we want you to have something," she says, voice steadier now, like she's decided to be brave. "Not because you need it. Because you deserve it."

I open my mouth, but nothing comes out. I feel the air has gone out of my lungs.

Jack clears his throat. "Cami and I want you to build out here," he says. "We want you to have your piece of Wilder land."

I stare at him and say softly. "What?"

He nods once, serious. "I have twenty acres with your name on it if you want it."

My breath catches. Wilder land is something I thought I'd never have. And I made peace with it. But this...this is unexpected. And far more than I deserve.

Cami squeezes my hand. "Tucker has his land," she continues. "Jenna has hers. Weston owns the entire Granger property, which now extends to the back of the Wilder Ranch and is part of it as well. We're building something here, Ollie. We want your family here, too."

Jack points across the field, toward a line of cottonwoods and a faint shape I didn't even notice at first.

"There's a cabin out there," Cami adds quickly. "It's small but has three bedrooms. It's not great, but it's solid. You could make it work until you build something else. Or fix it up. Whatever you want. It's yours to decide."

My heart pounds so hard it makes my ears ring. I look out and see Poppy and Owen here. Ellie in my arms and feel the quiet in my bones. The peace of this place. The fresh new beginnings that it is with Wilder Ranch and Jessop Ranches combined. We left the ghosts of the past and are building something new.

"You would do this?" I ask, voice rough.

Cami's face crumples as if she might cry again. "I'd do anything for you, Ollie," she says. "I love you. You're my family."

I shake my head slowly, trying to make sense of it. "But... it's yours. I can't afford this land."

Cami's expression turns fierce. The same look she gets when she's defending her ranch, her people, her heart.

"Now it's ours," she says. "You don't owe anything on it. It's yours and I really hope you say yes because Weston already drew up the papers."

Jack nods. "It was your family's, too," he says. "This land is meant to stay in the family."

My throat tightens. I stare out at the field again, and all I can see is a future I never let myself imagine because wanting it felt like it could never happen. Hell yeah, I want it. I want it more than anything.

I picture a porch light in the distance on a big red barn full of animals. Kids laughing, swinging on a tire swing beneath the big oak tree over there.

I blink hard and finally look back at them. "Yeah," I say, voice so thick it makes me choke when I respond. "Yeah, I want this."

Cami makes a sound that's half laugh, half sob, and she throws her arms around my neck so fast I barely have time to react. I hug her back, tight, because I don't know what else to do with the way my chest feels like it's splitting open.

Jack claps my shoulder with a heavy hand. "Good," he says gruffly.

Cami pulls back and wipes at her cheeks, then punches my arm lightly. "Don't make it weird, just take it."

"I'm not making it weird," I say, but my voice cracks, and she smiles at me like she sees right through me.

Jack starts the truck up again. "Come on," he says. "Let's go look at it."

We drive toward the cabin, the sun feeling somehow warmer and brighter now, my mind spinning. The cabin comes into view, and it's rough, sure. The porch sags a little. The roof looks like it's seen a few storms. But this place could be ours. I can't wait to tell Poppy. I've seen her dream board, and I know she has dreamed of us having a place of our own. She has chickens, a tire swing, a horse, and various other farm animals on that dream board. She wants a farm. And she's getting a farm.

Cami hops out first and walks up to the porch like she's already picturing a porch swing. Jack checks the steps with his weight, like he's already planning to help with repairs.

I stand back a second, staring at it. I've spent my whole life being the one who shows up, the one who holds the line, the one who makes sure everyone else is okay. I've never expected to be given anything like this. I expected to work like hell for everything I wanted.

Cami looks back at me. "Well?" she calls. "You coming?"

I nod and walk up to the porch, my boots thudding against the old wood. The door creaks open, and cold air rushes out, carrying the faint scent of old pine and dust.

I pull Cami in for another hug. "Thank you."

Jack claps me on the back and nods.

It's not fancy, but it's ours. And it's a damn beautiful start to our life together out here.

My phone buzzes in my pocket, and I pull it out. Poppy's name is on the screen.

I answer immediately. "Hey."

Her voice is warm, familiar, home. "Where are you?"

"At the ranch," I say, looking around the cabin, the walls, the windows, the way the light slants through. "Cami and Jack wanted to show me something."

"What kind of something?" she asks, suspicious in that way she gets when she thinks people are plotting behind her back.

I glance out the window at the field, the wide-open space, the sky that looks too big to be real.

"A big something," I say, and my voice goes soft without me meaning it to. "Can you come out here later? Around sunset?"

There's a pause. "Ollie," she says slowly. "Are you about to spring something on me?"

"Maybe," I admit.

She huffs. "You better not be pranking me. I'm tired."

I smile. "I'm not pranking you, baby. Bring Owen and Ellie when you come."

"Okay, we'll be there. Can I at least get a clue?"

"Nah, you're going to love this. Just come out. Love you, honey," I say again, quieter. "I'll see you soon."

Her tone changes. Softer. "Okay, I'll get the kids."

My chest tightens in the best way. "Okay," I say. "I'll meet you by the lodge."

"I love you," she says, like it's easy now, and the sound of that coming from her lips makes me close my eyes.

"I love you too," I say, and mean it with my whole damn chest.

I hang up and stare at the cabin again, and for the first time in my life, the future doesn't feel like something I'm running toward. It feels like something I'm walking into.

* * *

A truck crunches along the dirt road and pulls up. Poppy climbs out first. She pulls Ellie out of her carseat and bundles her up in a blanket. Owen follows, already bouncing on his heels like he can't stand still, eyes darting across the land like it's a playground the size of a dream. He's going to love what I'm about to tell them, but first I have to tell Poppy.

"Okay," Poppy calls as she approaches, narrowing her eyes at me, but she's smiling. "What's going on?"

I step closer and take her free hand, rubbing my thumb over her knuckles. "Come with me. Just us. Cami's gonna take Ellie and Owen to the barn."

She lets me lead her to the barn, Owen following behind us with a million questions, Ellie making soft little noises against Poppy's chest like she's talking to her, too.

"Hey," Cami says as she walks out of the barn, ruffling Owen's hair. "There's my Owen and Ellie."

"Hey, Cami. Do you know what the mystery is about?" Poppy asks, her eyes darting to me and back to her as if she has some answers.

"I do, but I'm not telling," she singsongs.

Cami takes Ellie from Poppy and straps her to her chest. "Let me take my sister. You're never too early to start learning about horses, baby."

"Come on," I tell Poppy, grinning as I take her hand. "There's something I want to show you."

Owen pops up instantly. "Me too?"

I stop and look at him, really look at him. He's watching me closely, hopeful but cautious like he always is when things feel big.

"Yeah, buddy," I say. "You especially."

That does it. His face lights up.

I hold the truck door for Poppy, and she hesitates before climbing in. "You know I hate surprises, Ollie."

"I know," I say easily. "But I think you're going to like this one."

Owen bounces in the back seat the whole drive, peppering me with questions I dodge badly on purpose. When we finally crest the rise in the field, the cabin comes into view, tucked near the cottonwoods like it belongs there.

Poppy goes still beside me.

She looks from the cabin to me, confused. "What is this?"

I park and cut the engine. "This," I say, turning to face them both, "is ours."

Her mouth parts. Her eyes go wide. "Ollie," she whispers. "Are you serious?"

But I'm watching Owen now. He's leaning forward between the seats, staring out the windshield like he's afraid it might disappear if he blinks. "You mean... like... we'd live here?"

I turn fully toward him. "Only if you want to."

That gets her attention.

Owen looks at me, searching my face. "We wouldn't have to move again?"

"No," I say quietly. "This would be home. Our family's land."

He swallows. "With you?"

"With me," I promise. "And your sister and Ellie."

His shoulders drop like something heavy just slid off them. "Then yeah," he says quickly. "I want that."

Poppy's hand tightens around mine.

I look back at her, my chest full. "Cami and Jack offered us twenty acres. There's a cabin. It's not perfect, but it's solid. A place to live while we save up to build something bigger for our family."

Her eyes fill instantly. "You're kidding."

I shake my head. "Nope."

She steps out of the truck, still holding my hand like she's afraid this is a trick. Owen bolts ahead, circling the cabin, already claiming it in his head.

"Why would they do this for us?" she whispers, voice shaking.

"Because they love us," I say simply. "And because they're our family."

She looks back at Owen, laughing now as he runs up onto the porch. Her eyes shine when she turns back to me. "Ollie..."

"And because I think they want you to have what you never got," I add softly.

She meets my gaze. "And what do you want?"

"A future," I say. "A place that's ours."

Owen comes bounding back. "Can I pick my room?"

I laugh. "We'll see."

Poppy laughs too, breathless and disbelieving. "I want this so much," she says.

I lift my hand and wipe a tear from her cheek. "We're going to be happy here," I tell her. "All of us. Together."

She exhales, a shaky laugh breaking free.

I cup her face and kiss her, slow and sure, like I'm making a promise with my mouth. She kisses me back like she's finally letting herself believe she's allowed to have this life.

"I can't believe this," she whispers.

I rest my forehead against hers. "Believe it," I say. "This is real. And it's good."

Behind us, Owen yells, "I'm calling dibs on the biggest bathroom if there is one."

She laughs again, warm and free, and something settles deep in my chest.

For the first time in my life, I know what good feels like.

And it's standing right here in front of me.

Chapter 37
Poppy
3 Months Later

Joy Of My Life by Chris Stapleton

In three months, everything can change, that's for sure. I stand in the middle of the shop with my hands on my hips, staring at the new sign in disbelief that this is actually my life. The letters are clean and bold, freshly mounted above the bay doors that have been here longer than I have.

Wilder Auto Body

Not Murphy's. And this shop is not my dad's. It's mine. And the Pine River Motorcycle Club.

Ollie leans against the tool chest beside me, arms crossed, watching my face like he's waiting for the moment it really sinks in. His hair's a little longer than it used to be, his jaw rough with stubble from a shift that ran long. He looks tired and steady and completely, undeniably mine. It still feels surreal that this is my life.

We've partnered with the local college to bring in interns, young adults excited to learn. They remind me of what I dreamed this place could be like. I still teach at the high school, and in the summer, I get to work in my shop. I love it. I love seeing that moment when something clicks for them, a puzzle is solved and repaired, and they realize they're capable of more than they thought.

The bay door opens, and one of the interns waves on his way out, calling a cheerful goodbye. When the door shuts again, the quiet feels good.

I glance at the office wall, where a framed photo now sits—Ellie in Ollie's arms, with chubby cheeks and a crooked grin. Owen was standing beside him, taller every day, his arm slung around Ollie's shoulder at their final basketball game.

Ellie is officially ours. I signed the adoption papers last week, my hand shaking as I wrote my name, tears dropping onto the page. She's big and happy and loud now, full of squeals and drool and determination. She smiles when she sees Ollie walk into a room like he's the best thing that's ever happened to her.

She's not wrong. He's the best thing that has happened to any of us.

Owen is thriving in a way I didn't know how to hope for. He got a horse for his birthday and talks about her like she's a person, like she understands every word he says. He's out at the barn as much as he can be, brushing her, feeding her, learning responsibility. He's so happy, and that's all I've ever wanted for him.

He laughs more, and he's confident.

Ollie and I are officially his guardians now, and we're working with Weston on adoption, too. That court date is coming up. It feels surreal to say it out loud. The Wilder name is all of ours, and Owen's soon.

We're still living above the auto shop and it's crowded but we're happy.

It's officially time to retire the last name Murphy. I didn't realize how heavy that name had been until I got rid of it. Things are different now that we've changed everything up. It feels good.

Ollie clears his throat, pulling me from my thoughts. "I've got something to show you."

My brows knit together. "What kind of something?"

"The good kind," he says, already smiling like he knows he's about to undo me.

He takes my hand and leads me out to the sidewalk, past the shop, and down the street toward the town square. Then it comes into view. My breath catches in my throat and my heart feels like it's beating so fast.

It's my mom's bench, the one that used to sit half faded and forgotten. It's been stripped and refinished, the wood warm and smooth, bright, and beautiful again. And carved neatly into the backrest are two words that make my knees go weak.

Grace Eleanor.

No Murphy. Not anywhere. That name isn't welcome here anymore. We're wiping it away.

Ollie watches my face, his expression soft and careful. "The town wanted to surprise you," he says quietly. "Maggie got together with a bunch of people and had it done."

I sink onto the bench, my fingers tracing the letters like they're real, like she's real. Tears blur my vision, but I don't wipe them away. I don't need to.

"She'd love this," I whisper. "She would have hated how Sully turned out."

"I know," he says, sitting beside me and pulling me into his side. "But she'd be so proud of you. You are the greatest gift of my life, Poppy."

I lean into him, pressing my face into his shoulder, breathing him in. For the first time in my life, pride fills me of where I'm at and what we're doing. We're building a legacy that we can all be proud of. Owen gets a better shot at life than he would have if Sully stuck around. We are going to make it out, break this generational curse, and build a good new one.

"Never in my life have I craved someone's presence like I do you," I tell him as he kisses me like I'm his prize.

* * *

Walker and Violet's backyard is strung with white lights, even though the sun's still high, the lake glittering behind the house like it knows something special is happening. There's smoke curling up from a flat-top grill out back, the sharp, mouthwatering smell of soy sauce and garlic mingling with the clean lake air. Japanese steakhouse right here in Bridger Falls, with a personal chef. Only Walker and Violet could pull this off. He's over the moon excited about their new baby that he'll give Violet whatever she's craving.

I stand near the patio doors holding Ellie, watching everyone mingle, laugh, and chat. Maggie's telling a story with a cocktail in hand. Owen's already gotten the chef to give him a shrimp skewer off the grill and is talking his ear off. That's Owen. Our little unofficial mayor, who never met a stranger. Jack's helping Walker carry out trays of food while pretending he isn't sneaking bites too. Cami's laughing so hard at something Violet says, and she waves when she sees me.

Ollie comes up behind me after he sets out a tray of food and presses a kiss to my temple. "You okay?"

I nod, smiling. "This is an amazing baby shower."

He grins. "Yeah. I noticed Walker really went all out with the chef."

Ellie lets out a happy squeal and reaches for him, and he takes her without hesitation, settling her against his chest while she bats at his chin with her chubby little hands.

Violet waddles out onto the deck, one hand on her eight-month belly, the other holding a lemonade with fruit in it and an umbrella hanging off the side. "Okay," she announces, glowing and dramatic. "Who wants to see the nursery?"

Everyone cheers like they haven't already seen it twice. She's so proud of that nursery, she's redone it like three times. None of us knows what they're having, and they aren't finding out.

We pile inside, laughing and bumping into each other, and Violet leads us down the hall with the pride of someone who built something sacred. The nursery is soft and warm and perfect. Pale wood. A hand-painted mural of mountains and water. A crib Walker put together himself, after she gave away the nursery to us the first time. They refused to let us pay them back, so I told them they all get free oil changes for life. Walker responded by saying, "We'll see."

Violet presses her hand to the wall. "I wanted it to feel calm in here," she says. "Like he or she is going to be so relaxed and at home."

Cami's eyes go shiny immediately.

Maggie smiles. "It sure is beautiful, sugar."

Violet's mom and dad are here, and they're a hoot. Her mom reminds me of my mom and having her around heals something in me I didn't know needed healing. She's taken Ollie and I under her wing and says she'll visit us, too. I just adore her.

I press my lips together, feeling something deep in my chest loosen. I love seeing all of them so happy.

Back outside, food is served, and drinks are passed around. Sutton sits beside me at the long table, Crew asleep in her arms. She watches him for a moment, then sighs with a smile that doesn't quite reach her eyes. She's been coming around more often, and we love having her here.

"I have this editing conference in Vegas next month," she

says quietly, glancing toward Maggie. "And I'm thinking about canceling."

Maggie swivels in her chair so fast she almost spills her drink. "Why would you do that?"

Sutton pauses then says, "I've never been away from him. Not even overnight. I don't like the thought of leaving him."

Cami leans across the table, eyes bright. "You should go. You deserve a break."

I nod. "Crew will be just fine. Didn't you say your parents were keeping him?"

"More than fine," Maggie adds. "He'll be spoiled rotten with your mom and dad."

Violet smiles at Sutton, soft and knowing. "You don't stop being you just because you became a mom."

Sutton chews on her lip. "I don't want to be selfish."

I reach over and squeeze her hand. "It's not selfish to still want things for yourself."

Cami leans back and says with authority. "Let your hair down. Go be wild in Vegas."

Jack chokes on his drink. "How wild are we talking? Vegas can be pretty wild."

Everyone laughs.

"I don't think I even know how to be wild." Sutton sighs. "I know work and motherhood. That's it."

"And that's exactly why you need to go," Violet says.

"Go meet all the romance authors," Cami continues, undeterred. "Get new clients. Have fun. Dance. Sleep in. Eat room service. That sounds like a fun time to me."

Sutton's eyes fill, but she's smiling. "Okay," she says softly. "That does sound pretty great. I can get dressed up, meet new authors, and get some rest."

Maggie raises her glass. "That's my girl."

As the sun dips lower and the lights come on, I step back for a second and take it all in. Violet is laughing with Walker, one hand on her belly, his arms around her, whispering into her ear. Sutton, rocking Crew gently, with a peaceful look on her face, takes in everyone. Cami is leaning into Jack, content and fierce. Maggie and Mack are bickering like it's their love language about whether or not they should get alpacas.

Ollie stands near the grill with Ellie, talking to Walker. He looks over at me and smiles, and the look in his eyes makes my chest ache in the best way.

I spent years thinking I had to carry everything alone. Turns out, I just hadn't found the right person to carry it with me.

I look at Ollie and realize it was always you. And now, it's always us.

Epilogue

Ollie
Buy Dirt by Jordan Davis

Boxes are stacked everywhere, half labeled, half not, and Owen barrels past me with an armful of something fragile, yelling that it definitely needed bubble wrap. Ellie toddles behind him on unsteady legs, holding onto boxes and furniture, clapping like she's the one in charge of this whole operation. Poppy laughs from the kitchen, where she's trying to figure out which box holds the coffee maker.

It's been over a year since I got her to agree to be my pretend wife. There was nothing pretend about that for me. I knew I loved Poppy a very long time ago. I just needed to get her to believe it and see the future that I saw. No matter what came our way. Sibling adoption, new jobs, a surprise baby...whatever has come our way, we've powered through it together.

Ellie will be one in a few weeks. She's got one of my ball caps on that keeps slipping over her eyes, and she is a curious and happy baby. Owen has his own horse at the big barn and a grin that doesn't leave his face anymore. He runs out there every morning like he's afraid she might disappear if he doesn't check on her fast enough. He rides her everywhere and they're practically inseparable.

The house is done for the most part. We still have to paint a few things and add on some hardware, but that's nothing. We made the cabin work, and now we have a barndominium. The barn is being built next, but for now, we can use Jack's until we can save up. We've got plans tacked up on the fridge with magnets shaped like cows and horses. Poppy keeps adding animals to the list like it's a joke, but I know she loves it. I used to be scared of wanting this much. Turns out, there was nothing to be scared of because it's a pretty great life.

Poppy still teaches at the high school, and she loves it. She comes home talking about students and projects they're working on. She runs the shop part-time now, too, confident and respected. She didn't give anything up. She gained space to breathe. We are a team and work hard to make everything happen. We rented out the loft above the shop, and that income is helping us save up for the new barn.

I watch her cross the living room barefoot on the hardwood floors we picked out together. This life fits her. It fits all of us. Her dream became our dream.

By late afternoon, the housewarming party is in full swing. Jack and Cami are playing bartender and handing out drinks behind a makeshift wooden bar that Tucker and Jack built that has wheels, and we can use for all of our family parties. Maggie's set up in the corner, holding court. Walker and I are manning the grill, cracking jokes as we sip our beers and fill trays of burgers and hot dogs.

Weston stands near the back porch, quiet and observant, nursing a drink and watching everything like he's taking notes.

Weston's usually the quiet one of the group. But this time he sees a little quieter.

Then the bikes roll in. Engines cut, and a few of the guys from the club step out carrying gifts from their saddle bags. Jack and Weston stiffen, unsure of the visitors. I'm not. They've been around, they respect the hell out of Poppy, and they run the business fairly and work hard alongside her. I have had no problems with the Pine River MCs.

Jonesy hands Poppy a ridiculous oversized stuffed horse for Ellie, and she laughs so hard and gives him a hug. Another gives Owen a pair of riding gloves, which he immediately puts on and Poppy shakes her head. "You're not riding a bike," she says, ruffling his hair.

Jack leans toward me. "You good with this?"

I nod. "Yeah. I am. They've been all right."

Because people can change when they choose to, I've seen it. I've lived it. And others don't change and that's just the way life goes.

As the sun drops and the lights flick on, Poppy finds me by the porch and slips her hand into mine like it's instinct. Ellie toddles between us, holding onto our legs, safe and certain.

I look around at the house, the land, the people who showed up and stayed. The life I never let myself imagine because it felt like tempting fate. I was wrong. I thought love would cost me everything. Turns out, it gave me everything.

About the Author

Erin Branscom is a creator of happily-ever-after's, crafting spicy, Hallmark-like romances that make readers fall head over heels for charming small towns. When she's not writing heartwarming stories, Erin can be found anywhere there are dogs, with a cup of coffee in hand, or lost in a good book. As a passionate Scorpio, she brings intensity and heart to everything she does. Dive into her world and discover love, warmth, and a touch of spice in every story.

Acknowledgments

To my family. I love you all and you are my reason for working hard every day. I'm so thankful for all of you and your support. To all my readers, thank you for always showing up for me and being excited!

Want more Poppy and Ollie?

Check out this bonus scene for Always You when you sign up for Erin's newsletter!

Scan the QR code to get your bonus scene:

Chapter 1: The
Pumpkin Spice Spell

Willa

The bells over the heavy wooden door to my bookstore and coffee shop jingle as I finish pouring a maple leaf design onto a pumpkin spice latte in a cauldron-shaped mug. I've lost count of how many pumpkin spice lattes I've made all day, already sealing the sweet, warm scent of cinnamon and clove into every corner of the shop. Fall has moved into Wisteria Cove, and honestly, I couldn't be happier. Sure, this means we're swamped, and all our shops are jam-packed from open to close, but it's my favorite time of year.

And what's better than a cozy bookstore and coffee shop in the fall? Absolutely nothing, that's what.

Inside Wisteria Books & Brews, I've collected mismatched armchairs and carved out little comfy reading nooks, each softened with blankets, pillows, and cushions that invite everyone in to explore the new and old books. Tall shelves with a ladder hold my carefully curated collections, while other shelves hold paperbacks mixed with hardcovers, new finds, and dog-eared favorites. Warmly lit lamps illuminate every corner, and no overhead lights glare in here. This is the ultimate escape for anyone needing a place to call home and curl up with a warm mug and a good book. My shop is eclectic, warm, welcoming, and alive.

This morning, a small coven of incredible women gathered here, as they often do, to celebrate each other's wins, sip coffee, and pull tarot cards between bursts of laughter and knowing nods. They're a tight-knit, deep-soul group who loves fiercely, supports endlessly, and leaves the air humming with good energy. I can't help but smile every time they're in the shop.

Nothing makes me happier than pouring someone their favorite coffee or tea and watching them choose from murder mysteries, fairy tales, gardening guides, or our local Wisteria Cove seaside lore. And I may or may not be reading their futures while they are here in the shop. But I don't tell them that. That's for sure.

My mother, Lilith Maren, and my two sisters and I are all notoriously known as the Maren Witches of Wisteria Cove. People love to make up stories about us flying on brooms and wearing witch costumes. But that's not true. But that's also *not not true*, either. While we don't fly on brooms or wear costumes, we all have unique gifts that we use in our day-to-day lives.

But life has been hard enough for all three of us. We don't need to make it harder by over sharing the things that make us weird. Well, *weirder* to the outside world, but just normal to us. History has called witches weird as a negative connotation in the past. But if being intuitive, helping others, and loving apothecary makes us witches, then I guess that's what we are.

It wasn't always easy growing up as the daughter of Lilith Maren, the town sea witch, as the tourists like to call her. She's infamous around here. Nobody takes our gifts seriously until they need us for something, whether they need a spell from my mother, or something apothecary from my sister, Rowan. I have gifts of discernment and intuition, and Ivy has gifts of care and art. She paints and designs tarot cards and loves to write.

Every year, we host the annual Harvest Moon festival, which attracts even more tourists. Can I move things and fly on a broom? *No.* Can I manifest things into happening? Yeah, I've been known to do that and see things that are going to happen before other people do. But mostly, I just run my coffee shop and bookstore. I find beauty in the magic of everyday things. Like a steaming mug of tea, a conversation with a friend, and curling up with a great book. There's magic in the small, everyday things, and I wish more people knew that.

In the back of my kitchen, my soup station bubbles away. Today's special is butternut squash with sage and cream, served in to-go containers with a fresh sprig of thyme. And in the glass case, we have fresh sandwiches that people can grab and go. This week I was feeling roast turkey, savory brie, and cranberry relish. Their aroma from the neatly stacked sandwiches draws customers in off the street. By the end of the day, the customers will have bought everything. We sell out of everything constantly, and it's been a good problem to have.

Across the shop, my sister Rowan emerges from the back, handing me a wooden box of precisely labeled apothecary jars. All clean line labels with: Ground, Clarity, and Calm. Rowan grew and cultivated all of them carefully from her garden and greenhouse.

"Another tea delivery?" I smile, relief washing over me. We've blown through nearly every blend this week, and my shelves are desperate for a restock. Rowan's tea is phenomenal, grown in her sun-drenched greenhouse and the little garden behind her cozy little cottage.

When she's not teaching yoga classes down at the community center, she's been pouring her heart into opening a yoga and apothecary shop in the vacant building right next door to

Wisteria Books & Brews. I can already picture it, the warm scent of herbs against the red brick walls drifting through the door that will connect both of our shops, the hum of music from my shop mingling with her laughter.

Rowan's already the go-to in town for everything from loose-leaf teas to lavender tinctures and magnesium sprays. If you can dream it, she can create it. Potions and remedies that seem to carry a little bit of Wisteria Cove's magic in every drop.

"Not everyone can suffer through your pumpkin spice lattes," she says dryly, her dark wavy hair that matches mine pulled back in a simple knot, her velvety brown eyes shining, silver rings clicking as she sets the jars in place. "But I'll give you props...you sell out of everything, so there's that. People love their pumpkin spice, but I'm not one of them. I'm more of a tea kind of girl."

I theatrically roll my eyes. "And there's nothing wrong with that. I love your teas, too."

My younger sister Ivy bursts in through the front door, her reddish-brown hair wild under an askew knit cap, grinning at us. She's walking dogs today, one of her many part-time jobs. The barking of the dogs has begun outside as they bark and look in the window, their leashes tied to the old iron lamppost out front. And there seem to be three extra loose dogs congregating with the ones tied up.

"Should I even ask, or do I just accept that you're the town's official puppy dealer now?" I grin.

"You guys, it's an emergency." Ivy's infectious grin is bright. Leave it to Ivy to smile through an emergency.

"Mrs. Tourney's golden retrievers escaped and fell into step behind me, so now I look like I'm running Wisteria Cove's unofficial Golden Girls Club."

I chuckle and reach for the phone to call Mrs. Tourney. This kind of thing happens often. Ivy's basically the unofficial dog whisperer of Wisteria Cove—well, all animals, really. I swear there's not a single pet within thirty miles that doesn't know or adore her. She's everyone's go-to for dog walking, pet sitting, you name it, though that's just one of her many gigs.

Ivy's what I like to call a serial job holder. She's worked just about everywhere in this town at least once, and somehow, she's charmed everyone while doing it. If Wisteria Cove has a job, Ivy's probably done it, quit it, and sometimes come back for another round. She always leaves on good terms, though. I'll give her that.

As I hang up the phone with Mrs. Tourney, who tells me she's on her way, Rowan sighs. "Remind me why you prefer dog walking out in the cold and don't want to teach yoga classes this week?"

"Because these dogs are adorable," Ivy shoots back with a grin. "Maybe if you considered goat yoga like I suggested, I'd fill in more."

I make Ivy's favorite drink for her, a Moonrise mocha, pop a lid on it and slide it over to her. She smiles gratefully and takes it, immediately taking a sip. "Mmmm, thank you," she says, closing her eyes.

We all turn and look as all the dogs she's walking peer in the window at Ivy, tails wagging, waiting expectantly.

"Look at them. It's like in Nordic countries where parents leave the babies in strollers outside in the fresh air to sleep," she says proudly of her charges as she sips her coffee.

"Yeah, except they aren't sleeping. They want their pup cups that you've taught them they get every time you come here," Rowan says with a smirk.

I pull out my small paper cups and fill them with whipped cream. Rowan, Ivy, and I carry them out and hand them out since they waited patiently like the good doggies that they are. I pet them and scratch their ears, grateful for the break from the busy day. One of them jumps up to sniff Ivy's coffee, and the outdoor table trembles, the glass lanterns shaking. It's the perfect friendly chaos that I crave in the shop. Magic in everyday moments.

Later, I go back to my cozy, cluttered peace. I glance around, grateful for the magic in the mid-morning mundane. The shop is empty of customers right now, but I'm sure we'll get another rush.

I love this street and always have. From the window of the shop, I can see the way Wisteria Cove folds in on itself, part fishing village, part small-town postcard. Shops like mine, tucked snug between weathered clapboard houses painted in shades of white, gray, and seafoam, line the cobbled street like they've been here forever. The air carries salt and woodsmoke, crisp with the warm autumn air.

Further down, the barber's striped pole spins lazily, bright against the red brick. A gull swoops overhead, its cry louder than the occasional car rumbling by, reminding me that here, the sea always has more presence than traffic. It's the rhythm of this place with the harbor bells, the rustle of dry leaves scraping along the stone, the quiet hum of neighbors calling out hellos.

It's not perfect in a shiny Hallmark way. It's better. Quirky, weathered, stubbornly itself. The shingles are faded from salt wind, the paint peels here and there, and the whole town smells faintly of fish no matter how many pies the bakery turns out. But it's *ours*. And I wouldn't trade it for anywhere else.

My gaze drifts down the street to the Holloway place. The windows stare back at me like eyes that have seen too much. It's different now with overgrown hedges, a porch in need of repair. When I was a girl, I used to run across that yard and lose whole afternoons in their backyard. Just seeing it now sends a wave of nostalgia washing over me, bittersweet as the bite of sea air. The house feels like a ghost of another time, one that's tethered itself to me whether I like it or not.

The Holloway house has sat empty for so long that it almost feels like part of the scenery now, with weathered shingles, faded paint, and a crooked mailbox with "Holloway" still scrawled across it in peeling black letters.

For a long time after Tate Holloway left, I would glance out, expecting to see a light in a window. Watching for a shape moving past the curtains. Or him stepping out onto that porch like no time had passed at all. But that hope faded years ago when he left and disappeared without a word. People around town said that he took a job offshore somewhere doing deep-sea fishing. And eventually, I stopped watching and waiting for him. But part of me wonders—if the old Holloway house could speak, what stories would it tell? Stories of sadness, grief, and a family robbed of time and memories.

I've poured myself into this place instead, focusing on the dried orange slices hanging from the windows, the books stacked just so, and every cinnamon-sugar swirl on the foam of a latte. I try to romanticize everything in my life and make every day count. That's the only romance I have these days. Wisteria Cove isn't exactly full of eligible bachelors, and even if it were, I'm not sure how many would want to date a sad and lonely witch. I live above my shop in a tiny studio apartment, and this is as exciting as it gets, boys and girls.

The bookstore witch is boring.

I built this life...this sanctuary...this shop filled with the hum of conversation and the scent of coffee, books, and pumpkin spice.

And most of the time, it's enough. But lately it just feels lonely. There has to be more than this, I just don't know what.

About five years ago, a severe storm destroyed my father's fishing boat. There were no survivors, and the boat was never found. My family and this town have never been the same. There were seven people, including our neighbor, Phil Holloway, Tate's father on the Salty Siren that night. That was one of the worst storms in New England history. And that night changed the course of both of our families' lives forever.

The Holloways and Marens were like family to each other once upon a time. We shared family dinners and holidays—even our mothers were friends. My sisters and I and Tate grew up together. Everything changed after that night, though. I have always suspected that the Holloways blamed my father for the boat sinking. He was the captain, and people still talk about it occasionally, whispering that they held him responsible. But nobody will ever know what really happened, because they're gone.

Watching my mother, Lilith, wait out on the widow's peak for him to come home for weeks after the storm was awful. She refused to believe he was gone. She said she could still feel him out there. Part of her died that night with him. The mother that we had after that night wasn't the same mother that we had before the storm, with him gone. He left a crater-sized hole in all our lives. Losing a parent is the worst, and not a club anyone wants a membership to.

April, Tate's mother, moved to Florida right after they declared Phil legally dead. She left the house for Tate, and he stayed for a few years, fishing locally. But then, without warning, he was just gone. Things were never the same between us after the accident. We still talked, but our friendship and closeness took a hit.

I move behind the counter, wiping my hands and brewing a fresh batch of coffee for customers while keeping an eye on the simmering soup. Donna Bennett, the town's self-appointed fairy godmother and my mother's best friend, appears at the counter. Donna is also a famous author who has penned over a hundred romance novels in the past several decades. Most of the locals know her, and it's not a big deal, but she keeps a low profile for the rest of the world.

"Hi, Willa, I need five pumpkin spice scones to go for Remy and Junie," she declares cheerfully, plopping her purse down on the counter.

"Hey, Donna, how are you doing?" I smile as I wash my hands and dry them.

"I'm good, sweetie. Just left a meeting about the upcoming Harvest Moon Festival. It's going to be amazing this year," she says. "Also, why didn't you tell me that Tate's coming back?"

I drop a scone on the floor that I was scooping into the bag.

What did she just say?

My chest tightens, and my hands shake.

"I didn't know about Tate," I say.

"Oh, I figured you knew since you two were always so close," she says, raising her eyebrows.

"Nope," I hand her the bag of scones and head to the register to ring up her order.

"Well, keep me updated. It'll be nice to have him home," she says as she hands me her card to pay.

I nod, even though my outside reaction is not even close to my inside reaction. I am freaking out and trying to keep my hands from shaking right now.

"Gossip is as hot a commodity here as the coffee, but I'm trying to reign in my chaotic emotions, so I give Rowan a nudge, who's sitting at the coffee bar, reading a book.

"Donna, tell me about your tarot session with Lilith," Rowan asks sweetly, getting her to change the subject.

"Thank you," I mouth to her behind Donna.

Donna brightens and, luckily, moves on to that, telling everyone what happened. Before I know it, Lilith Maren, my mother, sweeps in with all the dramatic flair she can possibly muster. She's a petite woman, barely five-three, though she carries herself like she's towering over everyone in the room. A velvet shawl drapes around her shoulders like she's stepping onto a stage, and dried wisteria vines loop over one arm as if she's bringing an offering. Her wrists are stacked with silver bangles that clink and jangle with every gesture, punctuating her words like exclamation marks.

Her hair, long and wild, falls in loose waves the color of burnished copper streaked with silver. She insists it's "witch's hair," untamed and full of secrets, and she refuses to let anyone tame it with scissors. Her eyes are storm-gray with flecks of green and have that mischievous spark that makes people wonder if she knows more than she lets on. Spoiler: she always does.

She's not thin but not full-figured, either; she has that ageless, solid, earthy presence of a woman who's lived fully and refuses to apologize for it. There's something both comforting and chaotic about her, like she could whip up soup to cure your cold while also casually working on a spell for your love life in the same afternoon.

Today she's wearing a layered plum and midnight blue skirt, the hem brushing her boots, and a blouse patterned with tiny, embroidered moons and stars. Rings glitter on nearly every finger, amethysts, garnets, and a chunky turquoise she swears is enchanted. Everything about her says: *I belong to this town, and I am at home here.* She's timeless, a little eccentric, and entirely unforgettable.

"The vines signal love and renewal," she says, planting them firmly on top of the counter as I wince. She doesn't even notice the dried leaves that rattle onto the floor. "I'm sensing you have both on the horizon, Willa."

"Mom, why are you bringing in outside things?" I wince, digging into my resilient politeness at her eccentricity. But this is what happens when you have a witchy mother. They *know* things.

My mom just smiles, hugs Rowan and then reaches to pull me into a hug, as well. "A little magic never hurts anyone, except the boring ones," she winks at me.

"I am not boring," I say as I swipe up the wisteria leaves into my hand.

Rowan arches a brow, her lips twitching. Before she can say anything, I shoot her a warning look, and she chuckles.

My mom laughs. "Not boring? Darling, you wouldn't know fun if it hit you like a broomstick. You hide out in your bookstore and hardly ever leave. You practically have to *schedule* fun. If that isn't boring, I don't know what is."

"Introverted," I correct, brushing the dried petals into a neat pile. "It's called being a homebody."

"Mm-hm." Lilith tilts her head, her hair spilling over one shoulder in a cascade of silver waves. "You're becoming a spinster with cats."

Rowan snorts. "She already has the tragic spinster vibe. Just missing the cats."

"Excuse me?" I glare at both, though my lips threaten a smile.

Lilith plants her hands on her hips, rings glittering. "I am simply saying, my darling daughters, that life is short, and you should be living it as though it were dipped in honey and rolled in cinnamon sugar."

Rowan leans against the counter, smirking. "You mean like Ivy? Trying out job after job?"

Lilith waves a hand as if brushing away a gnat. "She's figuring out what makes her happy." Her eyes sparkle with mischief as she looks between us.

Rowan rolls her eyes, but she's smiling. "That's one way of putting it."

I try to hold firm, but Lilith's infectious grin threatens to break me down. "You're impossible," I mutter.

"And you," she counters, reaching out to tap my nose like I'm still a little girl, "are delicious when you're ruffled. Don't waste your life on order when chaos is so much more fun."

This is exactly what it was like growing up in the Maren household. Chaos and comfort mixed into something like home. And I love it.

When the store finally clears out for the night and everyone is gone, I flip the closed sign, lock the door, and get my homemade chamomile tea. My good life doesn't require much, just a steaming mug of tea, a good book, and some quiet solitude in my favorite place.

I pull a cracked wooden ladder from the shelf, flip open a hidden latch, and climb up to the small loft with windows catching the moonlight over the harbor. Here is where my quiet solitude reigns. A plush armchair and worn quilt wait for me by a small reading lamp, as if ready for me and waiting for the day to end. A cozy bed, stacks of books, a tiny kitchen, and a bathroom. It's all I need, and it's mine.

This is also a perfect view of the Holloway place and the harbor just beyond it. The dark shutters tug at me again. Is he really back? I so badly wanted to ask Donna more, but Donna is not the one to ask. Donna is wonderful, but a big matchmaker, and almost as bad as my mom. Those two together are just about impossible when they get an idea.

I sip my tea and imagine what would happen if Tate showed up, knocked on the door. What would I even say to him? Maybe we'd talk, and he'd be nice. Maybe he'd be better and not the broody fisherman man he was when he left Wisteria Cove. Maybe he's changed. Or maybe he's not even here at all, and Donna is mistaken.

The harbor outside is calm, the moon silver and reflecting

across the dark water. A lone gull shrieks. My eyes seem to play tricks on me, as I think for a second I see a single upstairs light flare and fade. Maybe a coincidence, maybe not.

I feel mostly peaceful, other than the thought of Tate Holloway being back in town after all these years. I haven't exactly been pining for him. However, it is hard when his house is still there and serves as a constant reminder.

I light a small candle on my table for hope, lay out a leaf for fall rootedness, and sea salt for openness.

Yes, my life is full. Cozy, fun, and I am happy. But deep down? I'm deeply lonely.

I miss him.

Continue reading here:

High Road

Want more of Bridger Falls?
Scan the QR code to read Weston and Sutton's story:

Freedom Valley Series
Falling Inn Love
Baked Inn Love
All Inn Thyme
Love Inn Books
Forever Inn Love
Snowed Inn

Bridger Falls
Forever To Me
Wild As Her
Always You
High Road

Wisteria Cove
The Pumpkin Spice Spell
Mistletoe & Magic
Hexes & Honeysuckle

Cozy Creek Collection
Fall Too Well
Bagpipes & Buns

Coconut Beach
Just Another Summer Escape

You can find all of Erin's books on her website:
Erinbranscom.com